## About the Author

Susie Murphy is an Irish historical fiction author. She loves historical fiction so much that she often wishes she had been born two hundred years ago. Still, she remains grateful for many aspects of the modern age, including women's suffrage, electric showers and pizza. A Class Liberated is her seventh published novel.

ISBN-13: 978-1-915770-07-3



**www.susiemurphywrites.com**

Join the Susie Murphy Readers' Club
for free stories, exclusive updates and bookstore discounts:

**https://bit.ly/susie-murphy-readers-club**

# A Class Liberated

## A Matter of Class, Book Seven

### Susie Murphy

*For my precious niece and nephew, Emily and Denis,
whose names made it into my books before they were even born.
Sometimes, the universe aligns just right.*

# Chapter 1

Dressed in her nightgown, Bridget sat on the wide, cushioned stool at her dressing table and gazed into the mirror, half of her reflection in shadow, the other half lit softly by the oil lamp sitting to her right on the table's surface. Her lady's maid, Polly, bustled around the bed behind her, turning down the bedcovers and plumping up the pillows. She lingered over this task every night, giving Bridget sufficient time to change her bandage without being scrutinised.

With a small sigh, Bridget pulled open one of the drawers in the dressing table and withdrew a fresh white strip of cotton. She laid it on the table and proceeded to unwrap the used bandage from her cheek, loosening the knot behind her ear that helped to keep it in place. It fell away and she gathered the material in her hand to examine it. There wasn't a speck on it, no blood or pus or residue of any kind.

Swallowing, she reached for the oil lamp and slid it across the table until it illuminated the left side of her face. Summoning her courage, she made herself look into the mirror again. The light brought the scar on her cheek into sharp relief. More than three months had passed since Sullivan's blade had sliced into her flesh and she had to admit that the wound had healed very well during that time. What had once been an open, bloody gash was now a thin line of healthy pink scar tissue. Two inches long, it gleamed in the glow from the oil lamp.

And she knew the day had come. In fact, the day had already passed but she had been reluctant to acknowledge it, preferring to continue to hide behind the bandage, to rely upon its power to protect her like a shield from staring eyes. But that had become its only function – there was no longer a grievous injury to cover up, only the ugly reminder it had left behind, which she could not keep concealed forever.

She sighed again and placed the fresh strip of cotton back into the drawer, shutting it with a bitter sense of resignation. Polly came over from the bed and faltered when her gaze landed on Bridget's uncovered cheek.

'I'm sorry, my lady, do you need more time?'

'No, thank you,' said Bridget. 'You may take away the used bandage and there is no need to keep a supply of them in the drawer anymore.'

Polly nodded solemnly. 'I understand, my lady.'

As she accepted the used bandage from Bridget, a soft knock came on the door – not the one that led out to the corridor but the inner one that linked Bridget's bedchamber to Cormac's. They officially had a suite of rooms each but, ever since they had taken up residence at Bewley Hall, he had joined her in the lady's chamber every night, leaving the master's chamber unoccupied. After they had returned from their gruelling experience in Ireland, he had made a habit of knocking on the connecting door before entering, to allow her ample privacy to complete her night-time regime without intrusion.

Polly glanced at Bridget. 'Shall I...?'

Bridget gathered up the flailing strands of her courage. 'Yes, please let him in.'

Polly crossed to the door and opened it. Cormac stood on the other side; he had removed the coat and cravat he had been wearing at dinner earlier that evening, but he still wore his waistcoat, shirt and trousers. His gaze shifted from Polly to Bridget still sitting at the dressing table and she caught the almost imperceptible widening of his eyes.

Before he could speak, Polly interjected smoothly, 'Come in, sir. Her ladyship is ready to go to bed.' Then she blushed at the unseemly implication of her words. 'That is, she is ready for slumber,' she corrected herself hastily. She swivelled back to Bridget. 'Is there anything else I can do for you, my lady?'

Bridget shook her head. 'That is all. Thank you, Polly, and goodnight.'

Polly curtseyed and departed from the room through the outer door to the corridor, taking the used bandage with her. As she shut the door quietly behind her, Cormac stepped across the threshold of the inner door. He took only a few paces into the room before he halted with an air of uncertainty.

'Do you want me here tonight?' he asked. 'If you would prefer solitude...'

Though a large part of her wished to hide her scarred face from him, she stifled her self-consciousness and put out her left hand in invitation. He approached and took it, raising it to press a gentle kiss to her knuckles. While this was an act of extreme politeness in public, here in the seclusion of their bedchamber it became a tender gesture. Tonight, it even seemed to border on reverence, the way his lips lingered on her skin and drifted to her gold ring. Her whole body tingled at his touch; he had a remarkable capacity to make her feel attractive, even though she was nearly thirty-nine years old and well past the peak of her beauty.

She hiccupped as she recalled that age was no longer the greatest obstacle to her physical appeal. With that thought, her ripple of desire faded. She drew her hand out of his grasp and turned back to the dressing table mirror. The lamplight fell upon the shiny seam of her scar.

After a pause, Cormac stepped up behind her and their gazes met in the mirror.

'Why today?' he asked, his voice soft.

She twisted her mouth wryly. 'Because it was already long overdue. I should have done it days ago, perhaps even weeks. I was only using the bandage to hide. I couldn't pretend any longer that it was anything but cowardice.'

'That is not a word I would ever use to describe you,' he murmured, bringing his hand up to rest on her shoulder, the weight of it warm and comforting. 'Not in a thousand years.'

She tried to conceal her scepticism but the thinly pressed lips of her reflection betrayed her.

He raised a challenging eyebrow. 'A coward wouldn't have endured the trauma that you did on that farm and then carried on with scarcely any rest to strive to save dozens of famished tenants. A coward wouldn't have persevered with that gargantuan task while struggling through the grief of losing a cherished friend.'

His bluntness took her breath away. With a swell of sorrow, she recalled the freshly dug patch of brown earth in St Mary's graveyard that covered Liam's starved body. He had succumbed to famine dropsy before she and Cormac could get him the sustenance he so desperately needed.

Cormac's hand squeezed her shoulder gently. 'A coward certainly wouldn't have entered a warehouse full of dangerous men to rescue her two beloved boys.'

She swallowed hard at the memory of the nightmare she had suffered through in New York City.

He tilted his head as he looked at her in the mirror. 'I don't even think a coward would have climbed a giant oak tree just because a cheeky little boy dared her to do it.'

He winked and she felt her mouth curve into a small smile.

'He was a very cheeky boy, wasn't he?' she said.

'The cheekiest. Irredeemable.'

She turned her head and kissed his fingers that still clasped her shoulder. From that long-ago day to this, Cormac had shaped her life like no other. He had given her a love that was as vast as the heavens above, an exceptional, limitless gift that somehow still expanded more every day. He had given her three miraculous children, two in his likeness and one in hers, all three more precious to her than breath or heartbeat. He had given her devotion and passion beyond her wildest imaginings. Even when the inevitable heartaches had come, he had washed them away with kisses and the strength of his conviction that they could make it through any hardship because of the powerful bond that united them. She didn't know what she had ever done to deserve this extraordinary man.

His fingers drifted, gliding up the side of her neck, caressing the rim of her ear, meandering downwards again to stroke the delicate line of her jaw. He paused and once again made eye contact with her reflection. The lamplight flickered over his brow and cheekbones as he steadily held her gaze, waiting.

She knew what he was asking. There had never been a part of her body out of bounds to him, not since they had made their lifelong commitment to each other as they sailed away from London with Emily over a decade ago. She also knew that if she did not grant her permission, he would accept that. But the very notion was inconceivable. Every part of her belonged to him, just as every part of him belonged to her. Even the damaged parts. Perhaps especially those.

She nodded once, purposefully, a definite signal of her consent. His eyelashes lowered as he dropped his gaze from the mirror to her face. His fingers still hovered by her jaw. He raised them and let the tip of his index finger touch her scar so lightly that she could hardly feel it. He traced it along its full length. Then he bent and placed a careful kiss upon it.

'I never want you to be in any doubt,' he murmured, his breath warm on her cheek. 'When I look at you, I do not see this. I see only you, *a rún mo chroí*. Your pure heart and your generous soul are so dazzling that they outshine everything else.'

Her throat tightened with emotion. He coaxed her chin towards him and kissed her mouth. She kissed him back softly, melting into his embrace as he wrapped his other arm around her. His stooped position couldn't be very good for his back – he was almost thirty-nine too, after all, and no longer a sprightly youth – so she shifted along the stool to let him sit too. He lowered himself onto it with his back towards the mirror and brushed his lips against hers again. She responded with greater eagerness this time as her desire flared up once more, ignited by his nearness, their bodies wedged close together so that neither would fall off the edge of the stool.

They had not forged a physical connection since her abduction. She hadn't felt in any way inclined to engage in the act and he, of course, had not pressured her, understanding that she was in a fragile state after her ordeal. By day, she had been keeping her thoughts occupied with the charity event she was planning to help the Irish people who were starving from the potato blight. It distracted her enough that she often believed she had put the hideous episode behind her. However, by night, she could not prevent her dreams from straying back to that barn on Sycamore Farm. When she woke with fright, Cormac simply held her. Neither of them ever made a move to initiate anything remotely sexual.

But now, at last, her blood stirred. His torso pressed up against her, solid and warm, and his smell enveloped her, so familiar and, in this moment, extremely arousing.

She parted her lips and her tongue sought out his, grazing it with a suggestive stroke. He hesitated before reciprocating, skimming his tongue across hers. She sensed him holding back and realised he would need further encouragement to be persuaded that she was ready for this tonight. With a quiver of anticipation, she laid a deliberate palm on his thigh and then slid it up to cup him through his trousers.

His shoulders jerked at the touch, and so did the appendage within which hardened and strained towards her hand. She gripped him a little tighter. He broke their kiss to stare at her, his eyes wide.

'You want to?' he said rather breathlessly.

'I do,' she said, but then she faltered. What if his hesitancy was not due to gentlemanly restraint but insufficient appetite? Her looks had been spoiled by that blade – she was no longer pleasing to the eye. 'If—if you want to?'

His blue eyes burned with desire and his body throbbed in her grasp, thoroughly banishing her doubts. Their mouths joined together again, their tongues now entwining with fervour. As they kissed, she let go of him below to search upwards for the buttons on his waistcoat, undoing each of them one-handed. When she unbuttoned the last one and the waistcoat fell open, she felt Cormac's mouth widen into a grin and he once again pulled back.

'That was quite impressive,' he said.

She blushed. He reached his left hand up to brush the back of his knuckles along her cheek, briefly skimming her scar. She caught a glimpse of the braided leather band on his wrist, one of its seams containing strands of their hair.

'Will you come to bed with me?' he asked, his voice low and husky.

'I can't,' she said and he shot her a startled look. 'I must put in my pessary first,' she reminded him and his expression cleared.

'May I do it for you?' he asked bashfully.

It was her turn to be startled. She smiled. 'Very well, then.'

She reached towards her dressing table and sought out the pessary from one of its drawers. Withdrawing it from its box, she handed it to Cormac. Then, tugging up the skirt of her nightgown, she stood and put one foot on the stool, presenting herself to him. With careful tenderness, he spread her lips apart and inserted the pessary, pushing it gently upwards inside her.

'How does that feel?' he asked.

She set her foot back down on the floor. 'It feels fine,' she assured him. 'Please take me to bed now.'

'It would be my greatest pleasure,' he said.

Rising, he clasped her hand and led her across the room to the bed, where he let her slip under the covers first before sliding in after her. Propping himself on his elbows above her, he pressed his lips to her mouth and then trailed kisses all over her face, her nose, her forehead, her cheeks, and her scar, which was just another part of her now. It was nothing to be self-conscious about; that was what he was teaching her tonight.

She felt so safe in his grasp. A terrible thing had happened to her in Ireland, and she knew she was still healing in many ways, but she could believe now that she would survive it, that she would get past the trauma. Because she had Cormac. His strength, his solid presence, his fearless love, eclipsed everything else.

How incredibly lucky she was.

# Chapter 2

Rory stood in a corner of Emily's bedchamber, fumbling as he buttoned up his waistcoat. The garment was finer than anything he had ever owned, tailored to fit his tall frame perfectly. He reached for the cravat draped over the back of a chair, the linen sliding between his calloused fingers. As the son-in-law of the landlord of Bewley Hall, he was entitled to employ the services of a valet, but he had declined the offer almost before the words had left Mr McGovern's mouth. The very idea of having a personal servant to assist him in the basic act of clothing himself was horrifying to him.

As he attempted to knot the cravat around his neck, he couldn't help feeling as out of place as a fish flailing about on dry land. Conversely, Emily, who sat across the room at her dressing table while her lady's maid arranged her hair, acted with the grace of one who had been born into this life.

Which, of course, she had.

She wore a contented smile as she retrieved an ivory hairpin from the small pile resting on the dressing table and held it up for her maid to take.

'It's a marvellous morning, isn't it, Jennie?' she said merrily.

Jennie cast a dubious glance out at the somewhat blustery autumn weather beyond the window. 'As you say, ma'am,' she said, accepting the proffered pin.

She was very new to her role, having been just recently elevated from her previous position as housemaid. There had been only one lady's maid at Bewley Hall when Lord and Lady Bewley lived there, but now there were two ladies in residence; Polly Hawkins had been assigned to serve Emily's mother, leaving Emily to seek her own lady's maid. Rory had half hoped she might do without one altogether, which could have allowed them to maintain some sort of distance from the formal lifestyle they now led. However, after they married, she said she recognised the wisdom in having a measure of assistance in that regard. Rather than hiring from outside the household, she had chosen to promote Jennie, confiding in Rory that she had made this choice on account of Jennie's kindness to Gus and the part she had played in helping him to solve the mystery relating to Lady Dorothea's restless ghost. Emily's hope was that this sense of familiarity would promote a more relaxed environment for all concerned. Rory knew she had really meant for him though.

Jennie, for her part, seemed anything but relaxed as she twisted and pinned Emily's golden locks into an elegant style. She kept throwing disapproving looks in Rory's direction, her lips pressed into a thin line. He felt like an intruder, encroaching upon the space allotted for private female activities. But where else was he supposed to go?

Not for the first time, he brooded over their current living arrangements. Now that he and Emily were wed, would they continue to reside in her parents' home indefinitely? The thought of living under the constant scrutiny of his in-laws made his stomach a little queasy. He had the most immense respect for them but he longed for a space that he and Emily could call their own, where they could build a life together without the weight of her family's expectations, and those of wider society, bearing down upon them. This house was too grand for him – he was only a carpenter, the son of a deckhand, an Irish lad who had grown up sharing one bedroom with his entire family.

Still, he had married Emily – a choice he would make again without a second thought – and with that had come a commitment to a life he didn't really belong to but that he must somehow find a way to make peace with. Even as he acknowledged that, he was unable to stop himself from contemplating alternatives – could there be any chance of establishing a compromise of sorts?

As he shrugged into his coat, Jennie stepped back from Emily and critically eyed her handiwork. She shook her head.

'It could be better, but I'm still learning,' she said with a regretful sigh.

'It looks splendid,' Emily assured her. 'And remember, we are learning together.'

Jennie gave her a grateful curtsey. 'Thank you, Mrs Carey. I'll leave you to break your fast.'

She departed from the bedchamber, her expression guarded as she sidestepped Rory on her way out. Her air of vague discomfort compounded his own qualms about his and Emily's present circumstances and he resolved to raise the issue at once with his wife.

However, before he could utter a word, Emily sprang up from her seat, her eyes sparkling.

'Oh, I could hardly hold my tongue while Jennie was here,' she exclaimed. She came towards Rory, her hands clasped together – the walnut ring he had given her on their wedding day peeked out between her fingers. 'Do you think our efforts last night might have been successful? Wouldn't it be wonderful if we conceived a child from such ecstasy?'

She radiated pure joy as she beamed at him and he vividly recalled the passion they had shared the previous night. How the first time had been swift and urgent up against the wall of the bedchamber, spurred on by giddiness from the wine they had drunk at dinner. How the second time had been slow and languorous, tangled up in the sheets of the bed and each other's legs. How the third time had been later just before the dawn, when they were only half-awake and he had murmured 'I love you' into her hair over and over as he worshipped her body with his own. If a baby was to be the result of these fervent expressions of their love for one another, it would indeed be a wonderful thing.

All of his other concerns evaporated. He had no intention of dampening her enthusiasm this morning with misgivings of any kind. He wrapped his hands around hers.

'Please God,' he said softly and kissed her.

She kissed him back and then gaily led him towards the door. Resigned, he followed.

When they entered the breakfast room, Emily's parents and two younger brothers were already seated at the table, their plates full. Gus's was the fullest, piled high with fluffy scrambled eggs, although it looked like he had tried to conceal his generous portion by laying a slice of toast across the top.

Rory's gaze travelled over the silver cutlery, the lavish array of dishes on the sideboard, and the footman, David, standing attentively nearby, ready to assist. Reminding himself that this was all now part of his daily life, he joined Emily at the sideboard, filling a plate with scrambled eggs almost as liberally as Gus had. He might be uncomfortable at the idea of a servant being present to wait upon him, but his belly certainly had no objections to his rise in station.

As he and Emily took their seats beside each other, he became aware that the conversation at the table was centred upon the matter of Jack and Gus's education.

'It's September,' Emily's mother was saying. 'If we were still living in Boston, you would both be resuming your classes at Hawes School.'

'Is there a school in the village here?' Gus asked, scooping eggs into his mouth. The persistent wheeze at the edge of his voice was a constant reminder of the trauma he and Jack had endured when they had been forced by the Kelly Greens gang to climb sooty chimneys in New York.

She winced and her teeth nipped the tip of her tongue – Rory had noticed that she often did this in moments of speculation or anxiety.

'There is a small school in Gildham,' she said slowly, 'but it might not be appropriate for you. You see, your tuition will have to be a little different, now that you're living in this big house.'

'Why?' Speaking before he had swallowed, Gus sprayed bits of egg across the tablecloth. His eyes widened and he hastily used his napkin to clean up the mess.

Emily's father cleared his throat. 'You are expected to be taught certain things when you live at this level in society, things that the local boys and girls aren't required to learn. Classical languages, for example, and advanced mathematics. Etiquette as well.'

'What's etiquette?' Jack asked. He had stopped eating his breakfast entirely in order to pay close attention to what his parents were saying.

'Proper behaviour,' Mr McGovern replied. 'It covers quite a lot. How to make polite introductions. How to dress appropriately for a variety of occasions.'

'How to dance with young ladies,' Emily's mother chimed in.

Jack gaped, horror-struck, although Gus appeared intrigued by the notion, propping his elbows on the table with interest.

'And how to employ civilised table manners, of course,' Mr McGovern added, raising a pointed eyebrow at Gus.

Gus dropped his arms beneath the table and lowered his gaze to his egg-soiled napkin, chagrined.

Rory felt as dismayed as Gus looked. He was just as ignorant as the two boys in most of these areas. Emily seemed not to notice his discomposure as she thanked David for pouring her a cup of steaming coffee. Rory reached for the copper pot himself before David could pour a cup for him too.

'How do we learn the right way to do all these things?' Gus asked the table in a small voice.

Mr McGovern gave his younger son an affectionate grin even though he couldn't see it. 'There are two options before your mother and me. We could send you away to public school where you would study with other boys of your own age. Or we could hire a private tutor to instruct you at home.'

Jack waited solemnly, while Gus peeked up with some trepidation.

'We've debated the merits of both,' said their mother, 'and, given your limited exposure to the upper-class world thus far, we've concluded that a tutor would be the best option for now. This will allow you to remain in familiar surroundings while you receive a comprehensive education about that world before you have need to enter it.'

Both boys looked immensely relieved and resumed eating with gusto.

'When do we start?' Gus asked, his hand hovering near his mouth, ready to shield the table if necessary.

'We've already sent out enquiries,' said Mr McGovern. 'But you probably have at least another week or two of freedom.'

Jack and Gus shared a pleased look.

'That means we'll still be able to help Mr Comerford and Rory collect this quarter's rent from the tenants,' said Jack.

The land agent, Mr Comerford, had begun training Rory in earnest to become his deputy, which so far had entailed Rory shadowing him as he conducted estate business. Mr Comerford was a gruff man and took the work seriously, but he had a soft spot for the two younger boys and would not deny them the opportunity to 'help' however they could. So, until the new tutor arrived, he would continue to have three shadows.

'Speaking of Mr Comerford,' said Emily's mother, 'his sister is coming to the house this afternoon to officially begin her duties. Emily, would you care to join me in helping her to settle in?'

'I'd be delighted, Mama,' Emily said.

Mr Comerford's sister was Mrs Hawkins, Polly's widowed mother, and she had been hired as the new housekeeper to replace the despicable Mrs Sandler. Judging by her mother's suggestion, it seemed that Emily, too, would be doing her own share of shadowing.

Jack and Gus finished their breakfasts in a hurry and excused themselves from the table on the pretence of heading early to the stables to be fully prepared for their horse-riding lesson later that morning with their father. Thanks to an ill-judged comment on Gus's part at dinner the previous evening, Rory, along with every other person present, knew that the boys were in fact planning a staged fight with the younger stable hands in the hay barn. Still, no one seemed inclined to thwart their fun as they raced from the room.

After they were gone, Emily said to her parents, 'You're satisfied with your decision to engage a tutor for them?'

Her mother nodded. 'They're not ready to be thrust into that world yet. We're much happier to keep them within our protection for as long as possible.'

'We certainly are,' Mr McGovern said. He swivelled his attention towards Rory. 'I don't wish to cause any offence by saying this, Rory, but we were thinking that you might benefit from some instruction from the tutor as well.'

Rory stiffened. Emily gave him a quick sideways glance; she appeared not to have expected this either.

'Please do not view this as an insult in any way,' her mother said hastily. 'You've already demonstrated a remarkable capability to adapt to your new situation, and we truly believe you have great potential. But perhaps there are some gaps in your experience which could be remedied with the appropriate tutoring. You could go far with the right education.'

Though she delivered this in the kindest way possible, his pride was still stung. At twenty-two years old, was he to be sent to the schoolroom with the children? He knew he wasn't educated, that he didn't understand advanced mathematics or how to make polite introductions, and he comprehended that this was a tremendous opportunity to better himself, to gain the knowledge and skills that would help him navigate his new life. Emily's parents only meant well. And yet, their generous proposal made him feel about two inches tall.

He took a gulp of coffee to delay his response. Accepting the tutor's instruction would be an admission that he wasn't good enough for Emily. He had known this fact all along, but to have it confirmed in such a way left a bitter taste in his mouth that had nothing to do with the coffee. Bloody hell, this was mortifying. He threw a fleeting, embarrassed look at David, but the footman's expression was carefully blank, his gaze trained upon the wall opposite him.

Rory longed to say no. His father-in-law was already employing him as a deputy land agent; allowing him to fund his education would mean relying even further on his assistance. Rory wasn't a McGovern – he was a Carey, and now so was Emily. He wanted to be the man of his family, to be able to provide for himself and his wife as much as he could on his own terms. But he didn't have the means to accomplish that without help. And he would be a fool to turn this opportunity down.

So all he could do was swallow the coffee and, along with it, his pride.

He set down his cup. 'I appreciate the offer,' he said. 'And I accept. I'll do the very best I can to meet your expectations.'

Emily leaned in to link her arm through his. 'There are no expectations,' she said, and the sincerity in her voice made him feel a little better.

Mr McGovern gave a firm nod which seemed to indicate both agreement and approval. 'We'll make the necessary arrangements with the tutor then.'

'Thank you, Mr McGovern,' Rory said. 'And thank you as well, Mrs McGovern.' He stuttered. 'Oh, Christ, sorry. I mean, ah, Lady Courcey.'

She let out a peal of mirth. 'Heavens above, Rory, I'm your mother-in-law. Call me Bridget.'

He honestly didn't think he could. The respect he felt for her went too deep for such informality – even after everything she had been through, even with the exposed scar on her cheek that spoke of horror and pain and humiliation, she carried herself with a dignity that deserved the utmost admiration.

But he didn't want to outright refuse her wish either. Therefore, on this day of concessions, he said, 'Yes, Lady Bridget.'

She accepted his compromise with a soft chuckle.

He thought he would have more time to reflect on what had turned out to be quite a disconcerting breakfast. However, shortly before dinner that evening, David came to him with a message to call to Mr McGovern's bedchamber before the family gathered to dine.

'Did he say what for?' Rory asked, perplexed. Why his bedchamber, and not his study?

The footman gave an apologetic shrug. 'He passed on no other details.'

Following in David's wake, Rory left the east wing, which accommodated the bedchambers of Emily and her brothers, and proceeded to the west wing, where the master apartment was located. David directed him to a closed door and then departed down the corridor. Rory took a breath and rapped his knuckles on the door. At the muffled summons from within, he opened it and stepped inside.

Mr McGovern stood in the centre of the room, his arms outstretched as his valet, Mr Varley, helped him into his tailcoat for dinner. This was another part of the aristocratic lifestyle that baffled Rory, the rigid requirement to change clothing multiple times a day. Having said that, he did have to acknowledge that occasionally it was necessary as he glanced to the side and saw a discarded set of clothes on the floor covered in muck and hay. It appeared that Mr McGovern had also partaken in the boys' barn fight, and with great vigour.

'Thanks for coming, Rory,' he said now as Mr Varley smoothed down his coat at the shoulders. Though the valet was an older man, his wrinkled hands still moved with practised precision, if a little slowly. Once he was satisfied with the coat's fit, he shuffled over to a nearby table and retrieved a brightly polished pocket watch. Emily had told Rory the significance of the watch, that it had once belonged to her grandfather, Lord Courcey. Mr Varley handled it with care, draping the gold chain across Mr McGovern's waistcoat, the barest tremor visible in his aging fingers.

'Thank you, Varley,' Mr McGovern said. 'That will be all for now.'

The valet bowed and turned to pick up the discarded pile of clothing, his spine creaking as he did so. Then he slipped out of the room, the door clicking quietly shut behind him.

Mr McGovern regarded Rory with a wry look. 'I completely understand why you refused the services of a valet. I'm still not accustomed to it myself, but I retained Varley for his own sake. The fellow would have found it hard to acquire another position this late in his life.'

Rory nodded, waiting uneasily to hear why he had been summoned.

Mr McGovern fingered his watch chain meditatively. 'It's just one more surreal aspect of this whole surreal existence. Sometimes it feels as though I was plucked from my old life and dropped into this one like a marionette on strings. I keep expecting the puppeteer to emerge from his hiding place to snigger and declare that it was all a joke.' He raised his eyebrows at Rory. 'I imagine it's not too dissimilar to how you feel at times, is it?'

Rory hesitated. ''Tis a good way to describe it, sir,' he said eventually.

'And what about our conversation this morning? How did that make you feel?'

Rory gulped, unable to find the words to reply. How much of his inner turmoil had he inadvertently revealed at the breakfast table?

Mr McGovern crossed the room to the corner where a cane stood propped against the wall. It had a T-shaped handle made of brass and a beechwood shaft, and he picked it up with an air of reverence.

'Allow me to hazard a guess,' he said, turning back to Rory. 'I expect it brought you a measure of discomfort, or perhaps even shame?'

Rory felt blood rush to his face.

'Let me say first of all that it was absolutely not my intention, nor Bridget's, to stir up any such reaction. We raised the matter purely from a desire to offer you the best prospects going forward. But I think it was a struggle for you to accept. Am I right?'

Rory wished he already had a few lessons with the tutor under his belt so that he might have some hope of finding the right words for this painful discussion. 'It meant admitting I need help,' he muttered. 'So, for sure, it was hard to accept.'

A shadow of regret came into Mr McGovern's blue eyes. 'I'm truly sorry we inflicted that upon you. We ought to have found a better way of broaching the subject. But now that it's done, can I make one thing abundantly clear? There is no shame whatsoever in accepting help from those who are willing and able to give it, especially when it places us in a better position to support our loved ones. In fact, it's a sign of strength.'

Rory wanted so badly to believe it, but doubts crowded his mind. 'Seems like a sign of weakness to me,' he mumbled.

'Strength is not always about power. It also has roots in humility.' Mr McGovern held up the cane. 'Do you see this? It belonged to Lord Bewley. That gentleman helped me in more ways than I can count. His extraordinary bequest upon his death left me in control of an earl's estate, giving me the means to amply support my family at a level I could never have attained as a stable hand, nor even as a carpenter. But long before that, here under this very roof when I was your exact age, he gave me the education I'm offering you. I didn't fully comprehend then what a gift it was. It was only after the passage of many years that I recognised just how much it shaped me into the man I became, into the man I needed to be for Bridget, for Emily, for my two boys. Was it weak of me to accept Lord Bewley's help?'

Rory blinked, and it felt like he was blinking away a veil from his eyes. 'No, sir,' he said thickly, and then added more clearly, 'No, it wasn't.'

'Is it weak of you to accept my help?'

Rory felt a weight lifting from his shoulders. 'No, sir, it isn't.'

'I'm glad you can see it that way now,' Mr McGovern said with a sympathetic smile. 'Bettering yourself through education does not diminish your worth as a man or a husband. Rather than some kind of demeaning act of charity, look upon the tutor's instruction as an investment in your future and a path to achieving your goals.'

'Yes, sir,' Rory said, his back straightening. 'I will.'

Mr McGovern paused. 'At the risk of overburdening you with help, I do want to raise one further proposal for consideration.'

'What is it?' Rory asked, instantly cautious again.

'Your current accommodation.' Mr McGovern set the tip of the cane on the floor and leaned on it as he continued, 'You and Emily are a married couple now and I imagine this makes you crave some greater independence. You doubtless do not wish to have your living situation confined to one bedchamber, even if it is a room of generous proportions.'

It was downright eerie just how perceptive this man was about Rory's innermost thoughts.

'I'd like to put forward two recommendations, which I expect you to discuss with Emily before making a decision. Her preferences must be taken into account in this.'

Rory nodded firmly in agreement.

'Firstly,' Mr McGovern said, 'if you and Emily wish to find your own place to live, I am more than happy to assist you in accomplishing that. I could help you locate a suitable property in an area of your own choosing—you would not be beholden to remain within range of Bewley Hall, of course. The scale of the house and its level of luxury would be entirely up to you both. If you have a preference for something more modest, you might even like to furnish it with your own hands. I remember when I built the furniture for Acorn House in Boston. It was a labour of love, creating a home for my family.'

A vision entered Rory's mind of a cosy cottage filled with furniture crafted by himself, the air redolent with the scents of freshly sawn wood and beeswax polish. He imagined running his palm over the grain of a sturdy kitchen table, and he pictured Emily happily rocking their baby in a charming cradle. The idea of creating a haven for his wife and their future children, piece by piece, was very tempting.

Mr McGovern went on, 'Alternatively, if you decide you would prefer to stay here at Bewley Hall, we could arrange for a section of the house to be converted into a private suite for you and Emily. I'd suggest the upper floor of the east wing as it is rarely used. It would give you a sense of seclusion and independence while still being part of the household. A home within a home of sorts.'

The vision in Rory's mind blurred momentarily. When it reformed, several details had changed – the setting was far more opulent with big windows, plush drapes and elegant furniture too grand to be handmade...although perhaps the cradle might still be a possibility. Could this arrangement truly satisfy his need for autonomy? Putting that question temporarily aside, the important thing was that Emily looked just as happy as she opened a door and ushered in her parents, who beamed as they doted on their small grandchild.

Realising that Mr McGovern had presented him with two favourable futures, equally feasible and full of potential, Rory felt a lump come to his throat.

'This is all...'tis incredibly kind of you, sir,' he managed to say haltingly. 'I don't deserve—'

Mr McGovern came towards him, the cane tapping on the floor. He put his free hand on Rory's shoulder.

'You do,' he said. 'And I want to give it to you, without any loss of face or recompense on your part. Please be assured of this: I consider myself to have a daughter and three sons now.'

# Chapter 3

Bridget twitched back the fabric of the heavy velvet stage curtains and peered surreptitiously out between the drapes into the theatre. The stalls were beginning to fill with ladies and gentlemen dressed in their finery, and the air buzzed with their chatter and a sense of anticipation. She was grateful that so many had come, despite the freezing January night. London's upper classes were not without compassion after all.

Satisfied that she had not been spotted herself, she let the curtains fall back into place and turned to Frances Blythe beside her.

'It is a marvellous turnout,' she said, giving Frances a warm smile. 'Thank you for all your efforts to bring this vital event to fruition.'

Frances rejected the compliment with a dismissive snort. 'It is all thanks to you,' she said, her mannish jaw set in a way that conveyed she would brook no argument on the matter. 'You instigated the entire endeavour. I was merely your voice and your hands.'

'We achieved it together,' Bridget replied firmly. She, too, would stand her ground, for Frances had been indispensable these past months.

When she had initially conceived the idea of organising a charity event to aid the plight of the starving Irish people,

Frances was the first person who had come to her mind. Their time spent working side by side at St Swithun's Workhouse was so very long ago, and they'd had no communication since Bridget fled London with Cormac and Emily, but Bridget had written to St Swithun's in the hope that her kind-hearted companion might still work there. Incredibly, she did. In fact, it was like Frances's life had been frozen in time, for nothing substantial had changed – still unmarried, she continued to toil tirelessly to improve the lives of those fated to suffer within the walls of the unforgiving workhouse. In the space of a dozen years, Bridget had travelled to Boston, New York, England and Ireland, she had borne two more children, and she had lost her job as a seamstress and gained the wealth of a countess, all while Frances had doggedly plodded on in the same place every day, giving every moment of her life to serving others. Bridget felt utterly humbled by the magnitude of Frances's selfless, unwavering humanity.

In further proof of this, the response Frances had sent to Bridget's letter had been swift and wholehearted – she had readily accepted the role of overseeing the charity event and had even offered her own enthusiastic suggestions as to how it could all be managed. In return for her help, Bridget had promised to ensure that a portion of the proceeds would go to St Swithun's too.

She could not have picked a better representative to act on her behalf. She had known from the outset that it would be essential to appoint someone else to be the name and face associated with this venture; her own direct involvement would have only resulted in unanswered letters and closed doors. She could not risk anyone discovering that she had a connection to the event, lest the donors withdraw their financial contributions in self-righteous disapproval. Hence, she now stayed concealed behind the stage curtains instead of mingling among the crowd to thank them for their attendance. She didn't mind the lack of recognition; the most important thing was that the event would raise critical funds that could be sent to Ireland without delay.

Behind her and Frances, the actors were preparing themselves for their imminent performance, murmuring their lines or tracing their steps across the boards. Frances had negotiated with the theatre manager, Mr Puttenham, that three-quarters of the proceeds from the ticket sales would go to the charitable cause. According to Frances, he had only grudgingly agreed to this generous proportion after his aging grandmother, who had Irish heritage, had browbeat him into it.

Bridget espied him now, standing in the wings speaking with Cormac, whose hands were clasped behind his back in a stance of easy confidence. He, too, was an anonymous figure in these proceedings, his personal involvement stretching no further than arranging for the acquirement of the funds after the end of the performance. Mr Puttenham was not truly aware of who Bridget and Cormac were. Only the patrons currently seating themselves in the stalls would understand the significance of the names Lady Courcey and Mr McGovern, and Mr Puttenham had been instructed not to reveal these names publicly – Miss Frances Blythe was to be identified as the sole organiser.

Unable to resist, Bridget tweaked back the curtains again and peeked out at the audience who had no idea that they were supporting a cause spearheaded by a pair so notorious in their circle. A few rows from the front sat a lady with pursed lips and a rigid posture. Bridget recognised her as Lady Ainsley, the leader of the Ladies of Compassion Association which Bridget had joined back when she resided in London as Garrett's wife. Judging by her sour expression, Bridget speculated that Lady Ainsley wished she had been the face of this acclaimed event rather than the drab Miss Blythe.

Bridget's eye travelled further along the row and her breath caught as her gaze fell upon a familiar countenance dominated by a large nose: her old friend Lucy, Lady Newby. Lucy had been the one to help Bridget assimilate into London society when she first came to live there, and she had been a dear companion until Bridget had shattered their friendship by absconding from the city in a state of disrepute.

Bridget blinked and her breath caught again. Looking more closely at Lucy, she realised that her former friend was wearing a gown of dull black crape trimmed with a little grey. Lucy was in mourning. Who had died? Bridget glanced at the seats on either side of Lucy. She was accompanied by two young women – they had been only little girls when Bridget last saw them but they had to be Lucy's grown-up daughters, Angela and Valerie, for they both sported distinctive noses just like their mother's. However, there was no sign of Lucy's husband, Lord Newby. Good gracious, surely not. But then, Lord Newby had been Lucy's senior by fifteen years. The risks of old age and ill-health would both have been at closer proximity to him than his wife.

Moved by compassion, Bridget could not let the question remain unanswered. She dropped the curtains into place once more and turned back to Frances.

'You have already done so much, but I must ask for your assistance yet again.'

She had barely outlined her request, though, before the theatre manager and Cormac approached them.

'It is necessary to clear the stage now,' Mr Puttenham said in a pompous tone. 'The players are ready to begin.' He squinted at Frances. 'Do you still wish to address the audience before the commencement of the performance?'

'Yes, I do,' she said, looking a little nervous at the prospect. She touched Bridget's arm. 'I must go, but come find me at the interval. I'll do my best to help you then.'

'Thank you,' said Bridget. 'I would be so grateful.'

Cormac tilted his head at this unexplained exchange but he didn't question it as Mr Puttenham raised a meaningful eyebrow and he and Bridget were obliged to hurry from the stage into the wings. The actors also scurried off the stage, while Mr Puttenham and Frances waited expectantly in the centre where the velvet curtains met. As two members of the cast took up their positions close to where Bridget and Cormac stood, the curtains parted just enough to allow Mr Puttenham and Frances to slip through. Bridget sidled forwards, found the very end of the curtain where it hung inside the wings and tugged it back just a sliver to obtain a narrow view into the theatre. She could no longer see Lucy or Lady Ainsley from this angle, but she now had a better view of the boxes opposite her. Cormac stepped up behind her so that he could peer out above her head and she enjoyed the sensation of his body pressed close to her back.

She scanned the faces in the boxes and, with a jolt of surprise, found one she had not anticipated. Alone in the lowest tier closest to the stage, Garrett sat stiffly in his chair, exhibiting a notable lack of enthusiasm for his current situation. Bridget had advised Frances to issue an invitation to him out of courtesy, given that he had been the one to draw significant attention to the plight of the Irish at Parliament (an act which he had only undertaken on the condition that Cormac convince his recalcitrant son, Patrick, to finish his school studies), but she had not expected him to accept it. Perhaps he had realised that it would appear strange if he did not attend a charity event that was in aid of a cause he had so publicly advocated.

'You see him?' she mumbled over her shoulder.

'I do,' Cormac muttered back. 'I wonder why Pat isn't with him.'

'Has he already returned to Eton?'

'I don't think so—as far as I'm aware, the Lent Half doesn't commence until next week.'

There was no time to conjecture further because just then Mr Puttenham began to speak, his pompous voice booming out.

'Ladies and gentlemen, allow me to welcome you all here this evening. As you are aware, tonight's performance has been designated in support of the wretched creatures in Ireland who are unable to help themselves. Your benevolence towards your inferior neighbours is deeply appreciated.'

Bridget ground her teeth. Mr Puttenham gave a supercilious bow and then took a grudging step back to let Frances address the audience. Thankfully, she spoke with greater compassion. Clasping her hands tightly in front of her, she described how the potato blight had swept mercilessly through the Irish countryside, obliterating the people's main source of food and leaving them susceptible to severe hunger and disease.

'More than two years of unimaginable torment have left them utterly without hope,' she declared. 'Through no fault of their own, they have been afflicted by the most horrific calamity. With nothing in the soil but rotten tubers, they have been reduced to skin and bones. They shiver in the throes of deadly fever, desperately wondering how they will pay for the coffins of the next ones to perish.'

A number of female gasps rippled through the theatre. It was so reminiscent of the day that Frances had spoken to the Ladies of Compassion Association about the atrocious conditions at St Swithun's Workhouse that Bridget had to blink rapidly to recall herself to the present.

As relentless as ever, Frances carried on, 'None of us can even begin to conceive of the desolation these men, women and children are experiencing. Their anguish is simply beyond our comprehension. But it is not beyond our capacity to ameliorate it, and that is why I'm truly glad to see so many of you in attendance this evening. Your financial contribution to this event is accepted with profound gratitude. My associates and I will ensure that it reaches those who are most in need.'

Frances's hands were now clutched together so fervently that her knuckles had gone white. She unclasped them and stepped back with an awkward nod to indicate that her speech had come to an end, and the theatre manager darted forwards to take the limelight again. However, before he could open his mouth, another voice spoke up.

'I should like to add a few words, if I may.'

Bridget's gaze shot upwards to the box above the stage. Garrett had risen from his chair and was standing with his palms resting on the front of the box. His earlier stiff demeanour had been replaced by an air of composure. He looked out across the stalls, where a sea of faces were now upturned to him.

'While I commend Miss Blythe for her zeal,' he said evenly, 'I feel compelled to highlight the fact that her efforts do not stem from a place of authenticity. She speaks only on the word of others for she has not witnessed any of these circumstances herself.'

Bridget gripped the velvet curtain in horror as Cormac sucked in a breath behind her. What on earth was Garrett doing? Did he mean to dismantle everything they had worked so hard to achieve?

His gaze swept coolly over his captive audience. 'I, on the other hand, have been to Ireland this past year. I've beheld the conditions that pervade the country. And I can tell you that Miss Blythe has not done justice to the situation. This isn't an oversight on her part—it's merely that there are no words in our language to accurately describe how appalling it is.'

Bridget's horror turned to bewilderment.

'I can already surmise that the contributions gathered here tonight will not be sufficient, not by a considerable margin.

Which is why I am pledging a further donation. I intend to match the total sum of the funds raised from the ticket sales and thus double the figure that will be sent to Ireland. I urge you to do the same.'

Complete silence greeted this astonishing announcement. Then, after several long moments, a female voice responded.

'I shall make the same pledge,' she said firmly.

Bridget wasn't able to see the speaker but she recognised the voice – it was Lucy. In the wake of her declaration, a smattering of other voices concurred, and then several more, until the whole theatre was resounding with applause interspersed with cries of 'I shall make the same pledge!' Bridget couldn't guess how many were merely caught up in the fervour of the moment and how many might actually make good on their promises, but she was certain that their charitable cause would wind up with more money at the end of the night than if Garrett had not spoken at all. She watched him as he took his seat again in the box – even at this distance, she could discern that his lip was curled. Was it an expression of disdain? Or perhaps discomfort?

Cormac leaned in close to her ear, speaking in a normal tone so that he could be heard above the applause. 'What game is he playing?'

'I don't know,' she replied. 'This is quite extraordinary.'

'There must be something in it for him,' Cormac muttered.

'There very likely is, but we oughtn't to look a gift horse in the mouth. Whatever his motive may be, I think we should welcome the benefits of it now and deal with its consequences later.'

Looking rather stunned, Frances and Mr Puttenham retreated through the gap in the curtains and left the stage, exiting into the wings opposite Bridget and Cormac. As the applause began to die down, Bridget overheard the two actors nearby grumbling to each other.

'...demeans the nobility of our art to say that we perform it for those pathetic creatures across the sea.'

'Indeed, such an embarrassment.'

'I've heard it said that this blight is God teaching the Irish a lesson. We shouldn't be interfering in his righteous plan.'

'I have half a mind to refuse to go on stage. We are above such a humiliating endeavour.'

Next to Bridget, Cormac said to her in a raised voice, 'You know, I believe that a notable critic from *The Times* is attending tonight's performance. What an opportunity for the players to showcase their talents.'

The grumbling actors went suddenly mute, their faces alight with anticipation. Neither of them made a move to stalk from the wings in protest.

Bridget and Cormac exchanged looks of mingled amusement and glumness. With a resigned shrug, Cormac dismissed the bigotry they had just witnessed.

'What help do you need from Frances at the interval?' he asked as the actors cleared their throats noisily and shook out their limbs with exaggerated movements.

Bridget bit the tip of her tongue. 'I caught a glimpse of Lucy in the audience. I would not venture to approach her, only for the fact that she is in mourning attire. Poor, dear Lucy. I don't know who she has lost, but she was such a strength to me during my years in London that I should dearly like to offer my sympathies. You will probably say it is quite a risk but I've asked Frances to contrive a way for me to speak with her.'

'It is a risk,' Cormac agreed with a grimace, 'but we'll do our best to minimise it. I'm sure there's a space backstage where you can meet her in private and not be observed by the rest of the audience. Let me go and search for one while they are all in their seats.'

Just then, a stagehand strode past them and started hauling on a rope to pull open the curtains from this side. All went quiet in the front of the theatre, so Bridget thanked Cormac silently with a squeeze of his arm and a kiss on his cheek. He slipped away through the wings and out a door at the back of the dim space, while the stagehand grunted and secured the rope in place. As he marched back past her, Bridget tucked herself discreetly next to a piece of scenery in order to watch the performance from the wings.

But her mind was already drifting away as the two nearby actors strutted out onto the stage, their sense of self-importance evident even beneath the veneer of their characters. What reason could there be behind Garrett's very public and atypical display of philanthropy? Would Frances be able to convince Lucy to meet with her? And how would Lucy react if they came face to face?

# Chapter 4

Cormac entered the warren of hallways backstage thinking that this wasn't the first time Bridget's deep capacity for compassion had led her into complicated situations. Even though it had the potential to be problematic, he could not help but love her for it. With any luck, this encounter would not draw any untoward consequences upon them.

He turned onto a corridor with several closed doors on either side but he had hardly taken five paces along it when he heard sounds that were highly inappropriate for the location – a loud moan and a female voice gasping, 'Keep going, I'm almost there!' This was followed by an inarticulate, high-pitched exclamation that left Cormac in little doubt: behind one of the doors further down the hallway, a woman was reaching the climax of her pleasure.

He started to back up – this was someone else's private business and he had no interest in interfering. But then he heard footsteps behind him and, ducking his head out into the corridor he had just come from, he perceived a stagehand approaching, his arms full of fake swords and daggers. Cormac withdrew before the man spotted him and dithered on the spot. He had no idea who the woman was, nor why she would risk her reputation in such a public venue, but he could at least attempt to preserve her modesty, despite her own blatant disregard for it.

Decision made, he waited until the footsteps were nearly upon him and then he barrelled around the corner right into the stagehand. Startled, the man dropped his props, which landed on the floor in a loud clatter of wooden thumps.

'Damn it, my apologies,' Cormac exclaimed. 'I wasn't looking where I was going.'

The man opened his mouth, his expression livid, but whatever rebuke he had been about to hurl at Cormac dissipated when he looked at him properly and took in the fine cut of his clothes.

'No matter, sir,' he muttered and stooped to pick up the fallen props.

Cormac cocked his ear back down the corridor of closed doors. It was utterly silent now. He bent down to gather up the props too, which made the stagehand gape in confusion.

'Sir, there's no need—'

'It's the least I can do after causing the collision,' Cormac said with a grin.

Offering an uncertain grin in return, the stagehand nodded, and together they scooped up all the wooden swords and daggers. After they were securely piled in the man's arms again, Cormac stood back to let him pass. The man trotted away down the length of the corridor and didn't even glance back when one of the doors opened behind him.

A woman emerged from the doorway and glided up the corridor in Cormac's direction. Draped in expensive jewellery, she appeared to be in her mid-forties but the satisfied glow in her cheeks lent her a more youthful air.

'Oh dear, I seem to have lost my way,' she said with impressive equanimity. 'Has the performance already started?'

'Only just now,' Cormac replied, giving her a polite bow. 'Do you require an escort to your seat?'

'That is very kind but I ought to be fine from here, thank you.' Coasting past him, she strode into the other corridor with a surety that suggested she in fact knew these halls quite well.

He turned back to see another figure emerging from the doorway, a young, black-haired man straightening his cuffs with an air of smugness. Cormac's stomach plummeted.

'Patrick,' he said, unable to conceal the disappointment in his tone.

His nephew looked up in surprise. A guilty expression crossed his face but he covered it quickly with a nonchalant toss of his head. He came towards Cormac, his manner totally relaxed.

'Hello, Uncle,' he said. 'What happened to your determination to call me Pat?'

Cormac's jaw tightened. 'That name was to aid your reinvention, to help you develop into the new and better man I know you're capable of becoming. This behaviour looks remarkably like your old self to me.'

Patrick's whole body tensed. 'I don't need a lecture from you. I'll get plenty of those when I return to Eton.'

'So you still intend to complete your final two terms?' Cormac said, privately relieved. He didn't know what kind of a rage Garrett might fly into if Cormac's side of their bargain didn't bear fruit after Garrett's patent success on his part.

'Yes,' Patrick muttered, looking like he was already regretting the decision.

Cormac waved a hand in the direction that the woman had disappeared. 'Then why slip back into old habits? That was the Duchess of Northrop, I presume?'

'Yes,' Patrick muttered again.

'You were warned about pursuing her. You know it is both unwise and unscrupulous. Why revive the liaison when it is a part of the dissolute lifestyle you were supposedly leaving behind?'

Patrick shrugged. 'She asked me to.' He emitted a sigh of exasperation. 'Look, it's not as bad as before. We're being careful this time, meeting in secret, not flaunting it for the whole city to see.'

'You're not being careful enough,' Cormac said levelly. 'You were very nearly discovered by a stagehand just now. Perhaps you might deem such an exposure to be inconsequential, but how long until a person of greater influence catches the two of you together? I expect the duke would be extremely keen to exact retribution, not just on you but on your father as well.'

Patrick looked uncomfortable. 'She's lonely. Her children are more or less grown and her husband pays no attention to her. I'm able to help her feel happy, if only for a little while.'

That gave Cormac pause. 'Are you in love with her?'

His nephew let out a snort. 'Don't be daft. Love doesn't exist, except for the feeble-minded who mistake lust for something more. I suppose you could say I'm in lust though, and that's satisfying enough for me. And for her.' He grinned suggestively.

Cormac felt sorry for the lad, who was demonstrating just how immature he still was. 'Love does exist,' he said quietly. 'And I promise that it will hit you like a ton of bricks when that realisation eventually dawns.'

Patrick rolled his eyes and said nothing.

Cormac repressed a sigh. 'You should go take your seat,' he said. 'The performance has already begun.'

Patrick started to stalk past but then he halted. 'Tell me, did my father make a speech beforehand?'

'He did,' Cormac said with a slight frown. 'Did you expect him to?'

'I asked him to,' Patrick said, 'but I wasn't sure if I'd convinced him.'

He made to carry on up the corridor, but Cormac put out a hand to stop him.

'Wait a moment,' he said, bewildered. 'That speech was your idea?'

'If he talked about making a donation to match the ticket sales, then yes, it was.'

Cormac did his best to conceal his astonishment. 'What compelled you to recommend such a generous measure?'

Patrick glanced away. 'I don't know,' he mumbled. After a long pause, he added in an even lower murmur, 'It just seemed like the right thing to do.'

'The right thing for whom?' asked Cormac.

Patrick grimaced at him. 'You know. The people in Ireland. The ones who are suffering.'

Unable to hide his reaction this time, Cormac regarded his nephew with no small degree of amazement. Patrick glared back.

'Don't look at me like that. I may be a degenerate but I'm not completely devoid of morals.'

'It appears not,' said Cormac. 'Despite your efforts to persuade everyone of exactly that in the past.'

Patrick's glare dissolved into a rueful smile, which made his handsome features much more attractive. 'Fair point. I suppose I have only myself to blame for your scepticism.'

Cormac chewed the inside of his cheek as he considered his nephew. What a paradox he was. Could this surprising development be credited to a budding recognition of his mother's lower-class background? Was he beginning to acknowledge a tiny shred of kinship with the Irish people? After all, their miserable hunger could have been his fate had he not been taken from his first family and raised in upper-class circumstances. Whatever his motivation, Cormac knew better than to push him to admit it. Patrick had proved himself to be as headstrong as a bull if anyone tried to steer him too overtly – he would only improve his character by increments and on his own terms. Still, this was quite a significant step.

Cormac cleared his throat lightly. 'When will you finish your studies at Eton?'

'June,' Patrick replied. 'Along with classmates who will be a year younger than me,' he added glumly.

There was no need to point out that, yet again, he had only himself to blame for that situation.

Cormac moved on smoothly. 'Bridget and I are planning to organise another charity event like tonight, but we are hoping to locate the next one in Dublin. It will probably be the summertime before it can be arranged. If the date falls after your graduation, would you care to attend?'

Patrick hesitated. 'Maybe,' he said at last.

It was as much of a commitment as Cormac could expect. He held out his hand and Patrick shook it. 'Until our next meeting,' Cormac said. 'Good luck with your studies, Pat.'

Patrick's hazel eyes flicked towards Cormac's; Cormac couldn't be certain but he thought that the lad looked a little pleased. Nevertheless, he just nodded offhandedly and walked away around the corner into the next corridor. He would now be terribly late to the performance but at least he could slip into his box unnoticed by anyone except his father. Cormac presumed that the duchess was wealthy enough to have her own box too – whether the duke was waiting there for her or not was a different matter.

Mindful of the fact that he was in no position to judge an adulteress, Cormac made his way down the corridor, returning to his original purpose in coming backstage. He prudently bypassed the door that the duchess and Patrick had emerged from and instead found another room further along that was empty apart from rows of brass rails draped with cloaks and shawls. Mundane but discreet, it ought to serve adequately.

# Chapter 5

Bridget hovered in the cloakroom, her nerves fluttering with apprehension. Cormac had returned to her in the wings before the interval and told her about the room, which she thought would be very suitable since the theatre's patrons would not need to retrieve their outer garments until after the performance was over. As soon as the interval came and the drop curtain was lowered, she had sought out Frances in the other wings and relayed the location to her. Cormac had then led her to the cloakroom and left her there alone. And now she waited.

She imagined how Frances might navigate this sensitive mission. In her mind's eye, she pictured the woman weaving through the milling crowds in the lobby, her plain clothing in blatant contrast to the glittering attire surrounding her. The gazes of the patrons might land upon her and recognise her as the speaker prior to the beginning of the play, but they would likely glance away again, either deeming her unworthy company in which to be seen or wishing to avoid holding to their earlier pledges. Frances would disregard them for now as she searched for Lucy, but Bridget knew she would pounce on them like a terrier later before they departed.

Once Frances found Lucy, how would she broach the matter of requesting her company for a private meeting? Would she reveal to Lucy exactly who wished to meet her, or would she keep Bridget's identity anonymous in the hope that curiosity might sway Lucy to consent? There was a strong likelihood that Lucy would refuse outright – she could look upon the first scenario as repugnant and the second as ill-mannered. Or she might not wish to leave her daughters unaccompanied. After ten minutes had passed, Bridget began to doubt. After another five, she became entirely convinced of the failure of the mission. Her shoulders slumped. Before much longer, the theatre bell would ring and the audience would be expected to return to their seats.

The door opened.

She straightened, quickly angling her face a little to the side. Whether it was Lucy or a theatre attendant entering, she didn't wish for either of them to observe her scarred cheek if she could help it. She distinguished Frances's mannish jaw first as the woman peered around the doorway, and then Frances stepped aside and ushered Lucy into the cloakroom.

A crease between Lucy's brows smoothed out as her gaze fell upon Bridget. 'I suspected this mysterious request had come from you,' she said, her tone neutral. 'Tonight's event has your stamp all over it, even if the majority of the assembly out there do not recognise it.'

'But you still chose to come meet me?' Bridget said, a tiny spark of hope igniting in her gut. Could Lucy be prepared to forgive her after all these years?

Her erstwhile friend gave a noncommittal shrug. 'I will hear what you have to say. That is all.'

The tiny spark sputtered out. 'I appreciate that,' Bridget said quietly.

'I'll leave you two be,' Frances said. 'Do bear in mind that the bell will ring soon.' She backed out, closing the door behind her.

Bridget and Lucy regarded each other in silence, and Bridget took the opportunity to scrutinise her old friend more closely.

The small details that she could not make out from the stage now presented themselves plainly: the bloodshot tinge to her eyes, the downward curve of her mouth, the faint droop in her posture. Lucy had once been a person of great vitality and optimism – now she was but a pale imprint of that vivacious woman. It was all Bridget could do not to rush forwards and embrace her, to try to coax life back into her wilted form.

'Oh, my dear Lucy,' she murmured. 'Who did you lose?'

Lucy cast a sad, self-conscious glance down at her mourning attire.

Scarcely wanting to ask, Bridget managed to squeeze out, 'Was it Lord Newby?'

When Lucy looked up again, Bridget read the pain and acknowledgement in her expression.

'Dearest, I am so deeply sorry,' she said, conscious that the sympathy of a disgraced former friend would surely hold little value.

'Thank you,' Lucy said mechanically. It seemed like she would not say anything more but, abruptly, a small sob cracked out of her. 'Oh, goodness,' she mumbled, stifling it at once. 'I do apologise.'

'There's nothing to apologise for,' Bridget said earnestly. 'You are grieving. This is an extraordinarily difficult time for you.'

'It has been...very hard.' Lucy grimaced. 'I ought not to still be so distressed. He passed a year ago. But apart from church, this is my first public outing since my transition from full mourning to half mourning. I must confess I'm finding it rather overwhelming.'

'That is understandable,' Bridget said, wanting so badly to wrap her hands around Lucy's to give her comfort. 'He accompanied you on many occasions to events such as this.'

'More than once tonight, I turned to the seat beside me, meaning to share my appreciation of a witty line with him. I had to catch myself when I found Valerie there instead.'

Bridget pressed her lips together in compassion. 'How are the two girls faring? But I shouldn't call them girls, of course. They're grown women now.'

'They are,' Lucy said with a watery sniff. 'They were distraught at the loss of their papa, naturally, but they had been flourishing before that. Both of them are engaged to be married.'

'Oh, that is happy news,' Bridget said, keeping her enthusiasm muted.

'Their weddings had to be delayed until they were out of mourning, but now they can move forwards with the preparations. I expect them both to be married by midsummer. They have made respectable matches—a viscount for Angela and an earl for Valerie.'

Bridget would have supposed it to be a source of joy for Lucy to see her daughters make such advantageous alliances, but her sorrowful air did not abate. If anything, she seemed to grow gloomier.

'It is terribly selfish of me,' she said, 'only I cannot help but dread the day they both leave our home for good. I fear my loneliness will press even more heavily upon me in an entirely empty house.'

'But I'm sure you will still see them often,' Bridget said in an encouraging tone. 'After they have settled into married life, they will be only too delighted to have their mama come to stay. And they will positively fight over you when their babies come along and they desperately need your advice.'

At last, Lucy mustered a small smile. 'I do look forward to becoming a doting grandmother.' Her smile fell away, no doubt as she remembered that there would be no doting grandfather by her side. She shook her head. 'I am being quite ridiculous. Deep down, I always knew this day would come. Ronald was much older than me, after all. But when I was a green bride, I didn't spare a thought for the likelihood that I would end up spending more of my life as a widow than a wife.'

Bridget had no words of consolation in response to this. Lord Newby had been Lucy's senior by fifteen years, which put him in his mid-fifties at the time of his death. Objectively speaking, it was a reasonable age to attain, but of course that was no solace to his lonely, grieving widow.

Another grimace twisted Lucy's countenance. 'At least I may remain in my home for now. Ronald's nephew inherited the Newby title and is still a bachelor, so he has no need of it yet. But I shall be obliged to remove to the dower house once he marries. I cannot decide whether that will be easier or harder to bear.'

Bridget felt her pity swell even more. Perhaps the dower house would be less painful for Lucy without memories of Lord Newby nestled into every corner, but it would also be an undeniable signal that her life had become superfluous without a husband to attend to nor children to rear.

Bridget swallowed. Emily was already grown, and Jack and Gus were only a few short years away from manhood. How would she feel if, God forbid, Cormac passed away and she found herself in Lucy's unenviable position, redundant in the roles of both wife and mother?

She banished the thought uneasily. 'Now that you are out of full mourning,' she said, 'perhaps rejoining society will ease some of your despondency? You might be able to find a sense of purpose in resuming work with the Ladies of Compassion, or even simply in socialising with others again. I'm sure Cassandra and Alice will be delighted to—'

'I am no longer much acquainted with either of them,' Lucy said rigidly.

Bridget blinked. 'Whyever not? I understand that your contact with them would have been more limited this past year, but—'

'Our discord began before my husband's passing.' Lucy wrinkled her large nose. 'And I was the one who initiated the division. It pains me to admit this but I do not esteem them as highly as I once did.'

Bridget forced herself not to gape. Lucy, Cassandra and Alice had been close friends with each other before Bridget had ever joined their group and she knew that they had maintained their association long after that – Cormac had related to her how the trio had crossed paths with him when he came to London in pursuit of Emily. His spontaneous rescue of Alice before she was crushed beneath the wheels of a speeding carriage had resulted in the ladies identifying him as the man who had impersonated Oliver Davenport, and he had very swiftly found himself in a prison cell.

Lucy reached out and fingered the fur of a shawl hanging on the nearest brass rail. 'No doubt Mr McGovern has already told you this, but the three of us were in attendance at the Old Bailey when he was tried for fraud.'

'Yes,' Bridget said cautiously. 'He said that Alice was called upon as a witness.'

An expression of disgust rippled over Lucy's countenance. 'She was, and she told such a barefaced lie that it left me stunned with disbelief. I could hardly credit the fact that she sat there in a court of law and went so far as to commit perjury in her ambition to ensure Mr McGovern's conviction.' Lucy shot Bridget a wry look. 'I know he is far from an innocent man, but in this he was blameless. She actually announced to the judge and jury that there had been a secret engagement between herself and Mr Daven—Mr McGovern. It was such a spiteful act on her part to try to punish him for not reciprocating her feelings. Much as Cassandra and I had tried to engineer that match, it was evident that he never paid more particular attention to Alice than any other lady. Apart from you, of course.'

Bridget winced. 'You had begun to suspect our liaison before the truth came to light.'

Lucy's fingers clutched the shawl's fur more tightly. 'I had, and that was something else I could hardly credit. Surely our dear friend, our admirable heroine of the workhouse, could not be engaged in a scandalous affair. How utterly absurd. For so long, I refused to give it any credence.'

Bridget felt the old sting of shame prickle across her skin. 'But you ultimately confided your suspicions in Lord Newby.'

A shadow of hurt filled Lucy's bloodshot eyes. 'And he broke that confidence to inform Lord Wyndham. It was the one time when I felt he placed the value of male fellowship above that of marital loyalty. We went through a difficult period after that, though we eventually found an even keel again once I was ready to forgive him.'

Bridget noted that Lucy did not seek forgiveness for her own actions. Why would she? She did not approve of Bridget's adulterous conduct with Cormac, so she would see no need to apologise for the disclosure of her misgivings that had led, albeit inadvertently, to their discovery.

Deciding that there was nothing to be gained from dwelling upon past deeds that could not be undone, Bridget said, 'Did you confront Alice about her dishonesty?'

Lucy gave a grim nod. 'She simply would not admit that her behaviour had been appalling. When I asked her how she would have felt had his conviction been secured based upon her false testimony, she said that she would have been entirely satisfied. To my shock, Cassandra concurred. According to her, the method did not matter so much as the verdict and she felt heartily disappointed that they had been cheated out of the spectacle of seeing the scoundrel being led away to a prison ship or a gallows.' Lucy's mouth twisted sardonically. 'I cannot deny that Cassandra has on numerous occasions displayed a discouraging degree of shallowness in her character. But it truly astounded me that she could value her own thirst for entertainment above a basic sense of justice. I told her so, and she did not take my bluntness well. After exchanging some rather cutting remarks among the three of us, we ceased all familiar association. Since then, I have only met either of them in society situations where we have all taken care to keep our distance.' Lucy sighed. 'Initially, the loss did not seem so great. But now I feel like a building whose buttresses have all been torn down. Once my daughters' husbands take them away, I shall have no pillars left to prop me up. It will be only a matter of time before I fall into isolated ruin.'

'Oh, dearest, do not think that,' Bridget said impulsively. 'You shall always have my friendship if you ever wish to seek it.'

Lucy's gaze became shuttered. Bridget ought to have known better than to suggest such a notion – in Lucy's eyes, her character was as soiled as Alice's and Cassandra's. Lucy let go of the shawl and took a step back.

'Why did you want to meet me tonight?' she asked. 'And in this clandestine way?'

'To express my condolences, that's all,' Bridget said with sincerity. 'There was no ulterior motive, I swear. As for the surreptitious nature of it, that was regrettably necessary. I'm sure you can see that it would not benefit our charitable cause were it to be discovered that I or Cormac had any connection to it.'

'And you trust me not to divulge this fact to the other patrons once I return to the lobby?'

Bridget hesitated. In truth, it had not even occurred to her that revealing herself to Lucy might jeopardise her anonymity at large. Now, the naïveté of this venture struck her with full force. 'I hope that you would not do so,' she said weakly.

Lucy did not respond and in the silence that followed they heard the distant ringing of the theatre bell.

'I must go,' she said.

'Lucy—' Bridget started, beginning to panic.

'I will not betray your identity,' Lucy said stiffly. 'I believe that this is a cause worth supporting and therefore I won't do anything to impair its success.'

'Thank you,' Bridget said, relieved.

'Although I scarcely dare to imagine how Lord Wyndham would react if he became aware of your involvement. Doubtless, he would immediately withdraw his generous donation and encourage everyone else to do likewise.'

Bridget endeavoured to maintain a bland expression at this as they heard a soft knock on the door.

'Ladies, the bell,' came Frances's uneasy voice.

Lucy started to move towards the door. 'Do not worry, I won't breathe a word of this to him when I go back to the lobby.' At Bridget's palpable confusion, she halted to add, 'I left Angela and Valerie in the company of Lord Wyndham and his son when Miss Blythe lured me away.'

'Why were you speaking to Garrett in the first place?' Bridget asked, perplexed.

The corners of Lucy's mouth drooped a little more. 'You are not the only one who wished to express condolences this evening. Tonight has been our first contact since the funeral. He and Ronald were long-standing companions, remember?'

Bridget did indeed remember. In fact, their bond had been so steadfast that Lord Newby had stood up with Garrett at his and Bridget's wedding. With a jolt, she realised that Garrett had lost his closest friend upon Lord Newby's death and that he must surely have been in a state of grief too. He had made no mention of his bereavement during the course of the events the previous summer, but then he had been justifiably distracted by the ordeal of his near hanging, courtesy of a group of angry, starving Irishmen.

Suddenly, Bridget's mind caught on another detail that Lucy had mentioned. 'His son was with him?' she said with a touch of apprehension. Cormac had told her about his brief encounter with Patrick backstage – it sounded like the boy was still as reckless as ever in sexual matters, and Bridget didn't like the idea of him being in close proximity to Angela and Valerie, who were all Lucy had left to bring her joy. 'I must warn you—'

The door opened a crack and both the theatre bell and Frances's voice grew louder as she hissed urgently, 'The audience will be returning to their seats. It's past time to go.'

Lucy hurried to the door and Bridget followed in her wake. 'Please take heed,' she said quickly. 'Do not leave your daughters alone with Patrick Lambourne.'

Lucy's eyes widened but there was no time to say anything else as Frances whisked Lucy away down the corridor and Bridget was left alone once again in the cloakroom.

She let out a shaky breath. Much as she hated to show a lack of faith in Cormac's nephew, he had not yet demonstrated that he had the maturity to act like a gentleman. And Lucy's daughters were still unmarried – heaven forbid that Patrick might take a fancy to one or the other and pursue a conquest without a thought for the consequences.

Because the consequences of sullying a chaste young woman would be so much graver than dallying with an already-married duchess.

# Chapter 6

The bristles of Emily's brush whispered across the canvas, forming new peaks in the oil paint and adding more depth to the still life she was painstakingly creating. She glanced up at the table set alongside the wall of her parlour, upon which she had arranged a jar of yellow crocuses, accompanied by a silver candlestick, a pearl necklace and a decorative fan, all against the backdrop of a velvet cloth the colour of rich burgundy. She had assigned herself quite a challenge; capturing the details of this composition, from the lustre of the pearls to the texture of the fabric, would be a robust test of her abilities.

Nevertheless, she was determined to persevere until she got it as close to perfection as possible. She had been practicing diligently every day because she intended to apply soon to an art academy in England, now that it was absolutely certain that she and Rory would not be returning to America. Though this had been looking very likely anyway, their definite decision to remain on this side of the Atlantic had only come after much discussion between them, following the revelation of her father's two generous proposals for their living arrangements. Evaluating his suggestions from all angles, they had eventually opted for the private suite at Bewley Hall, and it made her so glad that she would stay close to her parents and brothers.

She sometimes wondered if Rory would have preferred the other option of residing separately from her family, but he had encouraged her to express her preference and seemed quite content to go along with it. It made a lot of sense for him too, after all, taking into account his training as the estate's deputy land agent and the fact that the tutor had since joined the household. Dwelling here meant that he could fully commit to both of those paths in situ. On the back of all this, he had written to Boston to cancel the lease on the carpentry workshop; that era of their lives was now well and truly over.

Their suite, on the upper floor of the east wing, had undergone a remarkable transformation over the past several months. What had once been a collection of unused rooms had now become a cosy sanctuary for her and Rory, comprising a drawing room, a bedchamber, a bathing room, and an additional chamber that remained empty for the time being but that would, she hoped fervently, serve as a nursery one day.

Though her womb was still empty for now, she reminded herself that these things could not be rushed as she carefully applied more chrome yellow to the crocus petals. The gentle March sunlight filtered through the parlour windows, casting a warm glow upon her work, and she found herself lost in the peaceful rhythm of her brushstrokes.

Her peace was broken when a knock came at the door, but she didn't mind because it was her dear mama who entered the room. Her heart swelled with gratitude every time she looked upon her mother and remembered how she had survived such a harrowing nightmare at the hands of those starving men on that farm in Ireland. Although her mother had emerged with both external and internal scars, Emily was just thankful that she was alive, and that she had a smile on her face as she crossed the parlour to where Emily sat on her tall stool.

'How is the latest masterpiece coming along?' she asked, peering over Emily's shoulder at the incomplete painting propped on the easel. 'Oh my, the sheen you have accomplished on Lady Bewley's pearls is superb.'

She stepped over to the table and bent to look closer at the items arrayed upon it, but she didn't touch anything. The pearl necklace occupied a particular place of honour in the still life owing to the fact that Polly, who was very protective of Lady Bewley's possessions, had offered it with great solemnity when Emily had enquired if there was any piece of pearl jewellery in the house which she could include in the arrangement. It was elegantly simple, just two strings of pearls draped across the velvet backdrop, but it had once adorned the neck of a lady whose greatest riches had been her kind heart and her generous soul, and thus Polly, Emily and her mother all treated it with the utmost reverence. Emily had actually tried to refuse it but Polly had insisted, saying that Lady Bewley would have been only too delighted to support Emily's artistic endeavours.

As though her thoughts had been following the same thread, Emily's mother said, with her gaze still locked upon the necklace, 'You know, it is a true sign of Polly's esteem that she permitted you to have this. She believes you are destined for international renown with your remarkable talent.' She straightened and turned back to Emily with an expression of pride. 'Of course, I could not agree more. You have an extraordinary gift and I hope you will always find time to nurture it, even when other blessings come into your life.'

Emily felt a flush of warmth through her chest. She harboured enormous ambitions for her art that were nearly too lofty to speak aloud, so it meant a great deal when others articulated their faith in her abilities, even if those voices were tremendously biased.

Her mother approached her at the easel again. 'I'm sorry I disturbed your work, but I came to let you know that our plans will be able to go ahead this summer. We have just received confirmation from Mr Dunhill at the Theatre Royal in Dublin. He has agreed to not one, but two charity performances at his theatre this July.'

'That's wonderful news,' said Emily. 'It will have such an impact on the cause.'

'I do hope so,' said her mother. 'Did your father tell you he has invited Patrick to attend?'

'Oh, indeed,' Emily said neutrally. Her feelings towards her cousin were complicated, to say the least. Most of the evidence she had seen demonstrated that he was an arrogant, self-centred lounger, and yet he had played a minor role in freeing her mother at the farm, so she had to acknowledge that there must be a modicum of decency buried deep within him. The worst thing she could say about him was that he was too like his father, whom she would never forgive for having deceived her with his letter full of lies that had lured her from Boston to London, and had very nearly resulted in her own father's conviction at the Old Bailey courthouse. To be frank, if she never saw either of them again, it would be too soon. But Patrick was family, so allowances had to be made.

'Will he reside with us in Dublin or might he have an alternative for accommodation?' she asked, discreetly crossing her fingers around her paintbrush.

'If he comes, I expect he will reside with us. He is unlikely to want to stay at Anner House—I imagine Lord and Lady Anner will have no wish to see him.'

That was a realistic assumption – when Garrett and Patrick had publicly announced their biological connection, the Anners had been exposed as frauds for having falsely claimed Patrick, whom they had named Edward, to be their nephew and heir. No, they certainly would have no desire to welcome him back under their roof.

'And where shall we stay while we're in the city?' Emily asked. The previous year, her mother had sold the Dublin townhouse belonging to the Courcey title in order to raise funds to support the struggling tenants on the Oakleigh Estate.

'I have already made enquiries about that. I wrote to my uncle's second cousin, the new Lord Walcott—' Her mother cut herself off with a rueful laugh. 'How silly of me, he's not "new" at all—he has held that title for over ten years now. I suppose I still find it hard to conceive of anyone but my dear, lavish uncle being the Lord Walcott.' Emitting a wistful sigh, she carried on. 'I wrote to his cousin at Lockhurst Park to enquire about his townhouse in Dublin, on Rutland Square. We visited it when you were younger, do you remember?'

Emily could recall a few sparse details from that time – her colossal granduncle reclining on a chaise longue, his small dog barely able to manage a weak yap, and an extravagant amount of food for breakfast.

'He confirmed that it is vacant at present and that he is willing to rent it to us for the duration of our stay in the city. We shall not need it above a few weeks—after the performances are over and the money has been collected, I hope we'll make our way down to Oakleigh. The boys still have never been there and I long for them to see it.'

That lifted Emily's spirits again. How special it would be for her brothers to finally stand in the place that meant so very much to their parents, the place where the first seeds of their close-knit family had been sown. Jack and Gus may have been born and raised in America and currently living in England, but Ireland was nonetheless their native land.

Buoyed by this pleasant notion, she brought her brush back up to the canvas. However, her mother was not finished.

'Gooseberry,' she said, an endearment which Emily had become fond of again, now that she had grown out of her adolescence. 'We believe we'll be able to have a more visible presence at these events in Dublin. Do you think they might be a suitable occasion for Rory's first foray into society?'

Emily's hand stilled. She turned to face her mother. 'That's a good idea,' she said cautiously. 'He's making fine progress with the tutor. This could be the ideal opportunity to put his new skills to use.'

Her mother studied her for a moment. 'But you're apprehensive about how he'll handle it?'

Emily winced. 'I know he'll be very nervous. He doesn't have a great deal of confidence yet. I think he just can't see himself fitting into that world at all.'

'I wonder if perhaps the best way to improve his confidence is to confront it straight on then?' her mother suggested gently.

'Perhaps,' said Emily. 'I'll speak to him about it.'

'Do, and remind him that we would all be there to support him. He wouldn't be facing it alone.'

Emily smiled. 'Thank you, Mama, I will.'

After her mother departed from the parlour, Emily stared absently past her easel out the window as she tried to picture her down-to-earth Rory mingling among pretentious lords and ladies. She had every faith that he was capable of doing anything he set his mind to – the obstacle most likely to trip him up would be his own lack of faith. He would need plenty of time to prepare himself mentally for the task.

It would probably be best to forewarn him now, she decided, and she slipped down off her stool to seek him out. Before she left the parlour, she used a rag to wipe off the excess paint from her brush, cleaned it with turpentine and water, and then laid it flat to dry – she had learned from frustrated experience that carelessly leaving her brushes standing in water for too long resulted in bent bristles. She wanted to prove that she was a serious artist at whichever art academy she attended next, and taking good care of her materials was a pertinent part of that proof. She refused to give them even the smallest reason to decline her application. That made her think darkly of her former instructors, Mr and Mrs Brubaker, who had recommended their daughter over Emily for a place at the National Academy of Design in New York, despite the other girl's lesser talent. Some impediments were beyond her control, she supposed, but in everything else she would do her utmost to meet the mark and, even better, surpass it.

Locking the parlour door behind her out of an abundance of caution for the security of the pearl necklace, she proceeded along the corridors of Bewley Hall until she approached the room that had been designated as the domain of the tutor, Mr Humphrey. Even before she reached it, she heard his cheerful voice with its subtle Scottish lilt drifting through the slightly open door. She sidled up to the gap and peered in to catch a glimpse of him standing in front of a large table scattered with books, pencils and a brass protractor. Rory, Jack and Gus sat around the table, their collective attention on Mr Humphrey as he elaborated on some sort of mathematical problem.

She'd had little interaction with the tutor herself, but Rory had confided in her that he had never met a man so determined to extract the positive from even the gloomiest horizon. Neither Rory nor Gus had been illustrious students to begin with, and Mr Humphrey had scrabbled to praise such things as their 'perseverance' and their 'enthusiasm' until they had begun to show signs of improvement. At least Jack's grasp of the academic material had been satisfactory enough that the tutor could take solace in him, and Rory had since reported that he and Gus were gradually catching up.

As she lingered at the doorway, Mr Humphrey wagged his finger at his three students and said, 'Bearing all of that in mind, now answer me this. If a merchant purchases a fabric at five shillings a yard, and then goes on to sell it at eight shillings a yard, how much profit will he make on a sale of 120 yards?'

Jack and Gus both reached for their pencils to start their calculations. Rory, on the other hand, remained still, a small crease on his forehead. Then he said aloud, '360 shillings.'

Mr Humphrey beamed. 'Aye, Mr Carey, precisely! Very well done. I wager you wouldn't have produced such a quick answer even a fortnight ago.'

Rory flushed with embarrassed pleasure. ''Tis getting easier,' he acknowledged.

'*It's* getting easier,' Mr Humphrey corrected. 'While I commend your arithmetical progress, you must also apply the same diligence towards your elocution. No challenge is too great for a capable young man such as yourself.'

As Rory nodded half-heartedly in reply, Gus chirped, 'The answer is 360 shillings!' His face was the picture of innocence but the page in front of him was blank, and Emily suspected that he had exercised his ears rather than his mind.

Nevertheless, she turned away from the door beaming as brightly as Mr Humphrey. It appeared that Rory was not only catching up, but forging ahead. She could not be prouder of him.

Rather than interrupting the lesson, she decided it would be best to wait until later to broach the subject of the Dublin charity events with him. However, she had hardly retreated down the corridor when she heard stampeding footsteps behind her and, whirling around, she saw Gus barrelling into view.

'Mr Humphrey let us finish a bit early!' he informed her as he ran by without stopping. 'We're going out to the paddock for a ride before dinner.'

Jack came jogging after his younger brother, offering Emily a patient smile. He carried on and the two boys vanished out of sight. Chuckling to herself, she retraced her steps to the door of the tutor's room where Rory was just emerging. His face lit up when he saw her and her insides fluttered in response. Though they were still in the early days of their marriage, she hoped that sensation would never fade.

'I was hoping to catch you,' she said shyly. 'Do you have a little time for us to speak together? Or are you going out to the paddock too?'

He gave her a lopsided grin. 'I could walk there very slowly.'

She grinned back and took the arm he offered her, a gentlemanly gesture that was most certainly a product of Mr Humphrey's tutelage. It wasn't that he hadn't been courteous before, only that he was starting to gain a better understanding of the precepts that now governed their lifestyle. She wouldn't have minded at all if he hadn't offered his arm, but she enjoyed leaning into him as they strolled along the corridor in Jack and Gus's wake.

'I may have eavesdropped on your lesson a few minutes ago,' she confessed. 'I overheard Mr Humphrey posing his mathematical question, followed by your very swift answer.' She squeezed her arm against his. 'He was impressed, and so was I.'

Rory ducked his head, a faint blush colouring his cheeks. 'I've been working hard,' he admitted. 'I want to be worthy of you and your family.'

Taken aback, she halted, which compelled him to stop as well. 'You *are* worthy,' she said, gazing earnestly up at him. 'Don't ever doubt that for a second. An education wouldn't make a blind bit of difference to what I think of you, nor to how much I love you. My parents would say the very same.' She giggled.

'Though, of course, their love for you is of rather a different nature to mine.'

He grimaced instead of laughing too. 'It'd make a big difference to what other people think of me though, like Bewley Hall's wealthy neighbours, or society in general.'

She sobered. 'Yes, well, that is in fact what I wanted to speak with you about.' She urged him to begin walking again, heading in the direction of the side door that the family used when they wished to go outside without the pomp and circumstance of being attended by the butler and the footman at the front door. 'Mama just told me that she and Papa are definitely able to proceed with their planned charity events in Dublin this summer.'

She felt him stiffen, and she knew he understood what that implied for him.

'How would you feel about it?' she asked quietly.

He didn't answer right away. They reached the side door where he placed his hand on the latch but didn't make a move to open it.

'I know 'tis the next natural step,' he said. 'And 'tis also an inevitability—if I don't go to these events, there'll be others in the future. So I'll make sure I'm ready for these ones.'

He opened the door. A gust of cool March air swirled into the corridor and she shivered. She had not brought her shawl so she didn't follow him when he stepped outside, choosing to hover on the threshold as he turned back to face her. The breeze tousled his shaggy brown hair, making it even more dishevelled than usual.

'I don't want you to feel pressured into it,' she said. 'You're under no obligation to attend if it will cause you discomfort.'

His mouth slanted in a wry expression. 'That's also an inevitability. But I'll be fine. 'Tis time for me to grasp that nettle.'

She worried at her lower lip with her teeth as she contemplated him. 'What troubles you the most about the prospect of it?'

He gave a casual shrug, but she discerned the shadow of uneasiness behind the gesture. She waited, still and patient.

At last, he said, 'Just that 'tisn't who I really am. You and I both know it, and everyone around us will probably figure it out too. I'm going to feel like an impostor from start to finish.'

She pondered that, wondering how best to assuage his concerns. It wasn't dissimilar to how she had felt on many social occasions in her life. The ball at Marlowe House in Boston came particularly to her mind, when she had donned a beautiful gown that did not belong to her and infiltrated the party pretending to be one of the guests. However, in contrast to Rory attending the upcoming events in Dublin, she'd had absolutely no entitlement nor invitation to be present at that ball. She had been a maidservant in the employ of Mr and Mistress Marlowe, and everything about that night had been an act. With that recollection, an idea occurred to her and she brightened.

'Rather than thinking of yourself as an impostor,' she said, 'why not believe that you're an actor? You will merely be playing a role, and interacting with your audience directly instead of performing to them from a stage.'

He eyed her doubtfully.

'I'm not jesting,' she said. 'I mean it. Let's invent a character for you to play. He can be someone who is entirely at ease in society situations, who doesn't care how the upper classes perceive him, who is able to converse effortlessly with lords and ladies alike. You can slip him on like a glove, and remove him at the end of each night.'

He ran a hand through his hair. 'It's that simple, is it?'

'It could be,' she said, undaunted. She waved her arm through the air as though she were brandishing a wand like a sorceress. 'Think of yourself as a lord, and you shall become one.'

Playing along, he straightened his shoulders and raised his chin at a lofty angle. 'What power you wield. I can feel the change happening already. Am I an earl like Lord Bewley was?'

'Heavens, why stop there? You shall be a duke!' She gave him a deep curtsey on the threshold. 'I am so very pleased to make your acquaintance, your Grace. What an honour it is to be in the presence of the admirable Duke of' – she cast about for a name that sounded suitably noble – 'Desmond,' she finished grandly.

He made an exaggerated bow in return. 'The honour is all mine, fair lady.'

She fluttered her eyelashes. 'With such a distinguished title, I imagine you must be exceptionally rich. Pray tell, where is your vast estate?'

'A fertile land called County Kerry,' he replied. 'Don't judge it for being located in Ireland. 'Tis—I mean, *it's* a place of glorious beauty.'

'Oh, I've no doubt there isn't an estate in all of the British Isles to rival the splendour of Desmond Hall. I do hope I shall be able to visit it sometime.'

He squinted at her. 'Isn't it improper for a lady to invite herself into a gentleman's home?'

She let out a tinkle of laughter. 'Indeed, it is. I am also playing a role—that of a wanton woman who wishes to be ravished in the wilds of Kerry.'

'Well, in that case...' He stepped up to the threshold and braced his forearms against both door jambs, leaning over her. 'This duke would be very happy to oblige.'

He bent his head and locked his mouth upon hers in a kiss that was instantly hot and fierce. The passion of it stole her breath away and she grabbed his lapels, pulling him closer. Her skin heated, banishing all awareness of the cool weather until the breeze swept a lock of his shaggy hair across her forehead, tickling her eyebrows. She tittered and drew back from their embrace.

'I wonder,' she said, brushing his unruly strands back with her fingers, 'whether the Duke of Desmond might favour a slightly shorter cut?'

He nodded in resignation. 'I reckon he probably would.'

# Chapter 7

Rory stared at his reflection in the tall, freestanding mirror and adjusted his white cravat with some consternation. He just couldn't seem to get it right this evening. With a grunt, he whipped it off and started again.

In the mirror, he observed Emily approaching behind him. They were in the bedchamber allocated to them for the duration of their stay at Rutland Square and Jennie had already left, having fulfilled her role with stunning success – Emily was a vision in some sort of soft pink material that Rory couldn't name but very much wanted to run his hands all over. Perhaps there would be time to indulge before they went downstairs, if only he could tie this bloody cravat correctly.

'I think you almost had it two attempts ago,' she said tentatively. 'May I help?'

Wordlessly, he held out the long strip of cloth to her and she shook it out to remove the creases he had created in his previous unsuccessful efforts. Then she reached up to loop it around his neck; he bent his knees but she still had to stand on her tiptoes. Her knuckles grazed his recently shaven chin as she knotted the cravat with agile fingers, making it sit securely at his throat. When she dropped back to the balls of her feet, he examined himself in the mirror and saw that she had achieved the desired look at last. Relief swept over him – he had enough to be worrying about this evening without fretting over his attire too.

'There you go,' Emily murmured next to him. 'You look dashing, your Grace.'

He mustered a weak smile. The concept of bluffing his way through tonight and tomorrow night had seemed doable a few months ago, but now the occasion was upon them and he feared that the Duke of Desmond would not be enough to save him from making a fool of himself.

He didn't voice his apprehension as he busied himself donning his gloves, but Emily must have sensed it.

'Don't let your confidence fail you now,' she said bracingly. 'Just keep reminding yourself that it's for an important cause—the proceeds raised across these two nights will help so many people still suffering on account of the blight. You can do this. And I'll be right beside you.'

He took a deep breath and nodded. Casting one final glance at the mirror, he noted with regret that his shortened hair exposed his big ears more and he felt a greater degree of self-consciousness about them than he had in a long time. Seizing his top hat like it was a piece of armour that would shield them from ridicule, he jammed it on and then he and Emily left the bedchamber to go downstairs.

The rest of the family had already gathered in the entrance hall, a tall footman lingering unobtrusively in the background. Mr McGovern and Lady Bridget stood close together, the former carrying Lord Bewley's cane and the latter rubbing nervously at the scar on her cheek. Jack hovered with his back to the wall, while Gus wandered about restlessly; still too young to be out in society, neither of them would be going to the theatre. Rory wished he could stay behind with them.

And there, leaning nonchalantly against the newel post at the bottom of the stairs, was Patrick. He had only arrived in

Dublin earlier that day, and his reception had been mixed. Emily had greeted him coolly, but her parents had been quite cordial, while her brothers had welcomed their cousin with enthusiasm – his cavalier air made him immensely appealing to two impressionable young boys. As for Rory, he had followed Emily's cue and done nothing more than civilly shake Patrick's hand. Patrick couldn't be reproached for his unavoidable connection to Garrett, but he had ample reason not to be particularly proud of his own character.

He seemed unconscious of any need for humility, however, as he grinned at Rory and Emily coming down the stairs.

'You look dazzling, cousin,' he said to Emily. 'Part of me wonders why my father did not suggest a marital union between us as a solution to his quandary back when he lured you to London. And another part of me wonders whether I might not have been unwilling.'

Rory gritted his teeth. Mr McGovern, too, looked unimpressed.

'There'll be no talk like that under this roof or any other, Patrick,' he said in a pointed tone.

'I only meant to pay a compliment,' Patrick said innocently. He bowed to Rory and Emily as they reached the ground level. 'And to offer my felicitations on your nuptials, which I neglected to do earlier. Congratulations to you both.'

Emily curtseyed stiffly and Rory inclined his head, wishing he could throw a punch instead.

'You seem happy in your choice of husband, cousin,' Patrick added with a wicked glint in his eye. 'I'm pleased for you. I imagine he's a very good listener.'

Rory felt himself go red all the way to the tips of the unfortunate recipients of that taunt.

Emily smoothed the pink skirts of her gown. 'Thank you. While I yearn to return your compliments in kind, I'm afraid I do not have such skill in callous words.'

Patrick went white. He opened his mouth but she turned away, not allowing him the chance to respond.

'Is the carriage waiting for us?' she asked her parents.

'It is,' her mother replied, looking uncomfortable at the prickly exchange and eager to move on from it. 'If everyone is ready, we shall go.'

The footman hurried to open the front door, admitting the balmy July evening air as well as the sound of hooves clopping along the street below.

'Thank you, Simon,' Lady Bridget said. She gave Jack and Gus tight hugs and a warning to behave while the family were out, and then she and Mr McGovern led the way down the steps to the carriage outside, which bore the Walcott family crest on its door panels.

Five would have been a tight squeeze, so Mr McGovern elected to sit up front with the coachman while Lady Bridget, Emily, Rory and Patrick climbed into the carriage. In a blatant effort to keep their distance from Patrick, Rory and Emily occupied one bench, her voluminous skirts taking up much of the space. As they settled themselves, he took the opportunity to brush his knuckles along the pink material amassed next to his thigh – even through his gloves, he could perceive its extraordinary delicacy. Opposite them, Patrick sank back against the seat next to Lady Bridget, his face still pale. He fixed his gaze out the window as the carriage began to move.

They rode to the theatre in silence. It was not a very auspicious start to the evening.

When the carriage rolled to a stop before the pillared façade of the Theatre Royal, Rory swallowed hard. Numerous carriages thronged the street in front of the theatre and well-dressed gentlemen and ladies were flocking towards its entrance. His palms began to sweat inside his gloves. Bracing himself, he alighted from the carriage and offered his hand first to Lady Bridget and then to Emily. Patrick emerged last, looking annoyed.

'I would have helped Lady Courcey,' he muttered to Rory.

Rory just shrugged in response as Mr McGovern jumped down from the coachman's seat and joined them. He offered his arm to Lady Bridget to escort her into the building, and Rory did the same to Emily. Patrick followed them, emanating a mien of indifference that was rather overdone.

The crowd milled around them, and some gazes swung in their direction, but neither Mr McGovern nor Lady Bridget attempted to avoid notice. Before travelling to Ireland, they had declared their resolve not to conceal themselves for these events, citing both a cautious optimism that Dublin society would not be quite as judgemental as the London ton and a desire to stand openly in solidarity with their suffering countrymen. Rory hoped that their faith wasn't misplaced, or else he would not be the only one in for a difficult evening ahead.

On the face of it, it appeared that their connection to the events had not significantly harmed sales, for the throng only became thicker when they presented their tickets to the doorman and entered the lobby of the theatre. The place teemed with patrons conversing animatedly and fluttering their fans. The aromas of multiple perfumes mingled with the smoky scent of the gas lamps. On the walls hung large, gilded mirrors and great bills showcasing the main performers playing at the venue – considerable prominence was given to illustrations of an angelic being alongside imposing lettering which proclaimed the figure to be 'Angelica: the girl with the voice of an angel!' From beyond the closed set of ornate doors at the far end of the lobby came the faint strains of the orchestra tuning their instruments. In the midst of such glamour and gaiety, Rory felt utterly out of place. What on earth was he doing here? A dart of panic began to climb his throat.

Then he sensed a small pressure on his arm and glanced down. Emily wasn't looking at him but her gloved fingers discreetly stroked the inside of his elbow in a soothing gesture. Although his panicky feeling didn't vanish, it did lessen to a certain extent, and he experienced a rush of gratitude for his discerning, compassionate wife.

They moved further into the lobby, losing sight of Mr McGovern and Lady Bridget as the press of bodies tugged them in opposite directions, though Patrick managed to remain close to them. Caught between several clusters of people, they lingered where they were, unsure what to do next.

'Maybe we could go take our seats for the performance?' Rory suggested. It would be a way to truncate the most excruciating part of the evening. He tried not to dwell on the fact that he would have to go through it all again the following evening.

'I think it's too soon yet,' Emily said apologetically.

Patrick beckoned to a passing theatre attendant who was carrying a stack of handbills. He took three and gave one each to Rory and Emily.

'It's easier if your hands are occupied,' he advised.

Rory shot him a wary look but there was nothing malicious in Patrick's manner as he opened his own handbill and perused its contents.

'It seems we are being treated to a variety of acts tonight,' he remarked. 'A solo singer, a ballet presentation, a woodwind trio, a number of Shakespeare monologues. They should be useful conversation topics if you find yourself stumped at any point.'

Again, Rory looked for the insult behind the words, but they appeared to have been delivered without spite. Frowning at Patrick's capricious behaviour, he unfolded the handbill to study it himself and, in the process, somehow managed to elbow the back of a gentleman standing nearby.

'Oh, bloody h—I beg your pardon,' he blurted as the gentleman turned towards him.

'No harm done,' the gentleman said genially. 'It's quite the crush in here, isn't it?'

'I-indeed,' Rory stammered. 'I wasn't expecting such a gathering.'

The gentleman chuckled. 'You ought to have—Angelica always draws a crowd. Or are you not aware of her reputation?'

'Uh,' said Rory, glancing down desperately at the handbill. What smooth response would the Duke of Desmond come up with?

'We've not yet had the pleasure of hearing her perform,' Emily chimed in serenely. 'We've only recently arrived in the city.'

'Ah, newcomers,' said the gentleman. 'And what has brought you to Dublin?'

At least that was a question Rory could answer, but Patrick interjected before he could speak.

'Oh, Mr Carey here is a man of the land,' he said. 'He's been holed up on the estate for so long that it was high time he experienced the diversions of city life.'

The gentleman raised an eyebrow with interest. 'Indeed. Where is your estate?' he asked Rory directly.

Rory's mind went blank. He couldn't very well claim Bewley Hall as his own, and neither was he prepared to lie to a stranger about the fictitious Desmond Hall. Hot anger rose in him at Patrick for dropping him into this awkward position.

'Well, I—' he began, but once again Patrick cut him off.

'He's due to come into a fine property in Carlow, and in the meantime he's the deputy land agent on an enormous estate in

Bedfordshire. Been working tirelessly to improve the place. Isn't that right, Mr Carey?'

Rory clenched his jaw. He refused to feel grateful to Patrick for extracting him from the predicament into which he'd tossed him in the first place. 'Yes, I'm learning the ropes, so to speak. It's been quite an undertaking.'

The gentleman nodded. 'I can imagine. Estate management is no small feat. What sort of challenges have you faced?'

Rory's thoughts raced as he tried to come up with something that sounded impressive. 'Well, there's the matter of modernising the agricultural practices, for one. And dealing with tenant concerns, of course.'

Patrick stepped in. 'Mr Carey's being modest,' he said with consummate self-possession. 'The estate owner is exceedingly pleased with the progress he's made.'

Emily beamed at Rory, her pride evident. 'He's worked so hard, and it shows.'

The gentleman looked impressed. 'It sounds like you have a bright future ahead of you in estate management, Mr Carey. And for now, you get to enjoy the fruits of your labour with a spell of well-deserved leisure in the city.'

Rory fidgeted with the edges of the handbill. 'I'm looking forward to experiencing all that Dublin has to offer.'

'There's no better place to start than at one of Angelica's performances,' the gentleman said with a wink. 'You're in for a treat.'

With a friendly bow, he excused himself and melted back into the crowd. Rory let out a breath, his shoulders sagging.

'You did very well,' Emily murmured, squeezing his arm. Grudgingly, she added to Patrick, 'And I suppose we ought to thank you for your assistance, although you nearly did more harm than good.'

'I didn't speak one word of a lie,' Patrick said defensively.

'What about that bit about coming into a fine property in Carlow?' Rory retorted.

Patrick regarded him as though he might be a little dim-witted. 'Aren't you married to the heiress of Oakleigh? When she inherits it, it'll become yours.'

Pursing his lips in a manner that conveyed he felt he had been unjustly maligned, he stalked away into the surrounding throng, leaving Rory to gape at Emily.

'I, uh, never realised that before,' he said weakly. Maybe he was dim-witted after all.

'Which is another reason why I love you so very much,' she said. 'You most certainly did not marry me for wealth if it never even occurred to you what you would legally gain in the future.'

He was at a loss for words.

She glanced into the crowd where her cousin had disappeared. 'For all his faults, Patrick seems to know exactly what to say to navigate the fraught waters of polite society. I do believe that was his unorthodox way of apologising for the offence he caused back at the house.'

Rory gave a grunt of reluctant agreement. 'Maybe someday he'll behave in a way that doesn't require him to apologise.'

# Chapter 8

Cormac sensed the low hum of tension radiating from Bridget as they wove their way amid the milling patrons. Though they were not as uninitiated as Rory, it had been a very long time since either of them had been out in public for a social occasion like this. When he looked over his shoulder, he realised that Emily, Rory and Patrick had been swallowed up by the crowd. He hoped they would fare all right among these people who kept such a tight hold of their high standards and their critical opinions, and he hoped the same for himself and Bridget.

They found a small pocket of space near a wall emblazoned with a great bill about the sweet-voiced Angelica ('Stunning! Astounding! You won't believe your ears!') and halted there to orientate themselves and scan the lobby. Cormac noted some inquisitive glances and a few whispers hidden behind gloved hands as others caught sight of the notorious Lady Courcey and her lover, and yet no one seemed appalled enough to openly rebuke them for attending. He lifted his chin and returned their stares levelly.

'I don't see Madeleine anywhere,' Bridget murmured, her relief palpable.

He knew that the spectre of her old friend, with her cutting remarks and superior airs, had haunted Bridget's thoughts in the weeks leading up to tonight. The last time they met in

Dublin, Madeleine had made it plain that she was repulsed by Bridget's decision to desert her wealthy husband in favour of a lower-class man whom she had once witnessed begging on the street; nor had she approved of the shame it brought upon those who were forced to acknowledge an association with Bridget. Indeed, the scandal of it had horrified her to such a degree that she had ended their friendship on the spot. What if she showed up at the Theatre Royal and attempted to sabotage the two events by persuading the patrons not to give their money to a tainted cause? Thankfully, however, it seemed as though she had placed a greater value on preserving her own reputation and had kept her distance instead.

'We ought to look for Mr Dunhill,' Bridget said next. Having made most of the arrangements by letter, they had finally met the theatre manager the previous week after their arrival in the city. They had confirmed the percentage of takings that would be set aside for donation from both performances, and had agreed to collect the money from him backstage at the end of each night. Still, it would be prudent to meet him beforehand as well, if only to be assured that no complications had arisen in the meantime.

Cormac started to raise his hand to draw the attention of a nearby theatre attendant who could seek out the manager, but stopped when a female voice spoke close by.

'Bridget?'

They both swivelled towards the voice and found a pair of women staring back at them. The women were identical in every respect: the same height, the same shape of face, the same colour eyes, and the same expressions of mingled surprise and wariness.

'Good gracious!' Bridget exclaimed with somewhat exaggerated delight. 'Julia and Eleanor, what an age it has been since we last met!' She turned to Cormac. 'The Misses Hyland were both presented as debutantes at Dublin Castle on the same evening as I. And they visited Oakleigh for Garrett's birthday celebration the summer my mother and I returned there.'

He vaguely recalled the presence of the twins on the estate that summer, but so much remained unsaid in this brief summary. Were they aware of the scandal that perpetually hung over Bridget like an ominous cloud? Did they share Madeleine's disgust? Did they know who he was? Could they identify him as the lowly youth who had saddled their horses at the stables?

One of them offered a polite smile. 'Eleanor is still Miss Hyland, but I have become Mrs Hyland after my marriage to our cousin.'

'Oh, indeed, congratulations,' Bridget said. 'So much time has passed—I imagine we have all lived very busy lives since our last acquaintance.'

The second woman, Eleanor, pressed her lips together wryly. 'I think ours have perhaps not been quite so busy as yours.'

Bridget visibly quailed and Cormac braced himself for the inevitable condemnation that would come next. However, the corner of Eleanor's mouth turned up in amusement.

'Do not fret,' she said. 'You shall receive no words of censure from us.'

'Oh,' said Bridget, her face flooding with relief. Then she gave a dubious frown. 'Why not?'

Julia's mouth mirrored her sister's amused expression. 'It's possible that you are not the only one who has skirted the boundaries of propriety over the years.'

This enigmatic comment filled Cormac with a powerful curiosity. Bridget blinked at her two old friends as Eleanor linked her arm with Julia's and gave them a most unladylike wink.

'Let us only say that we have exploited the advantages of our being twins to the fullest. We have just been rather more successful—'

'Or lucky,' Julia interjected.

'—at remaining beneath the notice of society's eagle eyes.'

Bridget gaped. 'I find myself speechless,' she said faintly.

'Quite,' Eleanor said with a chuckle. 'There is no need to respond. All of this is merely to affirm that we cast no judgement upon you for seeking happiness with your paramour.'

They both inclined their heads in Cormac's direction; he simply stood in dumbfounded silence.

'As opposed to Madeleine,' Julia added, 'who has done her utmost to persuade everyone in her acquaintance to shun this pair of events.'

Eleanor made a disparaging sound with her tongue. 'But we, in turn, have done our best to undo her hard work, for we recognise what a valuable cause it is. You are not without allies in this city.'

'Keep up your efforts,' said Julia, 'and we shall do likewise.'

They curtseyed demurely and drifted away into the crowd wearing identical secretive smiles.

'Well, you could knock me down with a feather,' said Bridget. 'How forthright they were.'

Cormac blew out his breath, nonplussed. 'I suppose they knew their disclosure was safe with us,' he said. 'After all, we are in no position to criticise them or spread rumours, even if we were the kind of people to do so.'

'That is very true.' Bridget released a baffled burst of mirth. 'Although they didn't reveal the exact nature of their indiscretions, it is nice to know that we are not the only sinners in this world.'

'Far from it,' Cormac said, raising a sardonic eyebrow.

'Who's been sinning?' Patrick suddenly appeared before them, his hazel eyes alight with interest. 'Is there some unseemly entertainment that I'm missing out on?'

'If there was, I would place you at the furthest distance from it,' Cormac replied with mock severity.

Patrick grinned. At the front of the lobby, a theatre attendant began to ring a bell, terminating any prospect of meeting Mr Dunhill before the performance commenced.

'May I escort Lady Courcey to her seat?' Patrick asked. 'I was deprived of the opportunity earlier.'

Cormac stood back and allowed his nephew to take Bridget's arm. As they made their way towards the auditorium, where the doors were now thrown wide open, he observed the determined set of Bridget's shoulders. The positive encounter with the Hyland twins seemed to have buoyed her up, and he was particularly grateful to the two women for not having drawn any attention to her scar.

Just before they entered the auditorium, they were joined by Emily and Rory who had managed to wade through the crowd to their side. Cormac led the way up the theatre aisle to the front row, where Mr Dunhill had ensured that five of the plush red seats would be reserved for their party. He had offered them a box but they had declined – such pretension would have been a step too far.

There was a sunken area between their row and the front of the curtained stage crammed with hard wooden benches. This pit was filling up with patrons who were filing in from a narrow side entrance instead of the ornate lobby doors, their clothing plain and, in some cases, a bit shabby. Glancing upwards, Cormac spotted a similarly dressed clientele swarming into the auditorium's uppermost gallery. Unlike the venue in London, Dublin's Theatre Royal appeared disposed to sell tickets to all classes of society.

These patrons were also of a rather more boisterous nature; instead of a hum of muted chatter, the auditorium rang with their loud laughter and lively conversation as they took their seats. Cormac cast a furtive look behind him into the rows of stalls, but the more affluent attendees did not seem unduly disturbed by the noise, suggesting that it was a regular occurrence to which they were accustomed. He found himself relaxing a little in the casual atmosphere, which was far removed from the stuffier London event.

They took their seats, Bridget to his left and Patrick to his right, with Emily and Rory on Bridget's other side. Rory looked immensely relieved as he sat down but his face fell when the stranger next to him struck up a conversation. Cormac felt a dart of sympathy and fondness for the lad – tonight presented a challenging situation for him but at least he seemed to be holding his own as he nodded sagely at whatever the stranger was saying. Cormac discerned Emily's fingers surreptitiously stroking Rory's sleeve in a soothing motion and recognised that she was playing her own part in helping him through the evening. The pair of them had come a very long way since the misunderstanding over her missing doll, Mabel, which had engendered such hostility between them during the years they had lived in Boston. Cormac smiled to himself and settled more comfortably into his seat as the orchestra, nestled in a hollow below the stage in front of the audience pit, concluded their final tuning adjustments.

The stage curtains rustled and Mr Dunhill, a rotund man with a round face and rosy cheeks, emerged through the slit at their centre. He wore his top hat at a jaunty angle and he gave the audience an expansive smile as he gestured down at the orchestra. At this signal, the conductor raised his baton and the musicians began to play.

The opening strains of 'God Save the Queen' filled the theatre. Cormac stiffened. A wave of muttering rippled through the crowd, permeating the air along with the stately melody. Decorum prevented him from peering back over his shoulder to gauge the reactions of the upper classes, but he had a good view of the people in the pit; while a few loyal souls stood, most remained seated, their expressions carefully neutral.

As the final notes faded, the orchestra transitioned smoothly into a spirited rendition of 'St Patrick's Day'. Now, a greater portion of the audience leapt to their feet, a surge of Irish pride swelling through the auditorium. One man in the pit even clapped his hands along to the lively rhythm.

Cormac exchanged a sideways glance with Patrick and caught the glimmer of awareness in his eyes. He was not unfamiliar with the resentment that existed in this country towards its domineering neighbour, having witnessed the men on Sycamore Farm attempt to hang his father for being an English landlord.

On the stage, Mr Dunhill remained entirely unperturbed as he beamed out over the audience. When the tune came to an end, he flapped his hands to encourage everyone to resume their seats.

'Ladies and gentlemen, distinguished guests, esteemed friends, welcome to the Theatre Royal for this evening's grand charity show!' he exclaimed, his voice resounding through the auditorium. 'It is with great pleasure that I, your humble host, present to you a night of unparalleled entertainment. Together, we shall journey through a delightful array of performances, from the enchanting melodies of our celebrated musicians to the mesmerising grace of our dancers. Prepare to be captivated by a variety of acts that promise to stir your hearts and your minds. And now, without further ado, allow me to introduce our first performer, a young lady blessed with a voice of pure angelic beauty. I give you...Angelica!'

Enthusiastic applause erupted from the crowd as the curtains drew back and a slender figure glided onto the stage, her head bowed. She wore a gown of shimmering white with a pair of feathery wings sewn onto the back of her bodice, and her black hair was pulled up into an elegant twist. Taking up position in the centre of the stage, she dipped into a graceful curtsey. When she straightened and raised her gaze to her adoring audience, Cormac's heart stopped in his chest.

The girl on the stage was Henrietta Brennan.

He felt like the whole theatre was crashing down around him. He would not have been surprised to look around and see dozens of bodies crushed beneath rubble, such was his absolute shock. *Henrietta?*

When his heart resumed beating, it pounded against his ribs and thundered in his ears. Disbelief, bewilderment and guilt warred for supremacy within him. He could not conceive of any logical explanation for her presence here. Was he experiencing a hallucination of some kind?

That might well have been his conclusion, only for the sudden muffled gasp he heard to his left. Bridget had recognised her too. Henrietta was real.

Through his disorientation, he clutched desperately for any strands of reason that could ground him in reality. These were the facts that he knew: Henrietta was the child of Thomasina Brennan, the prostitute he had bedded in Dublin during the darkest period of his life when he had worked for the money lender Cunningham. The girl was not his own progeny, though Thomasina had tried very hard to convince him that she was – instead, Henrietta's father and namesake was Henry Munroe, another of Cunningham's lackeys, last seen languishing in London's Newgate Prison. When Thomasina had died, Cormac had taken it upon himself to choose a guardian for Henrietta, placing her in the custody of her grandaunt, Mrs O'Hara, a decision he had come to sincerely regret. Over a year ago, Bridget had paid a visit to O'Hara's

Tobacconist and Lodgings and learned that Henrietta had run away from her cruel slave driver of a grandaunt.

And Cormac hadn't made any effort to find her since.

He had kept telling himself that he would begin his search for her soon, once he and Bridget had secured enough funds for the Oakleigh tenants and for as many other people suffering from the blight whom they could help. But their preparations for the event in London had occupied so much of their time, and then they had started preparing for the two events in Dublin, and of course there were ongoing matters to take care of at Bewley Hall, as well as Jack and Gus's education, and Emily and Rory's living arrangements, and he had continued to push Henrietta further down his list of priorities. He had not quite forgotten her, but neither had she risen to the surface of his mind very often.

And now here she was, waiting serenely on the stage while the orchestra played the introductory notes to her first song. He blinked, absorbing her appearance in greater detail. At fifteen years of age, her body displayed obvious signs that she had developed from a child into a young woman – her white gown accentuated the curves at her bust and hips, and the glow from the footlights at the front of the stage revealed her full lips and her pale, unblemished skin.

Good God, how she had grown up since he had last laid eyes on her. On that occasion, she had been just eleven years old, gangly and pimply, when he had brought her down to Carlow to visit the Oakleigh Estate along with Emily and Rory. Though he had tried to encourage her to be sociable, she had grown more sulky and withdrawn throughout the trip. At the end of it, he had proposed that she travel to Boston with them but she had rejected his offer, taking only his money and leaving him with a strong sense that he had failed her, despite the fact that she was neither his daughter nor his responsibility. And yet somehow, in spite of his inadequacy and her grandaunt's mistreatment, she had managed to find her way into this situation of prominence, exuding total composure as a sea of faces gazed up at her in admiration and anticipation.

She parted her lips and the melody emerged from her as pure and clear as a bell. He had heard her sing as a child, and had comprehended even then that she could hold a tune very well, but she must have received training in the meantime for now her voice possessed a power and a resonance that projected out into the auditorium. It was a traditional air which began tranquilly enough but swelled in volume and energy during each subsequent verse until she was belting it out with vigour and her captive audience were joining in enthusiastically for the choruses. She encouraged this, opening her arms out as though trying to embrace them all. Mr Dunhill stood to the side of the stage, watching on with an expression of delight.

Cormac tore his gaze away to look at Bridget. She stared back at him, flabbergasted. Beyond her, Emily's astounded face was riveted upon the stage – she had not failed to recognise Henrietta either.

He itched to jump out of his seat but forced himself to remain stationary as the first song concluded, at which point the crowd broke out into rapturous applause and cries of 'Angelica!' from the pit and 'Brava!' from the stalls behind. Henrietta bowed her head demurely.

Mr Dunhill let the ovation echo around the auditorium for at least a minute before he stepped forwards and pressed his finger to his lips. The audience quietened, their claps and cheers dispersing as an expectant silence took their place. He gave Henrietta a kindly nod and retreated once more to his unobtrusive position near the wings.

She took a deep breath and embarked upon her next song without any accompaniment from the orchestra. It was a ballad with a much slower tempo and a plaintive melody that wafted over her listeners, who seemed to hold their collective breath while she related a sorrowful tale of a young fisherman and his fiancée who were full of hope for their future together until his boat capsized at sea. His heartbroken lover could not accept that he was gone and each evening she lit a lantern by the shore, a beacon of her undying love and her faith that he would someday return to her. Decades later on a cold winter night, she was discovered lifeless by the water's edge, a smile on her lips as if she had finally found peace.

Gooseflesh rippled over Cormac's arms as the haunting tune twisted around him, making him feel the lover's devastation as profoundly as if it were his own. Glancing about, he discerned that he was not the only one moved by the tragic song; a few audience members in the pit were openly weeping. Tears trickled down Henrietta's own face, though she did not let the emotion impair her performance. Every note was pitch perfect, delivered with exquisite poignancy. When at last her voice died away, there was utter stillness in the theatre, unbroken by any rustle or whisper.

Then the audience erupted. Their roars of admiration resounded from every side, and several spectators at the front threw red roses onto the stage. Henrietta glided forwards to gather them up, her cheeks wet and her demeanour shy and grateful.

Mr Dunhill permitted this round of applause to carry on for even longer. Cormac clapped along mechanically, his mind in a whirl. Bridget, too, appeared to be clapping in a daze. On her other side, Emily's head was bent close to Rory's as she spoke rapidly behind her cupped fingers. Next to Cormac, Patrick, who was unaware of the family's connection to the angel on the stage, looked quite impressed as he expressed his own appreciation for her performance.

The clamour continued unabated, passionate exclamations of 'Angelica!' interspersed with pleas for 'More! More!' until eventually Mr Dunhill shouted over the din, 'Very well, just one more, for you are being a wonderful audience!'

He took the flowers from Henrietta so that she could wipe away her tears and then he gestured to her and the orchestra to begin the third song. This one revived the lively atmosphere of the first, with a stirring beat and a soaring melody, and she carried the audience along with her on a wave of such exhilaration that by the end of it they were nearly in a frenzy. As soon as the musicians played the final flourish of notes, the crowd leapt to their feet in a thunderous standing ovation.

Cormac rose too, watching Henrietta carefully as her beaming face shone almost brighter than the lamps. She curtseyed multiple times, her gaze roving over the sea of her enthusiastic admirers.

And then it landed upon him.

For the first time that evening, her poise slipped. A flash of astonishment and confusion swept across her countenance and she blinked furiously before managing to regain her composure. Mr Dunhill was just approaching her to hand back the bunch of roses; she plucked them out of his grasp and hurried from the stage, the feathers on her back fluttering as a voice hollered from the upper gallery, 'I love you, Angelica!'

After she had disappeared into the wings, Cormac turned to Bridget. Her dark brown eyes were guarded but, when she read the emotion in his own, she nodded without hesitation, understanding at once what he needed to do.

'We shall be obliged to wait until the interval,' she said, her words barely audible beneath the animated chatter of the audience who were retaking their seats.

'I know,' he said. Though he longed to charge out of the auditorium right away, instead he sat back down with a deep sigh of frustration as Mr Dunhill started to introduce the next act.

A troupe of ballerinas flitted onto the stage, but Cormac hardly registered them. He sat rigidly in his seat, every muscle tense with the urge to take action. Beside him, Bridget was equally on edge, like a coiled spring.

The performances continued, the ballet succeeded by a trio of woodwind players who were followed by a monologue from Hamlet. He comprehended none of it. Guilt burned inside him. He may not have denied Henrietta like Munroe, nor abused her like Mrs O'Hara, but he still had not made a great enough effort to protect her. He had abandoned her just like everyone else. It was a marvel to behold the life she had managed to create for herself despite all of that neglect.

That having been said, he still harboured numerous concerns. Theatre was not an industry well known for its respectability. To many, the path Henrietta had chosen wouldn't be viewed any higher than the one her mother had been compelled to follow. She received enormous acclaim in the limelight, but what were her circumstances behind the scenes?

The moment the interval was announced, Cormac shot to his feet. Bridget stood quickly too and together they hastened past the legs and skirts of the people sitting in the front row. Cormac caught Patrick's look of surprise but he didn't stop to explain – Emily would enlighten him on the reason behind their abrupt departure.

After exiting the auditorium, they made their way towards an inconspicuous door in the lobby which led backstage, where they found their progress impeded by a burly theatre attendant.

'No guests backstage,' he intoned.

Cormac kept a tight hold on his patience. 'We are actually acquaintances of Mr Dunhill. We're collaborating with him on tonight's charity event, and tomorrow's as well.'

The attendant narrowed his eyes doubtfully.

'We met with him last week when he brought us through this very door to speak in his office. It's up the stairs and past the dressing rooms.'

The attendant's expression cleared. 'Ah, fair enough,' he said, reaching for the door and adding, 'I'll bring yous straight there.'

Cormac would have preferred to avoid engaging with the theatre manager until after he and Bridget had seen Henrietta, but the burly man didn't leave their side as he marched them through the door, along the corridor beyond and up a flight of steps. When they passed the row of dressing rooms, Cormac perceived that one closed door bore the nameplate 'Angelica'. He flinched; they had walked right by it the previous week without an inkling of its significance.

Arriving at Mr Dunhill's office, they found the door open and the room empty. The attendant dithered in indecision.

'We're happy to wait here until Mr Dunhill comes,' Cormac assured him, even though he had no intention of doing so. 'The interval has only just begun so he probably hasn't left the wings yet.'

Henrietta, on the other hand, would have had plenty of time to return to her dressing room by now.

The attendant still seemed unsure but then he brightened as he peered past Cormac's shoulder. 'Ah, Mr Dunhill, sir! This gent wants to talk to you.'

Cormac and Bridget swivelled to see the round-faced theatre manager striding up the corridor towards them. Damn, his presence was a complication they didn't need. The attendant, however, gave a satisfied nod and marched away to resume his post at his door, while Mr Dunhill approached them with a puzzled smile.

'Mr McGovern,' he said. 'Lady Courcey. It's a pleasure, but I thought we had agreed that you would collect the money after the show was over?'

Cormac swallowed back his annoyance. This was a further obstacle, but if they had to go through Mr Dunhill to get to Henrietta, then they would.

'We had agreed that, yes,' he said, striving for amiability, 'but we wish to speak with you on another matter—your solo singer, Angelica. It's imperative that we meet with her.'

Mr Dunhill's welcoming countenance became wary. After a pause, he said, 'I'm afraid that won't be possible.'

At this, Cormac's qualms only increased. Thus far, the theatre manager had seemed harmlessly jovial, but now Cormac was filled with distrust. What was the man trying to conceal?

'I, in turn, am afraid that we will have to insist,' he said with icy civility.

'We know her, you see,' Bridget interjected in a more placating tone. 'And she knows us. From a long time ago.'

Mr Dunhill frowned. 'She said she had no family.'

Which was no doubt a factor in him seizing the opportunity to take advantage of her, Cormac thought, growing angrier by the second. Although she had appeared well nourished, Mr Dunhill could be exploiting her in a myriad of other ways.

'We do not share blood, and yet I have reason to claim a sense of responsibility towards her,' Cormac said, clenching his fist to keep his temper in check. 'You cannot prevent us from seeing her.'

Mr Dunhill shook his head. 'She's resting before her performance. She must not be disturbed.'

'But she has already performed,' Bridget pointed out.

'She'll go out again for the encore,' he replied. 'It's not in the billing but our regulars know to expect her reappearance.'

'Please let us have a few minutes with her,' said Bridget. 'We don't mean her any harm. We just need to talk to her.'

'I have a duty to protect my performers,' he said stubbornly. 'I can't take the risk that you're trying to deceive me.'

'We're not,' Cormac snapped. Part of him wondered whether clashing with the theatre manager might put their charitable cause in jeopardy, but he was prepared to gamble. 'We've known her since she was three years old. We know where she's lived for most of her life. And we know that Angelica is not her real name.'

Mr Dunhill's eyes widened with uncertainty. Nevertheless, he said, 'Be that as it may, I cannot allow—'

'It's all right, Mr Dunhill,' came a soft voice from behind them.

They all pivoted and found Henrietta standing there in the corridor. She was still wearing her shimmering gown but she had shucked off her feathery wings. This close to her, Cormac was struck by how similar she looked to Thomasina with her black hair and full lips, although it had to be said that her mother would not have favoured such a modest neckline.

She came forwards and gave the theatre manager a reassuring nod. 'I'll speak with them.'

His brows knitted together. 'Are you sure, my angel? You don't have to. I can send them away.'

'I'm sure,' she said. 'They're telling the truth—I do know them. And I know they won't stay long.'

She inflicted this sting with a sweet smile that made it all the more painful. Cormac felt the weight of his shame settle even more heavily upon his shoulders.

'Hmm,' Mr Dunhill said dubiously, before relenting and patting her cheek. 'Off you go, then. But keep it short—the second act will begin soon.'

With a swish of her white gown, she turned and led the way back down the corridor towards her dressing room. Cormac and Bridget followed, exchanging uneasy glances.

They trailed after her into a cramped, windowless room just big enough to fit a dressing table on one side and a low cot on the other. A wall-mounted gas lamp revealed a large, slightly tarnished mirror standing on the table, which was scattered with powder boxes and pots of rouge, a well-worn hairbrush, and the bunch of red roses she had received earlier from her adoring audience. A costume rail stood against the back wall, crammed with several white dresses and a few pairs of wings. The air was thick with perfume, the scent of roses, and stale sweat.

There was a stool in front of the dressing table – Henrietta pushed it in to give them a bit more space, although they were still obliged to stand in close quarters, unless any of them wished to sit on the cot, which was strewn with rumpled blankets and a shift stained under the armpits. Cormac eyed the cot in dismay.

'Is this where you sleep?' he asked.

She arched an eyebrow. 'Judging me already, are you?'

Turning to the dressing table, she carelessly pushed the roses out of her way and perched upon its surface, crossing her legs beneath her gown and surveying them with a cool expression.

'You'll have to forgive Mr Dunhill,' she said. 'He's extremely protective. We've had quite a few instances of men trying to force their way backstage because they want to "meet" me. Of course, it always turns out that they want much more than that. He's had to shield me from some very unwelcome advances, so now he has strict rules about who's allowed back here.' She twisted her lips. 'To be honest, he treats me like a child, constantly fussing over me as if I'm made of glass. Still, I'm happy to put up with it—he's the only man I've ever known who hasn't let me down.'

That hurt even worse than the last sting, especially because Cormac was in no position to deny it. How could he hope to make amends to the poor girl when he had disappointed her so thoroughly?

'Henrietta,' he began.

She folded her arms. 'I don't see anyone in this room who goes by that name.'

'Henny,' he tried, but she stared back, impassive. After another beat, he said, 'Angelica.'

'Yes?' she responded sweetly.

He chewed the inside of his cheek. 'I'm very glad to see that you are healthy and well—'

'Are you?' she said with a faint sneer. 'I bet the sight of me on that stage was a nuisance more than anything. Time to pretend you care for a couple of minutes, but I guess now you'll be off the hook again for another few years. Truth be told, it was a bit rich what you said to Mr Dunhill out there, acting like you were my long-lost da or something. I probably haven't even crossed your mind since you saw me last.'

'On the contrary,' said Bridget, 'we have tried to visit you in the meantime, only to learn from Mrs O'Hara that you had run away from her lodgings.'

'Oh,' Henrietta said, taken aback. Then her face darkened. 'Are yous here to take me back there? 'Cause I swear to God, I'll kick and scream every step of the way. I never want to lay eyes on that old bag ever again.'

'On that we are agreed,' Cormac said tersely. 'Placing you in her care was a tremendous error on my part, though at the time I believed it best for you to remain with your own flesh and blood. I can only express my deep remorse at the ill-treatment you suffered at her hands.'

Her brows shot up. 'So yous don't intend to tell her where I am?'

'No, we don't.' He made the decision on the spot – after all the abuse Mrs O'Hara had inflicted upon her grandniece, she no longer had any entitlement to the knowledge of her whereabouts. 'You have my word on that.'

She sagged with palpable relief. His heart went out to the vulnerable girl hidden beneath her prickly exterior.

'You should have come with us,' he said gently, 'when I offered to take you to Boston.'

She picked up a rose and twirled it between her fingers; the admirer who had thrown it onto the stage had removed the thorns so its stem was smooth.

'You didn't really want me to come,' she said at last. 'I know you just made the offer out of pity.'

'That's not true,' he countered. 'I sincerely wanted to make your life better. You didn't deserve the one you had ended up in—it was my fault you found yourself in that objectionable situation, but I had the means to liberate you from it.'

She shrugged. 'I didn't need you. I figured out my own path.'

'And we are most impressed with what you have managed to achieve,' Bridget said. 'Are you willing to tell us how you came to be here?'

Henrietta cast her a mistrustful look before she said, 'I suppose so.' She tossed the rose back onto the pile next to her and smoothed her palm over the skirt of her gown – at this proximity, Cormac could make out the tiny pieces of reflective silver metal that had been sewn into the material to give it its shimmering appearance. 'When I ran away, I had a plan. I'd heard of great singers who were adored everywhere they went and that's what I wanted for myself. So I sought out the theatres in the city and worked my way inside them by whatever means I could. I swept floors, dusted seats, cleaned out dressing rooms, anything to just get in the door. At night, I found different hiding places to sleep—under the stage or up in the gallery or in the costume storage room, which was the best 'cause I could make a nest out of the clothes. I was only ever caught once or twice.'

Cormac pictured her huddled in the darkness of a theatre building, small and alone and determined to succeed somehow. She had certainly inherited her mother's grit.

'I saw actresses come in for auditions but didn't know how to get one myself. Then one morning, I was sweeping the boards here at the Theatre Royal and I thought the place was empty so I put down my brush and flung my arms out and pretended I was singing to a full house. And after I stopped, I realised that Mr Dunhill was standing in the wings watching me. I was sure he'd kick me out but he said he'd never heard a voice as angelic as mine.' She flushed with pride. 'He took me under his wing, put me in the chorus, and arranged for me to get proper training in singing and acting. He made a big fuss when I was ready for my debut solo performance—I think he could tell I'd bring him a lot of money. It's not about the money for me, though. When I stood up on that stage and sang by myself for the first time and heard the clapping and cheering from the audience, I knew I was finally where I was meant to be. This was where I belonged.'

Her voice broke, and her eyes brimmed and spilled over. Cormac longed to put his arm around her. Then she threw them a wicked grin through her tears.

'I've gotten pretty good, haven't I?'

He cleared his throat, feeling foolish. 'I commend you on your talent and your resilience. You've made something of yourself against all the odds. Nevertheless, it must be a lonely existence without any family by your side.' Avoiding Bridget's eye, he carried on, 'If we asked again, would you come with us this time?'

She contemplated him, her countenance carefully controlled. 'No,' she said. 'I'm Angelica now. This is my home. And I *do* have a family—Mr Dunhill and the other theatre performers are all the family I need.'

This response wasn't a surprise really, but he still felt disappointed. He yearned to become a worthier person in her life than he had been up to now.

'Will you think about it?' he asked, his tone just short of pleading. 'We'll be back for tomorrow night's performance. May we speak to you again then?'

She jerked one slender shoulder in an approximation of a shrug.

Accepting that he would get no greater commitment from her than that, he said, 'We'll let you rest now. We look forward to hearing you sing again at the encore. You truly do have a marvellous gift, Hen—Angelica.'

He discerned a hint of her uplifted expression before she smothered it beneath a nonchalant nod. Smothering a whole host of his own emotions, he left the dressing room with Bridget and found Mr Dunhill hovering in the corridor, his round face anxious. In all likelihood, the man had no need to worry that his angel might fly away; Cormac highly doubted that a day's reflection would be enough to sway headstrong Henrietta.

He extended his hand and Mr Dunhill took it hesitantly.

'Thank you,' Cormac said, 'for taking care of her. I beg you, please don't ever let her down. She needs someone she can wholly trust.'

'I swear she is as precious to me as my own daughters,' the theatre manager replied.

They shook hands and, after confirming once more that they would meet after the show to arrange the collection of the charity funds, Cormac and Bridget made their way back to the lobby to rejoin the glittering mass of patrons who had no idea that the girl with the angelic voice had built a wall around her bruised heart.

# CHAPTER 9

The next morning, Emily sat in the sun-drenched drawing room of the house on Rutland Square, her pencil and sketchbook in her hands. She had not brought her easel from England, so for the duration of their stay in Dublin and at Oakleigh she would have to be content with sketching. At least she had completed the still life with the pearl necklace before they had departed from Bewley Hall, and it had in fact travelled with them, for her mother had implored her to permit it to be the first new artwork to grace the walls of Oakleigh Manor, whose previous paintings had been destroyed in the terrible fire that had also taken the life of Emily's grandmother. Her mother had even said that she would commission further pieces for the manor and that it would delight her to be Emily's first official patron.

Although the prospect of this honour greatly pleased Emily, right now her thoughts were focused less on the ideas she was idly sketching for it and more on the events of the previous night. What a shock it had been to see Henrietta on that stage. Her parents had not said very much when they returned to their seats after the interval, only that Henrietta was well and that they hoped to meet her again the following night. But Emily could tell from her father's morose face that the reunion with Henrietta had not been a particularly heart-warming one and she could only imagine what the girl might have said. In their previous interactions, Emily had found her to be sullen and unfriendly, and she could even vaguely recall that Henrietta had pinched her once when they were both little girls. Was she still the same as that contrary child, or had she matured in the interim?

Jack's voice broke into Emily's musings. 'No, that's an illegal move,' he said patiently to Gus, who was sitting opposite him across a chess table nearby. 'The knight can't go in a straight line—remember it has to make an L-shape.'

'Fine,' Gus grumbled, prodding his knight back and pushing his tricorne up his forehead to scrutinise his pieces more closely. While Emily may have left her easel behind, there hadn't been a doubt in the world that Gus's beloved three-cornered hat would accompany him to Ireland. He pointed to another square on the board. 'Can I put it there?'

'Yes, but look again at your other pieces. You've got one that could make a really good move against mine.'

Gus's eyes widened and he pored over the board in deep concentration. Beyond his curly head, Emily observed Rory wearing a similar expression as he sat at a round table with a newspaper spread out in front of him. Mr Humphrey had not travelled with the family, but he had left all three of his students with the enthusiastic instruction to continue sharpening their minds in his absence.

Patrick was also present in the drawing room but he had chosen to sit apart from the rest of them, lounging in a chair over by the window. Emily marvelled at his ability to be content doing absolutely nothing. During the interval at the Theatre Royal, she had apprised him of her father's connection to 'Angelica'; he had absorbed the news with obvious astonishment but his only response had been to say,

'My uncle is a man of many hidden layers.' Now, he glanced out the window with a preoccupied gaze.

Suddenly, Rory let out a low whistle. 'Listen to this,' he said to the room in general, his tone grave. 'There's been a rebellion down in Tipperary.'

Emily's head whipped towards him. 'A rebellion? Led by whom?'

'The Young Irelanders. It says here that they split away from the nonviolent Repeal Association to take more radical action in ending British rule in Ireland. They decided that an armed rebellion would be the only way to achieve their goal.'

Jack and Gus abandoned their game of chess, their young faces solemn.

'Did it work?' Jack asked, his voice small. 'Did they manage to end British rule?'

Rory let out a short, bitter laugh. 'If it was that simple, they'd have done it long before now. According to this, they planned the uprising poorly and didn't get enough local support.'

'No surprise there,' Patrick contributed unexpectedly, turning in his chair to face them. 'What did they expect, with the people starving in their hovels? They're only thinking about where their next meal is coming from, not who's holding sway in Dublin Castle.'

Emily gaped at him. He threw her a look of annoyance.

'Oh, I'm sorry, am I the enemy here?' he said tartly. 'Does my English blood offend you?'

'Of course not,' she said hastily.

'And you're half Irish anyway,' Gus piped up. 'Because you're Auntie Mary's son. Da told us all about her—she was his big sister, just like Emily's ours.'

Patrick's expression became shuttered. He jerked his chin at Rory. 'What transpired with the uprising?'

Rory scanned the newspaper article again. 'It collapsed after a skirmish between the rebels and the constabulary. There was a stand-off when the rebels cornered a troop of constables in a farmhouse in Ballingarry, but reinforcements came for the constabulary and the rebels scattered. The leaders have been arrested and will be tried for high treason.'

'Was anyone killed?' Gus asked, his countenance pale beneath his tricorne.

Rory hesitated. He glanced over at Emily, caught the subtle shake of her head, and said delicately, 'Uh, it doesn't say.'

Gus looked relieved. His gaze dropped back to the chess board and he blurted, 'Oh, I should move my bishop!'

He slid his bishop in a diagonal across the board and captured one of Jack's pieces with a flourish. His exclamation of triumph broke the heavy mood that had swelled just moments before, and Rory turned the page of his newspaper while Emily returned her attention to her sketchbook, wondering uneasily whether the Young Irelanders' short-lived rebellion would have longer-lasting ramifications.

Jack gave his younger brother a smile of approval before scrutinising the board again himself. As his hand hovered in indecision between two of his pieces, Gus swivelled towards Emily and pleaded, 'Will you tell us more about the ballerinas?'

He had asked a hundred questions at breakfast about the previous night's glamorous occasion, begging for specific details on every aspect of the experience, from how soft the cushioned seats had been to whether food was allowed inside the auditorium. Now, at Emily's tolerant nod, he embarked upon another flurry, and she responded as patiently as she could. Out of the corner of her eye, she glimpsed Patrick observing them and wished he would make a sociable effort to offer some answers himself. After she had addressed the matter of the dancers' satin slippers and how quiet their steps had sounded on the stage, Gus emitted a sigh.

'I wish we could have been there,' he said longingly. 'Do you think Ma and Da might let us go tonight?'

'I doubt it, I'm afraid,' she said. 'You and Jack are not quite old enough yet to attend the theatre.'

'It's your turn again, Gus,' Jack said, but Gus wasn't listening.

'I suppose it's for the best,' he said, his expression pensive. 'There might have been some judgemental stares, what with us being illegitimate and all.'

Emily's heart clenched at his matter-of-fact tone. 'Have Mama and Papa talked to you about that?'

Jack nodded, lacing his fingers together on the edge of the chess table. 'They said it's better for us to understand what it means, so we're prepared for how society might treat us in the future. They said it probably won't be easy.'

'If only we had a good story like cousin Pat,' Gus said. 'Then we'd be able to get away with it and no one would know the truth.'

Patrick gave a snort of amusement, but then he blinked as Gus's words sank in properly. 'Wait, what do you mean by that?'

Before Emily could intervene, Gus went on breezily, 'You know, how your da lied about marrying Auntie Mary so he could tell society that you're his legitimate heir.'

The room went still. Rory's head snapped up from his newspaper. Emily's pencil slipped from her numb grip and bounced onto the drawing room rug. Patrick's face drained of all colour.

'What did you say?' he said, his voice coming out in a croak.

Gus gulped, seeming to realise that he had divulged something profound. 'Um, I-I thought you knew. Your da never actually married our auntie. He just let everyone believe he did.'

He looked frantically at Jack and asked in a carrying whisper, 'Was that supposed to be a secret in the family as well?'

Emily watched Patrick as his countenance filled with incredulity for the merest second before it was replaced by dawning horror. His hazel eyes went wide.

He hadn't known the truth.

She thought back to the day Garrett had introduced her to Patrick in the gardens at Berkeley Square, when he had sought her assistance in getting his son to acknowledge him. After the arrogant boy, who at the time had still insisted upon being called Edward, had departed from the gardens, she had asked Garrett directly if he had truly married her aunt. Even when he had avowed it to her face, she had harboured doubts. The meagre number of witnesses, their willingness to sign written statements so many years after the wedding had supposedly taken place, the fire that had destroyed the church's marriage register – it had all struck her as too convenient. On the ship back to Boston, she had expressed her scepticism to her father and he had declared it all to be an elaborate lie. Mary had confessed to him that she had never been married and that she had stolen a wedding band from a dead woman she found lying in a gutter to hide her unmarried state from her family.

But Mary's death meant that she could not deny Garrett's version of events and there was no other concrete evidence to contradict the narrative he had put forth to the world, that he had wedded her in secret and been a widower when he had married Emily's mother. He had maintained that his first marriage had been valid, and that any issue from that union was consequently legitimate, and society had believed him.

And, evidently, so had his son.

In his shock, Patrick let down his guard for once and Emily was able to easily read the emotions that now played across his face – confusion, anger and shame all fought for dominance. However, she discerned the one that prevailed over every other by the two rare spots of red that appeared high on his cheekbones: he was deeply embarrassed.

How could he not be? It had been an act of true naïveté that he had accepted his father's story without question. Still, the blame for that lay at Garrett's feet – regardless of the front he was obliged to present to society, why had he never revealed the truth to Patrick in private? How mortifying for Patrick to now confront the reality of his illegitimate birth, especially in the presence of others who had already known it.

He gripped the arms of his chair so hard that his own arms trembled with the exertion. Despite her mixed feelings towards her cousin, Emily was moved to compassion. She rose, dropping her sketchbook onto her seat, and took a few tentative steps towards him.

'Pat,' she started, even though she had never felt compelled to use that more familiar form of his name before.

His gaze swung in her direction. 'You knew?' He stared past her to Rory. 'You all knew?'

The silence that greeted him was answer enough. He let go of the chair to run both of his hands through his black hair, his features full of anguish. Gus's lower lip wobbled as he apprehended the damage he had inadvertently caused.

'I'm really sorry,' he whimpered.

Patrick's jaw clenched. 'It's not your fault,' he muttered without looking at Gus. 'It's mine, for being such a damn fool.'

'You're not—' Emily tried to say, but he leapt up from his chair, his face livid.

'No?' he flung at her. 'What else would you call me? A halfwit? A simpleton? An idiot? Any one of those would fit the bill.'

Rory got to his feet too, bristling. 'Mind where you're pointing your temper.'

Emily made a shushing motion at him before approaching Patrick cautiously, as if he were a wounded animal. 'Don't let this define you. It doesn't actually change anything.'

'It changes everything,' he snapped. 'I'm not entitled to my father's title or his estate, or the education he paid for me, or an ounce of recognition from the upper classes. I have no right to any of it.'

'But society isn't aware of that,' she said, surprised by the ache of sympathy in her chest that urged her to alleviate his distress. 'Only your father and our family know the truth. And we won't tell anyone.'

'Your secret's safe with us, we swear,' Jack said earnestly.

'Why bother keeping it?' Patrick scoffed. 'It's a lie, and what's new about that? My whole life has been built on one lie after another. I was never Lord and Lady Anner's nephew, and now I learn that I'm not even my father's lawful heir. None of it has been genuine.' He swallowed. 'I'm nothing but a bastard.'

Emily flinched, not at the vulgar word itself but because it could also be applied to her two innocent brothers. Patrick's vehement reaction would only serve to plant insecurity in their impressionable minds.

'You mustn't call yourself that,' she said.

'Fine,' he retorted. 'If I'm not the bastard, then *he* is.' He curled his hands into fists. 'He's a damn liar. He led me to believe I'm someone I'm not, just to serve his own purposes.'

Emily could practically see the bedrock of Patrick's identity, already nebulous, shifting and crumbling beneath his feet.

'His choices are not your burden to bear,' she said, striving for a calmer atmosphere. 'We can't be held accountable for our parents' actions.'

'That's easy for you to say—you don't have a blackguard for a father. I do. His blood runs in my veins. His deceit, his sins...they're a part of me, whether I like it or not.'

With that, Patrick strode across the drawing room and stormed out the door, slamming it shut behind him with a resounding finality.

# CHAPTER 10

Cormac sat next to the coachman, Clancy, at the front of the Walcott carriage as it trundled through the Dublin streets towards the Theatre Royal. The rays of the late July sun slanted between the buildings – sunset was still an hour or two away. He twisted Lord Bewley's cane nervously between his palms, the grounds for his agitation twofold: he didn't yet know what he would say to Henrietta that evening, and he felt greatly troubled about his nephew sitting behind him in the carriage.

Emily had come to him earlier and imparted what had taken place in the drawing room. None of the family had seen Patrick for hours after the incident, although the footman Simon had confirmed that he had requested a bottle of claret to be brought up to his bedchamber. It wasn't until they were preparing to leave for the theatre that he had materialised, fully dressed and apparently sobered up, unless he was doing a remarkable job at concealing his inebriation. His steely expression had quelled any attempt to enquire after his wellbeing, and they had all headed down the steps to the waiting carriage in silence, leaving Jack to look after a guilt-ridden Gus, whose eyes were still red and puffy.

Until today, Cormac had not been sure whether Patrick had been aware of his illegitimacy. Now, he comprehended that he ought to have made a more concerted effort to ascertain this, rather than going on the assumption that Garrett would

102

undertake the difficult conversation himself. What a blockhead the man had been to avoid the matter entirely – he should have realised that the truth would eventually come to light. Gus, of course, could not be reproached for his blunder. After speaking with Emily, Cormac had sought out his younger son and told him as much, but it had still taken a lot to convince the boy that he wasn't to blame for the pain that Patrick was currently feeling.

And what would be the repercussions of that pain? Surely an afternoon spent drinking by himself was only the start. Could they expect to witness a full reversal of the progress he had been making, albeit by small degrees, to improve his character? Perhaps the knowledge of his baseborn status would remove all sense of inhibition and he would feel liberated to take his previous degeneracy to a new low. He and the Duchess of Northrop might well begin to flaunt their affair in public again, or maybe he would choose to pursue other women without discrimination. Would he frequent gambling houses and squander his inheritance? Cormac's thoughts were chaotic as he imagined all the ways that his nephew could fall into a headlong decline from which it might not be possible to retrieve him.

He was so distracted that he didn't notice the group of uniformed soldiers assembled in front of Carlisle Bridge until Clancy slowed the horses to a stop.

'What's this now?' the coachman muttered. 'It wasn't here yesterday evening.'

Cormac gaped at the sight of a barricade set up at the entrance to the bridge, creating a narrow passage which controlled the flow of vehicles and pedestrians across it. A union flag flew from the top of the barricade. Two soldiers detached themselves from the group and came forwards; one raised his hand in a commanding gesture at Cormac and Clancy, even though their carriage had already come to a halt.

'Where are you heading?' he asked in an English accent and an unfriendly tone.

'The Theatre Royal,' Clancy responded. 'Hawkins Street.'

Both soldiers narrowed their eyes, but then they took in the elegant cut of Cormac's clothing and the noble crest emblazoned on the carriage's door panels. The one who had spoken walked alongside the vehicle and threw a cursory glance in the window before he jerked his head back at the coachman and said, 'Drive on.'

As they moved off again, Cormac gritted his teeth at the union flag rippling in the summer breeze; it represented the United Kingdom of Great Britain and Ireland and was a glaring reminder of the oppressive British rule that the Young Irelanders had tried and failed to overthrow. Still, the hasty erection of the barricade was a sign that the rebellion had scared the British into stationing soldiers around the city. Perhaps they were on the lookout for hidden weapons or for straggling rebels who had evaded arrest in Tipperary and were now on the run. Cormac made a silent wish that they would remain free and that their flame of revolution would continue to burn. Needless to say, he approved of their endeavours – had he never left Oakleigh at the age of nineteen, it was possible that he might have participated in the Young Ireland movement himself. However, his life had followed an unexpected path and his capacity to help his countrymen had taken on a different form. Whether or not Irish independence would be achieved in this generation, the first priority was to feed the starving people so that there would be a next generation.

When they reached the Theatre Royal, he wondered if the fate of that important cause was in jeopardy. The crowd that milled around the theatre's entrance was noticeably smaller than the previous night's and their din was more muted. The aristocratic patrons in this city were most likely to be wealthy Protestants loyal to the crown – had the reports of the rebellion in Tipperary made them reconsider their willingness to relieve the plight of the suffering Irish? Did they view it as a sign of ingratitude? At least a certain portion had still turned up, though he could not tell whether altruism or the allure of 'Angelica' had enticed them to attend. Was he being too pessimistic? Perhaps the Young Irelanders' actions might not have quite as severe an effect here in Dublin, given its proximity to the crisis. However, it was very possible that news of the rebellion would cause charitable donations to dry up completely across the sea in England.

He chewed the inside of his cheek, sensing the undercurrent of tension in the air. 'Stay vigilant this evening,' he said to Clancy, who would drive further up the street to wait in a designated area until the end of the performance. Then he jumped down from the carriage to join Bridget, Emily, Rory and Patrick, who had just emerged from its interior.

Bridget turned her worried gaze towards him. 'What happened at Carlisle Bridge?'

'The British wanted to remind everyone who's in charge,' he said grimly. 'Shall we?'

He offered her his arm and they proceeded towards the theatre's entrance, followed by Emily on the arm of Rory, who was not looking very eager at the prospect of the night ahead, and Patrick, who brought up the rear, his shoulders hunched and his expression brooding.

The atmosphere in the lobby was not quite as merry as it had been the evening before, but it wasn't until they entered the auditorium that Cormac caught a proper sense of the mood of tonight's audience. While the wealthier patrons may have shown up in fewer numbers, the opposite was true for the lower classes. The pit and the upper gallery were absolutely packed, with still more streaming in from the side entrance. They squeezed close together on the benches and some even remained standing when they ran out of space. This time, there was no laughter; they buzzed with angry murmurs, punctuated now and then by more heated exclamations. Among them, from somewhere inside the pit, Cormac heard one voice burst out in Irish, '*Saoirse do mhuintir na hÉireann*!'

'Freedom for the people of Ireland': that was what preyed upon their minds, not the programme of entertainment ahead.

Warily, he led the way up the aisle to the front row where the same five seats had been left vacant for them again. As they sat down, he pictured Henrietta standing in the wings waiting to perform and wondered whether her angelic voice would be enough to soothe the restless crowd.

Next to him, Patrick grimaced. 'This place is like a powder keg,' he said, uttering his first words all evening. 'One spark is all it would take to ignite it.'

Surprised that his nephew had heeded what was happening outside of his own inner turmoil, Cormac nodded gravely. 'I didn't anticipate this level of tension.'

'I don't think it's appropriate for the ladies to stay,' Patrick said frankly.

Even as he spoke, several men in the pit started pounding their fists into their palms, resentment contorting their faces.

'I agree,' Cormac said, alarm rising within him. 'Let's escort them back out at once.'

Before they could make a move, however, Mr Dunhill emerged through the curtains on the stage. His top hat was still perched at a jaunty angle on his head, but his customarily rosy cheeks were pale and his smile seemed forced as he looked out over the agitated audience. Just as he had done the previous evening, he gestured to the conductor below him and the orchestra began to play. The majestic melody of 'God Save the Queen' swelled throughout the theatre.

Cormac wanted to groan. He supposed the playing of the tune was a tradition, or perhaps even an obligation, but could Mr Dunhill not have chosen to forgo it for one night? The jeers erupted immediately from the pit and the upper gallery in a cacophony of defiant boos and hisses. The conductor urged his musicians to play more loudly but that only incensed the audience further; they pounded their feet upon the floor in thunderous disapproval, trying to drown the music out. Mr Dunhill's frozen smile slipped from his face and he waved frantically down at the conductor. The orchestra cut off 'God Save the Queen' with a screech of bows against strings.

In the next instant, they struck up 'St Patrick's Day' and Mr Dunhill beamed, clearly convinced that this would appease his audience. The response was indeed raucous. Those sitting down leapt to their feet, stamping and cheering, and voices rose all around in a deafening roar. Shouts of 'Free Ireland!' and 'Get the English out!' peppered the clamour. Cormac's heart hammered as the commotion climbed towards its breaking point. The powder keg was ready to catch fire.

And then the spark occurred. From somewhere high above, a glass bottle was hurled down onto the stage. It narrowly missed Mr Dunhill and smashed into smithereens on the boards, sending chips of glass into the crowd in the pit. Bodies surged backwards, and there were bellows of fright and rage.

And after that came chaos.

The music stuttered to a halt as the throng heaved and pushed against each other, their limbs flailing and knocking over benches. Screams rang out from the stalls behind. Cormac sprang up from his seat, his only thought now to protect his family.

'It's time to get out of here,' he told them urgently.

He tucked Lord Bewley's cane under his arm and pulled Bridget to her feet. Patrick, Rory and Emily all stood hurriedly as well; Emily's blue eyes were wide with fear but Rory wrapped a protective arm around her shoulders. Other patrons in the stalls were also rising from their seats in panic and flooding into the aisles.

'We'll head straight for the lobby and all the way out to the street,' Cormac ordered. 'Don't stop until you're outside. Pat, please lead the way.'

Patrick looked startled, but then his gaze cleared as he grasped the situation – Cormac and Rory both had a lady to shield, whereas he was free to forge a path through the crush of people. He nodded and strode ahead to the end of the front row. As the rest of them followed, Cormac glanced up at the stage and spotted a horrified Mr Dunhill scurrying for safety back through the gap in the curtains.

The aisle was teeming with gentlemen shepherding ladies away from the mayhem as quickly as possible. Patrick pushed forwards, finding gaps wherever he could. Cormac held Bridget securely at his side as he shadowed his nephew, while Rory and Emily were so close behind that Emily's skirts pressed against the backs of Cormac's legs. The dense mass of bodies made the air stifling and difficult to breathe.

Not all of the wealthy attendees were averse to the unfolding chaos. A group of three young gentlemen had clambered onto the plush red seats in the centre of the stalls and were waving their cravats in the air, yelling, 'Give them hell!'

Objects rained down from the upper gallery, mostly harmless things like hats and handbills, with the exception of another glass bottle which plummeted downwards and shattered against a pillar. A shard flew into the face of a nearby man and cut his cheek; he emitted a snarl of pain and irrationally hit out at the closest person to him, a beefy fellow who whirled and punched him so hard that he fell back against the pillar. The people were losing all reason in the pandemonium.

Just before they made it through the ornate lobby doors, Cormac looked over his shoulder to snatch a final glimpse of the bedlam – men were climbing up onto the stage and shouting rallying cries down at the crowd. Then he and the others spilled out into the lobby where there was a little more space and it became easier to breathe.

'Keep going,' he said to Patrick and his nephew continued to lead the way, snaking between the milling, panicked patrons until they reached the theatre's entrance and finally emerged out onto the street. Cormac urged them to walk another thirty yards along the footpath before they stopped. Dusk had not yet fallen and the bright, calm outdoors seemed poles apart from the chaos inside the heaving theatre.

Bridget was shaking like a leaf in his grasp. He rubbed his hands up and down her arms and said, 'You're safe now.'

'It all happened so fast,' she said faintly.

Emily clung to Rory, her features pallid. 'Was this a reaction to the failed rebellion?'

'For the most part, we can assume,' Cormac replied. 'But that rancour towards the English is always simmering under Irish skin—it doesn't take much for it to break through to the surface. What occurred in Tipperary was a missed opportunity, though, and who knows when the next one will come along?' Despite his yearning for such a scenario, he couldn't think about future uprisings at this moment. Sweat soaked his clothes and his pulse thrummed in his ears; while his family were now safe, his anxiety had not yet abated. He focused his gaze on Patrick and Rory. 'Take Bridget and Emily further up the street—Clancy will be waiting there with the carriage.'

Alarm filled Bridget's expression. 'Why aren't you coming with us?'

'I have to go back for Henrietta,' he said.

She opened her mouth to protest, but then closed it. It wouldn't do any good, and he could tell she knew it.

'I'll be careful,' he promised without her having to ask.

'You'd better be,' she replied.

He produced Lord Bewley's cane from under his arm. 'I've got a weapon if I need it,' he said, only half in jest. The slender shaft of wood was not especially intimidating, but it would do in a pinch.

'I'm coming with you,' Patrick declared. 'Rory can bring the ladies to the carriage—that doesn't need two of us.'

Cormac thought of the enraged men who had climbed onto the stage and decided that Henrietta didn't have time for him to argue with his nephew.

'Fine,' he said. 'Let's go.'

He gave Rory a meaningful nod that conveyed the trust he was placing in him to guard the two most important women in his life. Then, with an encouraging smile at Emily and a brush of his fingers against Bridget's right hip, he spun on his heel to stride back to the theatre's entrance, Patrick at his side.

They found the lobby seething with bewildered patrons trying to distance themselves from the bedlam inside the auditorium, the racket of which carried through the open ornate doors. Cormac perceived the Hyland twins amid the throng; they were both hanging on to a gentleman who had his arms enveloped protectively around them. Seeing that they were out of harm's way, he charged onwards in his mission to save Henrietta.

This time, he went first and Patrick followed, darting in and out among the crowd until they reached the inconspicuous door that led backstage. The burly theatre attendant was nowhere in sight; either he had joined the fracas, or fled from it. Shoving the door open, Cormac barrelled along the corridor beyond and up the steps two at a time, Patrick striving to keep up behind him. The sounds of the riot were more muffled here. They made directly for Henrietta's dressing room and, finding her door ajar, dashed inside.

The room was empty. Cormac deflated; he had hoped she would seek safety here. Was she still in the wings? He supposed there was a possibility that she had already escaped from the building – the performers and stagehands probably had their own entrance which would not be overwhelmed by masses of people. However, he couldn't abandon his search on that assumption; he would have to make certain that she was safe.

'Let's carry on,' he said to Patrick, who backed out of the dressing room. As Cormac was about to leave himself, he glanced down at the rumpled blankets on the cot and glimpsed an object poking out from the folds of material: a small wooden limb with a lace cuff. He bent and twitched back the blanket to reveal a head with painted black hair and a sombre expression. He stared at it, astonished.

'Uncle?' came Patrick's voice from the corridor.

'I'm coming,' Cormac replied hastily and folded the blanket over the doll again before rejoining his nephew.

Together, they passed Mr Dunhill's vacant office and hurried deeper into the labyrinth of corridors. A pair of tearful ballerinas came scurrying around a corner, shrieked at the sight of them and scuttled away down a different corridor – the frightened girls couldn't know that Cormac and Patrick posed no threat to them.

By instinct or luck, they managed to navigate their way swiftly to the back of the stage. They slipped through a door into the wings, finding themselves in a dusty, dimly lit space cluttered with theatrical paraphernalia. The noise from the audience grew instantly louder, an inarticulate roar of hot-blooded hostility. Cormac edged forwards to gain a narrow view of the stage and saw that some of the rioters were attacking the velvet curtains in a frenzy. At first, he couldn't tell how they were tearing the heavy material, but then he discerned the lengths of splintered wood in their grips – they must have smashed up the benches in the pit. The jagged edges ripped at the fabric, and the rioters cheered and tossed the tattered fragments into the crowd below. They appeared to have lost all sight of the original motive for their anger; now they were just a mindless mob intent on random destruction.

Sidling further into the wing past a table stacked haphazardly with scripts, Cormac squinted through the gloom and distinguished Mr Dunhill hunkered down behind a piece of painted scenery, his eyes as round as his face as he peered out from his hiding place.

'Mr McGovern!' he croaked. 'Good heavens, what prompted you to come up here?'

'Where's Henrietta?' Cormac demanded. At Mr Dunhill's confused frown, he said, 'Angelica! Where is she?'

The theatre manager pointed a shaky finger across the stage into the opposite wing and Cormac discerned the tips of white feathers poking up from behind a rack of props.

'Stay here,' he said to Mr Dunhill. 'But be ready to move quickly.'

He beckoned to Patrick with a twitch of his head. They retreated to the back of the wing and hastened along the passage behind the stage's backdrop, keeping themselves concealed from the men shredding the curtains. Upon reaching the other side, they found Henrietta alone, crouching in the shadow of the props rack, her pale face in profile as her gaze darted frantically around the chaotic scene. When Cormac approached her side, she jumped and gave a screech of fear, rearing back from him.

'It's all right, it's me,' he said, putting up his free hand in a placating gesture.

She sagged with relief and, even in the midst of all the havoc, it gladdened his heart to see that reaction – she did not wholly detest him then. He dropped his hand and offered it to her, intending to lead her back through the passage unnoticed, but one of the rioters must have heard her scream for he suddenly whirled in their direction.

'Oi!' he said and started to advance on them menacingly, brandishing the length of wood in his fist. Cormac stepped forwards with the cane raised, shielding both Henrietta and Patrick.

'Stay back!' he barked at the man, his voice cutting through the din and catching the attention of the other men on the stage, whose heads swivelled towards him too.

The first rioter sneered and, without warning, hurled his piece of broken wood at Cormac. It whistled past his shoulder and clattered against the props rack. Henrietta gasped and ducked down low behind it. Cormac's own wrath mounted, along with alarm, as he realised that these men were beyond reasoning with. He had to get Henrietta out of there as fast as he could.

'Here, catch!' he exclaimed to Patrick and tossed Lord Bewley's cane to his nephew, who fumbled but managed to secure his grasp on it. Then Cormac strode to Henrietta, bent and swept her up into his arms, crushing her wings in the process. Her light frame trembled against him. That was when the rioters caught sight of her.

'Angelica! It's Angelica!' they cried, their expressions morphing from anger to a fierce, almost fanatical ardour.

'Don't come any closer!' Patrick yelled, pointing the cane at them as if it were a sword.

A young fellow with a wild glint in his eyes did the same with his own stick and bawled, 'We'll save you from these wicked men, Angelica, don't you worry!'

Cormac tightened his hold on Henrietta and eyed the opposite wing where Mr Dunhill was peeping out in terror. If they could get backstage again, perhaps the theatre manager would have a key to a room where they could lock themselves in until the danger had passed.

'We need to cross over the stage,' he muttered to Patrick. There was no advantage in trying to retreat via the passage behind the backdrop – it was a slower route to the exit and the time for concealment was past. The rioters crowded nearer, their vandalism of the curtains forgotten. Beyond them, through the ragged gap in the curtains, the riot in the auditorium raged on.

'Get ready to run,' Patrick replied, his jaw set with determination.

He stooped to snatch up the piece of wood that the first rioter had thrown and whacked it against the rack of props, knocking it over. An array of goblets, masks, crowns and lanterns tumbled down between them and the rioters, scattering across the boards and buying them precious seconds. They hurtled away across the stage and joined Mr Dunhill in the other wing, before dashing towards the door they had entered through only minutes earlier. Mr Dunhill thrust it open, Cormac followed with Henrietta's arms wrapped around his neck, and Patrick came last, still wielding the cane and the piece of wood. The sound of the bedlam in the theatre once again dimmed as the door banged shut behind them.

In an act of quick thinking, Patrick knelt and wedged the piece of wood under the door, just as the pursuing rioters started to beat their fists upon it. The wedge held in place and frustrated shouts rose from the other side of the door. Breathing heavily,

Cormac gave Patrick a nod of approval. Henrietta clung to him like a limpet; he could feel her heart thumping against his chest.

'Is there a safe place to hide?' he asked Mr Dunhill. 'Or a way to exit the building without detection?' At a push, they could go back through the lobby, but there was no telling if the rioters had spilled out beyond the auditorium by now.

Mr Dunhill seemed quite unsteady on his legs and it took a moment for Cormac's question to register. 'Y-yes,' he said at last. 'The stagehands have their own access to the theatre. Follow me.'

He stumbled down the corridor and they went after him, leaving behind the noisy pounding on the door. Cormac continued to carry Henrietta; her face was so white that he feared she might faint.

Their route through the warren of corridors eventually brought them down a stairs to an exit at the very back of the theatre. They emerged into an alleyway where several others were milling around – Cormac recognised the trio of woodwind players, all clutching their instruments protectively, as well as the burly theatre attendant, who seemed to have shrunk in on himself as he slumped on an overturned box. Twilight was setting in by this stage; in the weakening light, it was harder to read Henrietta's expression, but Cormac thought she looked embarrassed.

'I can stand now,' she said, her voice brittle.

He set her down on her feet. Her crushed wings drooped from her back. Nearby, Patrick was panting slightly as he leaned on Lord Bewley's cane. Mr Dunhill stared up at the building with his palms pressed to his temples.

'My beautiful theatre,' he moaned. Cormac imagined that the theatre's actual owner might have something to say about this sense of possession, but in reality Mr Dunhill, as the manager, had the deeper connection to it for he lived and breathed there every day. He shook his head in disbelief. 'Those thugs have ruined it.'

'Will it have to close?' Henrietta asked in alarm.

'For a while, at least,' Mr Dunhill said miserably. 'It's going to take time to repair all the damage. The cost of it all! What's more, the damage to its reputation will take even longer to repair. Ticket sales will certainly be down upon reopening, after word spreads about what's happened.'

Henrietta gulped. 'But I'll still be able to stay here in the meantime, won't I?'

'I'm afraid that'll be impossible, my angel. The performers will all need to leave until it's safe to come back.'

Cormac couldn't have been gifted a more perfect opportunity. 'You can stay with us,' he said to Henrietta. 'Until the theatre reopens, or for as long as you like. We're planning to travel down to Carlow soon.'

Her features were indistinct in the gathering darkness. She said nothing. Was she contemplating his offer? He waited with bated breath.

But then Mr Dunhill said, 'Or you could come with me, my angel. My family and I live on Frederick Street, which is but a short walk from here. I know that my wife and daughters would gladly welcome you into our home. You would feel comfortable there in no time for we are a tight-knit family.'

The wilted feathers on Henrietta's back rustled as she bobbed an uncharacteristic curtsey at Mr Dunhill. 'Thank you, sir, I'm very grateful.'

Cormac endeavoured to conceal his disappointment as he said, 'Are you certain? We'd be more than happy to—'

'I'm certain,' she interrupted. 'I want to stay near the theatre. This is where I belong and I'd like to get back here as soon as possible.'

'My girls will be delighted,' Mr Dunhill said. 'They're of a similar age, so you will get along very well, I think.'

Cormac grimaced, resigned. 'Do you remember what I begged of you last night?' he said to Mr Dunhill.

'I do, indeed. And I remember what I swore in return.'

Cormac certainly hoped so because Henrietta's happiness was wholly in this man's power.

'Will you write to us?' he asked her. 'Let us know how you are?'

'I'm no good at writing,' she mumbled.

'May we write to you at least?'

She shrugged. 'Fine.' She turned to Mr Dunhill. 'Can I go back to my dressing room before we leave? I have…things I want to bring with me.'

An image entered Cormac's mind of a wooden limb with a lace cuff as Mr Dunhill said, 'No, no, that's out of the question while those vandals are still inside. We must wait for the constabulary to put them to rout. You can borrow clothing from my Joanie for the time being—she's about your size.'

As Henrietta's shoulders sagged in acquiescence, Patrick straightened up. 'What now, Uncle?' he asked, his voice steady despite the chaos they had just escaped.

Cormac glanced at Henrietta, who lowered her head. 'We'll return to the carriage,' he replied to his nephew. 'Mr Dunhill, please accept my best wishes that your theatre will be able to reopen as soon as possible. Be safe, Hen—Angelica.'

Instead of giving her another chance to avoid his gaze or otherwise reject him, he pivoted swiftly and made for the end of the alleyway. Patrick caught up and wordlessly passed Lord Bewley's cane to him. Cormac gripped the beechwood shaft, resisting the urge to look back over his shoulder.

He prayed that, for once, he had left Henrietta in safe hands. Perhaps, in the care of the Dunhill family, she would finally find the refuge she needed.

# CHAPTER 11

With the unlit fireplace at her back, Bridget surveyed her family assembled before her in the library of the house on Rutland Square. Emily and Rory sat on the chaise longue that had once been her uncle's favoured spot, while Jack and Gus occupied the chaise longue opposite them, their guileless faces turned towards her expectantly. Patrick leaned against a glass-fronted bookcase to the side, his arms folded. Cormac stood next to Bridget and she silently praised God once more that he had not been injured in the previous night's melee.

'Thank you all for agreeing to gather here,' she said, although the remark was mainly for Patrick, the only one whose attendance might have been in doubt. 'There are some matters we thought it would be best to discuss together.'

'Is this about the big fight at the theatre?' Gus asked and added longingly, 'I wish we could've been there.'

'I'm most relieved that you were not,' Bridget said, shuddering at the idea of her two boys getting caught up in the violence that had occurred. It was bad enough that her precious daughter had been involved; thank goodness Emily hadn't been hurt, only shaken in its aftermath.

'We would have protected you, Ma,' Jack said seriously.

'I know, my lamb. But your father and Rory and Pat looked after Emily and me. We were perfectly fine.'

Gus shot an apprehensive glance across at Patrick before returning his gaze to Bridget. 'Next time, we'll show you we can be just as brave,' he said, straightening his tricorne and puffing out his chest.

'There won't be a next time,' she said firmly. 'We've decided that we should leave the city without delay.'

'Dublin doesn't feel safe at the moment,' Cormac added. 'Between the soldiers and the rioting, it's preferable to get away from it for the time being.'

Bridget's teeth nipped the tip of her tongue as she looked around at them all. 'We believe that the most prudent choice is to head straight to Oakleigh. Our initial plan had been to travel down there within the next week or two, but now we shall do so on the morrow.'

Regrettably, they would be travelling with less funds than anticipated. A disastrous consequence of the riot was that they could not obtain the proceeds from the second night of ticket sales that had been designated for their charitable cause – that money would now be required to go towards the repair work on the theatre or, more likely, to be refunded to disgruntled patrons who had been denied their evening of entertainment and been put in danger to boot. The vandals had done more harm than good to their countrymen by curtailing the resources that could be distributed to the tenants at Oakleigh and to other communities. Nevertheless, Bridget and Cormac would do everything they could with what they had, and Cormac had vowed to make up a portion of the deficit with some of the income from Bewley Hall. A warning echoed through Bridget's mind in the voice of the solicitor Mr Brereton, who had cautioned her before about landlords risking bankruptcy in their efforts to help the needy. She dismissed it from her thoughts.

'I'm excited to go to Oakleigh,' Gus declared. 'I hope there'll be a mystery to solve on the estate. My detective skills haven't been needed in quite some time.' He tapped the cocked brim of his hat meaningfully.

'I want to see the stables where Da worked,' Jack added eagerly. 'And go riding across the fields. And walking up the mountains. There are mountains, aren't there, Da?'

Cormac gave him a good-humoured nod. 'Yes, indeed. The Blackstairs. They're not far from the limestone quarry where your mother and I used to play as children—we must stop by there as well.'

'So much to do!' Gus said, beaming.

'And not an infinite time in which to do it unfortunately,' Bridget said. She'd rather not be the killjoy but someone had to keep a practical head. 'Even though we'll be travelling there sooner than planned, you'll still have to fit it all in before the summer ends, for you must return to Bewley Hall by the autumn to resume your lessons with Mr Humphrey.'

Gus deflated ever so slightly. 'Rory too?'

'You know Rory is not bound to the same curriculum of study as you and Jack. He will go back when he pleases.'

Rory shifted on the chaise longue and reached up to graze his hand over his stylishly trimmed hair. 'I'll be going back, but for a different reason.' His exposed ears turned a little red as everyone's attention focused upon him. 'I need to visit the solicitor in Liverpool. The current lease on the house on Penny Close runs out at the end of August so I have to sign some documents to renew it.'

'And I must also return to England by then,' Emily joined in. 'Before we came to Dublin, I sent out applications to a number of art academies, and I'm hopeful that I shall be invited to present my portfolio to at least one or two of them. With any luck, I may even secure a place for this coming year. So we shan't have very long to spend at Oakleigh either.'

'Then we'll have to make the most of our brief time together there,' Bridget said with a bright smile, even while she was conscious that the general mood on the estate would not be particularly cheerful. She sent Patrick a wary glance. 'Will you journey down with us as well, Pat?'

He slouched against the bookcase. 'Thank you for the invitation, but I won't.'

'Do you intend to go back to London?' Cormac asked.

Patrick let out a harsh laugh. 'I think not. I have no desire to see my father right now.'

An awkward silence descended. Gus's gaze dropped to his knees.

'But then where will you go?' Emily said with a frown.

Patrick brooded over this for a beat or two. 'Ashbrook Lodge,' he said at last.

Jack tilted his head with curiosity. 'Where's that?'

'It's my father's property in Kildare. The small one he purchased years ago with his father but never bothered to manage himself. I don't know if he's ever even set foot there since he bought it.'

Bridget perceived the bitterness in Patrick's tone and wondered if it could only be attributed to his aggrieved feelings towards his father, or whether he perhaps disapproved of Garrett's status as an absentee landlord.

'And what do you mean to do once you get there?' she asked. She knew that Garrett had once envisioned it as a place of banishment for his son when his behaviour had got out of hand with the duchess in London, but that was hardly Patrick's incentive.

He shrugged. 'Maybe I'll lounge about all day and drink myself into a stupor every night. Or I might ask the agent to acquaint me with the running of the estate. I haven't decided yet.'

Cormac cleared his throat but didn't say anything. Bridget didn't even know what he could say – she got the sense that Patrick was teetering on the brink of an abyss and that one misplaced word could tip him over the edge. His cavalier attitude was almost certainly a mask to conceal his deep pain. Perhaps what he needed above all else was some time alone to adjust to the reality of his new – and, to him, objectionable – identity. Still, the poor boy had no mother and a blatantly inadequate father; it was vital for him to understand that he had others upon whom he could rely.

'You know where we are if you need us,' she said gently.

He blinked. Then he pushed himself off the bookcase to make a stiff bow. 'I'll leave you to prepare for your departure. Thank you for your hospitality under this roof.'

He started to stride towards the library door. As he passed the chaise longue where Jack and Gus sat, Gus peeked furtively at him before looking away. Patrick paused and swivelled back. He stuck out his hand to Gus.

'There's no ill feeling between us,' he said. 'I mean it.'

Eyes wide, Gus stood and shook his cousin's hand. Then he threw his arms around Patrick's waist. 'I'm so relieved,' he wheezed.

Patrick appeared bemused but didn't resist the gesture. After a lingering moment, he patted Gus on his curly head, disengaged himself and left the library.

Bridget's heart brimmed with affection for her little boy. 'Come here to me, my miracle,' she said, putting her arm out.

He skipped over to her. 'I amn't a miracle,' he replied with his customary refrain, slipping into her embrace.

'On the contrary,' she murmured, pressing a kiss upon his crown. Then she glanced around at the others. 'Come, let's get ourselves ready. Oakleigh awaits.'

# CHAPTER 12

The journey from Dublin to Carlow the next day was a sombre one, the windows of the train offering glimpses of a countryside still marred by the devastating effects of the blight. Many fields lay barren, and dilapidated cottages stood abandoned. Emaciated livestock huddled in sparse numbers, the shape of their ribs visible beneath their hides. The few people Bridget spotted along the way bore the unmistakable marks of hardship and hunger in their gaunt faces and bony bodies; they watched the progress of the passing train with an apathetic mien. Sorrow sat heavily in the pit of her stomach as she wondered how many more years the blight would continue to return to the potato crop. And even after it finally retreated, how many decades might the country have to endure its repercussions?

They disembarked in the late afternoon at Carlow railway station, where they engaged a carriage to transport them the rest of the way to Oakleigh. Polly, Jennie and Mr Varley followed behind in another carriage, which conveyed their luggage and a portion of the charity funds (a precautionary measure they had taken after having learned from bitter experience that it was wisest not to store all their money in one chest).

At least when they began to travel through Oakleigh land, Bridget was heartened to see that the estate looked marginally better tended than it had last year. The surrounding fields, though not entirely spared, showed signs of careful cultivation and recovery. Cattle grazed in grassy pastures, their frames lean but more nourished than the other poor creatures they had passed. As they entered the manor grounds, she noticed clusters of vibrant purple foxgloves blooming at the base of the trees that lined either side of the gravelled avenue, and her spirits lifted further at this evidence of the estate's resilience in the midst of its tribulation.

The carriage lumbered to the top of the avenue where the red-bricked manor came into view. She doubted the day would ever come when the sight of the house didn't prompt a swell of joy within her. Even though the building that stood here was a replacement of the original one that had burned down and it possessed a new additional wing on the western side, it still radiated the essence of 'home'. She cast a covert glance at Jack and Gus as they gaped out the carriage window, taking in the view of the manor for their first time; how she longed for Oakleigh to one day mean just as much to them.

Two freckled lads in mid-adolescence were crossing in front of the house; the taller one carried a bundle of sticks across his shoulders while the shorter pushed a wheelbarrow half filled with cabbages. With a hiccup, Bridget recognised them as Liam Óg and Aidan Kirwan, the sons of Ellen and dear departed Liam. At the carriage's approach, Liam Óg set his bundle on the ground and hurried up to the manor's entrance, pushing open the black-painted double doors and disappearing inside. By the time the family had alighted from the carriage, he had re-emerged in the company of his mother.

Ellen and Bridget rushed towards each other and hugged fervently. A little over a year had passed since Liam had perished and Bridget felt the weight of Ellen's continuing grief in the tightness of her embrace and the shudder of her breath as she tried to hold back her emotion. When they pulled apart, she saw

that Ellen was wearing a black ribbon around her upper arm –
needless to say, Ellen and her children couldn't afford proper
mourning clothes like Lucy, so this was the simplest way that
she could express her widowhood.

'You are welcome back,' she said, her voice mostly steady.

'We are very glad to be home,' Bridget replied.

After Ellen greeted Cormac, Emily and Rory, she glanced to
the side and let out a gentle exclamation. 'Ah bless, are these your
two boys?'

Bridget smiled. 'Yes,' she said, putting a hand on each of their
shoulders. 'Jack, Gus, this is Ellen. She knew your father and me
long before either of you were even thought of.'

Jack looked thoughtful. 'If you knew them back then, you
must have all sorts of stories.'

'Did Da get into lots of trouble?' Gus asked eagerly. 'Because
Ma says we take after him!'

Although the boys' accents had softened over the past year,
they still held a mild American twang that sounded peculiar
here in the heart of Oakleigh. Ellen didn't blink, though –
instead, she gave a chuckle that rasped out of her like she hadn't
laughed in a long time.

'I'm sure I'll be able to think of a story or two. Come on inside
now.'

She turned and led the family towards the front doors, while
her sons carried on around the corner of the house with their
loads of sticks and cabbages. As she stepped across the threshold
into the entrance hall, Bridget was pleased to register the myriad
signs that the manor was being fully utilised by the tenants in
their time of need: one corner of the hall appeared to have been
designated as a storage area for blankets and spare clothing, and
another was occupied by sacks and baskets of food supplies.
Through the open door that had once led to the drawing room
in the house's previous incarnation, she could glimpse a row

of straw mattresses laid out on the floor. Footsteps sounded on the ceiling above, and voices drifted towards them from deeper within the house. Gone was the awful pall of the fever that had blanketed the place on their last visit – now there was a sense of optimism and bustling activity. The people were finding a way to cope with their ordeal and Oakleigh was playing its part to help them.

As Ellen led them forwards, she said, 'John and Mr Enright will be sorry to have missed your arrival, but they're away for a few days in Wicklow—there's an auction for farming equipment on an estate that's been broken up on account of the blight. They'd intended to be back in time, but you're quite a bit earlier than expected.'

'Yes, we'll explain the reason for that,' Cormac said gravely.

A door opened at the back of the entrance hall and a woman emerged through it at a brisk trot. She looked like she was in her early thirties and strands of her knotty brown hair fell around her face as she marched across the entrance hall, calling out to Ellen, 'Mrs Kavanagh said everything's ready for supper.'

Then she stopped short at the sight of the family, her gaze flitting over them all and anchoring upon Cormac like a lodestone. Her mouth dropped open.

Ellen gestured towards Bridget and Cormac. 'Cathy, you remember Lady Courcey and Mr McGovern, don't you?'

From the woman's throat spurted a rasping sound that was possibly supposed to be a laugh. 'I'm not likely to forget the fella who saved my life, now am I?'

'Oh, I remember the night that happened,' Emily murmured to Rory.

Bridget did too, and she recognised the gleam in the woman's eyes for it was an expression she had beheld several times before, most often in the eyes of Tess O'Leary, but also in those of Thomasina Brennan, Alice Caulfield and the farmer's wife

Maisie McKinty – women who had taken a shine to Cormac and, on occasion, stepped beyond the boundaries of propriety in their desire for him. Bridget had grown accustomed to it, and yet it was difficult not to feel a sense of possessiveness as Cathy's glowing face focused upon Cormac's self-conscious one with palpable adoration. Still, her reaction was understandable – Cormac had rescued her the night the abominable fire had destroyed the manor.

Now, although she was a grown woman, she stuttered like a bashful girl as she asked Ellen, 'W-will I tell Mrs Kavanagh to delay supper?'

'Please don't do so on our account,' Bridget interjected. 'We have no wish to impinge upon the plans you've already made.'

'Then will you share the meal with us?' Ellen asked. At Bridget's hesitation, she added, 'There should be a sufficient amount to go around. The situation is not so dire as it was when you were last here. We've been careful with the money you provided and have made it stretch far enough that the estate is beginning to recover. Some tenants even hope to be able to return to their homes soon to tend their own plots again.'

'That is such positive news,' Bridget said. 'In that case, we would be very pleased to eat with you.'

Despite what Ellen had said, their presence would surely put a strain on the evening's rations – they would amount to nine extra mouths once Polly, Jennie and Mr Varley joined them – but at least the fresh funds they had brought would remedy that circumstance in the immediate future.

'I'll go back down to the kitchens to let Mrs Kavanagh know,' Cathy said, throwing Cormac a warm smile.

'Perhaps we could tell her ourselves,' Bridget said, linking her arm through Cormac's. 'We should dearly love to see her—it has been too long.'

They hadn't met the cook when they were at Oakleigh last summer because she had chosen to endure the worst of the blight with her sister and brother-in-law who were tenants on the Rathglaney Estate over the county border into Wexford. But she had since returned to resume the post she had held for so many years before Bridget's mother had driven all her staff away with her tyrannical mismanagement of the estate.

Cormac nodded his agreement to Bridget's suggestion. 'And I'll go from there out to the courtyard to find a stable hand who can help me and the coachman take care of the horses and carriage.'

They knew that Oakleigh's stables were in use again for John Corbett had written to Bewley Hall several months ago to happily inform them that the manor had been able to purchase a number of horses to work on the land. It was a significant sign of recovery, considering that he'd had to sell all the previous animals in a desperate attempt to gather money to feed the famished tenants.

'I want to see the kitchens as well!' Gus declared, his eyes as round as the dinner plates he no doubt expected to discover there.

Thus, after depositing their hats and gloves in a pile on one of the spare blankets in the corner – for there was neither hatstand nor butler to take them – they all traipsed over to the door at the back of the entrance hall and down the kitchen stairs. When they entered the main kitchen space below, they were greeted by the familiar sight of Mrs Kavanagh bustling about her domain, which was dominated by an enormous cast-iron stove. She didn't have a team of maids working for her as she once did, but there were a couple of girls – daughters of tenants, perhaps – hurrying to and fro as they laid out dishes on the big table in the centre of the room. Liam Óg was also there, stacking his bundle of sticks next to the stove, while Aidan was carrying an armful of cabbages in through the back door, his wheelbarrow visible on the cobbles outside.

Mrs Kavanagh turned when the family entered, her big bosom joggling as she clapped her floury palms together with delight.

'Well now, look who it is!' she said, beaming.

Old age had settled upon her and deep lines etched her face, but her cheeks bloomed from the heat of the stove, lending her a residual touch of youth. She strode forwards, wiping her hands on her apron, and affectionately cupped both Bridget's and Cormac's cheeks. It made Bridget feel very young again to be petted like a child, although she had to admit that she quite enjoyed it; she hadn't received the warm attention of a mother figure in such a long time. Part of her worried that Mrs Kavanagh might remark upon her scar but the cook didn't even seem to notice it as she shifted her welcoming gaze to Emily.

'You're not much taller since I saw you last but I can tell you've grown in other ways,' she said with a wink down at the walnut ring that adorned Emily's left hand.

Emily coloured. 'It's so nice to see you again, Mrs Kavanagh. This is my husband, Rory Carey.'

Mrs Kavanagh gave Rory a piercing stare. 'Hmm, I'll need time to take the measure of you, although I'm sure you wouldn't have made it to the top of the aisle without the thorough approval of this lad.' She patted Cormac's arm.

Rory looked baffled that anyone would have the temerity to call Cormac a 'lad'. He mumbled something completely unintelligible but it didn't matter because Mrs Kavanagh had already moved on to Jack and Gus.

'The image of your da,' she said to Jack, chucking him under his chin. 'And the image of your ma,' she said to Gus, ruffling his chestnut curls. 'What a beautiful family you all make.'

Gus gazed up at her with an expression bordering on awe. 'Da says you make the best tarts in the whole wide world,' he said in a hushed voice. 'Is that really true?'

She chuckled wistfully. 'There hasn't been any occasion for baking tarts of late. This is much plainer fare,' she added, gesturing to the table, where the assembled dishes consisted of pitchers of water and plates of sliced brown bread along with pots of stew that emanated the faintly sweet smell of turnip.

'I haven't yet found a food I don't like,' Gus said in total seriousness.

With that statement left hanging innocently in the air like a challenge, the final preparations took place ahead of supper. It turned out that Liam Óg and Aidan had followed in their father's footsteps and taken on stable hand duties at the manor, so they accompanied Cormac and Rory out to the front of the manor where the second carriage was expected to have arrived by now. The luggage needed to be unloaded and the horses rested, fed and watered before the coachmen could make their journey back to the railway station.

Meanwhile, Bridget, Emily, Jack and Gus helped Cathy and the other two girls carry the supper dishes upstairs to the dining hall in the tenants' wing. This room contained a long table that spanned almost the full length of the space, with benches lining either side of it. Tenants milled around, laying out wooden bowls, spoons and cups on its surface. Bridget recognised many of them from her and Cormac's last visit; although they still bore a thin, pinched appearance, their frames had filled out over the past months so that their skin no longer clung so tightly to their bones. Moreover, they seemed to be in good spirits as they talked among themselves, which was a stark contrast to the deathly silence that had pervaded the manor the previous summer.

A figure detached himself from the others and approached the family with a veritable spring in his step.

'Welcome home, my lady,' he said to Bridget, offering her a smile and a neat bow.

'My goodness, Denis!' she said, surprised and pleased to see him.

Once a young footman at Oakleigh, he was now a man of forty or so, and yet he still retained a certain boyishness in his features as he grinned at her in a manner that was utterly guileless.

'I'm glad to find you in decent health,' she said. 'Where have you been? You weren't here when we came a year ago.'

His expression dimmed. 'I was desperate enough to enter a workhouse. The hunger was bad, but the shame and misery were worse. I can tell you, I was never so happy to leave a place. Now I look on every new day as a blessing.' He raised his chin resolutely. 'And better times are ahead of us all, I'm sure of it.'

She marvelled that he had managed to preserve such a wholesome outlook – it appeared that neither age nor the workhouse had hardened him.

By the time they had brought the rest of the dishes up to the hall (which took several trips as the fare was plain but plentiful), Cormac and the others had rejoined them, along with Polly, Jennie and Mr Varley. The family took a bench near one end of the table, while Ellen and her children, including her youngest, Bridie, sat around the corner of the table next to them. The rest of the tenants took their seats too and every man, woman and child bowed their heads to mumble a few words of grace before they began to ladle the turnip stew from the pots into their bowls. Bridget noticed that Ellen's lips had not moved during the prayers but she made no comment as they both reached for pitchers to pour cups of water for their families.

When everyone's cups had been filled, Cormac raised his own and looked around at them.

'To Liam,' he said.

They lifted their cups and echoed him. A little further down the table, Denis overheard and made the same gesture.

'To Da,' whispered Bridie, her freckled face lowered as she huddled at the end of her family's bench. Jack, who was seated just around the corner from her, cast a solicitous glance in her direction but didn't say anything.

After that, they tucked into the meal and at the same time embarked on a more detailed discussion of the estate's affairs. Ellen imparted how Oakleigh's stewards, Laurence Enright and John Corbett, had overseen the planting of alternative crops to the failing potato and ensured that the produce would not be exported, unlike the continuing policy on so many other estates where the landlords' greed for profit trumped the tenants' need for food. They had also implemented a temporary suspension on collecting rents. In turn, Bridget and Cormac shared news of the charity events they had organised in London and Dublin and the riot that had severely diminished the funds they had intended to bring.

'We hope what we've brought will still make a significant impact though,' said Bridget. 'Here, and further afield as well.'

Cormac nodded. 'We'd like to distribute it to other struggling communities who are also in need of it. It occurred to me that it might be especially worthwhile to send some to Ballingarry in Tipperary, where the Young Irelanders' rebellion took place. The locals may be experiencing a dearth of resources in its aftermath.'

Ellen winced. 'I've no doubt they are. Even though few of them supported it, they're likely feeling the brunt of the authorities' ill will anyway.'

As they spoke, Bridget noticed that Bridie had already devoured her portion of stew and brown bread and was looking forlornly down at her empty bowl. A twinge of guilt stabbed Bridget's stomach; there was nothing left in any of the pots. She was about to rise and bring her own bowl over to the girl when, without any fuss at all, Jack passed his slices of bread to Bridie, placing them gently into her bowl. Bridie stared at him in bewilderment but he had already returned his attention to his father, who was talking about taking a cart with provisions to Tipperary within the next week. After a moment or two, she gobbled the bread up, her expression one of baffled delight. Bridget's heart squeezed with a deep, fierce love for her son.

# Chapter 13

Later that night, Ellen brought them to an upstairs chamber which contained straw mattresses for the whole family. She apologised so many times that Bridget eventually had to be quite stern in her insistence that their accommodation was altogether satisfactory, even though she discerned Emily's and Rory's downcast faces at being obliged to share a room with Emily's parents and brothers. To be fair, it was not an ideal scenario for any of them, but privacy and personal comfort were secondary concerns when others had greater needs.

This was a principle which they fully embraced over the next few weeks, devoting every waking hour to any task, big or small, that would contribute to the improvement of the estate and the lives of its tenants. They used the money they had brought as wisely as they could, purchasing more food, bedding, medicine and seeds, and distributing these among the tenants according to the sizes of their families. They assisted the people in making their homes habitable again, helping to repair ramshackle roofs and walls and planting seeds on their plots of land. They ensured that the local doctor, Dr Lynch, had all the supplies he needed to continue tending to patients still suffering from the effects of fever and malnutrition. Although it would be a long time before life at Oakleigh resembled the way it had prior to the coming of the blight, they would reclaim it little by little.

Bridget and Cormac made the conscious decision not to shield Jack and Gus from either witnessing the deprivation nor participating in the toil. While they didn't think that their more humble living situation back in Boston had faded from the boys' memories just yet, it was prudent to remind them that their comfortable lifestyle at Bewley Hall was a privilege that shouldn't be taken for granted, and that it also came with its own obligations. Cormac articulated this one morning as the family rode along the lane leading to the village of Ballydarry, carrying provisions for the villagers in their saddlebags.

'Tenants are supposedly meant to serve their landlords,' he said, 'but it's more appropriate that landlords serve their tenants by seeing to their welfare. Nothing on the land will thrive—neither the estate nor the people—if the roots are not well tended.'

Jack and Gus nodded intently. Emily and Rory were listening closely too; after all, the responsibility of Oakleigh would someday be theirs.

Emily was the only one of them who looked ill at ease atop her mount. John Corbett had made sure to give her the most docile animal from Oakleigh's stables, but Rory still kept his own horse close beside her for her reassurance.

Their first sight of Ballydarry was its two church spires, which came into view as they began to descend the lane's gentle slope towards the village. St Canice's, the Church of Ireland establishment, was the larger of the two and they passed it first when they entered the small settlement. This was where the funerals of each of Bridget's parents had taken place. After a moment of indecision gazing up at the steeple, she resolved to bring Emily, Jack and Gus to visit their grandparents' grave before the summer was through. She supposed that her mother's spirit might not welcome the presence of the illegitimate boys at her graveside, but she knew without a shadow of a doubt that, were he still alive, Lord Courcey would have doted upon all of his grandchildren, no matter their scandalous origins.

They carried on through the village to the crossroads where the Roman Catholic church, St Mary's, stood. Its sombre façade stirred further memories of lost family members whose graves they would also visit, though these were on Cormac's side: his father and brother buried in the church's graveyard, and his sister Mary lying in unconsecrated ground beyond the wall. Sadly, there were two absent from their number – Cormac's mother and his sister Margaret had perished in Dublin but, in desperate need of money, Tess had given their bodies to medical men whose lackeys frequently prowled the city's tenements seeking corpses upon which they could practise their skills. Bridget shuddered as her mind unwillingly conjured up gruesome images of what must have happened to them. She banished them again as quickly as she could.

A stooped figure emerged unsteadily from the church's porch, accompanied by a much younger man. Bridget was surprised and glad to recognise the older one as the priest, Father Macken – he had to be eighty if he was a day, so the fact that he was still alive at his age and in these impoverished times was a marvel. He dipped his trembling fingers into the holy water font by the church door and feebly flicked them over the head of his companion, who was easily distinguishable by the medical case in his hand. Dr Lynch accepted the sprinkling of water without objection, although Bridget thought she discerned a hint of discomfort in his stiff posture.

Father Macken squinted past the doctor, caught sight of the family and commenced a slow, shuffling walk down the church path towards the road. They halted on their horses; Emily pulled rather too abruptly on her reins but her placid mount didn't startle. Dr Lynch followed the priest, keeping to his pace and eyeing him warily as he shambled over the treacherous cracked stones of the path. They reached the family without incident, and Father Macken's wrinkled hand quivered as he made the sign of the cross in the air before them.

'May God bless you and keep you,' he said, his voice thin and shaky, 'for your kindness to the people here. You bring hope where it's needed most and the Lord sees your good deeds.'

They bowed their heads respectfully, while Bridget privately noted that the priest was being quite selective about her and Cormac's deeds – after all, they had committed adultery and they shared two illegitimate children, both grievous sins in the eyes of the Catholic Church. Perhaps he felt that resources were too scarce to spurn their goodwill and so he chose to turn a blind eye instead.

Dr Lynch cleared his throat and adjusted his grip on his medical case. 'Remember what I said about resting, Father,' he said. 'You don't want that cold to turn into influenza. Your parishioners need you healthy.'

Father Macken shot the doctor a remarkably piercing look, given his otherwise frail state. 'I'll heed your advice,' he said, his tone just short of sullen. '*After* I've called into The Pikeman.'

It might have seemed incongruous for the priest to declare his intention to visit the local drinking house, only for the fact that The Pikeman had become a meeting point for the distribution of provisions to the villagers. Having sent word in advance, it was where the family were now heading.

Undeterred by Father Macken's defiance, Dr Lynch said, 'How fortunate—that is also my next destination. Allow me to accompany you there.'

The Pikeman was almost directly across the road from the church so they would not have to walk far, but Bridget sensed

Father Macken's resentment and wondered what was afoot between the two men to cause their palpable tension.

'Who is in need of your services?' she asked the doctor with some apprehension. Though outbreaks of fever had become far less frequent among the estate's inhabitants of late, she dreaded every day that she would hear of another poor soul who had succumbed.

'Annie Bracken. She's not ill as such, but she's got an anxious sort of nature, especially since her mother passed last year.' He waved his free hand in a nonchalant manner. 'It's nothing to be concerned about. Ben just asked me to look in on her.'

Bridget gave a sympathetic nod, understanding the doctor's trivialising of the situation. She had been told in confidence by Ellen that Annie Bracken was in actual fact prone to bouts of hysteria, but it would do her no good at all if word of that got out – women who suffered from such an affliction were usually carted off to the asylum. It was a mark of Dr Lynch's compassion that he chose to quietly treat her instead of exposing her condition, and Bridget was glad the estate finally had the aid of such a decent doctor. If the supercilious Mr Abbott, who had once served Bridget's mother, had deigned to minister to Annie, he would have sent her away without a second thought.

Bridget gave Dr Lynch a smile that she hoped conveyed her gratitude and urged her mare backwards a few paces to allow him and Father Macken to cross the road in the direction of The Pikeman. Then she and the rest of the family followed, almost immediately passing the two men who were hampered by the priest's slow progress. They stopped in front of the drinking house and proceeded to dismount. As they tied their horses to posts and removed their saddlebags, she endeavoured not to think about the frightening incident that had happened to her here many years before, when several of The Pikeman's unsavoury patrons had intimidated her on account of her English blood. Thankfully, those men no longer lived on Oakleigh land and the tenants who remained did not espouse the same abusive sentiments – at least, not to her face. She was not so naïve as to believe that every single person on the estate welcomed her presence, but they surely had to put their grievances aside when she was in a position to offer substantial assistance during the current crisis. Her close connection to Cormac, a local man born and raised on Carlow soil, was also advantageous in swaying the wider community's opinion of her.

The doctor and the priest finally reached the building too and made their way inside. Cormac led the family after them, stepping beneath the sign of a man wielding a pike and pushing on the heavy wooden door, which creaked as it opened wider, revealing the dim interior where knots of villagers huddled around.

Ben Bracken stood behind the bar, his weather-beaten skin still a prominent feature of his appearance, despite the fact that he was now the proprietor of the drinking house instead of a labourer on the land. His expression lifted at their entrance and, wiping his hands on a rag, he came around the end of the bar to shake Cormac's hand. Cormac returned the gesture with sincerity, which was no wonder, for he owed Ben more than he could ever repay – it was Ben who had given him the crucial information that had helped him to locate his lost family after Lady Courcey had thrown them all off the estate.

Now, Ben pressed a leathery palm to his chest and said, 'We're most obliged to ye for coming here today.'

'We hope we've brought enough,' Bridget replied, her gaze sweeping the room. More had come than she'd expected: there were mothers with children clinging to their skirts, a pair of ginger-haired lads who looked barely out of adolescence as they shuffled their feet in embarrassment, a solitary girl with her palm resting protectively over her pregnant belly, and a few elderly men hunched in the corner. Father Macken had joined this last group and was murmuring something to them, but Dr Lynch was nowhere to be seen.

The family began to unload the provisions from their saddlebags, setting them on the surface of the bar, and the villagers came forwards eagerly. Bridget and Cormac divided up the rations of beans, salted meat and apples (the first of the season from Oakleigh's orchard) and passed them to Emily and Rory, who moved through the crowd to hand them out, subtly prioritising the most vulnerable among them. Jack and Gus, keen to help, followed their lead. As they distributed all the food, it became clear that what they had brought on this occasion was not going to be sufficient. The villagers stared at the dwindling supply with hollow eyes, and Bridget felt a sharp pang of remorse that their efforts were falling short.

Jack and Gus came back to her side, their hands empty. Jack's forehead was furrowed; he dithered for a moment before reaching into his pocket and pulling out a small parcel of bread and cheese. Gus eyed it with concern.

'That's your lunch,' he reminded his brother in an alarmed whisper.

Jack chewed on his lip. Then he stepped back into the crowd of milling villagers and handed the parcel to the pregnant girl, who accepted it dumbly. When he returned, he shrugged at Gus's horrified expression.

'Isn't it better to give it to others who need it more?' he said in a quiet voice that only Gus and Bridget could hear. 'I don't mind being hungry for a few hours. These people know what it's like to be hungry for a lot longer than that.'

Gus's face fell. He curved his palm defensively over the bulge in his own pocket.

'Do I have to give mine away as well, Ma?' he asked in dismay.

'That's entirely up to you,' she said.

As he struggled with the decision, she spotted Dr Lynch descending a rickety stairs at the far end of the drinking house, a woman ambling in his wake. Annie Bracken was only a wisp of a thing, her skin as smooth as her brother's was weathered. She plucked nervously at the worn material of her skirt as she trailed after the doctor, who made his way over to Ben and handed him a small bottle. Ben pocketed it with a solemn nod of thanks.

A resigned sigh drew Bridget's attention back to her sons. With an effort that seemed to require all of his willpower, Gus extracted his parcel of food from his pocket. Taking a deep breath, he squared his shoulders, crossed the room to Annie, and placed the parcel in her hands without a word. She gaped at him with startled eyes before giving him a timid smile. He offered her a formal bow, which he had undoubtedly learned from Mr Humphrey, and then trotted back across the room, looking noticeably less gloomy than when he had set out.

After they had dispensed the last of the provisions, the family bade farewell to the villagers and remounted their horses. They proceeded onwards to McKinty Farm, where they had made a prior arrangement to assist Farmer McKinty in clearing a plot of land that had fallen into neglect. Cormac and Rory helped the gentle farmer to remove rocks and break up the soil, while Bridget and Emily joined the farmer's wife, Maisie, in planting neat rows of vegetable seeds in the freshly turned earth, and Jack and Gus followed behind, using trowels to cover the seeds with soil. Throughout their labours, Bridget kept a surreptitious eye on the flirtatious Maisie, but the woman did nothing more than throw Cormac a few teasing winks, which he pretended not to notice. Bridget thought that the McKintys had a number of children but there was no sign of them anywhere on the farmstead and she hesitated to ask after them, lest it transpire that they had perished from the fever.

Much later, when they had finished toiling on the farm and were riding back to the manor, Bridget surveyed her two boys, who drooped wearily in their saddles, their cheeks streaked with dirt.

'You both did fine work today,' she said, 'but most especially when you acted with such selflessness at The Pikeman. I'm proud of you.'

Gus's stomach rumbled loudly in response and Cormac threw a worried glance over his shoulder. 'I think we're being hunted by a pack of ferocious lions,' he said in alarm.

Gus giggled. 'It's only my hungry belly!'

'In that case, you'll be pleased to know that Mrs Kavanagh has stocked her pantry well with the funds we gave her,' Bridget said. She leaned conspiratorially towards Gus. 'We've insisted upon continuing to eat simple fare on the whole, but I may have mentioned to her that I know someone who is particularly fond of mince pies.'

Gus's eyes widened. 'Mince pies?' he repeated in beatific anticipation.

Bridget smiled as they carried on down the road and the imposing manor came into view on the horizon.

# CHAPTER 14

The following morning, there was a stir of excitement when a package of letters arrived, forwarded from Bewley Hall. The family gathered around, and Bridget watched Cormac's face change as he thumbed through the correspondence, saying, 'That's Mr Comerford's scrawl, I was expecting this from Mr Carruthers, and—ah!' His expression glowed as he held up two letters. 'Chicago!'

One of them was from Derval Carey to Rory, who took it and turned away to read it hungrily, Emily peering past his elbow. Cormac opened the other letter addressed to himself, which had come from Orlaith. His eyes glistened as he scanned the page, and Bridget could tell how much he was missing his youngest sister. How eighteen months had gone by in a blink.

'It sounds like they're thriving for the most part,' he said to Bridget, with Jack and Gus also listening eagerly. 'Charlie's fighting fires and Orlaith's patching up the injured. The twins turned one in May and are speaking their first words.' He smiled but then frowned as he read on. 'Maggie is almost four, though she doesn't talk much at all. Bronagh didn't want to write a note but sends her love.' Bridget suspected that Orlaith had embellished that slightly, knowing Bronagh's reserved nature. 'Tess has regular work at a laundry and hopes to open her own place someday. That's very good to hear.' When he finished, he stared down at the sheet of paper with longing. 'God, I wish I could read it twenty times over. But Rory and I really have to go.'

'I'll mind it while you're away,' Bridget promised, and he reluctantly surrendered it to her so she could tuck it into her pocket.

The letters had arrived at the perfect moment, as Cormac and Rory were in the midst of preparing to leave that morning, heading for Tipperary with a horse and cart carrying supplies, intending to do what they could to help the Ballingarry locals in the aftermath of the Young Irelanders' failed rebellion. They would be gone for a few days, maybe more. At least now they set out with a little extra warmth in their hearts. And although Bridget, Emily and the boys would miss them greatly, there was no shortage of tasks to occupy them in their absence.

Indeed, they had scarcely departed when Laurence Enright and John Corbett requested a meeting with Bridget to discuss the current state of affairs at Oakleigh. The drawing room was still occupied by straw mattresses and there was no space yet in the new house designated as a study, so she invited the two stewards to sit with her at the table in the tenants' dining hall once it had been vacated after breakfast. They took the bench opposite her – John seemed totally at ease in this setting, while Mr Enright made a valiant effort to appear so, even as he struggled to swing his legs over the bench.

'Thank you for meeting with us, my lady,' he said, straightening his spectacles. 'We know there have been many demands on your time.'

John gave her a paternal wink. 'I wager you've hardly remembered to sleep since you got here.'

She shrugged self-consciously. 'It's difficult to conceive of resting when there is always more work to be done.'

Mr Enright folded his hands on the surface of the table. While most of his nails had grown back normally, she discerned the uneven ridges on both of his thumbnails, silent reminders of the brutality he had suffered twelve years ago when two malicious tenants had wrenched off all of his nails in retaliation for the evictions Lady Courcey had compelled him to carry out.

'What you and Mr McGovern have achieved has been nothing short of remarkable,' he said, his voice full of respect. 'The estate had been teetering on the brink of ruin a year ago, but now it is beginning to revive, thanks to your concerted efforts.' He cleared his throat. 'However, this comes with its own concerns. Oakleigh's recovery is attracting attention from further afield—'

'We're doing all we can to help other communities too,' she interposed. 'Cormac departed for Tipperary barely an hour ago, and we mean to send Mrs Kavanagh to Wexford very soon with provisions to help the tenants on the Rathglaney Estate. I hope no one suspects us of hoarding the charity funds for Oakleigh's benefit alone.'

'Begging your pardon, my lady, that is not the point I was leading towards. The problem is that poor folk from other regions are flocking to Oakleigh. They've heard that the people here are faring better under your guardianship, and they seek refuge. Your benevolence is, of course, wholly commendable, but it has had the unintentional consequence of inviting an even greater strain upon your resources.'

'Oh, I see,' she said, nonplussed.

Her mind drifted back to the pair of ginger-haired lads she had seen in The Pikeman the previous day. They had seemed so embarrassed – had they been outsiders chancing their luck? What about the unfortunate pregnant girl by herself? Could she have been an outcast forced to seek sanctuary elsewhere, in a place rumoured to be more hospitable? It might explain why the family had run out of the food they were distributing. And yet, if that was the case, how astonishing it was that none of the villagers had raised an objection to the presence of strangers in their midst.

'Why would the local residents abide it?' she asked aloud. 'If these extra mouths mean they themselves might have to go without?'

John shook his head. 'I can't speak for every individual on the estate, but I know they won't turn them away from Ballydarry, not if Ben has anything to say about it. The Pikeman has become their focal point, and 'tis his establishment so 'tis his rules. He wouldn't have the heart to cast out anyone in need. Neither would the majority of the villagers, in fairness. They're decent folk and they understand the desperation of others, for it wasn't too long ago they were in as bad a predicament.'

'My goodness,' she said, 'that is truly admirable conduct on their part.'

'Indeed,' said Mr Enright. 'As admirable as your own, housing the tenants throughout the manor during the worst of this calamitous blight.'

She tilted her head. 'I believe I can guess what you're about to say next.'

He smiled faintly. 'Yes, my lady. The time has come when these tenants must return to their own dwellings and commence paying their rents again, and the manor must be restored to its original function as the home of a noble family.'

'Noble?' she said with an amused twist of her mouth. 'My family is about as far from noble as can be, at least in the traditional sense of the word. However, I take your point.'

'I'm glad you do. Oakleigh deserves to reclaim its former splendour. Perhaps that could begin with you furnishing the house again as it once was?'

Perceiving his dubious glance around the dining hall, she said firmly, 'This wing shall remain. Even once the blight passes, there will always be some tenants in need, and so there must always be a place for them to find succour until they can support themselves again.'

'We won't argue with you on that, my lady,' John said with equal firmness, and Mr Enright gave a conceding nod.

Bridget's gaze wandered to the empty walls. Yes, it would soon be time to breathe life back into the manor, to make it a place where people lived rather than just survived. It needed to be filled once more with beauty and art. She thought of Emily's painting which they had brought with them from England – how proud she would be to see her daughter's work displayed in a place of honour at Oakleigh. She relished the prospect of reviving the grandeur of the house with elegant furniture, of making its rooms cosy with drapes and rugs, of restocking the library's shelves with books...but the days were passing too quickly.

'Unfortunately, there won't be much time to embrace this endeavour before we leave at the end of the summer,' she said. 'While we should like Oakleigh to be our primary home in the future, we have to go back to England in the short term. Cormac has ongoing obligations at Bewley Hall, and the boys must resume their studies with their tutor.'

Mr Enright leaned forwards. 'Then why don't you stay longer, even after the others must go? The work here is far from finished and the estate would benefit from your steady presence.'

She mulled over his suggestion. To stay where she was most needed certainly appealed to her, but Cormac would baulk at the idea of her travelling separately from the family, given what had happened the last time she came to Ireland in the regrettable company of Mr Sandler. If she was being honest, the notion didn't thrill her either, much as she wished she had the courage to dismiss her apprehension.

'I don't know whether it would be wise for Polly and me to journey alone...' she said, trailing off as her hesitation billowed up between her and the two men.

John gave her a reassuring nod. 'I'll personally see to your safety,' he said. 'I can escort you and Miss Hawkins all the way from here to the front door of Bewley Hall if needs be.'

That made her feel a hundred times better, and she knew Cormac would have no objection to such a scenario either.

'Let us consider it, then,' she said with a grateful smile.

'Very good, my lady,' said Mr Enright. 'In that case, another task you ought to take into account is the matter of household management. A proper complement of staff must be hired to help the manor function properly again. You have a cook, but what about a housekeeper, a butler, maids, gardeners? These are essential positions, and filling them will bring employment to many of the local people.'

After a pensive pause, Bridget said, 'You are quite right. Please leave this with me.'

Once their meeting had concluded, they left the tenants' dining hall and Bridget made her way below stairs to the kitchens. As she approached the door to the main kitchen, she detected the savoury scent of cooking meat, along with Mrs Kavanagh's voice raised in exasperation.

'Gus McGovern, if I catch you pilfering from my pantry again, I swear to the heavens—'

'I'm not pilfering!' came Gus's responding protest. 'It's for the villagers, I promise!'

Mrs Kavanagh's tone softened. 'Ah, you're a good-hearted lad, just like your da.' Then she became stern again. 'But there are rules, even when it's for a worthy cause. You've got to ask first, understand?'

Bridget stepped into the kitchen and Gus froze at the sight of her, a basket of loaves in his arms and what looked like a pot of honey sticking out of his pocket. Perhaps in an effort to avert a potential scolding, he rattled off at full tilt, 'Jack and I are going back to Ballydarry with Liam Óg and Aidan because we want to bring more food to the villagers and I should have asked Mrs Kavanagh first but I definitely will next time and we'll see you later, Ma!'

With a winning smile, he darted out the back door of the kitchen into the courtyard.

Mrs Kavanagh chuckled and gave Bridget a wry look. 'I'm sure I'm not telling you anything you don't already know but, good Lord, it's nigh on impossible to stay vexed with that lad for long.'

'It is,' Bridget agreed with a sigh, contemplating whether Gus's cheeky behaviour warranted a light smack on his rump. 'Shall I call him back to return what he's purloined?'

Mrs Kavanagh waved a dismissive hand. 'After hearing about yesterday's shortage, I'd baked that additional bread specifically for the villagers.' She winked. 'But he wasn't to know that, was he?'

Bridget laughed. 'I'm glad he accidentally did the right thing. On another matter, I'm looking for Ellen. Is she about?'

'I think she's out at the stables giving her two lads strict orders to look after your two while they're on their expedition to the village.'

Mrs Kavanagh had scarcely finished speaking when Ellen came through the back door, the ends of the black ribbon on her arm fluttering as she crossed the threshold in a hurry. As soon as she saw Bridget, she said quickly, 'I was just going to seek you out. Our four boys are heading to Ballydarry but I have Liam Óg and Aidan well warned not to get up to any mischief.'

'That's perfectly fine,' Bridget said. 'I know Jack and Gus will be safe with them. Could I have a word with you, if now is a convenient time?'

'Oh, of course,' Ellen replied without question, and she followed Bridget out of the main kitchen and down the hall to an empty room. There were several spaces such as this below stairs that had yet to be utilised since the manor had been rebuilt. This one was not very large but it had a fireplace and the potential to be quite snug once it acquired some furniture.

Bridget glanced around it before focusing her gaze on Ellen. 'It's time for Oakleigh to thrive once more as a proper home for both family and staff. I believe this room could work very well as the housekeeper's office. Would you agree?'

Ellen appraised their bare surroundings with a crease between her brows. 'Yes, I think it would be quite suitable. It's close enough to the kitchen that the housekeeper and Mrs Kavanagh would be able to coordinate together with relative ease, and yet it's at enough of a distance that she could consider it to be her own domain.'

'Excellent,' Bridget said. 'I'm glad it pleases you. Needless to say, it must be furnished first before it's ready to be occupied. You will want a writing desk, certainly, and cabinets for the linen and household inventories, and maybe a comfortable chair by the fireplace?'

Ellen's mouth dropped open. 'Wait...you mean...?'

Bridget gave her a warm smile. 'Indeed, I do.'

'But I'm not—I couldn't—'

'You could, and you would do a marvellous job.'

Ellen stared at her, stunned. 'Would you not wish to hire a proper housekeeper with experience?'

Bridget's jaw tightened as she remembered Mrs Walsh, the housekeeper who had worked at the manor during her mother's guardianship. She had no idea where the woman was now, nor if she was even still alive, but she would make no attempt to trace her whereabouts – she could still recall the sound of the key clicking into place when Mrs Walsh had helped Garrett lock Bridget into her bedchamber to prevent her from running away with the McGovern family.

Bridget took Ellen's hands in both of her own. 'You have done so much to lead the tenants here this past year, despite everything you have suffered yourself. Your strength and dedication are extraordinary. You are more than capable of filling this role, and Oakleigh would be honoured to have you do so.'

Ellen let out an unsteady breath. 'The honour would be mine.'

Bridget squeezed her fingers. 'It will probably mean that you and your children ought to remain living here at the manor, even after all the other tenants return to their own homes. With Liam Óg and Aidan already working as stable hands, that makes the most sense. As for Bridie, she is too young to begin employment yet, but perhaps in the future she might take up a position in the scullery? That would keep her near you, and she could rise through the maids' ranks over time.'

Emotion welled in Ellen's eyes. 'Thank you,' she managed to whisper.

One consequence of this arrangement was that the McGovern family cottage would lie empty in the long term if the Kirwans did not return to it. Bridget sincerely hoped that someday it would become a home again, possibly for one of Ellen's children whenever they married. She pictured the horseshoe above its door – had it rusted over the years? It was supposed to bring luck, and yet not everyone who had lived within those walls had been lucky. Still, maybe it would bless another family with better fortune in the future.

But for now, they would concentrate on reviving this beloved home.

She gave Ellen a thoughtful look. 'And Denis?' she asked. 'What do you think of my appointing him as butler?'

Ellen emitted a watery chuckle. 'I think he would jump over the moon with pride.'

Bridget felt her heart glow. Little by little, they would piece together a new and enduring community at Oakleigh.

# Chapter 15

Rory made his way through the winding streets of Liverpool, the late August breeze carrying the fishy, salty smells of the docks along with him. He had left Emily behind in the care of her father – she'd looked very green after their journey across the Irish Sea, so Mr McGovern had suggested that she get some sustenance at an inn (a proposal which Jack and Gus, or rather their bellies, had thoroughly supported) while Rory went about his business. Once he returned from his visit to the solicitor, they would see about getting the train to Bedfordshire.

Jennie and Mr Varley had travelled with them from Ireland, although Polly had remained with Lady Bridget, who had arranged to stay a couple of months longer at Oakleigh. Rory could tell that Mr McGovern hadn't been enamoured with that plan, but his and Lady Bridget's essential responsibilities compelled them to be apart for the time being. Rory wondered glumly what it would be like if he and Emily were also obliged to follow separate paths in the name of duty – what if, in the distant future, he had to continue to fulfil his role as deputy land agent at Bewley Hall, while she was required to go to Oakleigh when she became the Lady Courcey? Then it occurred to him that they might be separated much sooner than that, depending on the responses she received to her applications to the art academies. He pushed the dispiriting thought aside for now. After spending several weeks sharing a bedchamber with her family, his chief ambition was to get back to Bewley Hall and ravish her in their private suite as soon as possible.

But first, he had to call upon Martins & Martins Solicitors to sign the new lease.

It was still somewhat baffling to him that he owned actual property, a house that was entirely in his name and not obtained by means of his marriage to Emily. Number 5 Penny Close was a humble dwelling, to be sure, but he was nonetheless its landlord.

And his tenants were his bigamous father's second wife and their three illegitimate offspring.

He could only feel sorry for Maud Pratt, who had been so deceived by Rory's father that she'd had no inkling of the existence of his first wife and four children living in Boston until Rory had appeared on the doorstep in Penny Close. Brian Mór's subsequent death at sea had resulted in the solicitor Mr Martins probing into his deceased client's past and exposing his second marriage as illegal, leaving Maud in a precarious position without a husband or the protection of the law. Rory knew he had done the right thing by allowing the family to continue to reside in the house on Penny Close – he had no need of it, while a roof over their heads was the very minimum they needed to survive.

When he reached the solicitors' office, he took a deep breath that had nothing to do with the exertion of his walk. This was only a formality, so why did he feel daunted all of a sudden? He had assumed after the charity events at the Theatre Royal that his adopted persona of the Duke of Desmond would lie dormant for a lengthy period, but now he wondered whether he ought to summon the duke's confidence for this meeting. Squaring his shoulders, he pulled on the cord to ring the bell.

When he was admitted into the presence of Mr Martins a short while later, he found the solicitor searching through a stack of papers on his desk.

'Mr Carey, please take a seat. I had my hand on the contract earlier this morning—ah, here it is.'

He slid a page out from among the others and laid it flat on the surface of the desk in front of Rory.

'Circumstances have changed since we last corresponded, so I was obliged to draw up a new lease, but you'll find all the details are in order.'

Rory frowned. 'What circumstances changed?'

'The former Miss Pratt is no longer the signatory on the document. In consequence of her recent marriage, the signatory is now her husband, a Mr Tommy Jones.'

Rory gaped at him. 'She got remarried?'

'Married,' Mr Martins corrected primly as he straightened two pens on his inkstand. 'One cannot remarry if one has never been wed before.'

Rory found himself bristling at the solicitor's judgemental tone. What happened to Maud hadn't been her fault – she'd been ignorant of the truth and his blackguard of a father had been entirely to blame.

He shifted uncomfortably. It seemed a betrayal of his mother to come to Maud's defence, even in his thoughts.

'Who is this fella?' he demanded, before catching himself and adding, 'Uh, this fellow, I mean.'

Mr Martins consulted an open book on his desk that was filled with neat handwriting. 'He's a stoker,' he said at last. 'At the Rigby Foundry.'

That answered very little. How had Maud met this man? Why had she married him less than two years after Brian Mór's death? Although she might not have been a widow in official terms, surely she was still in mourning. Rory didn't know much about their relationship – and nor did he want to – but he had been able to tell that she'd loved his father deeply. She must have done this for other reasons, and that filled him with a sense of unease.

Mr Martins tapped the bottom of the lease and pointed to the inkstand. 'When you're ready, Mr Carey.'

Rory rubbed his jaw. The Duke of Desmond would be canny in a situation like this. 'I'm not really inclined to sign an agreement with a man I've never met.'

'I'm afraid I have no personal knowledge of Mr Jones, so I can't provide any reassurances as to his character.' Mr Martins shrugged. 'You're not obliged to be loyal to these tenants and are well within your rights to seek alternatives. Perhaps you would prefer to lease the house to your own kind?'

'My own kind?' Rory repeated, taken aback.

'Indeed. There are plenty of them swarming the town nowadays, since that infernal blight sent them running from their own country.'

Rory gritted his teeth. 'I don't want to evict Maud and her children,' he said, his voice brittle. 'I'd just like to learn a bit more about this stranger before signing anything. I think it'd be best if I pay a visit to Penny Close.'

Mr Martins looked annoyed at the delay in concluding their business, but he said grudgingly, 'As you wish.'

After a curt farewell, Rory strode away from the solicitors' office, feeling both perturbed and resentful as he marched deeper into Liverpool's warren of streets. The unexpected revelation of Tommy Jones had disconcerted him, but so had the solicitor's disdainful attitude towards Irish immigrants.

Though he had never been particularly drawn to politics, Rory had dwelled a great deal on the plight of the Irish since his and Mr McGovern's trip to Tipperary. What he'd witnessed in Ballingarry had been far worse than anything he'd seen at

Oakleigh. In the wake of the failed rebellion there, the people had appeared shockingly gaunt and listless, ravaged not only by hunger but by the crushing weight of demoralisation. It seemed that the British authorities were determined to reward Irish nationalism with total deprivation of both food and hope.

The needlessness of it made Rory so angry. Although the potato crop was struggling, the British still had the power to stop the export of other thriving produce out of the country and to adequately feed the people, but they chose not to, content to leave them to starve instead. They didn't just view the Irish as inferior – they viewed them as expendable. This sentiment was pervasive throughout the country, but Rory had seen it magnified tenfold when it came to the unfortunate inhabitants of Ballingarry.

And now, here in Liverpool, he had beheld yet another demonstration of that same contempt, albeit on a smaller scale. The solicitor's sneering tone had delivered his underlying message so casually: 'we tolerate you, as we must tolerate the rats in the gutter'. Little did the man seem to realise that it was the ruthless policies of his own country's government that had driven the desperate Irish to flee their homeland in the first place.

Rory's feet pounded the footpaths at such a pace that he reached Penny Close sooner than he'd anticipated and before he'd decided what he would say. He paused at the top of the narrow alley lined with cramped terraced houses and exhaled slowly, endeavouring to stifle the bitterness that had burgeoned in him in reaction to the solicitor's derogatory remarks. He needed to commence his conversation with Maud in a non-accusatory frame of mind.

Once his blood had cooled, he proceeded into the alley and approached the door of Number 5, rapping twice with more assurance than he felt. After a few seconds, it opened and his gaze dropped to the short figure on the threshold – a girl of about seven with a mane of frizzy hair. She looked up at him in silence and, momentarily tongue-tied, he said nothing either.

A voice drifted out from the interior of the house. 'Is it Elsie, May? She's early—she said she wouldn't be coming by until later to borrow that yarn. Let her in, love.'

'It's not Elsie,' the girl said in a timid squeak.

Rory heard a scrape that could have been a chair or a stool scuffing against the floor and then a woman appeared in the doorway. Hair as frizzy as her daughter's, Maud stared out at Rory with shock and, if he was not mistaken, a degree of fear.

'R-Rory!' she stammered. 'What're you doing here?'

'I've just come from the solicitors' office,' he said, and the fear in her expression mounted further. He knitted his brows. 'Can I come in?'

Although she looked very much like she wanted to say no, she nodded and stood back, tugging May to her side as she did so. Rory stepped over the threshold and into the one room that took up the whole lower floor of the house. It was smokier than he remembered, but otherwise it remained the same: the table with the five stools, the fireplace with its blackened bricks...the floor where Brian Mór had landed after Rory had punched him on the chin. Nothing marked the spot, but Rory wouldn't ever forget a single detail from the day he had struck his father – not only had he uncovered the awful truth of Brian Mór's bigamy, but he had also learned that he had three half-siblings.

He glanced around. 'Where are your two boys?'

'Upstairs,' Maud replied. 'Frankie's abed with a broken leg. He had an accident last week.' She grimaced. 'You know how careless ten-year-old boys can be. Alfie just went up a few minutes ago to bring him some bread and dripping. He'll be back down soon.'

She bustled past him and cleared a few swathes of fabric from one of the stools, dropping them onto the table among several balls of yarn. 'Have a seat.'

He sat on the stool, which was a little short for his long legs. He tried not to appear uncomfortable as he hunched on it. 'Uh, so like I said, I was at the solicitors' office—'

Maud interrupted him quickly. 'May, why don't you bring that yarn over to Elsie now? It'll save her calling by for it later.'

She plucked one of the balls of yarn from the table and handed it to her daughter, who gave Rory an assessing stare before she trotted out the door, closing it behind her. Maud turned back to Rory.

'Did you sign the lease?' she asked, crossing her arms to grip her elbows.

He hesitated. 'Not yet. I wanted to speak to you first. Mr Martins told me about... Tommy Jones.'

She smoothed her palms down the long sleeves of her dress, flattening them over her cuffs. 'It must've given you a surprise to see Tommy's name on the contract. I'm sorry I didn't get a chance to tell you beforehand. I got married a month ago. I'm Maud Jones now.' She attempted a smile.

Should he congratulate her? She didn't seem very happy, but that could well be on account of his presence rather than anything else – being face to face with the son her duplicitous 'husband' had fathered by another woman probably never got easier. Not when that son owned the roof over her head.

'It did give me a surprise,' he admitted. 'Have you known Mr Jones long?'

'Oh, forever,' she said with a light laugh. 'His aunt lives across the close at Number 2.'

That made Rory feel a little better. At least there was a long-standing connection between them.

'I'm glad—I mean, I hope that—it was for the right reason,' he said haltingly. 'And not 'cause of wanting security or—or if you were worried about being on your own without a man, that is. You were definitely safe here. I wouldn't have evicted you.'

She gave him a pitying look. 'It's sweet that you think that was enough. But what do you imagine life's been like for me, suddenly unmarried with three illegitimate children? People I knew all my life started crossing the road to avoid me. The grocer refused to serve me and I had to find another further from home. Elsie was the only one who stuck by me and she's mad as a hatter, which made her as much of an outcast as me.'

He winced. 'I'm sorry. It can't have been easy.'

'It wasn't. So when Tommy showed an interest, I encouraged him. Why wouldn't I? He has a steady job. He's well liked in our community. Since we married, people have started talking to me again. And then there's...'

She trailed off and placed a palm on her stomach.

Ah.

'I can guess what you're thinking,' she said. 'I already had three stained with sin. What was one more? But I couldn't carry the weight of my shame any longer. I needed this one to be lawful.'

He wanted to tell her that the shame wasn't hers, that it belonged to Brian Mór alone. He wasn't sure if she'd appreciate it coming from him, though. If Emily were here, she would know the right words. Moreover, she would probably have surmised that Maud was with child far sooner than him, maybe even back at Martins & Martins Solicitors – she was much more in tune with these kinds of things, especially since she was so eager to conceive herself.

The door opened and Maud flinched. Then her expression softened as May came trotting back in. 'Thanks for doing that, love. Did Elsie have any message for me?'

'No, but she said the cat winked at her this morning, which means trouble's coming.'

Maud raised an eyebrow at Rory as though to say, 'See? Mad as a hatter.' However, May crossed her small arms and levelled him with a suspicious look. Before he could protest his innocence, footsteps came stamping down the stairs and a boy of about twelve emerged onto the ground floor, carrying a plate that was empty apart from a greasy streak and a few crumbs. He didn't possess his mother's frizzy hair; instead, he had the same brown hair as Rory, which they had both inherited from Brian Mór.

As soon as he saw Rory, his countenance filled with a suspicion that matched his little sister's. 'What's brought you here?' he demanded.

'Don't fret, Alfie,' said Maud. 'The lease needs to be renewed on the house so he called by to check that all's in order before signing it.' She turned her expectant gaze to Rory. 'And now you know everything's fine, you'll go back to the solicitors' office, won't you?'

He had just opened his mouth when the door opened again and this time Maud, Alfie and May all flinched. A short, stocky man marched in, his face and clothes filthy with soot. For a third time, Rory found himself on the receiving end of a suspicious glare.

'Who's this?' the man barked.

Maud crossed the smoky room to him and put a placating hand on his arm. 'This is Rory, Tommy,' she told him. 'Rory Carey. Our landlord.'

Tommy Jones's face cleared at once and he grinned at Rory, revealing a large, misshapen tooth that jutted out from the right side of his mouth. 'All right, mate? Good to finally meet you.'

He strode forwards and stuck out a sooty hand, black grime buried deep underneath the fingernails. Rory stood and shook it.

'Nice to meet you too,' he said. 'I hope you don't mind me calling by?'

'Not at all! I'm sure my wife's been treating you well.'

Tommy gave Maud a wink and she flushed. 'He's not here long,' she said. 'I didn't get a chance yet to offer him anything.'

'I don't need—' Rory started to say as Tommy exclaimed, 'Well then, why don't I take him up the road for a pint?'

'No, honestly, 'tis fine,' said Rory, putting up his hands in polite refusal.

Tommy flung a friendly arm around his shoulders, their differences in height making the movement a little awkward. 'Why not? Is my money not good enough for you?' He let out a boisterous laugh.

Rory forced a smile. 'I'm just short on time. My family's waiting back at the docks—we've got to catch a train to Bedfordshire.'

'Ah, fair enough,' Tommy said, clapping him on the back and dropping his arm. 'Whereabouts do you live in Bedfordshire?'

'The Bewley Estate,' Rory replied, hoping Tommy would assume he lived as a tenant on the land, rather than at Bewley Hall itself. He had no desire to get into an explanation about how that extraordinary set of circumstances had come about.

Tommy just nodded and said, 'And do you have other business in Liverpool apart from signing the lease for this place? I suppose that's squared away already?'

Rory swallowed. 'I, uh, just wanted to call by first. Make sure all was well with the house and...everything.'

Tommy darted a glance from him to Maud and back. 'And have you found that all is well?' he asked lightly.

'Of course he has,' Maud said, her own voice equally light. 'Although now that I think of it,' she carried on, swivelling towards Rory, 'we've been having trouble with the fireplace—it's smoking more than it should be, as you can no doubt tell. The flue is probably blocked.'

'That's an excellent point, my lovely wife,' Tommy said, throwing Rory a smirk. 'You can take care of that, right?'

Rory didn't object, in spite of Tommy's smugness; it was the landlord's responsibility to ensure that the house was habitable for his tenants.

'For sure,' he said. 'I'll leave instructions with Mr Martins to arrange a chimney sweep to fix it, and to send the bill to me.' He looked around. 'Is there anything else? Do the youngsters have all they need? Do they get any schooling?'

This went beyond the level of concern expected from a landlord, but he genuinely wished to know. They were his kin, after all, even if he didn't like the way that fact had come about. Alfie and May both stared at him, their suspicion supplanted by astonishment.

'Schooling?' Tommy whistled, his large tooth vanishing momentarily behind his pursed lips. 'No time for that. There are more important things to be doing, like putting food on the table. Right, Alfie?'

'Yes, sir,' Alfie mumbled. He was still holding the plate and he gripped it tightly in both of his hands as he peered up at Rory. 'I deliver newspapers every morning. The printer expects them to be out by dawn, so I start early. When I'm done, I come back home and help Ma.'

'You'd better not be helping your ma with any more of that sewing,' Tommy said. 'That's women's work.' He tousled Alfie's brown hair, a bit more roughly than was necessary.

'No, sir,' Alfie murmured, discreetly stepping out of arm's reach.

Maud made no comment on this exchange, although her lips tightened. Rory eyed her, doubt coiling in his gut.

'I'll head back to the solicitors' office so,' he said, '...if that's what you want me to do?'

She blinked and then beamed at him. 'That would be terrific.'

'Appreciate it, mate,' Tommy added cheerfully. 'Glad we got to meet in person.' He gestured to his stepdaughter. 'May, love, help this old man get his boots off, there's a good girl.'

He dropped heavily onto the stool Rory had vacated and stuck out one of his legs. May knelt in front of him and began to unlace the boot, her fingers blackening from the soot at once.

Maud accompanied Rory to the door. 'Thanks for coming,' she said, her eyes not quite meeting his.

He lifted the latch, crossed the threshold and turned back to bid her farewell. She was already reaching out to close the door and, as she did so, her cuff shifted up her forearm. For the briefest moment, he caught a glimpse of a dark bruise circling her wrist, stark against her pale skin. His stomach clenched. She quickly tugged her cuff back down.

'Goodbye,' she said hurriedly and shut the door.

# Chapter 16

Bridget stood in the doorway to Oakleigh's main bedchamber, gazing around at the room within. Transformed since its previous occupants had left, every trace of their straw mattresses had been removed and it now contained a mahogany four-poster bed that matched the mahogany mantelpiece above the fireplace, as well as a wardrobe and washstand. The bed was dressed in crisp linen and boasted two pillows, while new drapes framed the windows, although the walls and floor were still missing mirrors and rugs, leaving the room unfinished for now – practicality had taken precedence over luxury. She recalled the cosy sheepskin rug that had once adorned the floorboards of her old bedchamber and thought it would please her to obtain something similar in the future, when she could acquire more discretionary furnishings.

She stepped inside. Despite its bareness, she felt a sense of satisfaction in claiming the space. This bedchamber, the domain of the lady of the manor, was connected to the master's chamber next door in much the same manner as the suite of rooms at Bewley Hall. The next time she and Cormac stayed at Oakleigh, this would be their private sanctuary.

With a small sigh, she acknowledged the ache of his absence, while taking comfort in the fact that she would be seeing him again very soon. The past three months had been a whirlwind of activity, involving several trips to furniture makers in Dublin in her quest to fill the manor with essential items. Though it was a long way from resembling its former glory, she had made very reasonable progress. But now the end of November was fast approaching and she had begun formulating her plans to return to England. She wanted to get back in time for Christmastide and, before that, Gus's birthday.

She heard the light tread of footsteps behind her and turned to find Polly on the threshold.

'Are you pleased with it, my lady?' she asked, glancing about the room.

'Very much. Part of me wishes I had a bit longer to enjoy it, but I do believe it is time for us to go back to Bewley Hall.'

Polly's face lit up at the news. Bridget experienced a dart of unease.

'Oh, my dear Polly, have you been unhappy at Oakleigh?' she asked in concern. 'You ought to have said—'

'No, not at all,' Polly hastened to assure her. 'We've been doing valuable work here. I suppose I'm just eager at the thought of going home, and of seeing...everyone.'

Of course, her mother and uncle worked in the Bewley household, which meant that Bridget and Polly would both be returning to their families.

'It will be splendid for us all to be reunited for the Christmas season,' Bridget said with a smile. 'John Corbett has promised to accompany us, so we shall be quite safe on the journey.'

Another set of footsteps sounded out in the corridor and this time Denis appeared in the doorway. Since his promotion to butler, he had started wearing a black tailcoat with a charcoal waistcoat and a crisp white shirt, dark trousers and polished shoes, all of which he had acquired at a tailor's in Tullow, the nearest town. Bridget would not have objected if Denis had chosen to wear less formal attire, but he earnestly wished to live up to the honour that had been bestowed upon him and so she had provided him with the funds to do so, although he had begged for the final sum to be taken out of his wages in partial payments until it had been repaid in full. As Ellen had predicted, he had embraced his new role with a fervent sense of pride.

The one aspect where they had eschewed formality was his name. Bridget would continue to call him Denis – as was her wont when her fondness transcended the typical employer-servant boundary – though the staff would now refer to him as Mr Nolan.

Polly stepped aside to allow him to enter the bedchamber and he came forwards, holding out a sealed note to Bridget. 'A letter has arrived for you, my lady.'

She accepted it and saw that it had originated from Ashbrook Lodge. That gladdened her – Patrick had been silent for so very long. Then she turned the note over and registered the wax seal with surprise: Wyndham. She flipped it back, examined the handwriting on the address more closely and recognised its owner.

Garrett was in Ireland?

Mystified, she broke the seal and unfolded the page. In three terse sentences, Garrett enquired after her health, requested an audience at her earliest convenience, and confirmed his readiness to call upon her at Oakleigh as soon as he received her reply.

'My lady?' Polly said, her tone nervous. 'It's not bad news, is it?'

Bridget frowned and gave an unconvincing shake of her head. In a daze, she wandered over to the mahogany bed and lowered herself onto the edge of it, gaping down at the page.

Her mind whirled with so many questions that she could hardly pin them all down. What had brought Garrett to Ireland? Had he pursued Patrick when his son hadn't returned to England? If Garrett was now at Ashbrook Lodge, had Patrick deserted the place, unwilling to remain in the presence of his disappointing father? Or could Garrett and Patrick possibly have reconciled? What did Garrett wish to speak to her about and with such urgency?

Given that they'd had no interaction with each other since the conclusion of the charity event in London, she could probably assume that his demand for a meeting concerned Patrick in some way. After all, Patrick had been under her and Cormac's supervision when Gus had let slip the truth about his illegitimate origins. Did Garrett mean to rage to her about this blunder that had led to an estrangement with his son? If so, she would defend Gus to the hilt. The failings in that scenario belonged to Garrett and no one else.

Perhaps, if Patrick was refusing all contact with his father, Garrett wanted to visit Oakleigh to seek her and Cormac's intercession in the matter. He had written to Bridget but it could well be Cormac's assistance he desired, considering the past success Cormac had achieved with his wayward nephew. Although there were ways and means for Garrett to have established that the mistress of Oakleigh was in residence before he'd sent his correspondence, it was less likely that he would have been able to determine if any of the rest of the family were also present. Thus, upon his discovery that Cormac was actually in England, Garrett might deem this a wasted trip.

Should she grant his request to visit nonetheless? There was no justifiable reason not to – they did share a tentative accord at present in the sense that no outright antagonism currently existed between them, and if there was something she could do to benefit Patrick's welfare, then of course she would wish to do it. She would have to make it clear, however, that Cormac would not be available to offer his help, and that, as Oakleigh transitioned from a sanctuary for tenants back to a manor home, Garrett must be prepared for a humble reception.

She looked up from the letter to find both Polly and Denis gazing at her with troubled expressions.

'Nothing to worry about,' she said, waving the page as she gave them a wan smile. 'But we shall be obliged to delay our departure for Bewley Hall a little longer.'

Three days later, she sat in the drawing room, awaiting Garrett's arrival. There was no sofa yet as the upholstered furniture she had ordered in Dublin would take a while to be sourced and delivered. Instead, she had arranged for two wooden chairs with arms to be positioned in front of the crackling hearth and she had cushioned them with the pillows from her bedchamber. A low table stood between the chairs, appropriated from the housekeeper's room below stairs. There was nothing grand about these circumstances, but they would have to make do; she had not expected to receive visitors in a formal capacity so soon. If Garrett found fault with the room's current state, the inconvenience was his to bear.

He had still arranged to come, even though her reply to his letter had conveyed Cormac's absence. What did he want with her in particular? Patrick had always been polite with her but they possessed no special bond – she doubted whether she would be able to exert any great influence in a situation where Garrett aspired to reconnect with his alienated son. She shifted the low table an inch to the right and continued to wait, absorbed in her misgivings and hating that Garrett could still inspire such unease in her.

A knock sounded on the door and Denis entered.

'Lord Wyndham to see you, my lady,' he announced with a solemn bow and stepped aside, revealing Garrett in the doorway, dressed immaculately from head to foot.

He strode into the room and bowed as Bridget rose and came forwards to meet him.

'Lady Courcey,' he said stiffly. His hand twitched and, realising the gesture he wished to make, she offered him her own. He took it and kissed the air above her knuckles.

'Lord Wyndham,' she greeted in return and curtseyed, marvelling at their mutual civility. A casual spectator would not be able to tell that they shared such a turbulent history. Without warning, she recalled the attraction that had bubbled up inside her the first time she caught sight of him across a crowded ballroom. In the next instant, she remembered his merciless grip on her shoulders the day he had burned the wooden bird. Firmly, she banished both memories from her mind.

She turned her gaze to Denis. 'Please tell Ellen we will take refreshment whenever it is ready.'

He bowed once more and retreated from the room. Bridget indicated the two chairs and Garrett settled his long frame into one, making no remark on the unsophisticated nature of them. She took the opposite chair. For several moments, the only sound came from the flames crackling in the fireplace. The fire was well set, and yet she found that its warmth couldn't reach her on this chilly November afternoon.

Garrett cleared his throat. 'Allow me to offer my felicitations on your recent birthday.'

Her mouth dropped open in astonishment. Indeed, he was correct. She had left behind her thirties this month, as Cormac had the previous month. Though they had been apart for both occasions, they had each written to the other, with expressions of passion that would have left her scarlet had any eyes bar theirs read them.

But it had been twelve years since she and Garrett had lived under the same roof. How had he even remembered? 'I—thank you,' she stuttered.

'A not insignificant milestone,' he added.

She tensed. While it was ungallant of him to draw attention to her actual age, she was more perturbed by the implication of his words. It reminded her horribly of the day she turned twenty-one and he had forced her to sign a contract conferring guardianship of Oakleigh onto her mother in perpetuity. Was forty consequential for some legal reason of which she was not aware? Was this why he had come? She pressed her cold hands into the folds of her skirts.

To her surprise, however, he didn't pursue the subject any further. Instead, he rested his elbows on the arms of his chair and said, 'I had the opportunity to survey conditions in the countryside along my journey here. Oakleigh appears to be faring better than most.'

She nodded. 'It's been a long road to get to this point—the situation was a great deal grimmer a year and a half ago. We've done our utmost to support the tenants, and it's a relief to see the estate beginning to recover.'

He glanced around the bare drawing room. 'And the manor? I'm impressed by the quality of the reconstruction. It would be a shame if this new building didn't get to fulfil its proper purpose.'

'Steps are being taken in that direction, now that the tenants have returned to their own dwellings, but furnishing the entire house will take time.'

He steepled his fingertips together. 'I imagine all of this is stretching the estate's finances to an extreme degree?'

And there it was. As the legal owner of Oakleigh, he had a stake in its prosperity. Naturally, the matter of how its money was being expended would be of chief importance to him.

Her teeth clamped down on the tip of her tongue. 'Charitable donations have helped to provide sustenance to the tenants, as you know. I sold Courcey House on Merrion Square last year, which was an enormous help in obtaining resources. Oakleigh's overall income has admittedly been depleted by the suspension in collecting rents, but those are resuming in increments, and in the meantime Cormac can alleviate the deficit from Bewley Hall as needed.'

'Too munificent for your own good.' He shook his head. 'You might both be paupers before this crisis is through.'

'Would you have us stand idly by while the tenants starve?' she demanded. 'Our efforts pale in the face of what still needs to be done. The country as a whole continues to suffer.' A hopeful thought occurred to her. 'I wonder would you be willing to make another petition to Parliament?'

He didn't answer right away. 'I'm afraid it wouldn't do any good,' he said at last. 'I've already exercised all the power I have in that regard, and Parliament has domestic concerns that it deems to be of higher priority. Pity. It might otherwise have been an expedient solution.'

His expression turned meditative and she frowned. Just then, there was another knock on the door and Ellen came in, a ring of keys jangling at her waist. Her face was inscrutable as she set a tea tray down on the table between Bridget and Garrett.

'Is there anything else you need, my lady?' she asked.

A crystal ball would be helpful to divine the thoughts of the man brooding opposite her. 'Not for now, Ellen, thank you.'

Ellen exited the room and Bridget leaned forwards to pour the tea. She pushed a cup and saucer across the table towards Garrett but he didn't take it, his mouth pressed to his steepled fingers as he gazed absent-mindedly into the fire. Lifting her own cup to her lips, she sipped and waited. As the silence stretched between them, she began to wonder what on earth was happening. He had instigated this meeting, and yet now he sat like a statue opposite her as though he didn't intend to say anything else.

Her patience grew thin. She set down her cup. 'You wrote from Ashbrook Lodge,' she said. 'Can I assume then that you have seen Patrick?'

His hazel eyes shot to hers before skittering away again.

'Come now,' she said, her tone on the verge of complaining. 'You didn't come all this way for no purpose. If it's not about the estate's finances, surely it must be about Patrick? When he stayed with us this past summer, he made an unpleasant discovery about the circumstances of his birth. I presume you know this?'

Garrett scowled. 'I do.'

'I hope you don't place any blame upon my son for his inadvertent disclosure,' she said hotly. 'He wasn't to know that you had concealed the truth from yours.'

Garrett's jaw tightened. 'I'm thoroughly aware that I was the one at fault. I absolve your son of any guilt.'

She faltered, snapping her mouth closed. She had expected a more fiery altercation than that.

Garrett sat back in his chair with a frustrated exhalation of breath. 'However, I would have appreciated an alert from you after the disclosure occurred. I didn't realise anything was amiss with Patrick for quite some time.'

She winced. Yes, perhaps that would have been the considerate thing to do. But she had been so preoccupied with fleeing Dublin following the riot, and helping the tenants upon reaching Oakleigh, that the notion hadn't even occurred to her.

'How did you find out?' she asked guiltily.

'Blanchard, the land agent at Ashbrook Lodge, wrote to me. He said that Patrick had shown up at the estate without any prior warning and declared that he intended to take up residence there "until further notice". Blanchard treated him with all due courtesy but felt it was his duty to inform me of the situation, as he got the distinct impression that my son desired to keep me ignorant of his whereabouts.'

Bridget shifted uneasily in her chair, feeling the pillow slip at her back.

'I was perplexed by Patrick's subterfuge as I wouldn't have opposed his inhabiting the Lodge for a time, if that had been his preference. In fact, it would have pleased me to grant it as a reward for completing his education at Eton. So I wrote to him. And I received no reply.' Garrett paused. 'I wrote again. Silence.'

Bridget read the hurt in his slumped shoulders.

'I corresponded further with Blanchard but he could offer no illumination. He said the boy was tight-lipped about everything bar the management of the estate, in which he had started to take a keen interest, especially in addressing the effects of the blight. When two more of my letters went unanswered, I concluded that I must speak with my son in person. Hence, I travelled to Ireland.'

'And?' Bridget said cautiously.

'And he flatly refused to see me.'

She swallowed. Garrett rubbed his forehead, and she wondered if it was an attempt to obscure the stain of humiliation on his cheeks. Seizing her cup, she gulped another mouthful of tea. This development certainly indicated that he was here to seek help in bridging the rift between him and his defiant son. She wasn't the most ideal person for that, but maybe he would ask her to relay his plea to Cormac.

Garrett let his hand drop. 'Being a parent is quite the humbling experience, is it not? One thinks one has mastered the challenges of this world, and then one's child demonstrates the capacity to reduce one to less than nothing.' He shook his head, his countenance bleak. 'I couldn't deduce how I had let him down on this occasion, but my sense of worthlessness was all-encompassing. Men who long to be fathers cannot conceive of the pain to which they are laying their future selves bare.'

She was startled by his frankness. Why would he reveal such vulnerability to her? 'Do you regret bringing him into your life?'

'No,' he said vehemently. 'I have always desired this bond. If anything, I yearn for it even more, the harder he pushes me away.' He sighed. 'I was utterly desperate for him to open up to me at Ashbrook Lodge. If I could only learn what I had done to offend him, then I would do whatever I could to remedy it. So I refused to leave, effectively trapping him in his bedchamber until he was prepared to come out and face me.' His mouth twisted wryly. 'I know—my tactics have never been deserving of glory, and this ploy was just as unsavoury. Even when my intentions are well-meaning, I still manage to be a failure of a father.'

She hesitated. 'Not a failure, in this instance. Misguided, perhaps.'

He raised his eyebrows at her. 'You are being generous. Of all people, you have the most right to cut me down.'

A hum of dissent vibrated in her throat; Cormac's sister Mary would arguably lay greater claim to that entitlement, if only she were still alive. 'What good would it achieve for me to cut you down? I don't have the stomach for it today, and it would certainly be of no practical use to Patrick, who is our primary concern at this juncture.'

They exchanged a long, lingering look, and she sensed the memories crowding in again. Was it generosity, or foolishness, that compelled her to seek out the better parts buried inside this mercurial man? There was no denying that he had played a substantial role in her and Polly's rescue from Sycamore Farm, at what had turned out to be an immense risk to his own person. Moreover, she knew without a flicker of doubt that he had adored James for the duration of their baby's tragically brief life.

But with Garrett the scales always ended up tipping back. She couldn't forget how he had inveigled Emily into running away to London with his deceitful letter. How he had testified as a witness against Cormac in his trial at the Old Bailey. How he had spurned Mary when Patrick had been a newborn in her arms.

She pinched the bridge of her nose. 'Did he eventually come out of his bedchamber?'

'He did, issuing a tirade of vitriol that still haunts me. In truth, even though I had cravenly shied away from telling him, I hadn't anticipated that he would react with so much revulsion to the knowledge of his illegitimacy. After all, he has no need to worry that it will be exposed—those who know have either been paid off or are trustworthy enough to keep the secret. But it appears that his level of integrity is more elevated than mine.'

Garrett had accused Bridget of naïveté in the past, but for once she could say the same of him. He ought to have foreseen that Patrick's sense of identity was already too fragile to suffer a blow like this without consequence.

'What exactly did he say?' she asked, keeping her voice neutral.

'He said that he was ashamed of me. I felt it like a physical strike to my chest. It seems to ache even now.'

She didn't scoff at his hyperbole; she suspected he really meant it. 'Does it make you ashamed of yourself, too?'

Garrett gritted his teeth. 'Yes. I'd much rather not. It's an abominable feeling.'

An incredulous laugh cracked out of her. He threw her a glare.

'I'm glad my humiliation amuses you,' he retorted. 'In all honesty, I don't understand what changed his attitude. He had always admired my guile before.' Letting out a huff, he added in a mutter, 'I suppose being around your saintly family might have rubbed off on him.'

'I do apologise if you believe our morals are contagious,' she said tightly. 'How dreadful of us to exert such an unwelcome influence, even though it was precisely what you begged Cormac to do when you came to him at Bewley Hall. May I infer from your delivery of that insult that you are not in fact here to seek our help with regard to Patrick?'

He pressed his lips together. 'Allow me to express my regret for my thoughtless remark. It was undeserved.'

Taken aback by his immediate contrition, she realised that his desperation must be even greater than she had first guessed. 'So you do seek our help?'

He cleared his throat, unable to meet her gaze. After a lengthy pause, he said, 'Might I suggest we take a walk outdoors? It's cold but dry. It would be refreshing.'

She blinked. What was there to gain from prevaricating?

'Very well,' she said with a shrug. 'I must warn you, though, that the grounds are not what they used to be. Pretty gardens were no one's priority once the blight came. However, I've begun the task of hiring additional staff, both indoor and outdoor, so I do hope that the gardeners will be able to bring the grounds back to life in the spring.'

'The state of the grounds will not trouble me,' he said indifferently.

She put down her teacup. His own was still untouched. They both rose and made for the drawing room door, which he opened for her. Out in the entrance hall, they heard the brisk tapping of shoes on the floor and Denis appeared, standing to attention before them, not unlike his long-ago predecessor, Mr Buttimer. A few minutes later, they stepped out the front door into the biting November air, Bridget in her cloak and bonnet, Garrett in his overcoat and hat, and both of them wearing gloves. She shivered as the wind tried to sneak between the folds of her cloak. To her relief, he did not offer his arm for her to lean on.

She had not mentioned the orchard because she had no intention of leading him anywhere near it, even though it was the one place on the grounds that had continued to thrive – the apples it had produced this autumn had been a triumph amid the rest of the neglect. Instead, she steered him directly towards Oakleigh's gardens, which had been unscathed by the blaze that had burned the manor down but had still suffered from several subsequent years of abandonment.

They passed underneath the arch that marked the entrance to the gardens, ducking around the vines that had been left to drape untamed over it. The way ahead was lined with hedges whose untrimmed foliage protruded on either side, and weeds had overtaken the once-pristine flowerbeds that bordered the gravel path. Bridget recognised the tall spires of foxglove stalks among them and was pleased that the wildflowers had taken root here, just like on the avenue, even if there was no colour or life in them at this time of the year. She would ask the gardeners to retain the foxgloves if possible when they revived the beds.

Keeping a few inches of distance between each other, she and Garrett followed the pathway. She waited for him to elucidate exactly how he expected her and Cormac to aid him in his predicament with Patrick, but he remained taciturn. By the time they reached the sculpture of Venus perched on a wide plinth, lichen and bird droppings blemishing the limestone body, she realised he would need some encouragement to coax it out of him. The man was too proud by half.

'Do you want to tell me what happened after Patrick's outburst?' she asked, striving for a gentle approach.

Garrett made no response at first. It must have been quite the harrowing encounter for him to have such difficulty talking about it. For a long minute, the only sound was the crunch of the gravel beneath their feet.

'He stormed off,' he said at length, his voice strained. 'I gave him a few hours to calm down and then I sought him out again, but his scorching anger had merely hardened into cold contempt.'

Garrett's posture sagged. Against her will, Bridget felt a dart of pity for him. He had brought this shame upon himself, true, and yet to be so roundly rejected by one's child was a painful experience that no parent could easily bear. Regrettably, she knew just how it felt. Although Emily had not vilified Bridget and Cormac to their faces, her actions had conveyed clearly enough that she had been unhappy with the life they had built for her in Boston when she ran away to London in desperate pursuit of a better one. That they had so thoroughly failed their daughter had been an appalling realisation.

Thus, she was not surprised when Garrett continued, 'It truly left me nauseated. I implored him to tell me what I needed to do to regain his trust. He said that such an aspiration was futile as he could finally see that I always placed my own desires before every other consideration, including him. I swore that I would do whatever it took to prove to him that he was more important to me than anything else.' Garrett heaved a sigh, his breath puffing out in the chilly air. 'And so he set me a challenge. One that he fully believes I cannot rise to.'

'A challenge?' Bridget repeated, intrigued.

The path widened to accommodate a bench to the side, its wooden seat discoloured with moss. As they passed it by, he muttered, 'I must demonstrate that I am capable of acting selflessly, that I can do something for the benefit of another that brings me no personal gain. If it's to my obvious detriment, so much the better. Should I find myself unable to do that, then

I'll have proven that selfishness is the most fundamental trait of my existence.'

She frowned, as doubtful as Patrick that Garrett could pass such a test. 'And what is this miraculous deed?'

'He didn't specify. I must determine it for myself.'

Now she was powerfully curious. How could a man as self-centred as him even envisage the type of endeavour that would meet Patrick's criterion? 'And have you settled upon your course of action, or are you still contemplating your options?'

He gave her a sidelong glance, his eyes narrowed as though he could discern her scepticism. 'I have spent much time grappling with it,' he said, without answering her question. 'After our second confrontation, Patrick permitted me to temporarily stay at the Lodge on the proviso that our paths could not cross. Thus, we take our meals separately, we ride out on the estate at different times, and he even instructed the housekeeper to accommodate me in the opposite wing from his own bedchamber. It's been quite a headache for the staff, but I haven't disputed the matter with him, not in his current volatile state.'

Garrett paused at a gap in the hedge which afforded a view of the neglected lawn in the centre of the gardens, the grass overgrown and choked by weeds. She halted too and stared at him as he gazed out across the wild expanse, his gloved hands clasped behind his back. Though still remarkably handsome, he seemed older than his forty-six years, his shoulders bowed as if weighed down by the gravity of fatherhood.

'A petition to Parliament might have been a neat way to resolve this quandary,' he said, almost to himself, 'but on balance I don't believe it would be acceptable in Patrick's view, not when I have already undertaken it on a prior occasion.'

She didn't comment, but she agreed with his reasoning – there would be a pall of insincerity over such a repeated act.

Garrett grunted and then straightened, turning to her. 'I wish to grant you a divorce.'

She looked at him uncomprehendingly. 'Pardon?'

He pursed his mouth. 'You heard me correctly.'

She took an uncertain step backwards. 'You cannot mean it.'

'I do.'

'But—' Her mind flailed as she tried to grasp the implications of his declaration. 'But why would you? There would be absolutely no—'

'No benefit to myself,' he finished for her. 'Isn't that precisely the point?'

She gaped at him. Surely he did not mean to answer Patrick's challenge with the most immense response imaginable? There had to be myriad other manoeuvres he could make on a smaller scale that would demonstrate unselfishness to his son without relinquishing so much power.

'You would lose Oakleigh,' she said. Although the estate had been in dire straits these past few years, it was still a hugely valuable property.

'I would,' he said.

'You would face enormous stigma in society,' she said, baffled. So would she, of course, but she didn't move in the same elevated circles he did.

'Yes,' he said. A muscle twitched in his jaw.

'You would forsake your control over me.' The words came out in barely more than a whisper.

Shame crossed his face. 'I suspect the way I have held onto that so tenaciously is one of the things Patrick despises most about me.'

She shook her head in disbelief. 'I cannot accept that you would be willing to follow through with this. You must know what I would immediately do with my freedom.'

'You would marry again,' he said without inflection. 'And I would have facilitated the happiness of a pair whom I believe truly command Patrick's respect.'

Her legs shook. Fearing they would not support her for much longer, she stumbled back along the path the way they had come until she reached the moss-covered bench and collapsed onto it, heedless of the stains it would leave on her cloak. Garrett did not follow her at once, giving her a few moments to hunch over her knees and process the enormity of what he had just offered her.

It had to be a trick. This was no different to the insidious letter he had sent to Emily in Boston – it was merely a lie cloaked in temptation, a promise that concealed a trap. If he really meant to do it, which she highly doubted, then there must be some advantage in it for him, despite what he claimed to the contrary.

The gravel crunched nearby. She sat bolt upright.

'*You* wish to remarry!' she exclaimed. 'That's why you're doing this.'

Garrett came to a halt several paces away from her. He raised his arms in a gesture of innocence. 'Most assuredly not. I can guarantee you that I have no ambitions whatsoever in that regard.'

She squinted at him with distrust. To her surprise, the hazel gaze that met hers was unguarded and, as far as she could tell, sincere.

'I don't...understand...' she said weakly, bewilderment sweeping over her. 'The man I married would never...'

She trailed away, struck dumb as she once again read shame in his expression.

'That man would never have been capable of this,' he admitted. 'But I'm not entirely sure if he's the same man anymore.'

'What changed him?' she asked, pleading for some scrap of insight.

Garrett glanced away. 'He nearly died.'

She opened her mouth but no words came out. Abashed, she realised that she had never given much consideration to how his experience at Sycamore Farm might have affected him in the long term. Dismay coursed through her that her antipathy towards him had led her to dehumanise him to such a degree. What had gone through his mind in those agonising, interminable seconds when the rope had constricted his windpipe and his lungs had struggled vainly for air? What regrets? What fear? It would be more astonishing if he had *not* been changed by it.

When he looked back at her, his countenance was pale. 'I can no longer deny that the horror of that day left an indelible impression on me. I tried to pretend for a long time that I was merely furious at what had transpired, but eventually I had to admit that it had terrified me. Especially when I acknowledged to myself that I had quite possibly deserved such a brutal ending.' His throat bobbed. 'And if my death had occurred, what legacy would I have left behind? Who would have mourned me? Had I done enough for my only living child?'

Her pulse quickened at his confession. She had not anticipated such introspection from him. He lifted his shoulders self-consciously as though he could discern the trajectory of her thoughts.

'Yes, it seems I've become something of a philosopher.' He indicated the bench. 'May I?'

She nodded mutely and he sat beside her, leaving space between them so that their elbows did not touch.

'I have always wanted a son, you know that. But simply having him as my heir is no longer adequate. Now, I desire his esteem. Heavens, I even crave his filial love, though I doubt that will ever be within my reach. In its place, I would settle for the genuine regard he holds for his uncle.'

Startled, she peered at him askance.

'Oh, he hasn't said so in as many words. But I can tell. Somehow, the man has won the respect of my son in a handful of meetings and letters. He is even fashioning him into a better person by degrees, and thus is managing to succeed where I have repeatedly failed. It might be exactly what I requested of him, but that makes it no less difficult a reality to endure. Yet again, he has bested me.' The bitterness was evident in Garrett's voice.

'It's not a competition,' she said, reining in her exasperation. 'That's the wonderful thing about love. The more it grows, the more room there is for it. It would be perfectly possible for Patrick to hold both his uncle and his father in high regard.'

'I haven't given him much reason to, though, have I?' Garrett muttered.

She grimaced, unable to contradict him. 'But you hope to change that fact with this divorce?'

He kept his gaze trained on the ragged hedge opposite them. 'I think it would be a step in the right direction.'

Her heart fluttered madly against her ribs. Could she trust him? Was this truly a possibility?

He crossed his legs at the ankles, though the rigidity of his torso belied the casual gesture. 'The spectre of death is a curious thing,' he said, his tone falsely light. 'It has the power to focus one's mind in a manner which nothing else can.' His expression became sober. 'I have cogitated upon it at great length since Newby passed away. It was a struggle for me to accept the expiration of a man who had been my closest companion since I left my boyhood. I witnessed how it shattered his wife and daughters. I grieved in a way that I hadn't since—' He cut himself off, seemingly incapable of uttering their precious boy's name. He shook his head. 'It made me recognise the impermanence of life, though still at a somewhat remote distance—such a fate was surely a long way off for me, after all. Then, mere months later, the events on the farm occurred to give me a more concentrated viewpoint. For several ghastly moments, I believed my own time had run out.'

He declared this quite coolly but she detected that muscle twitching in his jaw again and knew his composed façade was a mask to cover deeper emotion.

'It must have been petrifying,' she murmured. She had brushed with death at the age of nineteen, when a fever had nearly taken her after she fell in the limestone quarry during that ferocious storm, but she had never had a rope coiled tightly around her neck with murderous intent.

He exhaled a shaky breath. 'Would you believe me if I said all I could think about was Patrick?'

She bit the tip of her tongue. If truth be told, his stark candour throughout this conversation had made her more receptive to the notion than she might have been an hour ago.

His hand drifted up to his throat. 'I was terrified that the men would string him up after they were done with me. What if my last act on this earth had been to deliver my son to the place of his death?' His voice cracked along with his composure and he turned his face fully away from her, but not before she caught a glimpse of his rapidly blinking eyelids.

She gave him a brief respite to gather himself before she said, 'It was a most disturbing experience. I can understand how it might have altered your perspective on life since then.'

'It altered Patrick too,' he said gruffly, still not looking at her. 'You may have noticed a difference in him when he resided with you this summer. He playacts the degenerate more often now than he embodies it. He does not squander his time or my money at Ashbrook Lodge—rather, he has insisted that Blanchard instruct him in its management. Moreover, I think you are aware that my speech about matching ticket sales with donations at your charity event in London was made upon his demand.'

'Yes,' she said, 'he told Cormac so when they met backstage. Putting aside his more dubious conduct, that admirable act reflected well on him. It reflected well on you too, in that you granted his request when you could have refused him.'

Garrett shrugged. 'He badgered me into it. I would not otherwise have done it. I confess, I felt profoundly uncomfortable with the praise I subsequently received, as it hadn't come from a place of generosity—or, at least, not mine.' At last, he glanced back at her. 'My son is a better man than I. That is as I would wish it, though it hardly leaves me feeling very proud of myself.'

She studied his face, searching for artifice and finding only chagrin in his downcast eyes and the tight lines around his mouth.

'That may be true,' she said hesitantly, 'but there's still time for you to become a better man as well.'

His lip curled wryly. 'You don't deem me to be a lost cause?'

'I don't know. Do you?'

'I have my reservations.' His forehead creased. 'However, I do appreciate that you haven't dismissed me as unsalvageable just yet. You would be well within your rights, given our history.'

'Maybe so, but you now plan to make reparations regarding that, yes?' She arched her brow, challenging him to renege on his promise.

'Yes, I do.' He inclined his head in a small bow.

Hope surged in her; she was actually beginning to believe him. 'What are the steps involved in obtaining a divorce?'

'I will have to petition Parliament to pass an act. It will take many months, perhaps much longer. The wheels of bureaucracy turn slowly, and there will be plenty of hurdles to overcome, not least the expense of it.'

'How much could it cost?' she asked in a quiet voice, thinking of the funds that were already strained from supporting the tenants and furnishing the manor.

'I shall cover it.' Before she could decide whether she ought to demur, he said, 'I can't imagine Patrick will count this as a selfless act if I charge you for your liberation.'

She nodded, privately relieved.

'I must warn you,' he added, 'the proceedings will be held in open court and it will be a scandal in the papers. I shall be obliged to publicly accuse you of adultery in order to present reasonable grounds for divorce.'

She sighed. 'Well, it's what I'm guilty of, isn't it?'

He emitted a humourless sound that could not be construed as a chuckle. 'Quite. There's also a point to be made in relation to your second marriage, whenever that may occur—you understand that it will not give your sons legal status? They will regrettably remain illegitimate.'

She narrowed her eyes at him. 'Why do you say "regrettably"?'

'Because children shouldn't be punished for their parents' misdeeds. I'm confident that this sentiment resonates with both of us.'

He was right. Regardless of the pain and hostility that had long existed between them, that was most certainly their common ground.

'Indeed, we are in accord,' she said.

'What a remarkable rarity,' he said dryly. He sat in pensive silence for a few beats before swivelling towards her. 'Shall we shake hands on it?'

She faltered, then said, 'I think we can manage that level of civility.'

The corner of his mouth twitched. He rose from the bench and removed his gloves, dropping them onto the seat. She stood too and did the same, the cold November air caressing her exposed skin. He extended his right hand; when she offered hers, he grasped it with a light pressure. His fingers were cool as he met her gaze.

'Did you ever believe we would arrive at this point?' he asked.

'No,' she said, 'and yet here we are.'

He placed his other palm over their joined hands. 'I carry a lot of regrets in my life, Bridget, and many of them involve you. But I think, for once, I am making the right choice.'

Her breath caught and she didn't say anything. He pressed gently and relinquished his hold, reaching for his gloves.

'I'll keep you informed of my progress. Will I write to you here or at Bewley Hall?'

'Bewley Hall,' she replied a little unsteadily. 'I'm returning there for Christmas and expect to remain for at least a few months after that.'

'Very well. Shall we go back to the house now? I judge our business to be concluded.'

His familiar curtness was almost a relief after such heartfelt honesty – she felt like she was regaining firmer ground. She donned her own gloves again and then took the arm he offered her with only the slightest hesitation.

They followed the path back through the neglected gardens, her heart racing as she envisioned the possibility that lay in her and Cormac's future.

# Chapter 17

'I can't believe we've put a whole tree inside the house!' Jack said, his voice full of amazement.

Emily smiled at him as she stood back, admiring the fir tree that dominated the drawing room and filled the air with the scent of pine. Her father had initially been dubious about this new trend as it had been made popular by the royal family, but she had eventually convinced him to put aside his Irish ideals on this one occasion because she found it so charming. She and her brothers had just finished decorating the tree's branches with candles, which the family would light on Christmas Eve (only on her father's strict condition that they keep several buckets of water close at hand), and candied fruits, which they would have to monitor vigilantly to prevent Gus from making off with them at his first opportunity. At least for now he was distracted by a plate of mince pies sitting on a round table near the roaring hearth.

'December is the greatest of all the months,' he declared thickly, his cheeks bulging. 'There's my birthday, and Christmas, and an excuse to eat mince pies every single day. It's like the year is saving the best for last!'

Emily felt a pang of sadness and her hand drifted to her stomach. She had hoped to have special news to share before the year's end, but it was not to be. Her hand moved to her pocket, where a piece of paper crinkled beneath her fingers, and she drew cheer from the memory of the entertaining letter she had received from Matilda, her staunch companion from her days as a housemaid in Boston. Dictated to the housekeeper at Marlowe House – since Matilda couldn't write herself – the letter gaily reported that their old pigeon friend was alive and well and sent his greetings by dropping a special 'gift' onto her cap.

The door opened and Emily's father entered the drawing room, carrying a box.

'I've just completed the last one,' he announced, crossing the room and setting the box on the table next to the rapidly emptying plate of mince pies. A few stray wood shavings clung to his sleeves as he lifted the lid of the box and withdrew several wooden ornaments, carved in the shapes of stars and angels and doves.

'They're perfect, Da,' Jack said, beaming. Then his fair eyebrows furrowed. 'How will we hang them, though?'

Their father produced a roll of ribbon and a scissors from his pocket with a flourish. 'Courtesy of Mrs Hawkins,' he said. 'And I've already chiselled holes in the tops of the ornaments, see?'

Emily took the items and set to work at once, snipping the ribbon into lengths and threading them through the ornaments' holes. She then passed them to Jack and Gus, who circled the fir tree, seeking empty branches. As she licked the frayed end of a piece of ribbon to smooth the strands, her father used the poker to push a burning log further in from the grate and paused to stare meditatively down at it.

'What's on your mind, Papa?' she asked, although she was certain the more pertinent question was 'who'. He and her mother had been apart for more than three months now and his mood had palpably slumped when her latest letter had indicated that she would be delaying her return to Bewley Hall a little longer, though she had not explained why.

However, when he turned away from the fire, he said, 'I was thinking about Henrietta.'

Emily blinked. 'Oh. What about her?'

'I was just pondering what Christmas will be like for her in the Dunhill household,' he admitted. 'I hope they'll include her in their festivities and make her feel part of the family.'

'I'm sure they will,' she said without conviction. Henrietta had a tendency to push people away with her prickly temperament. 'Has there been any word on the reopening of the theatre?'

'I've exchanged correspondence with Mr Dunhill. He's optimistic that it will reopen in the new year.' A somewhat guilty expression crossed her father's face. 'I also sent him some sheet music as an early Christmas gift for Henrietta—a Scottish song called "The Parting Glass". I heard it being sung when I was passing a tavern in Bedford after a recent appointment at the bank, and the poignancy of it reminded me so much of her ballad about the young fisherman's lover that I sourced a composition of it. Even if she cannot read the notes herself, someone at the theatre should be able to teach it to her.'

'I'm certain her sweet voice will do it justice,' Emily replied and said no more on the subject, although she wondered whether her father was fully aware of the obvious paternal nature of his conduct.

She was going to ask instead what business had brought him to the bank when Gus skipped over to collect another ornament and a mince pie.

'Ma's cutting it close to get back in time for my birthday tomorrow,' he said with the pronounced wheeze that always laced his voice during the winter.

'You mustn't be disappointed if she doesn't make it,' Emily said soothingly. 'You remember what her letter said—she was unavoidably detained but she would still try her best.'

'She'll make it,' he said with total confidence before turning to their father. 'When will we get to go back to Oakleigh? I didn't solve a mystery there over the summer, but I'm positive there's at least one ghost, if not more, haunting the giant's claw. I need to do more investigating.'

'And we never got to go walking up the Blackstairs Mountains either,' Jack called over his shoulder as he slipped the ribbon of his angel ornament over the end of a branch.

'Hmm,' said their father. 'And those are your noble intentions? This has nothing to do with the fact that travelling to Ireland would mean missing your lessons with Mr Humphrey?'

'That would be regrettable but unavoidable.' Gus carefully enunciated each syllable with round, innocent eyes and Emily burst into giggles.

'Don't you encourage him,' their father said, fighting a grin.

The door swung open again and this time Rory, David and Mr Comerford came in, all three of them bearing large pails chock-full with branches of holly. The sight of Rory reminded Emily of the Christmas gift she lacked but had so dearly yearned to give him. Bottling up her despondency, she mustered a bright smile.

'Those will make such beautiful garlands,' she said. 'Let's start with the mantelpiece and the window sills.'

David and Mr Comerford brought their pails over to the hearth, so she directed Rory towards one of the drawing room's large windows and helped him pull the holly branches from his pail, taking care not to prick herself on the spiky leaves. As she arranged the branches along the sill, positioning them so that the bulk of their vibrant red berries faced into the room, Rory sidled close to her.

'What was that look?' he murmured. 'When we came in?'

She cringed. He knew her so very well now, but sometimes she wished she could conceal her feelings a little better.

'Oh, nothing, really,' she said, striving for a light tone. 'I had just hoped that we would have more than one reason to celebrate this Christmas.' She blew out her breath. 'But we don't.'

His green eyes softened with understanding. He reached around her, ostensibly to tuck in a branch that was sticking out too far, but he used the opportunity to brush his body gently against hers, the closest they could embrace in a roomful of people.

'It'll happen,' he said, dipping his head to let his lips graze her ear. 'We don't know what next year will bring. Well, apart from what we do know.'

Drawing back, he gave her a clumsy wink and she suppressed a laugh, recalling the time she had walked in on him practising winking in their bedchamber mirror, which had most definitely not been a component of Mr Humphrey's curriculum.

'You're right,' she said, her spirits lifting. 'Next year already has so much to offer.'

Her insides glowed as she pictured the acceptance letter that lay proudly on her dressing table. In January, she would commence her attendance at the Blake-Fletchley Academy of the Arts in Harrogate, Yorkshire. The best part of this was that she planned to reside with her kind friend from the *Integrity*, Louise Shelby, who lived near Harrogate with her four-year-old daughter, Philippa. The worst part was that it would mean being separated from Rory for a time, but he had fully supported her decision and the Academy permitted its students to travel home once a month. She and Rory would just have to be very active on her visits to Bewley Hall if they desired next year to bring them additional cause for joy.

Mouth quirking as though he could guess the train of her thoughts, Rory picked up the pail and they moved on to the next window. As they laid out another set of holly branches, he said, 'I'm thinking of making a trip to Liverpool after you leave in January. My excuse for visiting Penny Close could be to check if all's well with the flue since it was unblocked.'

She bit her lip. 'But in reality you want to check on the family?'

'I do.' His Adam's apple bobbed. 'I'm really not sure if I should've signed the lease with Tommy Jones—I've been questioning the wisdom of it every day since. My gut tells me there's something off about that fella.'

He had described to her what had happened during his last visit, including the tension that had hummed in that smoky room and the bruise he had glimpsed on Maud's wrist. Could it have been produced by the vicious grip of a man's fingers? Or had she simply injured it in an innocuous accident caused by clumsiness? The evidence was only circumstantial, especially when Maud herself seemed to be insistent that all was fine.

'You'll need to act with caution,' Emily said sombrely as she gathered up a couple of berries that had fallen off the branches and rolled along the window sill. 'Maud married Tommy of her own free will. She's his property now.'

'But the house is my property,' Rory said. 'I might not have a say in how he treats what's his, but I do have a say in where he does it. If there's something rotten going on, I've got to figure out a way to confront him about it.' At Emily's hum of apprehension, he added, 'I'll be careful. The last thing I'd want is to put Maud and the young ones in a worse position.'

'I wonder what sort of Christmas they'll have—' Emily started to say when the drawing room door opened for a third time.

'I *knew* she'd make it back in time!' came Gus's wheezy crow of triumph.

Emily whirled to see the butler, Sheppard, ushering her mother through the doorway, along with Polly and John Corbett. Her mother's cheeks were flushed with cold and pleasure as Gus charged across the room and flung his arms around her.

'I've missed you, my little miracle,' she said, dropping a kiss onto his mop of chestnut curls.

'I amn't a miracle!' he chirped, beaming up at her as he made space for Jack to share their hug.

'My lamb,' she said tenderly, pulling Jack in close to her.

Beyond their cluster of bodies, Polly's face lit up as her gaze swung across to the hearth, where David and Mr Comerford had finished decorating the mantelpiece with holly. Her uncle strode forwards and they met in the middle of the room, his big hand cupping her cheek with affection.

'Welcome home,' he said gruffly and David echoed him, looking very pleased as he glanced away from Polly and started to stack the empty pails inside each other. 'Your mother will be mighty happy to see you,' Mr Comerford continued. 'Will we go find her?'

Polly nodded eagerly. As he escorted her from the drawing room to seek out Mrs Hawkins, John ventured further in, his expression dumbstruck. Emily's father approached him and said, 'Thank you for accompanying them all the way from Oakleigh. I sincerely appreciate it.'

John goggled at him. 'Jaysus, lad, this place is colossal. You're the landlord of all this? You could knock me down with a feather.'

Emily hid her amusement at the man's stunned disbelief as she hastened towards her mother. The boys hadn't let her go, so they ended up squeezed between both women as they embraced. When they separated, laughing, their mother's dark brown eyes sought out their father. He came to her at once, grasping her hand and lifting it to press it against his chest.

'Let's not be apart for so long again,' he murmured.

'Agreed,' she said softly in return. 'Can we...' She threw a fleeting look over her shoulder to the doorway. 'There's something urgent that cannot wait.'

He nodded without hesitation.

'John,' she went on, raising her voice a little, 'will you please excuse our momentary absence? A pressing matter requires our attention. David can show you to a guest bedchamber in the meantime, and we'll return shortly.'

Still drinking in his surroundings, John responded with a good-natured wave and they slipped out of the room, their hands clasped and their heads bent close together.

'Good gracious,' Emily whispered to Rory, who had stepped up beside her. 'They couldn't even wait until bedtime.'

***

Cormac stood staring at Bridget, his heart thumping wildly. 'Are you being serious?' he managed to croak.

Her smile bloomed. 'I am. And I think Garrett is too.'

He shook his head, trying to process the news. They had retreated to his study, where the remnants of his labours on the wooden ornaments were still strewn across his desk. The scent of the wood shavings lingered in the air, but he hardly noticed.

'I can't quite comprehend it,' he said hoarsely.

She squeezed his hand, which she had not released since he had taken hers in the drawing room. 'I know it's difficult to believe, given his previous vile conduct. But you should have seen him. He was so dejected, and astonishingly self-aware. I scarcely recognised him.'

Cormac frowned, trying to reconcile this image of Garrett with the version who had caused his family so much pain.

'Patrick's disdain has hit him harder than anyone could have expected, including him.' She pressed her lips together thoughtfully. 'It's forced him to confront his inadequacies both as a man and a father.'

Cormac winced. He knew all too well the power of a child's love, and the devastation of losing it – when Emily had fled to London, her actions had seemed a declaration that she was willing to claim Garrett as her father instead of him, and it had crushed him. Could Garrett be capable of feeling the bone-deep anguish and guilt of letting down his child? And was he genuinely prepared to take such a drastic measure to regain his son's respect?

Cormac chewed the inside of his cheek as numerous doubts crowded in. 'He may have good intentions right now, but that doesn't mean he won't retract them the instant he has another change of heart.'

'I'm still cautious,' Bridget admitted. 'His past record makes him far from trustworthy. Nevertheless, I can't help but feel a flicker of hope.'

He endeavoured to let himself feel it too. If Garrett followed through on this, Bridget would finally be free of him. She would be able to marry Cormac, lawfully and with no obstruction from any quarter. They would be forever tainted by the scandal, yes, but that was hardly unfamiliar territory. He envisioned the joy of giving her his name at last, of being able to truly call her his wife.

A giddy laugh bubbled up in his throat and he swept her into his arms, spinning her around in a circle. She let out a surprised yelp before her own laughter mingled with his. When he set her back on her feet, he cradled her face in his hands, his thumbs tracing the curves of her cheekbones, his right palm caressing her scar. She leaned into his touch, her eyes shining.

'What an incredible gift to receive this Christmas,' he said.

'The potential of it is so vast that it seems too big for Christmas alone,' she said, a little breathless. 'Perhaps we ought to view it as a gift for our recent significant birthdays as well.'

'From the least likely benefactor imaginable,' he said wryly, sobering again. 'We will need to temper our expectations for now. His capricious disposition and the slow pace of the law mean that nothing is guaranteed at this stage, nor for a very long time into the future.'

'I know, but we shall exercise patience and keep faith that it will ultimately be rewarded.' The corner of her mouth tilted upwards. 'We should go back to the drawing room now. We haven't been very good hosts yet for John and we have a great deal to show him before he returns to Oakleigh—he's eager to stay for at least a week and see as much of the estate as possible.' She brushed her fingertips over Cormac's chest. 'But later, I want you to do all those things you promised to me in your letter for my birthday.'

His whole body ignited at the heat in her gaze and it took a supreme effort to release her from his grasp and open the study door.

# CHAPTER 18

Rory strode down the corridor in the direction of Mr Humphrey's tutoring room, a multitude of plans running through his mind. The arrival of the new year had instilled a renewed sense of purpose in him, and he was eager to get started.

Emily had gone to Harrogate for her first term at the art academy but he wouldn't let that dishearten him – though he might be feeling lonely without her, she was pursuing her artistic dream and he would rather walk over hot coals than get in the way of anything that made her happy. Besides, he already had a clear idea for how to make the most of her next visit home, which involved spending a lot of time behind the locked door of their suite, appreciating a different kind of art form: every line and curve of her body.

He still intended to travel to Liverpool in the next week or two, although today he was more focused on having a discussion with Mr Humphrey about his tutoring. While he didn't want to leave Jack and Gus behind, their differences to him in age and aptitude had grown more apparent over the last few months. He had caught on to the principles of mathematics better than he had expected and he now desired a greater challenge in that area, especially if it would aid him in his training as deputy land agent. He hoped Mr Humphrey might be able to teach him geometry for land surveying, as well as accounting and financial forecasting, with the ultimate goal that he would become a much more useful assistant to Mr Comerford.

And maybe in the future a more proficient, confident Rory Carey would be able to give the Duke of Desmond a run for his money.

As he approached Mr Humphrey's room, he heard speaking from within and realised that he wasn't the first to arrive. Gus's earnest voice drifted through the open doorway.

'Mr Humphrey, don't you think it would be a good geography lesson to carry out a practical study on the effects of the frost on the river? We could observe the thickness of the ice, and take notes on how it's formed...and maybe we should bring our skates along for, uh, a thorough examination.'

Rory snorted quietly as he reached to push open the door further, but he halted when clipped footsteps sounded behind him.

'A moment, Mr Carey?'

He turned to see Mr Sheppard coming towards him, a look of consternation creasing his usually composed features. Stepping back from the door, Rory wondered what had caused the butler such disquiet and what it could possibly have to do with him. Then his heart jolted. Had there been a message from Emily? Had she fallen ill or had some sort of accident at the art academy? What if she was being mistreated there? She had told him when she received her acceptance letter that it was a male-dominated institution in terms of both students and instructors, which had made him even prouder of her accomplishment – but what if they had subjected her to harassment or ridicule for being a woman? He would race up to Yorkshire this very instant and tear into whoever had made her feel alone or unsafe.

But then Mr Sheppard said, 'You have a visitor, sir.'

Rory's anger transformed into confusion. 'A visitor?' he repeated. Who on earth would call upon him at Bewley Hall?

'Yes, sir. I thought it best for David to bring him straight down to the kitchens.'

Rory gaped, now at a total loss.

Mr Sheppard cleared his throat. 'He started to say that his name was Alfie Carey but quickly corrected it to Alfie Pratt.'

Rory blinked. That provided some illumination, at least, although it prompted a plethora of other questions. What the bloody hell was Alfie doing in Bedfordshire, and how did he get here from Liverpool? Had Maud sent him? What had happened to make him come all this way?

Uneasiness swirled in Rory's gut. 'Thanks for telling me. I'll go see him right away.'

Leaving the butler behind, he hurried off down the corridor, his planned discussion with Mr Humphrey forgotten. As he made for the servants' stairs that led down to the kitchens, his apprehension swelled. There could be no good reason for his half-brother turning up out of the blue like this.

Reaching the lower level, he passed by the offices belonging to Mr Comerford and Mrs Hawkins and entered the main kitchen, where the lingering aromas of bread and bacon mingled with the clatter of pans and dishes being washed in the nearby scullery. His gaze skated over the maids bustling about wiping down surfaces after the morning's breakfast preparations and landed on the shivering figure hunched on a stool in front of the large hearth.

Alfie's unkempt brown hair framed his face, which Rory could only see in profile, and yet even from this angle it looked too worn for his young age. He was wearing a threadbare coat, inadequate for the bitter January weather, with a thin scarf wrapped around his neck, and his feet were extended towards the blazing fire, revealing the gap where the soles of his boots had come loose at the toes. His right arm hung awkwardly in his lap, while his left hand clutched a thick slice of bread slathered with butter, which he was devouring in quick, hungry bites.

David stood over him with a worried expression. Relief flooded his face at Rory's appearance and he strode across the kitchen to him.

'I'm glad you're here, sir,' he said in an undertone. 'He's in a bad way but the girls have promised to make him a bowl of soup shortly. He says he's your...'

The footman trailed off uncertainly, but Rory responded with a firm nod – there was no point beating about the bush. 'My half-brother, yes.'

He led the way back over to the fireplace. Alfie started when Rory came into his line of sight and hastily swallowed the last of his bread.

'Crikey, Rory,' he said through chattering teeth. 'I'd no idea you lived in a place like this. Our whole house could fit in this kitchen.'

Rory grimaced. 'It's not mine—it belongs to my father-in-law,' he said, choosing not to mention the enormous property he would gain when Emily eventually inherited Oakleigh. 'Tell me what's happened, Alfie. Why are you here?'

The lad's gaze darted away. He huddled in on himself, his left arm cradling his right. Rory's eyes narrowed, remembering Maud's wrist and wondering if a similar bruise was concealed beneath the sleeve of Alfie's coat.

'You're hurt,' he said tightly. 'Did Tommy do that to you?'

Alfie jerked his head back towards him, fearful. 'How'd you know?'

'I just had an inkling,' Rory said, his voice grim. 'How bad is it?'

Alfie shrugged, wincing when the movement jolted his arm. 'It's not so bad, really. It's nothing in comparison to—' He choked, and his whole body seemed to wilt. 'Nothing in comparison to what he did to Ma,' he finished miserably.

Rory stiffened with alarm. 'What did he do to her?' he demanded, his mind hurtling through all kinds of awful possibilities.

Alfie tucked his feet under the stool, the soles of his tattered boots flapping against the flagstone floor. 'He beat her,' he whispered. 'He kept at it for so long that he beat the baby out of her. It's dead.'

Rory's stomach roiled with nausea. He put out a hand to steady himself on the mantel above the hearth. Next to him, David went pale with shock.

'Jesus Christ, Alfie,' Rory croaked. 'Is your ma—'

'She's alive,' the lad replied. 'But that's the best that can be said about her.' He gulped. 'There was a lot of blood. A-and she was screaming. May went for Elsie. After she came, Tommy headed out to the pub like it was just any normal evening. Elsie took care of Ma, got her upstairs and washed her and tried to calm her down. They left behind the...' Alfie shuddered. 'I put it on the fire. I didn't know what else to do.'

Rory could hardly think past the horror that engulfed him. Moved by utter pity, he dropped to a knee on the flagstones and grasped Alfie's left shoulder.

'I'm so sorry you had to do that,' he said as gently as he could, even as his fury burgeoned. Emily was desperate for a baby, and yet that bastard Tommy Jones had squandered his and Maud's child like it was nothing.

'I did the wrong thing,' Alfie said hoarsely. 'Ma came stumbling back downstairs 'cause she wanted to hold it. I-I had to tell her it was gone.' The lad's face crumpled.

Rory swallowed, unable to conceive of the guilt his half-brother must have felt, nor the grief Maud had experienced. How far gone had she been? Seven months? Eight? The tiny creature that had been forced so brutally from her body wouldn't have been fully formed, but would it have looked enough like an infant for her to cradle it and mourn the life that had been cruelly extinguished?

Still aghast, he realised he needed to stifle his feelings in order to establish the most important details of this appalling affair. He tightened his grip on Alfie's shoulder.

'I know 'tis hard to talk about, but I have to ask—when did this happen?'

Alfie stared down into his lap. 'On Christmas Day.'

Rory's conscience pricked as he recalled the merry festivities that had been taking place at Bewley Hall while terror was unfolding inside the little house in Liverpool. 'Is Tommy still at Penny Close?'

Alfie scoffed. ''Course he is, acting like nothing even happened.'

'Is your ma healing? Does she need a doctor?' Rory didn't even bother asking whether Tommy had called for one.

'Elsie's been looking after her. She's not able to move very well. She manages to get up in the mornings, but as soon as Tommy heads off to the foundry, she goes back to bed and just lies there. She stopped doing any sewing so I took over a few pieces that I knew needed to be finished.' Alfie cringed. 'Tommy came home early one day and caught me. He wrenched my arm and roared that men don't do women's work, not even soft weaklings like myself.'

Rory clenched his jaw. 'How long has he been this violent?'

'He's always been rough with us, ever since he moved in. He broke Frankie's leg back during the summer—kicked him 'cause he was in the way.'

'Good God,' muttered David.

How Rory wished Maud hadn't covered up her husband's ill treatment when he came to visit. Had he known, he could have dealt with the situation so much sooner, preventing it from escalating as grievously as it had.

'D'you know what sparked his temper on Christmas Day?'

Alfie chewed on his chapped lower lip. 'He accused Ma of getting special benefits at the grocer's and offering them in return. I didn't know what he meant and she wouldn't tell me after.'

'I see,' Rory said, exchanging a look with David and privately speculating about Tommy's level of paranoia.

'I'm worried it's only a matter of time before he beats Ma again. I've told her we can't carry on like this, but she says we're stuck and there's nothing to be done.'

A heavy silence fell, pierced only by the chatter and footsteps of the maids going about their work.

'So you've come to me for help?' Rory asked.

Alfie nodded, raising hopeful eyes to him. 'There must be something you can do, right? As our broth—I mean, as our landlord?'

'I'm sure as hell not going to let things stay the way they are,' Rory replied, though he didn't yet have a clear idea as to how he would proceed. He felt some of the tension in Alfie's body recede under his grip. 'How'd you know where to find me? And how were you able to get here all the way from Liverpool?' He surely wouldn't have had the money for a train ticket, not even in a third-class carriage.

'You told Tommy you lived on the Bewley Estate in Bedfordshire—that was enough to set off with.' Alfie's sheepish expression betrayed his awareness of how rash a move this had been. 'I was lucky and met a metalwork tradesman driving his cart out of town. He knew the route I needed to take and he was going as far as Birmingham himself, so he let me travel with him if I'd help load and unload his goods along the journey. Once he turned off the road to Birmingham, I walked the rest of the way.'

Alfie reached up to loosen the scarf around his throat, and Rory released his shoulder to let him unwind it. He dropped it into his lap before continuing on.

'In Bedford, a butcher gave me directions to the Bewley Estate. After that, I figured all I had to do was keep asking around until I found someone who knew you. When a girl in the nearby village told me to come up here, this wasn't what I was expecting to find.' He raised his eyebrows.

Rory shrugged. 'I married into money,' he said, opting for the simplest explanation, which didn't account for the fact that he had fallen utterly in love with Emily and would have married her even if she hadn't had a penny to her name. 'Does your ma know where you went?'

Alfie flinched. 'I crept out while she was upstairs in bed and warned Frankie and May not to tell her until after I'd gone. She would've only tried to stop me, and then nothing would've changed.' He squared his shoulders. 'But something's definitely got to change.'

'I agree.' Rory stood, his knee aching from the hard stone floor. 'We need to make a plan. But first, let's find a place for you to grab a bit of rest. You've been on the road for days—you must be knackered. In the meantime, I'll see if I can get you some warmer clothes, and better boots. I reckon you're about the same size as my wife's brother.' Alfie was maybe a year older than Jack, but his poorer circumstances left him slighter than he ought to be.

Alfie's cheeks turned crimson. 'No need for that,' he mumbled.

Rory perceived his shame, noting that the lad was prepared to receive aid for his family but not for himself. He tried to recall exactly what Mr McGovern had told him the day he'd offered his assistance to Rory. 'A wiser man than me once said there's no shame in accepting help from those who are willing and able to give it. In fact, 'tis a sign of strength.'

Alfie squinted up at him doubtfully.

'Believe it. You can trust that man's advice. I certainly do, and I know David here does as well.' Rory clapped David on the back and the footman nodded along. 'It was fierce brave of you to come this far,' Rory added. 'Had you ever been outside of Liverpool before?'

Alfie shook his head. 'Never in my life.'

'Maud is very lucky to have you as a son.'

Rory didn't consider himself to be good with words at all, but he could tell that for once he had said precisely the right thing by the way Alfie's face blazed with quiet pride.

At that moment, one of the maids trotted over with a tray, steam rising from the bowl of soup on top of it. 'For the boy,' she said to Rory, casting her concerned gaze past him towards Alfie.

'Thanks,' said Rory, stepping back to let her carry the tray to him. 'After he's finished, can you ask Mrs Hawkins to bring him to a room where he can sleep for a few hours?'

He wasn't sure whether it would be better for the lad to rest in a guest bedchamber or in the servants' quarters (although he knew where he would feel easiest if he were in Alfie's position), so he would rely on the judicious housekeeper to make that decision. The maid nodded.

He turned to David. 'D'you know if Mr McGovern's at home today, or did he go out after breakfast?'

'He's in his study, sir,' David replied promptly. 'Lord Sinclair came to pay him a visit not ten minutes before this young man arrived. They're likely still in conversation.'

'Thanks,' Rory said again. 'Alfie, d'you mind if I leave you for a bit? I've got to go figure out what to do next. The housekeeper will be along in a short while to look after you.'

Alfie had lifted the bowl of soup from the tray and was inhaling deeply, letting the steam bathe his face. 'That's fine,' he said absently. 'Crikey, this smells good. Is there any way for me to bring some of it back to Ma and Frankie and May?'

The maid glanced at Rory before saying, 'You eat all of that yourself, and we'll see about bottling up a couple of jars to take back with you.'

Rory sent her a look of gratitude and then spun around, leaving the kitchen at a quick stride. As he ascended the servants' stairs back to the family section of the house, rage surged up his throat, threatening to choke him. An ample portion of the rage was aimed at the despicable Tommy Jones, for sure, but more of it was directed at himself. Why hadn't he done something sooner? He'd had his suspicions about that man, but he had procrastinated, and now that unfortunate family had suffered abuses beyond comprehension. He shouldn't have waited so long to act.

'God damn it!' he burst out as he flung open the door that led into the back of the entrance hall.

Three heads turned towards him in astonishment. Mr Sheppard was in the middle of passing Lord Sinclair his hat and gloves, while Mr McGovern stood next to them, his hands clasped behind his back. Their bodies froze in this tableau as they stared at Rory.

'Sorry,' he muttered, mortified that his outburst had been witnessed by Mr McGovern's dignified guest. 'I didn't mean to interrupt. Please carry on.'

Lord Sinclair levelled a stern look at him from beneath his overhanging brow, before returning his attention to Mr McGovern.

'As I was saying, I'd highly recommend a visit to Aintree when you get the opportunity—if not this February, perhaps next year? There's no finer course for a race. The spectacle will leave a lasting impression on you.'

'I appreciate the recommendation,' Mr McGovern said, inclining his head politely. 'I'll most certainly keep it in mind.'

Lord Sinclair bowed and took his leave. As soon as Mr Sheppard had shut the door behind him, Mr McGovern swivelled towards Rory.

'What's the matter?' he asked, his gaze sharp.

Rory advanced further into the entrance hall. Without any dent to his pride, he said, 'I need your help, sir.'

# Chapter 19

Rory stepped down from the railway carriage onto the thronged platform at Lime Street in Liverpool, his breath fogging in the evening air. Mr McGovern had disembarked before him, and Alfie followed after, clutching a covered basket that contained three jars of what he had declared to be the best soup he had ever tasted. Steam hissed from the train as they made their way along the platform, jostled by the other passengers hurrying past them.

A day had passed since Alfie had turned up at Bewley Hall, and he was now dressed in sturdy boots and warm clothing appropriate for the winter season. Jack, of course, had been more than eager to help and had also pressed Alfie to take an extra pair of gloves. Not to be outdone, Gus had supplied a pair of his own gloves for Frankie, and together the boys had extracted a thick scarf from Emily's belongings, which they knew she would be only too delighted to gift to May. Alfie had accepted these offerings in silent bewilderment.

Mrs Hawkins had fashioned a sling for him out of a strip of cloth, allowing his sprained right arm to rest against his ribs. He was carrying the basket with his left hand, but Rory noticed him struggling to keep it upright in the midst of the heaving crowd and hastened to relieve him of it. He checked beneath the cover to make sure the soup jars and woollen garments were still nestled safely inside, and then he and Alfie followed Mr McGovern to the railway station's exit.

Beyond the exit, the smell of horse manure hit them, wafting from the row of hackneys that had lined up to take the train's passengers onwards to their next destination. However, Mr McGovern had already determined that it would not be advisable to hire one of these. Penny Close was within reasonable walking distance and a vehicle like that would only attract unwanted attention in the neighbourhood.

Alfie knew the twists and turns of Liverpool best, so he scurried forwards to take the lead and they set off along the street. Darkness had fully fallen, though it was scarcely five o'clock, and a soft mist began to drift down around them, glistening in the glow of the gas lamps. Rory glanced at Mr McGovern as they passed through a pool of light – his shoulders were rigid and his mouth was set in an angry line. He had been incensed when Rory had divulged the reason behind Alfie's unexpected presence at Bewley Hall.

'Being a husband doesn't grant a man leave to treat his wife like an animal,' he had fumed, his fists clenched and wrath seething in his blue eyes.

He and Rory had agreed that it was vital to intervene, for Maud and her three children were otherwise defenceless. They couldn't involve the authorities, who would only turn a blind eye to affairs of a domestic nature, and yet neither of them could stand idly by while Tommy's violence reigned unchecked. Whatever the law might say, that family did not deserve to live under the heel of a brute.

When they neared the vicinity of Penny Close, Alfie's pace slowed and he hunched his shoulders, peering about him covertly.

'His shift shouldn't finish until six,' he muttered to Rory, 'but sometimes the machinery breaks down so there's no telling when he might get let off early.' He cast a meaningful look down at his injured arm.

'We'll keep a watchful eye,' Rory said, remaining vigilant for any sight of a short, stocky figure looming out of the mist.

Thankfully, they proceeded without incident. Just as they reached the entrance to Penny Close, Mr McGovern gave a low whistle behind Rory and Alfie, bringing them to a halt.

'I'll go first to check whether it's clear,' he said. 'If Tommy happens to be in the street, he won't recognise me.'

He sidled past them and around the corner into the top of the alley, then ducked his head back out. 'It's completely empty. Everyone's probably staying inside out of this weather.'

They joined him and the three of them hurried down the narrow alley with its two lines of terraced houses. They didn't approach Number 5, however; instead, they made for Number 4 on the opposite side of the alleyway. Its façade was identical, apart from the numerous scratches that marred the lower portion of its door. Alfie shot a furtive glance over his shoulder before rapping his knuckles on the wood. As they waited, Rory became aware that the mist, deceptive in its softness, had stealthily saturated their caps and coats.

The door opened, revealing a woman with silver-streaked hair escaping its pins in wild wisps and a faded shawl festooned with short, ginger-coloured hairs.

'Alfie?' she said in a reedy voice that contained astonishment and suspicion wrapped in a thick Liverpool accent.

'Can I come in, Elsie?' Alfie asked nervously. 'And these fellas too? They're decent people, I promise.'

Elsie emitted a 'humph' of scepticism, but she stood back and let them enter, shutting the door behind them. They found themselves in a room very similar to Maud's, apart from one stark difference: a high-backed chair was situated in front of the fireplace and a ginger cat perched upon its backrest, glaring at them with unblinking yellow eyes.

'Your ma's been worried sick about you,' Elsie said reproachfully.

Alfie winced. 'I'm sorry—I didn't want her to worry. But I had to go get help.'

'Humph,' Elsie said again. 'And help comes in the form of this pair?'

She eyed them, letting her gaze drop to the floor where water was dripping from the ends of their coats and gathering in little puddles.

'It does,' Alfie said firmly.

'Then why are you here and not across the way?'

'We need to wait until we're sure Tommy's out of the house. Will you let us stay here for an hour or two so we can keep watch for him?'

'Humph,' she said for a third time. She tilted her head and frowned as though listening hard. 'Fine, then. The admiral will allow it.'

Rory blinked, but Alfie seemed to accept this statement without question.

'All we've got to do is stand guard at the window until he arrives,' he said, 'and be careful that he doesn't spot us. Right?' He glanced up at Mr McGovern.

'That's right,' Mr McGovern said. 'We'll stick to our plan. I'll take the first watch.'

He strode over to the single window by the front door and took up a position next to its peeling frame, twitching the thin curtain back just a sliver so that he could observe Number 5 across the alley. Knowing they might have to wait for some time, Rory set the basket on the floor, careful to avoid the puddles they had created. Meanwhile, Elsie shuffled over to the chair by the hearth and sank onto it, facing the fire. The cat immediately jumped down into her lap and she stroked its ginger fur.

'That Tommy Jones is a bad man,' she said. 'But Maud married him, the poor wretch, and the law's clear when it comes to a wife's obedience. Even the admiral thinks there's nothing you can do.'

'We're going to act outside the law,' Alfie said in a valiant display of confidence.

'Like your da?' Elsie said tartly, without looking over her shoulder.

Alfie blanched.

Elsie tutted. 'She's a dear friend, but God knows that woman has chosen her men poorly.'

This time, Alfie bristled. He opened his mouth as though preparing to retort, but Rory shook his head at him. Their plan required Elsie's cooperation – it made no sense to antagonise her. Moreover, the cat was staring at them from her lap, exuding a palpable air of malevolence.

Alfie gave a reluctant nod and instead said, 'How's Ma been faring since I left? I mean, apart from worrying about me. Has she tried to get up out of bed more?'

'Not really,' Elsie said with a sigh. 'There's been no further bleeding, but she's still very tired and weak.'

'And Tommy?' Alfie asked, his tone uneasy. 'What did he say about my disappearance?'

'Oh, apparently he effed and blinded for a few hours, and then swore you'd better not darken his doorstep ever again or you'd get a hiding that would have you begging the grave digger for an early plot. He reckons you've followed in your da's footsteps and gone to sea. He ordered Frankie to go to the printer's and take over your newspaper deliveries.'

Alfie chewed on his lip. 'And are Frankie and May—'

'He's here,' came Mr McGovern's low voice from the window. 'Or, at least, a man fitting his description is approaching Number 5.'

Rory hastened over to the window and Mr McGovern stood aside to let him take his place. Peering past the small gap in the curtain, he discerned a figure stumping up to the door of Maud's house through the misty gloom. He'd only met the man once but he recognised his stocky form.

'That's him,' he muttered. Anger sizzled in his veins as Tommy disappeared inside the house – he itched to confront the brute and make him answer for his abuse. But they had formulated a sensible plan and, for the sake of Maud and her children, they needed to keep to it. 'I'll stand watch now,' he said firmly.

Mr McGovern didn't demur. He crossed back over the room to the basket and crouched to retrieve one of the soup jars from beneath its damp cover. Rising, he approached the hearth and held the jar out to Elsie.

'Parsnip soup,' he said. 'A token of our thanks. It just needs to be heated up over the fire.'

'You won't believe how good it tastes, Elsie,' Alfie said earnestly.

Rory couldn't see the woman's face but her wild hair was just visible above the back of her chair – it quivered like she was nodding, and Mr McGovern turned to place the jar on the mantelpiece. Rory returned his gaze to his slim view of the now-empty alley.

'You reckon he'll be about twenty minutes, Alfie?' he said.

'Yes,' the boy replied. 'He won't care that Ma isn't well. He'll expect her to be up out of bed ready to put his supper on the table. As soon as he's scoffed it down, he'll head back out to meet his mates at the pub.'

'And you believe he's unlikely to return for a couple of hours?' Mr McGovern asked.

'At the very least,' Alfie said. 'There's been plenty of nights when he hasn't come back until near midnight.'

'Well, we won't gamble as far as that.' Mr McGovern's voice was grim. 'The quicker we can accomplish this, the better.'

The cat let out a soft hiss and after that the room fell silent. Rory kept his eyes trained on the closed door of Number 5, imagining the scene within – Tommy wolfing down his supper while Frankie and May endeavoured to stay out of his way, a pale Maud hovering nearby to wait on him when she was the one who really needed looking after.

He tried not to think too closely about the fact that this was the woman his father had had the gall to wed while he was still married to Rory's mother. There was no point in overcomplicating the situation. Maud was just a woman in distress, desperate for help that he was in a position to give. His mother would surely understand.

He continued to stand motionless by the window, the musty smell of wet wool rising from his coat and his collar clammy against the back of his neck. Outside, the mist thickened into a heavier drizzle and rivulets of water began to trickle down the window panes. What if the bad weather deterred Tommy from going out to the pub as usual? Would they be obliged to wait until he left the following morning to start his next shift at the foundry? Rory doubted whether Elsie or her cat would be eager to tolerate three house guests for the night.

A glimmer of light suddenly bloomed across the alley and he snapped to attention as a hunched shape emerged through the doorway of Number 5, silhouetted by the candlelight within. Rory breathed a sigh of relief as Tommy plodded away up the alley. The door closed after him and the light vanished.

'He's left the house,' Rory reported to the others without taking his gaze from the window.

'Very good,' Mr McGovern said. 'As discussed, we'll wait at least ten minutes to make sure he doesn't return for some unexpected reason.'

Rory heard a quiet click and guessed that Mr McGovern had pulled out his pocket watch to check the time.

'Well, well, it looks like we have a toff in our midst, Admiral,' Elsie murmured.

Rory felt offended on Mr McGovern's behalf – the man didn't deserve such an unwarranted insult. But he said nothing and so Rory didn't either, although he found himself wondering whether Elsie took advantage of her eccentric façade to get away with saying whatever she pleased.

The next few minutes crawled by, punctuated only by the faint ticking of the pocket watch and an occasional disgruntled meow. Nothing stirred out in the alleyway, boosting Rory's confidence that Tommy had by now settled himself at the pub with a pint in front of him.

'Ten minutes,' Mr McGovern said at last. 'Shall we proceed?'

'Good luck with your unlawful scheme,' Elsie said cheerfully, and Rory glanced over to spot her wispy hair disappearing from sight as she nestled deeper into her chair.

Mr McGovern snapped his pocket watch shut and tucked it away, while Alfie scurried to pick up the basket. Rory joined them at the door and caught one final glimpse of the cat's baleful glare before they slipped out into the alley.

# Chapter 20

Hunching their shoulders against the drizzle, Rory, Mr McGovern and Alfie hurried across to the front door of Number 5. As Alfie reached for the latch, Rory detected a dart of movement in his peripheral vision. Heart seizing, he looked towards the mouth of the alley where a shadowy figure loomed through the murk and seemed to be staring straight at them. In the next instant, he relaxed – tall and rail thin, the silhouette was nothing like Tommy's stocky frame. The stranger turned away and continued past the alley, footsteps fading into the night. Letting out a quick breath, Rory followed Alfie and Mr McGovern over the threshold into the house.

When they entered the room, which was still as smoky as his last visit, he spotted Frankie and May first of all, their short forms standing at the table. Frankie was dabbing his finger across the wooden surface, scooping up stray crumbs and licking them off his fingertip, while at his side May was dragging a grimy cloth over a plate, leaving smears in its wake. Then Rory's attention swung to the stairs, where Maud gripped the rickety banister as she climbed upwards, each step an evident struggle.

At their entrance, she twisted around and uttered a loud gasp. 'Alfie!'

Shock and relief filled her wan face. She hastened to descend the stairs and, in her rush, stumbled on the second-to-last step. Mr McGovern was the quickest to react, lunging forwards to catch her before she could fall to the floor. He steadied her on her feet and she stared up at him, bewilderment clouding her features.

'Who are you?' Her gaze darted from him to Rory and then to Alfie. 'You were gone for so *long*. God, I was scared out of my mind that he'd—' The words died in her throat.

Rory's chest tightened as understanding struck – Maud had feared that Tommy had done Alfie harm. In truth, her fear wasn't unfounded; he had already taken one child from her. A gentle swell beneath her dress showed that her body had not yet forgotten.

'I'm safe, Ma,' Alfie said reassuringly.

He offered a smile to his younger siblings. Frankie hobbled forwards with a distinct limp in his right leg, but May hung back by the table.

'I been looking after Ma and May just like you told me to,' Frankie said stoutly. 'And I been delivering the papers every morning. Takes me a bit longer 'cause of my leg, so I got to start earlier or else the printer fella will throw a fit.'

'Good job,' Alfie said, putting down the basket so he could clap his palm on Frankie's upper arm. 'I'm proud of you.'

Frankie beamed up at his older brother. In that moment, it seemed to Rory that Alfie transformed from the tentative boy who had come seeking help at Bewley Hall into the steadfast leader his family needed. He had leaned on Rory in their absence, but now they were relying on Alfie to step up as the head of their household. Tommy, of course, had never earned that role, and Maud, in her present state, could not fill it.

She extended a trembling hand towards Alfie and he moved closer to let her grip his sleeve, as though she were confirming he was real.

'I'm so glad you're home,' she said tremulously. 'Frankie and May told me where you went.' She threw a wary glance in Rory's direction. 'You shouldn't have gone.'

'I was right to go,' Alfie insisted. 'Rory and Mr McGovern are here to help us.'

Her shoulders curved inwards. 'There's nothing to be done. You know that.'

Rory clenched his fists at her palpable despair. 'That's not true,' he said. 'You aren't stuck, and you don't deserve to suffer any longer under the boot of that thug.'

She went rigid and, for a second, she seemed to forget to breathe. Wide-eyed, she stared at Alfie, letting her hand drop from his sleeve.

'You had no right to tell him,' she whispered. 'None at all. How could you—'

Her voice cracked, and she wrapped her arms around her middle. Alfie looked devastated, his confidence of moments ago withering into dust. Rory shot a grimace at Mr McGovern, who responded with a brief nod of encouragement.

'Maud,' Rory began, but she cut him off with a deep, anguished sigh.

'I'm Mrs Tommy Jones, and that's what I'll stay until they lay me in my grave.' Her chin lifted, though shame burned high in her cheeks. 'It doesn't matter what I wish now—I made my choice, didn't I? A poor one, I can see that plain enough...but there's no undoing it.'

May let out a low whimper, and Maud swivelled towards her. Her expression splintered with sorrow, but she drew herself up as though gathering her strength before holding out her arms. May set the plate and cloth on the table and scuttled into her mother's embrace. Maud pulled her close, one hand resting on the girl's frizzy hair, and then peered back at Rory.

'I've got to live with it,' she said, 'and it's my fault these three have to live with it too. All I can do is try to shield them from the worst of Tommy's ways.'

Rory shook his head. 'We're not going to stand idly by and let this situation continue.'

She blinked. 'Why would you care? Your da turned his back on your ma to take up with me. Surely you can't be all that bothered for my welfare.'

He shifted uncomfortably. 'I'm the landlord here,' he said, but his gaze drifted to the children – Alfie chewing his lip with anxiety, Frankie favouring his left leg, little May huddling against her mother like a small, frightened animal – and something tugged at him, something more than duty.

'Landlord,' Maud repeated. She studied his face. 'And what's a landlord able to do against a husband's say-so?'

'Nothing,' he admitted. 'Or nothing lawful, at any rate.'

Her nostrils flared and her focus swerved back to Mr McGovern with greater suspicion. 'Who are you?' she asked again, taking a conspicuous step away from him and drawing May with her.

'I'm no one to fear, I promise you that,' he said calmly. 'My name is Cormac McGovern. I'm Rory's father-in-law.'

She squinted in confusion. 'Why on earth are you here?'

'The law offers you no sanctuary, so I'm offering you one instead,' he replied, letting his words hang in the smoky air.

Rory cleared his throat. 'Mr McGovern owns the Bewley Estate in Bedfordshire. He's willing to take you and the children as his tenants.'

Maud's lips parted in sheer incomprehension.

'We've considered the situation from every angle,' Rory continued, watching her closely for her reaction. 'As your husband, Tommy holds all the power. His name's on the lease here and you've no legal way to refuse his presence in this house. I could evict him, true enough, but that wouldn't solve the problem of getting him away from you. You'd be forced to follow him wherever he went.' Rory swallowed. 'The only way to ensure your safety is to put distance between ye—proper distance. Somewhere else in Liverpool wouldn't be far enough. But Bedfordshire would be ideal. And if you and the children flee before Tommy comes back tonight, he won't have a notion where ye went and won't be able to pursue ye.'

She swayed on the spot. 'Alfie,' she said hoarsely, 'is this what you had in mind when you ran away to get help?'

'No,' he replied. 'This was their idea. I only hoped Rory might boot Tommy out of the house. But I see now—it wouldn't work, would it? Tommy'd just come marching back in soon as Rory was gone, and you couldn't do nothing to stop him. The peelers wouldn't lift a finger—they'd never stand between a man and his wife. So there's only one thing for it...we've got to be the ones to leave.'

She quailed. 'But Liverpool is our home,' she protested, her voice faint.

Rory's mouth tightened. 'Can you honestly say it's felt like home since that brute came along?'

She faltered, chin trembling, but then she said, 'I'm too weak to travel.'

'We'll travel by rail for the most part,' said Mr McGovern. 'It shouldn't prove too taxing.'

'Mr McGovern said he'll get a doctor for you in Bedfordshire,' Alfie added, reaching down to the basket. 'He'll see you right. For now, I've brought some parsnip soup to heat up. It's a start—it'll help put a bit of strength back into you.' He withdrew the two soup jars, along with the pair of gloves and the scarf. Holding the latter items out to Frankie and May, he said, 'Rory's family also sent these.'

'We don't need charity,' Maud said sharply.

'They're gifts,' Mr McGovern corrected, his tone gentle. 'From my children to yours.'

Frankie and May accepted the woollen garments uncertainly, and Alfie trotted over to the fireplace with the jars.

Maud wrung her hands. 'You need to go before Tommy returns from the pub. With drink in him, he'll beat you black and blue.'

'We've time yet,' Alfie assured her, setting a pot on the crane over the hearth and tipping the contents of the jars into it.

Rory frowned at the smoke curling through the room. 'What happened with the flue? Was the chimney sweep not able to clear it?'

Maud lowered her eyes. 'He never so much as touched it. When he showed up, Tommy talked him into telling your solicitor the job was done. Then, soon as the money came from you, Tommy split it with the sweep and spent his share on pints instead.' She shrugged. 'The sweep had a debt to clear with a pawnbroker, so he was happy enough to go along with the scheme.'

It was only further evidence of the scoundrel Tommy was, not that they needed any more.

'Ma, feel how soft it is!' May exclaimed, holding out the scarf.

While Maud admired the garments, and Frankie and May tried them on, Rory drew Mr McGovern aside.

'The idea of her having to stay married to that louse makes me sick to my stomach,' he muttered. 'Is there some way to help her secure an actual divorce from him?'

Mr McGovern winced. 'The expense would be prohibitive. Such a remedy is only a privilege within the purview of the upper classes.'

Rory deflated. Over Christmas, he and Emily had learned of Garrett's vow to obtain a divorce from Lady Bridget, but the way the lady had spoken of it had made it plain that the endeavour was monumental. For a woman of Maud's station, divorce was as unreachable as the stars.

'The soup's warming up,' Alfie called from the hearth.

As the smell of parsnip began to fill the smoky room, May spun in a circle, making her new scarf twirl, while Frankie flexed his gloved fingers. They were both laughing with delight. Maud turned to Rory and Mr McGovern, stricken.

'I don't even remember the last time I saw them smile like this,' she croaked.

'Isn't that sufficient incentive to leave?' Mr McGovern said softly. 'Think of the life they might have, away from that man's cruelty.'

Maud's expression wavered, fear warring with hope on her pale features.

The door crashed open.

Everyone whirled around and Rory's heart plummeted when he distinguished Tommy's short frame outlined in the doorway. A taller figure loomed behind him, skinny as a rail. Both of them were drenched from the rain that was now bucketing down in the alley beyond. Tommy marched inside, apoplectic with rage, his large, misshapen tooth prominent as his lips drew back in a snarl.

'I swear I'm going to—' he seethed, but halted when he spotted Rory. He blinked, confused. 'What're you doing here? I wasn't expecting you.' He glanced over his shoulder at his tall companion. 'Ned just told me he saw two men entering the house.'

And there was no reward for guessing the paranoid conclusion Tommy had jumped to. Rory suppressed a groan, cursing their bad luck for crossing the alley just as Tommy's friend had happened to pass by. He pictured Ned dashing to the pub to divulge what he had witnessed and Tommy storming out to confront his cheating wife. While they had been trying to convince Maud to leave, their time had been leaking away more rapidly than they had realised. Could they possibly still salvage the situation, and perhaps return tomorrow to complete the escape?

Keeping his stance as casual as he could manage, Rory said lightly, 'I had to make a trip to Liverpool, so I just thought I'd call by to check in on the family.'

'At this hour?' Tommy said suspiciously. 'And who's this fella?' he barked, jerking his chin at Mr McGovern. Then his attention pivoted to the hearth and landed upon Alfie. 'What the—you goddamn brat!' he snapped. 'The nerve of you, coming back here! I'll bloody skin you—' He caught himself as his eyes darted towards Rory. 'I mean, you had your mother at her wit's end, you rascal. Where've you been all this time?'

Alfie froze. In the ensuing silence, the only sound was the rain hammering on the ground outside. Rory could sense waves of terror rolling off Maud. Frankie and May clustered close to her, their earlier laughter extinguished.

'Well?' Tommy demanded.

'I-I didn't mean to—I w-went to visit—' Alfie's words tumbled out in a panicked stutter.

'He came to me 'cause he wants to learn a trade and he knows I used to be a carpenter,' Rory interjected, invoking the Duke of Desmond to make his voice nonchalant. 'I had a lot to show him, so 'tis my fault he was gone for so long. We should've sent word.'

Tommy's distrustful expression darkened like a thundercloud. He rounded on Maud, who shrank away from him. 'What the hell is going on?' he growled, advancing towards her. 'You think I'm stupid? You've been scheming behind my back, haven't—'

'That's enough.' Mr McGovern's commanding tone cut through the room. He stepped forwards, placing himself between Tommy and Maud. 'We're not here for a social call, Mr Jones. Your wife and her children are leaving with us tonight.'

Tommy snorted out a laugh of utter disbelief.

'This isn't a bluff,' Mr McGovern said, unmoved. 'Nor is it a negotiation. I suggest you make your peace with it and step aside.'

Tommy's mouth worked soundlessly for a moment. He half turned to Ned, who was still standing in the open doorway, as if seeking confirmation that he'd heard right. Ned took a couple of paces further into the room, his boots leaving wet, muddy prints on the floor.

'No way you're putting up with that kind of talk, Tommy,' he said bracingly, before flicking his gaze to Mr McGovern and Rory. 'Yous have some brass ones, coming in here thinking yous can just walk out with a fella's family.' He cracked his knuckles. 'The only place yous are heading after this is the hospital.'

Rory registered the man's Irish accent with surprise – he spoke with the same inflections as Tess and Orlaith. Mr McGovern, too, blinked at this unexpected detail about Tommy's companion.

'You're Irish,' he said. 'A native of Dublin city, if I'm not mistaken?'

'A Liberties man, born and bred,' Ned said, puffing out his chest. 'Fifteen years in Liverpool hasn't changed that, mind you, but I'll still stand by my English mate here if yous are going to cause trouble.'

Rory could practically see Mr McGovern's mind calculating the situation. Should they come to blows, the men were evenly matched in terms of two against two, but there were also four vulnerable people for Rory and Mr McGovern to defend, while Tommy and Ned had no such concerns. Mr McGovern's jaw tautened, and Rory hoped he could perceive a way out of this unforeseen predicament.

'Are you aware of what your "mate" did to his wife?' Mr McGovern asked coolly. 'If you've met her at any stage over the past few months, then has it not occurred to you to wonder why she is no longer big with child?'

Ned faltered. 'She lost the babe. Tommy told me so.'

'Did he tell you *how* she lost it?'

'Shut the hell up,' Tommy snarled.

Mr McGovern didn't flinch. 'Brute force at the hands of your "mate" is the reason why Maud is not expecting anymore.'

Ned's eyes widened and he glanced uncertainly at Tommy.

Tommy bared his teeth, his large tooth sticking out. 'It doesn't matter. The babe wasn't mine anyway. She's been having a fine time with the grocer for months. Thought she could pull the wool over my eyes, but I'm too smart for that.'

'That's not true,' came Maud's thin, quivering voice behind Mr McGovern's back. 'I was never unfaithful. You made all that up in your head.'

Tommy lunged for her, trying to duck around Mr McGovern, who grabbed him by both shoulders and shoved him backwards so violently that Tommy lost his balance and fell hard on his rear end. He stared up in shock and fury.

'I'm going to pound you into a pulp,' he spat.

He put out a hand to Ned, who helped him to his feet, despite looking a little repulsed. Tommy squared up to Rory and Mr McGovern, his face a mottled red.

'What the devil makes you think you can take my wife away from me? She's mine by law and I can do with her whatever I please.'

Mr McGovern's gaze turned to steel. 'That attitude is precisely why we are choosing to take matters into our own hands. The welfare of a woman and her children ranks far higher in our estimation than any man's supposed rights.'

'You haven't got a leg to stand on,' Tommy sneered. 'You've trespassed on my private property and tried to kidnap my family. The peelers will have you both behind bars.'

'It's not your property,' said Rory. ''Tis mine, and I won't allow your abuse to continue under this roof. You can walk out that door of your own accord, or they'll be the ones leaving—but either way, this ends tonight.'

Tommy crossed his arms. 'I'm not budging from this spot.'

Rory mirrored the gesture. 'Then make your farewells to them, 'cause you won't be seeing them again.'

An incredulous guffaw burst out of Tommy. 'And where are they going?'

'That's not your concern.'

Tommy's eyes narrowed with a dangerous gleam. 'I bet you're planning to take them to that estate where you live in Bedfordshire. No other place makes sense, not when you're being this goddamn protective of them. Though God knows why you'd want to add a weak woman and three runts to your responsibilities.'

'Again, that's not your concern.'

'You get that there's nothing to stop me from coming after them, right? I could drag Maud back here by her hair in front of a dozen peelers if I wanted. You wouldn't be able to do a bloody thing about it.'

'Why do you assume that our criminal activities end at trespassing and kidnapping?' Mr McGovern asked, so mildly that he might as well have been commenting on nothing more remarkable than the bad weather visible through the doorway. 'Do you not realise how easy it would be for us to hurt you?'

Tommy's jaw slackened, and for once he offered no retort.

Rory seized on the thread of threat, prepared to tell any lie that would extract them from this quandary. 'My father-in-law has connections in both influential and unsavoury quarters. Ruthless men will come after you if you try to come after Maud.'

The first genuine trace of apprehension crossed Tommy's face. However, he quickly covered it up with an ugly smile. 'You're saying this fella's hiding some level of clout behind his posh clothes and his posh words? I seriously doubt it. By the looks of him, he probably has someone to help him put on his breeches every day.'

Rory laughed grimly. 'God, you've no idea who you're talking about. This "posh" fella is capable of violence you wouldn't believe.'

Maud cowered at that, and he felt sorry for adding to her fright, but there was no way to communicate that she herself had absolutely nothing to fear from Mr McGovern.

The man in question stood in silent contemplation for several moments. Then he turned his attention to Ned. 'You say you lived in Dublin up until fifteen years ago? Did you ever hear of a money lender called Cunningham while you were there?'

Ned's countenance darkened. 'There wasn't a soul in my part of the city who didn't know that name. I was never stupid enough to borrow from him, but I knew others who had and who sorely regretted it after.'

'I have some good news for you,' Mr McGovern said. 'Cunningham is dead.'

Ned brightened. 'Well, now, that really is—'

'I'm the one who killed him.'

Ned's mouth dropped open comically. He took a step backwards, eyeing Mr McGovern as though expecting him to strike like a snake.

'Jaysus, Tommy, be careful with this one,' he said with an obvious shudder. 'The fella who took down Cunningham has to be either crazy for trying or even more diabolical for managing to pull it off.'

Tommy scoffed. 'There isn't a speck of proof that he's telling the truth. Don't be so gullible.'

'And you don't be a fool,' Ned flung back. 'I've got no interest in being dragged into this business if it's actually dangerous. We thought we were going to confront that grocer who's been having his way with Maud, and figured the second person had to be some namby-pamby friend of his, if the rumours about him are anything to go by. Sure, a pair of sissies would be easy to thrash. I didn't expect to come face to face with the fella who finished off that son of a bitch Cunningham. He could do us proper damage.' Ned retreated another step towards the doorway.

'I'm not afraid of him,' Tommy insisted.

Rory clicked his tongue in exasperation at the man's bullheadedness. 'You say you're not afraid, and yet you absolutely should be. You believe you're a strong man, when in truth you're just a coward bullying those weaker than you. You think you're not stupid, but by God you really are.'

Tommy's eyes flashed and he launched himself at Rory, seizing the front of his coat with one hand and boxing his ear with the other. Unprepared for the sudden attack, Rory couldn't evade the blow and his head rang from the force of it. Mr McGovern strode forwards to intervene, but Ned uttered a frustrated curse and leapt at him, hauling him back. As their own tussle ensued, Rory fought to wrench himself free of Tommy's iron grip on his coat, struggling to land a punch in return. Through the chaos, he heard Maud's sharp cry of panic and glimpsed her pushing Frankie and May over to the stairs, hustling them upwards to safety before turning and planting herself on the bottom step with her thin arms spread wide to shield them behind her.

'Run and hide, Alfie!' she screeched.

Rory couldn't see how Alfie reacted because Tommy filled his vision, his breath reeking of beer as he snarled into his face. Though Rory had height to his advantage, Tommy had muscle and he knew how to use it, his whole body radiating menace as he thrust his weight against Rory's. He swung his free arm around for another strike, but Rory succeeded in blocking it with his forearm and brought his fist down on Tommy's chest. Unfortunately, it was only a glancing hit as Tommy jumped swiftly back to avoid it. Then he bent forwards, ramming his shoulder hard into Rory's midsection. Winded, Rory stumbled backwards, pulling Tommy with him, and his spine slammed into the wall behind him. They both grappled to regain their balance but Tommy was quicker and he wrapped his bulky arms around Rory's torso, pinning him in place. The brute might have a predilection for picking on women and children, but he had evidently seen his fair share of brawls with tougher opponents too.

Beyond Tommy's shoulder, Rory caught sight of Mr McGovern and Ned circling each other, the latter flailing about as he threw wild shots in an attempt to breach Mr McGovern's steadfast defence. When Mr McGovern deflected yet another attack, Ned let out a bellow of aggravation and snatched up a stool by the table, hurling it at Mr McGovern, who neatly dodged it. The stool clattered away towards the open door, where rain gusted in from the dark night. Then Mr McGovern advanced with ominous intention and trepidation mounted on Ned's face.

Meanwhile, Tommy's arms continued to constrict until Rory's ribs screamed in protest. As he strove to escape the prison of Tommy's unyielding embrace, a scared-looking Alfie appeared beside them. He hooked his good left arm over Tommy's elbow and heaved on it, trying to drag Tommy away from Rory.

'You little blighter!' Tommy growled, purple with wrath.

Releasing Rory, he grabbed hold of Alfie's injured right arm in its sling and gave it a vicious twist. Alfie yelped in pain and Tommy cuffed him on the side of his head before swatting him away like a fly. He wasted no time in turning back to Rory, but it had been enough of a distraction for Rory to get in one decent punch to Tommy's temple. The other man recoiled but retaliated almost at once, shoving Rory back against the wall for a second time and closing his meaty hands around his throat. He squeezed tightly and Rory choked as Tommy's inexorable grip cut off the supply of air to his lungs. Dimly, he heard Maud shriek at Tommy to let go. Fear engulfed him as he felt the increasing pressure from Tommy's fingers and the burning sensation in his throat, and he comprehended that he was about to lose this fight.

A loud crack sounded nearby, followed by a grunt. Through his swimming vision, he managed to piece together what had happened: Mr McGovern had grasped the plate May had been wiping earlier and smashed it over Ned's head in a spray of ceramic shards. Ned now staggered and fell to his knees, swaying. One more blow would likely knock him out, which meant that Mr McGovern would very soon be free to rescue Rory. But he would be mere moments too late.

That was when a shrill yowl pierced the room. Tommy gave a yell and his hands dropped from Rory's throat as he lurched downwards. Sucking in deep lungfuls of precious air, Rory glanced down to distinguish a ginger blur with claws latched onto Tommy's trouser leg. Tommy scrabbled at the cat as it thrashed about, its tail trapped beneath his boot. Lifting his foot, he aimed a savage kick at the cat, but it shot away out of reach, its fur standing on end.

It had bought Rory vital seconds. Drawing back his elbow, he threw his weight behind his fist just as Tommy straightened, and the strike landed directly on his mouth. Tommy's head snapped sideways and a spurt of blood sailed through the air. An instant later, Rory heard a tinkling sound like a pebble skittering across the floor. When Tommy's head swivelled back to him, there was a bleeding gap where his large tooth used to be. He reached up to touch it and his eyes bulged.

Before he could say or do anything else, Mr McGovern strode over and wrenched both of Tommy's arms behind his back in an action that looked far too practised to be his first time. Beyond them, Rory discerned Ned's long, skinny form sprawled motionless on the floor, fragments of the broken plate scattered around him. Tommy bucked like a wild animal but Mr McGovern held firm, twisting harder and making Tommy wince.

'Your companion is out cold,' he said grimly. 'And you're next if you don't yield this instant. We're now two against one.'

Rory raised his fists in readiness, even as his throat blazed and his breaths came in ragged pants. The ferocity slowly drained from Tommy's body and his shoulders slumped in defeat.

'You win,' he muttered, his speech slurred through his bloody lips.

His tongue probed the gap in his teeth and he let loose a string of colourful curses at Rory, who accepted them stoically. Tommy then turned his vitriol on the cat, which had padded nonchalantly over to the fireplace as though interested in nothing more than the simmering pot of parsnip soup, now almost certainly burned. Tail raised with aplomb, it completely ignored the accusations Tommy hurled at its back.

Rory's hand throbbed and he looked down to realise that his knuckles had split open where they'd connected with Tommy's teeth. As he lifted his other hand to massage his aching throat, he glanced out the doorway and across the rainy alley. Standing on the threshold of Number 4 was the wispy-haired figure of Elsie; she nodded once at him before retreating inside her house.

'And as for you!' Tommy transferred his attention to Maud, who flinched but didn't abandon her protective position in front of Frankie and May on the stairs. Alfie joined her on the bottom step, his arm hanging awkwardly out of its sling, and glared at Tommy as the man spat, 'You're to blame for all of this, you miserable, pathetic bi—'

'Quiet!' Mr McGovern shook him forcefully and Tommy's jaw clacked shut. 'This is how it's going to be, Mr Jones,' Mr McGovern continued in a cold voice. 'You will stand here and not move an inch while Maud and her children pack their things and leave with us. You will not attempt to follow us, now or at any stage in the future.'

Tommy's expression smouldered with fury, but he grumbled, 'Fine, you have my word.'

'Strangely enough, I don't trust your word,' Mr McGovern replied. 'I wouldn't put it past you to concoct a dim-witted plan to force your wife to return to your side, even when faced with the blatant reality that she doesn't wish it.'

Tommy shifted within Mr McGovern's grip and said nothing.

'To avoid the occurrence of such a futile scenario, Rory has a proposition for you,' Mr McGovern said, nodding at Rory to proceed.

'I do,' Rory said, relieved to find that his voice still worked, although it came out in a noticeable croak. 'Ideally, I'd take great pleasure in kicking you out of this house, but that wouldn't be much of an incentive for you to toe the line. So instead, I'm offering you a deal—you may remain living under this roof at an extremely low rate of rent for as long as you keep your distance from Maud and her children. If you come after them, I'll evict you and you can go find full-price accommodation elsewhere, and you still won't get them back. You'll lose more teeth too, if I can manage it.'

Tommy glowered at that last remark, but then he squinted at Rory in appraisal. 'What kind of rent are we talking?'

'How about a shilling per quarter? Does that sound like a good enough reason to stay well away from the whole family?'

Tommy's eyes gleamed and his lips widened into a red smile. 'It sure does.'

Rory knew he was practically giving away the tenancy for free, and it galled him to reward the brute for his actions instead of punishing him. However, he figured that bribery was a language Tommy would understand, and this arrangement offered the best prospect of keeping him in a comfortable situation that he'd be loath to ruin for himself. With minimal rent to pay, he could afford to hire a woman to cook and clean for him, and he'd have enough spare to pay other women to cater to his carnal needs whenever he felt so inclined. If he no longer required Maud to fulfil those wifely duties, surely he'd be satisfied to leave her be.

Rory suspected Emily would rap him sharply on the wrist if he didn't give Maud the final say. He met her gaze straight on. 'Are you willing to come with us?'

She looked from her three children to Tommy and squared her shoulders. 'Yes. We just need a couple minutes to get our clothes and my sewing things, and say goodbye to Elsie.'

As the family hurried upstairs to fetch their few belongings, Rory turned and caught sight of Tommy's misshapen tooth on the floor near the fireplace. The admiral had curled up beside

it and was basking in the glow from the hearth, purring in
contentment.

# Chapter 21

Emily clutched her sketchbook and box of charcoal sticks to her chest as she rushed through the front doors of the Blake-Fletchley Academy of the Arts and navigated the teeming corridor beyond. February's bitter wind followed her inside, the draught sending a discarded scrap of paper skating across the floorboards. The distinct scent of turpentine hung in the air, mingling with the muskier odour of young men who smoked often and seldom washed.

The tide of male students parted around her, no longer with the exaggerated shock they'd displayed in January, but still with lingering glances that ranged from admiring to disapproving. She had learned to steel herself against both varieties and held her chin high as she hurried forwards, quickening her pace even further at the sight of a familiar brown bonnet ahead.

'Jane!'

The other woman turned, her expression filling with relief as she shifted her drawing case from one hand to the other. Emily and Jane were that term's only new female students, a shared circumstance that had swiftly united them among the sea of dark coats and sceptical stares.

'I was beginning to think you'd been deterred by the weather,' Jane said as Emily fell into step beside her. A particularly strong gust rattled the windows, as if to emphasise her point.

'And miss today's lesson?' Emily said. 'After all Mr Parrish's hints about a special demonstration, I would have fought through a blizzard to get here.'

Jane laughed, and they hastened in the direction of Room Eight, Emily's mind racing with possibilities. Throughout the past week, their drawing master had been dropping tantalising suggestions about a novel technique he was eager to share. She and Jane had debated at length over what it might be, and even their fellow students had lost some of their aloofness in their animated speculation.

When they reached the classroom, they found it already crowded and buzzing with an air of expectancy. Their male peers had claimed the prime positions, their easels forming a circle around the open space in the middle of the room. Emily and Jane were forced to weave their way to the back, where they found two spare seats behind a hulking fellow whose broad shoulders obscured half their view.

Mr Parrish swept in moments later and strode to the room's centre. He was followed by a handsome youth wrapped in a long robe, whose graceful posture drew Emily's eye at once. He assumed a position to the right of Mr Parrish, his spine erect and his shoulders back, holding himself with seemingly effortless poise.

'Gentlemen!' Mr Parrish clapped his hands together, his face alight with enthusiasm. 'Today, we break from our usual static poses. The human figure in motion—that is our challenge!'

Appreciative murmurs rippled through the room, and Emily and Jane exchanged a glance of excitement.

'Our assistant in this undertaking' – Mr Parrish indicated the youth, who arched a delicate eyebrow but didn't speak – 'is trained in the balletic arts. He will demonstrate a series of athletic stances, each held for mere minutes. You must learn to capture the essence of movement, the tension in the muscles and—'

The hulking fellow shifted sideways in his seat and the drawing master broke off, his mouth slackening when his gaze landed upon Emily and Jane. The room fell quiet. Emily felt heat creep up her neck as twenty pairs of male eyes turned towards them.

'Ladies,' Mr Parrish spluttered. 'You are not meant to be—highly inappropriate—under no circumstances can you be permitted to...'

He gestured fretfully at the young man beside him, and Emily comprehended that the youth must be naked beneath his robe, or, if not, nearly so. She also realised what an extraordinary opportunity this would be to practise life drawing, not just on a hand or a face but on the whole human form. To study its raw lines and curves, free from the distortion of garments, would be an experience of immeasurable value to her artistic education. Desperately, she looked around, yearning for a champion to intervene on her and Jane's behalf. The youth appeared unperturbed at the prospect of baring his body to female eyes, but disapproval radiated from every other countenance in sight.

Mr Parrish coughed loudly. 'Mrs Carey, Miss Lyndon, arrangements have already been made for you in Room Twelve down the hall. Kindly proceed there so we may commence without delay.'

Emily's grip tightened on her box of charcoal sticks. Words of protest rose in her throat, only to clog there as the hulking fellow swivelled on his seat and smirked at them. The idea of attracting even more attention to themselves, with the same inevitable conclusion, made her stomach churn.

Jane was already getting to her feet and snatching up her drawing case, her movements sharp with suppressed anger. Emily followed suit, sensing the weight of scrutiny and derision upon them. As they made their undignified exit, she was painfully reminded of her former schoolmaster, the repulsive Mr Miller. Mr Parrish might not have taken a leather strap to her palms, but his message was the same: 'You are inferior. You are unworthy.'

They proceeded in silence to Room Twelve, which was smaller, colder, and smelled of dust. In the centre before two lonely easels stood their consolation prize: a marble statue, its lifeless shape half hidden beneath an artfully draped swathe of cloth. The fabric concealed more of the figure than it revealed, as if even an exposed chest made of stone might prove too shocking for feminine sensibilities.

'Well,' Jane said, her voice tight, 'we're certainly guaranteed that this model won't move from his position.'

Emily stared at the statue's blank expression, thinking of the dynamic poses they were missing, the vital knowledge denied them. How were they ever to capture the true essence of the human form when they were restricted to studying this cold, partial echo of it?

'True, he won't move,' she said. 'And neither shall we, if we continue to endure the limitations put upon us.'

She tried to say it with audacity, as though she might whirl around, march back to Room Eight and insist on being allowed to participate in the lesson.

But her courage failed and she just stepped up to one of the easels in resignation.

Later that day, she scurried along the busy streets of Harrogate, heading north-east in the direction of the nearby village of Bilton, where her friend Louise Shelby resided. The icy wind stung her cheeks with the promise of imminent snow, and she hoped she would make it back before it started to fall. Perhaps if it had arrived earlier, she would have been obliged to remain at Louise's home that morning and thus would have avoided the day's humiliation.

How she yearned to confide in Rory. She knew he would be outraged on her behalf, even though what had happened was in reality nothing more than could be expected. The fact that Blake-Fletchley had opened its doors to her and Jane at all was remarkable enough – of course the institution's grudging acceptance would come wrapped in constraints, their presence merely tolerated and not deemed equal to their male counterparts. Still, in his unwavering loyalty, Rory would dismiss such rationalisation and call her drawing master a 'bloody idiot'.

Then she felt a twinge of guilt for being so engrossed in her personal concerns when Rory was carrying heavy burdens of his own. The previous week, on her first visit back to Bewley Hall since she had commenced her studies at Blake-Fletchley, he had divulged the dreadful truth of Tommy Jones's abuse and the confrontation that had taken place at Penny Close. She had beheld the lingering bruises on his throat with horror and thanked God that he and her father had escaped with their lives. Now, having uprooted Maud and her three children from their home, Rory was anxious to see them safely settled. Emily's father had secured them a cottage in Gildham, which had been recently left vacant after the passing of its elderly occupant, a neighbour of the redoubtable lacemaker Ethel Cobb. Rory hoped that Maud's sewing skills might serve her well in this new situation – Ethel's granddaughter had agreed to help her learn the intricacies of machine lacemaking, while Maud's children were to attend the small school in the village. Emily deeply admired her husband's compassion towards the woman, even as she comprehended how uncomfortably it conflicted with his fierce loyalty to his mother.

A few snowflakes swirled in the freezing wind and she tucked her sketchbook inside her cloak to protect it...not that today's sketches had been particularly inspiring. Dusk was descending quickly; loath to be out unaccompanied after dark, she pressed onwards into the quieter, more rural area of Bilton. Louise dwelled there in her parents' modest home, to which she had returned following the death of her husband, Roger, in America, not long after they had emigrated together.

Emily could have afforded to bring her lady's maid to Yorkshire and to lodge somewhere more refined, perhaps even nearer to the academy, but the chance to strengthen her friendship with Louise, and to spend time with her adorable daughter Philippa, outweighed most other considerations. Louise's parents, Mr and Mrs Fielding, had welcomed Emily with great kindness, aware of how she and Louise had become close companions aboard the *Integrity*. They politely rebuffed her offer to pay rent, but they were amenable to accepting odd gifts here or there, such as a new rug for the hallway or a footstool for the parlour. Emily's father had also arranged for a steady supply of coal to be delivered by the local merchant throughout the colder months. The result of this arrangement was a pleasantly warm house in both temperature and atmosphere.

The snow grew thicker just as Emily opened the front gate of the Fieldings' little garden. She paused to brush the accumulating flakes from her cloak before letting herself into the house. The first sound she heard when she entered was the unmistakable cry of a fractious child.

'Won't!'

The pitch of distress was enough to pull at her heartstrings. She hastened into the parlour to find Louise sitting at the square table, a plate of mash cooling in front of her as she tried to coax four-year-old Philippa into opening her mouth for a spoonful.

The child, however, twisted sideways in her chair, her curls bouncing as she shook her head vigorously, her lips sealed tight.

'Please, pet,' Louise implored, and Emily detected the frayed edge to her voice. 'Eat your dinner and I'll tell you the story again about how you were born on the big ship.'

Philippa pouted in a manner quite unlike her usually sunny nature. 'It's lumpy.'

'It's not,' Louise said, holding the spoon steady. 'I made it for you myself. Just two more bites.'

'Not hungry!'

Louise glanced over her shoulder, caught Emily's eye, and gave her an exasperated grimace. 'I hope your day's been going better than mine.'

Emily laughed lightly. 'I can assure you it has not.'

Footsteps sounded out in the hall and Mrs Fielding came bustling into the room, carrying an armful of clothing.

'Evening, Emily, love. I'm glad you got back afore the worst of that snow sets in.' She surveyed the battle being waged over the plate of mash. 'Still not eating?' She tutted. 'Reckon she's coming down with a cold. She's been sniffing ever since you took her walking on the Stray without her scarf—I'll tell you that for nowt.'

Louise closed her eyes briefly and Emily sensed that this was not the first time today that Mrs Fielding had aired her opinion. Taking a controlled breath, Louise turned back to her daughter.

'Philippa, pet, if you don't eat up, you won't get anything else until breakfast tomorrow.'

'Fine!' Philippa agreed.

Mrs Fielding crossed the parlour to her chair by the fire, murmuring, 'Might as well starve the poor lass.'

Louise threw her a sharp look but Mrs Fielding didn't seem to notice as she sat down, propped her feet up on the footstool in front of her, and started to sort through the pile of clothing in her lap. Emily perceived the anomalous current of tension within the room and wondered just how bad Louise's day had been. Mumbling an excuse about putting away her belongings, she retreated to her bedroom – a tiny room on the ground floor that smelled like it had once served as the pipe-loving Mr Fielding's sanctuary – to set down her sketchbook and remove her cloak and boots. As she withdrew the box of charcoal sticks from her pocket, she resolved to push her own disappointment to the back of her mind and endeavour to bring some cheer to the household.

Half an hour later, the snow was falling in earnest beyond the window, but the cosy room within resounded with giggles as Philippa delighted in the amusing sketches Emily created for her: the little girl's curly head topped with a crown of fluttering birds, her mother flying above the grassy Stray with a pair of wings instead of arms, her grandfather smoking a pipe ten times larger than himself. The mash still remained uneaten, but Louise's expression was nonetheless full of gratitude as she sat in the chair opposite her mother, working on the mending which Mrs Fielding had identified from the pile of clothes.

'Another one!' Philippa chirped, her small finger pointing eagerly. 'Do Gran!'

Emily smiled. 'Good idea. While I'm drawing her, will you have a spoon of mash?'

'Not hungry!'

Emily peered over at Louise, who shrugged as if to say, 'Well, it was worth a try.' With an answering nod of resignation, Emily began her next sketch. Philippa sniffed and swiped the back of her hand under her nose before leaning her arms on the table to follow Emily's progress.

As the charcoal stick darted across the page, Louise cleared her throat. 'Did something unpleasant happen today at the academy?' she asked, glancing from her darning needle up to Emily and back down again.

Emily grimaced. 'I suppose you could say that.'

Not wanting to dampen the newly cheerful mood, she kept her tone as blithe as possible as she described what had taken place in Room Eight at Blake-Fletchley. She chose her words carefully so that Philippa's young ears wouldn't pick up on the gravity of the incident, while she privately wondered whether such female constraints would have eased at all by the time the girl became a woman. She supposed that a more liberated future was doubtful so long as women continued to wear their shackles without protest, just as she and Jane had done.

Shame pricked at her, and yet she didn't know how else she could have responded to the situation. Had she planted herself on her seat and refused to move, she likely would have been expelled for her misconduct.

Was she greedy to crave equality with the male students as part of her admittance to the institution? It wasn't as though all artistic avenues were closed off to her – she had other options aside from life drawing that could be just as fulfilling.

'I am resolved not to be discouraged,' she said aloud, looking up from her sketch. 'I have passionate interests in other areas such as portraiture and still life, and perhaps even landscapes. I've also been practising a great deal with oils and I mean to continue to improve my technique.'

'You seem reet determined,' remarked Mrs Fielding, as she examined a smock of Philippa's with a rip at its hem. 'I wager nowt will get in your way in the long run.'

'Indeed!' Emily said with spirit. 'I am prepared to devote my entire life to my art.'

Louise blinked but didn't comment, her gaze focused on threading her needle through the heel of a stocking.

With a final sweeping gesture, Emily completed the sketch – a depiction of Mrs Fielding pouring a cup of tea for a fox wearing a smart waistcoat – and Philippa clapped her hands with glee. Snatching it up, she ran over to show her grandmother, smudging the charcoal in her haste.

'Look, Gran!'

'Well now, isn't that reet grand!' Mrs Fielding exclaimed. Then she clicked her tongue. 'You've got charcoal all over your fingers, you silly lass. Between that and your runny nose, I reckon we need to fetch you a hanky.'

She pulled herself up out of the chair with a grunt and ushered Philippa from the parlour, the little girl still clutching the sketch and beaming as her nose dripped. Emily couldn't help but feel a small twinge of loss at her departure – it seemed like the light in the room dimmed without her bright presence. When Emily looked away from the parlour door, she found Louise observing her.

'You're very good with Philippa,' said Louise. 'So kind and patient.'

'She's a gem,' Emily replied softly. 'What a joy she brings to your life.' She tried but failed to keep the longing from her voice.

Louise let her mending drop into her lap. 'You so dearly wish to be a mother.'

'I do,' Emily admitted.

'But do you understand what that entails? What you'd have to sacrifice?'

Emily stared at her blankly.

Louise leaned forwards in her chair, her expression tender. 'I consider you a beloved friend, and so I feel compelled to alert you to the blind point in your vision. You cherish two distinct ambitions, but can't you see that you'll only ever be able to realise one of them? If you pursue excellence in your art, it will demand so much from you that you will have no time to raise a family. If you choose motherhood, your artistic dream will wither from neglect.'

Emily opened her mouth to object, but Louise shook her head to cut her off.

'What do you think I have been doing all day?' she said, throwing her hands up in mild exasperation. 'My daughter woke me before the sun rose, and from that moment I gave her every ounce of my attention: I made her breakfast, washed her clothes, brought her out for a walk, read to her. More than an hour was taken up with our struggle over dinner. Right now, I am mending her stockings. Tonight, we must set up the bath before she goes to bed and that is an ordeal of its own kind. Has there been even a minute of my day devoted to myself?'

Emily's insides shrivelled. She comprehended Louise's well-intentioned reasoning for speaking her mind, but how her bluntness stung – not least because Emily could recognise the truth in her words, the truth to which she had unconsciously turned a blind eye.

Before she could find her voice to respond, Louise hurried on. 'I'm not saying this to hurt you, nor because I feel sorry for myself. My life is very different to what I'd once imagined it would be—there's no denying that. I'm a widow living with my parents and sometimes that is stifling.' Her posture slumped. 'Every now and then, when I have a particularly difficult day, I do wonder whether I might have thrived if I had stayed in America, even after Roger died. I was educated to a greater degree than my parents, and I think I could have been a good teacher. But I came back home to Yorkshire and have long since resigned myself to that choice.' She stroked the stocking in her lap and her expression lifted with fondness. 'Still, when all is said and done, Philippa is my beginning and my end, no matter where I live, and I wouldn't change that for the world. I don't have any grand ambition beyond being the very best mother I can be.' She glanced up. 'You, on the other hand...'

Emily swallowed. 'I understand what you are saying,' she said, scarcely louder than a whisper, 'and I have to confess that it had never occurred to me before now. Gracious, how utterly foolish of me.'

'I didn't mean to imply that you are foolish,' Louise said, her gaze earnest. 'I don't believe that at all. Only a bit short-sighted, perhaps.'

Emily wished she could laugh it off, but she didn't feel capable of mustering even a weak chuckle. Her stomach twisted as she realised that she had never given proper thought to how she would balance both of the aspirations she had nurtured for so long. Was it, as Louise stated, impossible? Would she either have to put her art aside to raise a family, or sacrifice family to fulfil her own potential?

She gulped as a memory stirred: her mother admiring her still life painting in the parlour, gently urging her to find time to nurture her gift even when other blessings came into her life. At the time, Emily had taken the remark at face value, missing the quiet caution tucked within it. Now, with Louise's words echoing in her ears, she finally comprehended what her mother had been trying to tell her.

'I know your circumstances are different to mine,' Louise said delicately, 'and maybe when you have a baby you intend to hire someone to take care of all the daily time-consuming tasks on your behalf. But then why would you desire a child so much if not to relish looking after every aspect of his or her wellbeing?'

Emily flushed at the idea that her privileged situation might lead her to transfer the more burdensome parts of motherhood to a servant. Before she could ask herself whether she would be prepared to do this, Mrs Fielding and Philippa re-entered the parlour and her heart leapt at the sight of the little girl. It was uncanny how the child prompted such a visceral reaction of tenderness and protectiveness in her.

How could she ever forego the possibility of bearing one of her own?

And yet, how could she give up the artistic dream she had yearned to attain since she was a child herself?

Dispiritedly, she had to acknowledge that both of her goals were, at present, beyond her control. Her body refused to cooperate in one pursuit, while the gatekeepers of the art world dictated the other, leaving her powerless to shape her own destiny in either realm.

Her breath snagged in her throat.

What if she would accomplish neither in her lifetime?

Philippa trotted across the room, her curls bobbing gaily about her head. She climbed into Louise's lap, knocking her mending to the floor, and wrapped her arms affectionately around her mother's neck.

'I'm hungry,' she declared.

Louise sighed and cast Emily a lopsided smile. Emily did her very best to smile back.

# Chapter 22

Cormac raised a questioning eyebrow at Bridget and, when she nodded back, he rapped his knuckle on the door to the tutor's room.

'Come in!' came Mr Humphrey's unfailingly cheerful voice, coloured by his gentle Scottish accent.

Cormac opened the door and allowed Bridget to enter first, before following after her. They found the tutor standing over the large table that dominated his room, an array of papers and books laid out in front of him. He beamed at them.

'Mr McGovern, Lady Courcey, thank you very much for taking the time to meet with me. Please, please sit!'

As they sat at the table in two of the chairs usually occupied by his currently absent students, Cormac glanced down at the papers and spotted Jack's name written in neat letters in the top right corner of several of the pages.

Mr Humphrey bounced on the balls of his feet. 'I appreciate you coming here, so that I could show you these examples as part of our discussion.'

He gestured towards the table. Cormac tugged a sheet closer to him and identified it as the beginning of an essay in Jack's handwriting on the qualities of a noble leader.

'It is not necessary to consider Mr Carey's eligibility,' Mr Humphrey continued, 'as he is past the age where it would be relevant, although I will say that I'm extremely pleased with his progress—he has a keen mathematical mind. Wee Master Angus, I'm afraid, has yet to demonstrate that he is capable of the concentration and discipline required for the broader educational path. Master Jack, however, is ready for that challenge, I believe.'

Next to Cormac, Bridget's fingers tightened on the edge of her chair. 'What is your recommendation, Mr Humphrey?'

The tutor took a seat at the top of the table and folded his hands on its surface. 'It is my opinion that Jack should commence attendance at public school. It will expand his horizons in a way that is not possible in his current situation.'

Cormac flattened his palm over Jack's essay. 'What do you mean by that?'

'I do not harbour any conceit about my professional abilities. My tutelage is satisfactory, to be sure, but it can only advance Jack to a certain point. You will see when you peruse his work here that he has grasped the fundamentals in many subjects such as philosophy, history and literature. However, a wider range of tutors with specialist knowledge in their individual fields of study would edify his mind to a far greater degree.' Mr Humphrey paused. 'In addition to this, I feel that a public school setting would promote another essential aspect of his education: his social development.'

A flash of concern crossed Bridget's face. Cormac frowned, his shoulders tensing.

'Please elaborate,' he said in a measured tone.

Mr Humphrey's expression grew more intent, his usual optimism giving way to an uncharacteristic sombreness. 'Since his recent twelfth birthday, Jack is no longer quite a child and yet neither is he ready to become a man. He lives rather a sheltered life here at the Hall. Indeed, so does Angus, but I do not worry for his social skills—that laddie could charm a monk into forgetting his vow of silence. Jack, on the other hand, has a more retiring disposition and I regret to say that he is not flourishing in his brother's shadow. It is my strong belief that he requires more space to grow.'

A ripple of apprehension ran down Cormac's spine. He and Bridget had striven to create a safe haven for their children at Bewley Hall, but it sounded like this may have left Jack unprepared for the trials that lay beyond its walls. Did their son need the hard lessons that only the wider world could teach?

Bridget bit the tip of her tongue, her cheeks pale. 'But is he not too gentle for school in that case? Wouldn't he be a prime target for bullying?'

'That's why I would advise you to choose the school very carefully. In fact, I already have an institution in mind: Balfour School in Scotland.'

'*Scotland?*' Bridget yelped. 'Good gracious, no, that is too far away.'

'Is that not what would make it an appealing option from the perspective of Jack's advancement? Besides, the continuing expansion of the railway renders travelling north much easier than it once was. The school is situated near the village of Carstairs, where a new station was recently built, making the journey more convenient than you might imagine.'

'It's still a substantial distance,' said Cormac, fighting the urge to dismiss it just as swiftly as Bridget had. 'What else leads you to recommend it?'

'I used to teach there before I began private tutoring,' Mr Humphrey said, smiling fondly. 'I am acquainted with the headmaster, Mr Cameron, and deem him to be a very fair man. He would guarantee an environment that would nurture Jack but also draw him out of his shell.'

Cormac couldn't quash the unease that burgeoned within him as he considered the reputation of these types of institutions, steeped in their supercilious traditions and notions of superiority. What if attending one planted seeds of doubt in Jack about his father's humble beginnings? Thus far, Cormac and Bridget had succeeded in raising their boys to disregard such prejudices. Would public school undo that hard-won perspective?

With a grimace, Cormac pushed back his chair and rose, striding over to the window that overlooked the avenue at the front of the house. The ground outside lay bare without a trace of snow, in contrast to the landscape further north in Yorkshire where, according to Emily's latest letter, there had been a recent flurry. Scotland was undoubtedly blanketed in it.

He chewed the inside of his cheek, contemplating the idea of sending Jack away to this Balfour School. At least Mr Humphrey had not suggested Eton, a place forever tarnished in Cormac's mind by the fact that it could count both Garrett and Patrick among its past pupils – neither of them had emerged from it as shining examples of virtuous youth.

Then again, Jack's nature was very different to Garrett's and Patrick's – he was pure-hearted, almost to a fault. Could that purity be his safeguard from corruption, or would it only make him more vulnerable? Furthermore, what message did it convey if Cormac and Bridget chose to keep him cooped up at Bewley Hall? Would they be protecting him, or would they be doing him a disservice not to let him spread his wings beyond the confines of their parental nest?

Cormac turned back to face Mr Humphrey. 'We will need to talk with Jack before coming to any decision,' he said firmly and Bridget gave an emphatic nod of agreement.

'Aye, of course,' said Mr Humphrey. 'I wanted to broach the matter with you in the first instance to see if you might be amenable. Should Jack prove willing to go ahead with it after your discussion with him, I could write to Mr Cameron. It is already February, but he may be in a position to enrol Jack for the academic term commencing this September.'

'Before we proceed further,' Cormac said warily, 'there's something you ought to know about our personal situation, as it might influence how Jack would be perceived at the school.'

Bridget took a measured breath. 'My husband, Lord Wyndham, is seeking a divorce from me.'

Mr Humphrey blinked. 'I see. Well, that is...unexpected.' He adjusted the papers on the table before him, clearly thrown.

'Would it compromise our son's suitability?' Cormac asked, though he suspected the answer already, and wondered furthermore whether they were about to lose the services of the tutor altogether.

Mr Humphrey wavered, but only momentarily. 'I won't pretend that such matters wouldn't draw notice,' he said. 'Still, as long as it didn't disrupt Jack's conduct or studies, I see no reason why it would affect his prospective place at Balfour. The school's priority ought to be his potential and his progress, not...his family's circumstances. I would make a strong case for him in my recommendation letter.'

As Bridget thanked the tutor for his solicitude, the muffled sound of hooves drew Cormac's attention back to the window once more. A smartly dressed rider had just reached the top of the avenue and was swinging down from his mount as a stable hand came hurrying forwards. Cormac glanced over at Bridget.

'Patrick's here,' he said.

They took their leave of Mr Humphrey, and a quarter of an hour later they were seated in the drawing room opposite Cormac's nephew, whose nonchalant attitude seemed a little forced as he reclined back against the sofa. The letter he had sent the previous week announcing his return to England and his intention to visit Bedfordshire had left them none the wiser as to how he had been faring since his fiery confrontation with

Garrett, and Cormac still could not tell as he surveyed the young man's guarded hazel eyes.

'Did you spend the Christmas season at Ashbrook Lodge?' he asked.

Patrick nodded.

'That must have been quite a solitary experience,' Bridget said, her head tilted with sympathy.

Patrick shrugged. 'It didn't bother me. I meant to uncork a '34 Bordeaux with Blanchard on Christmas Eve, but we became sidetracked trying to work out which crops would be best to plant in the coming year to reduce the estate's reliance on the potato.' He raised his eyebrows at Cormac. 'Would you have any recommendations in that regard?'

It took an effort for Cormac not to raise his eyebrows in return. 'I believe Oakleigh has planted turnips and barley to good effect. Are you familiar with the concept of crop rotation?'

'Yes. We've been going around the estate speaking to the tenants about it. It will take some persuasion to get them to commit to it, though.'

'Because they don't trust that it will be successful?' asked Bridget.

'Because they don't trust *me*,' he replied.

She cringed. 'Oh.'

His mouth twisted wryly. 'Who can blame them? My father has been an absentee landlord on the estate for over twenty years. Odds are they don't expect me to stick around for long either. Still, at least no one has tried to hang me yet.'

An awkward silence fell.

After a beat, Cormac said, 'Have you been in contact with your father lately?'

Patrick shifted on the sofa. 'I have. He came back to Ashbrook Lodge after his visit to Oakleigh and informed me of the conversation that had taken place. I approve of the objective he has chosen to demonstrate selflessness in his character, and so I've allowed the lines of communication to reopen between us.' He hesitated. 'This brings me to the reason for my presence here at Bewley Hall. Upon arriving in London last week, I went to Berkeley Square, where my father had some unwelcome tidings to impart. He has initiated his enquiries into the divorce proceedings but has encountered some impediments that he's reluctant to relay. He asked me to call upon you, thinking that the news would be better received from me in person than from him by letter.'

A heavy weight settled in Cormac's gut. Was their tentative hope to be extinguished so soon? They'd had scarcely two months to enjoy the prospect of this divorce.

But then Patrick said, 'He still believes it's possible to accomplish it. However, there are certain steps involved which would be...highly unpalatable. You will need to decide whether you are willing to become embroiled in them.'

He directed this at Bridget and she swallowed audibly. 'What steps?' she asked in a quiet voice.

Patrick adjusted his position on the sofa again, crossing his legs and uncrossing them before leaning forwards and clearing his throat. 'The process will begin in the ecclesiastical courts. If a legal separation is granted, my father can then petition the House of Lords to pass a private act of divorce. There will be much debate of the evidence before it can be approved. I'm sorry to say that a major part of that evidence' – he winced, looking genuinely contrite – 'is a public statement from you declaring your adultery.'

Cormac watched the colour drain from Bridget's countenance. 'I-is it not sufficient for him to accuse me of it?' she said falteringly. 'Surely they would deem a man's word to be worth more than a woman's.'

'No doubt they would,' replied Patrick. 'But it wouldn't be enough to satisfy them. They will want to see you humiliated.'

Bridget turned to Cormac with anguish churning in her eyes and his heart clenched at her palpable distress.

'Couldn't I do it on her behalf?' he demanded of Patrick. 'I'm a guilty party in this too.'

Patrick shook his head ruefully. 'My father's sources have told him that Lady Courcey is the one who must be disgraced.'

Cormac could picture the peers in the House of Lords salivating at the idea of bringing a woman to her knees for daring to break free from the shackles of a loveless marriage. His bile rose.

'It's out of the question,' he said through gritted teeth. 'They're not entitled to treat her with such contempt. Do they not see that their malice strips them of any claim to virtue themselves? Our sins are no greater than theirs.'

Patrick rubbed the back of his neck. 'You certainly can refuse to do it, so long as you understand that denying them means that they will not grant the divorce.'

A tiny whimper escaped Bridget's lips. 'But it was finally within our grasp for the first time. We can't relinquish this chance.'

She reached out compulsively to grasp Cormac's arm. He put his hand over hers, hating the desperate feeling of helplessness that hovered between them.

'It isn't fair,' Patrick muttered. 'They're forcing you to decide which holds more value to you: your reputation or your freedom.'

Bridget's chin lifted a fraction. 'We already know which of those is more important.' She squeezed Cormac's arm even tighter. 'Since when have we ever cared what society thinks of us?'

'Bear in mind that this would be very different,' Patrick cautioned. 'Up to now, you've managed to get by on a relatively minimal level of notoriety. This scandal, however, would be a total annihilation of your anonymity. The papers would revel in publishing every minute detail of the affair. People who may have supported you in the past would not be able to countenance such flagrant disregard of the established rules. Many would feel that you ought to have borne the repercussions of your mistakes, and they would look down on you for desiring otherwise. You would likely end up isolating yourselves to an enormous degree.'

Cormac's mind reeled at this merciless depiction of their future. Bridget, on the other hand, seemed emboldened by it. 'Let them judge us how they wish,' she said, squaring her shoulders. 'Their opinions do not signify in the slightest.'

Patrick blinked. 'I admire your fortitude, my lady,' he said, inclining his head. 'But please remember that it is not merely a matter of reputation. There are other material concerns at stake. For instance, you would forfeit all right to any property you brought to the marriage.'

Although Bridget quailed at this declaration, Cormac sought out the logic behind it.

'Was that not already the case?' he said. 'Oakleigh legally became Garrett's when they wed.'

'True, but the lady has been its guardian for many years. The divorce would wholly rescind that privilege. Having said that...' Patrick trailed away, his expression turning pensive.

'Yes?' Cormac prompted.

'Perhaps I'm in a position to prevail upon my father in that regard. I could press him to make the ownership of Oakleigh a part of the divorce settlement, conferring it irrevocably upon Lady Courcey.'

This time, Cormac did raise his eyebrows. 'Do you believe you hold that much power over him?'

'I believe he has a deep urge to show that he is capable of reform,' said Patrick.

Bridget gulped. 'I would grieve the loss of Oakleigh far more than the loss of society's esteem. If you could exercise any influence in this respect, Pat, I would be so grateful. At least the Courcey title itself will pass to Emily regardless, thanks to the entailment on the estate.'

'Leave it with me for now.' Patrick clasped his palms together. 'Speaking of your daughter, her own marital state would spare her from some of the consequences in all this. As your only legitimate offspring, she could have become enmeshed in the proceedings, given that she has not yet reached the age of majority. But her marriage last year removed her from my father's lawful control and placed her under her husband's authority instead, meaning your divorce would actually have no legal implications for her. Her reputation, however, wouldn't be so secure. She would be unavoidably tainted by the scandal. Your sons, too.'

Cormac felt queasy. They had only just begun to consider the idea of sending Jack away to school. What kind of damage could his parents' very public disgrace do to his social development? Would it be akin to throwing him into a lion's den?

With the accumulation of so many disadvantages, Cormac wondered unhappily whether there were enough benefits to outweigh them. What price were they prepared to pay for Bridget's freedom and the chance to marry at last? Were there other costs which had not yet even occurred to them?

He let out a long exhalation of breath. Beside him, Bridget's shoulders slumped.

Patrick grimaced. 'I'm not trying to dissuade you from this path,' he said apologetically. 'On the contrary, I wholly believe my father ought to remove the sword of Damocles he has left hanging over your heads for so long. But it would be remiss of me not to relay his warnings about the extent of its impact.'

'We appreciate your candour,' Bridget said with a feeble smile. 'And we realise this requires further careful deliberation on our part.' She cast an anxious sideways glance at Cormac. 'Especially in relation to Jack.'

Patrick's forehead creased. 'Why especially him?'

'His tutor has recommended that we send him away to school,' she replied uneasily.

Patrick looked horrified. 'You're not serious? With this scandal about to break? He would be crucified at Eton.'

'Not Eton,' Cormac said. 'A school in Scotland.'

'Ah.' Patrick's expression cleared. 'That's different. In fact, it makes much more sense. You'd be placing him as far away from the furore as possible. Yes, good thinking.'

Cormac sensed a tremor of surprise run through Bridget as Scotland's remoteness suddenly turned from a blow into a blessing. He tilted his head at his nephew.

'How soon do you need to convey our answer to your father?' he asked.

Patrick sat back, seeming a bit more relaxed now that his troublesome task had been executed. 'Not immediately. I do intend to return to London and then to Ashbrook Lodge after that for the spring planting of the crops, but I can spare a few days if circumstances require it.' His casual manner couldn't quite conceal the hopeful flicker in his gaze.

Cormac restrained a twitch in his mouth as he said, 'You're very welcome to stay here, if that's agreeable to you?'

'Thank you, Uncle, I'm amenable to that.'

# CHAPTER 23

'So, uh, are you settling in all right?' Rory asked, standing awkwardly opposite Maud with his hands shoved into his pockets.

'Oh, yes, all fine,' she said with false brightness.

They were in one of the two rooms that made up the little cottage in which she and her children now resided in Gildham. A narrow hallway separated the two spaces; when she'd cautiously answered the door to his knock, she had ushered him inside and made sure the door was firmly latched again behind him before steering him into the kitchen. Now, she hovered in front of the fireplace (whose smoke drifted serenely up the chimney), her fingers curled tight in the folds of her apron.

'Is the cottage to your liking?' He glanced around at the bits of furniture – a table, a wooden settle with a high back and arms, a couple of cupboards – that must have belonged to the previous occupant.

'It is,' she said. 'We've got everything we need. The villagers even brought us this set of fire irons, which was so kind of them.' She pointed behind her to the hearth where a poker, brush, tongs and shovel hung from an iron stand, the items mismatched and well used.

'And has the doctor been looking after you?' Rory knew that Mr McGovern had enlisted a doctor from Bedford to come to the village and tend her.

'He's satisfied with my progress. I have more energy now than I did after...' A flash of pain crossed her face and she blinked it away with an obvious effort. 'The children are at school right now. They'll be sorry to have missed you, especially Alfie.'

'I'm sorry too,' he said. 'I'll be sure to come back another time when they're here.'

A silhouette passed by the window and she stumbled backwards in fright, her heel knocking the brush off the fire irons stand. She hastened to pick it up, her fingers trembling as she fumbled to slot it into place again. When she turned back to Rory, her cheeks were still flushed from her sudden alarm.

'I think it was just someone walking by,' he murmured. Gesturing towards the empty window, he added, 'Whoever it was is gone now.'

She lowered her gaze. 'I keep expecting him to show up at any moment. Every shadow, every footstep, every knock on the door. One day it's going to be him.'

Rory clenched his fists inside his pockets, angry that the bastard continued to hold so much power over her. 'You're safe here. He's got a cheap rent at Penny Close and more money in his pocket than he's ever had before. If he has any sense at all, he's not going to throw that away.'

She shrugged, still looking at the floor. Then she glanced up, biting her lip. 'How's your throat?'

'Grand,' he said blithely. 'The bruises are mostly gone and so's the hoarseness, as you can hear.' He scrabbled about for a change of subject. 'D'you miss Liverpool?'

He wished he'd picked any other question when her expression turned wistful. 'I do,' she admitted. 'This village is nice but it's a far cry from a bustling port town.' She emitted a sad chuckle. 'I miss Elsie too, if you can believe it. She might be odd but she was always a steadfast friend.'

'Have you, uh, made any friends here yet?'

'Ethel Cobb next door has been neighbourly in a no-nonsense sort of way, telling me to keep my chin high and make the best of it. Her granddaughter Ettie is a godsend. She always holds a seat for me on the cart that takes the women into Bedford to the lacemaking factory, and she's been giving me a lot of advice while I'm getting trained on the machines.' Maud grimaced. 'It's very different to the kind of work I'm used to. I thought I'd be quicker at it by this stage, but Ettie says I've got a keen eye so I'm sure I'll get the hang of it. Once I do, I should be able to get full hours there.'

'That's good,' Rory said, shuffling his feet. 'I'm glad that—I mean, I hope that—uh, for sure.' Damn, he should have invoked the Duke of Desmond for this visit. What would the duke say at this juncture? 'If you need anything, don't hesitate to come up to the Hall. I'll be glad to help in whatever way I can.'

She nodded. 'Thanks very much again to you and Mr McGovern for looking out for me and the children. All of this is more than we deserve.'

He dismissed her words with a shake of his head. 'Ye do deserve it. After all ye've been through, ye have a right to be happy.'

Her eyes started to glisten at that, so he bade her a hasty farewell and left the cottage with a promise to come by again soon to see Alfie, Frankie and May. He heard her checking the latch as he walked away from the door.

He spent the ride back to Bewley Hall composing a letter in his head to his mother. He knew how to start it: he would ask after her wellbeing, and how Una, Sorcha and Brian were faring, and what life was like for them in Chicago. For Emily's sake, he would request tidings of Orlaith and Charlie and how they were managing with their twins, who had to be nearly two years old by this stage. Out of politeness, he would extend his enquiries to Tess, Bronagh and Maggie too. That much was straightforward enough.

Then it would be expected that he would share his news and yet he didn't have a notion how to go about it. 'I'm progressing well in my training as the deputy land agent on the estate, and the tutor says I've got a knack for mathematics, and by the way I've given refuge to the woman your husband left you for, along with her three children as well.' If he'd been physically writing the letter, the floor would be littered with crumpled sheets of paper by now.

He arrived back at the Hall no closer to resolving his quandary. Realising he would probably need Emily's help to find the right words, he decided to retrieve her last letter, stowed carefully beneath his pillow, to double-check the date she was next due to return from Yorkshire.

He entered the house via the side entrance nearest to the stables but had hardly taken ten paces along the passageway when he heard a loud bang from deeper within the building, followed by a rumbling din that might have been something heavy rolling across a floor. Mystified and slightly alarmed, he went in search of the noise's source and traced it to an open door on the next corridor, which led into a room he'd never seen before. It was lined with rich wood panelling and boasted a billiard table in its centre, gleaming with brass fittings and topped with green baize. Patrick and Jack stood beside the table clutching long wooden cues, while Gus was on his knees in a corner, salvaging a white ball that had rolled underneath a leather armchair.

'Got it!' he announced, holding it up.

'Great,' said Patrick. 'Next time, mind you don't hit the ball so hard that you knock it off the table. You're lucky you didn't damage the baize.'

Gus's face fell but brightened again when Patrick winked.

'I just need more practice!' Gus exclaimed, jumping to his feet and hurrying over to Jack with his hand out. 'Can I have another go?'

Jack surrendered the cue without protest and Gus dropped the ball onto the table's surface, standing on his tiptoes to get a better angle.

'Here, use this,' Patrick said, nudging the armchair's footstool over to the table so that Gus could climb onto it. As he put a steadying hand on Gus's shoulder, he spotted Rory hovering in the doorway. 'All right, Carey?' he said with a cool nod. 'Care to join us?'

Rory shrugged noncommittally but came further into the room.

'Pat's teaching us how to play!' Gus said, maintaining his balance on the footstool. 'He said every self-respecting gentleman should know his way around a billiard table. It's as important as being able to tie a cravat.'

That stung Rory more than he wanted to admit. He watched as Gus tried to line up the cue.

'Hold it with a lighter grip,' Patrick advised. 'It's about control, not force. Like this.'

He leaned over the table with his own cue, curling his fingers loosely around the smooth wood and resting the upper end on the bridge he formed with his other hand. Gus tried to copy him, his tongue peeping out of his mouth as he concentrated. He prodded at the ball and it rolled away a few inches.

'A decent attempt,' Patrick said, standing back. 'I think it's Jack's turn now.'

Beaming, Gus hopped down from the footstool. He passed the cue to his brother, who scarcely had time to step up to the table when footsteps sounded in the corridor outside and Mr McGovern appeared in the doorway.

'I reckoned this was where all that noise was coming from,' he said with a grin. 'Jack, will you come with me? Your mother and I would like to have a quick word with you.'

'He's not in trouble, is he?' Gus asked anxiously.

'No, but you are,' Mr McGovern replied, arching his brow. 'You're to report to Mrs Hawkins this instant and explain why she appears to be missing a whole jar of blackberry jam after checking her inventory.'

'Oh, I wanted to feed a robin that came to the window—' Gus began enthusiastically before wilting under his father's stern gaze. 'I've just realised I forgot to put the jar back afterwards.'

'Off you go and apologise,' Mr McGovern said and Gus scurried out of the room. 'Come along with me, *a mhac*,' he added to Jack in a gentler tone.

Brow furrowed, Jack handed the cue to Rory and departed from the room with his father, leaving Rory and Patrick alone.

Patrick coughed. 'Fancy a game?'

'I've never played,' Rory replied. 'I guess I'm not one of those self-respecting gentlemen.'

Patrick rolled his eyes. 'Let's not be sensitive today, shall we?'

He reached for the white ball Gus had hit, positioned it near the head of the table and leaned over once more with an easy confidence. His cue struck the ball, which streaked across the baize and knocked another ball, this one red, directly into a corner pocket. He straightened with a smirk. Rory was impressed but refused to show it. Patrick rounded the table, fished the ball out of the pocket and dropped it onto a random spot of the baize.

As he lined up his next shot, he said offhandedly, 'You know, you're something of a puzzle to me.'

Rory frowned. 'What d'you mean?'

Patrick hit the white ball and sank the red again. 'I mean, I can't figure you out. Why did you marry my cousin? Apart from her manifest charms—which hardly require marriage to appreciate—the answer seems obvious: for her money and all the privileges that come with it.' He waved his cue to indicate their surroundings. 'And yet you don't seem to indulge in those privileges at all. You don't even have a valet, isn't that right?'

'Do you?' Rory challenged.

'Of course. I left him behind in Bedford to make my visit to Bewley Hall, but he will join me now that my uncle has invited me to stay for a few days.' Patrick set the end of his cue on the floor and leaned casually on it. 'Why did you marry her, if not for a comfortable life?'

Rory reddened. He had no desire to explain himself to a fellow for whom he held little regard, but he couldn't leave his relationship with Emily undefended.

'Because I love her,' he said firmly, relieved that he didn't stammer over the words.

Patrick's mouth curved with amusement. 'It always fascinates me to encounter people who are determined to stake their whole lives on something entirely imaginary.'

Rory threw him an incredulous look. 'You think love isn't real?'

Patrick snorted. 'I know it isn't. It's just a fairytale romantics use to convince themselves that their entanglements are more than transactions of lust or convenience.'

Rory gaped. Notwithstanding his dislike of Patrick, he had always viewed him as a man of the world, with more sophistication and experience than Rory in numerous areas.

It stunned him that the fellow could be so naïve on this one matter.

He was ready to argue the point, but then Patrick said, 'When I first heard about your marriage, I assumed you'd got her with child so you had to hasten to tie the knot. Figured you couldn't keep your hands to yourself.'

Rory gripped his cue tightly, his jaw clenching. 'Watch your mouth.'

'It was a reasonable assumption,' Patrick said, undeterred. 'But no child materialised, which made me wonder whether the opposite was true and you were too afraid to do the deed. Or maybe you tried, but something's broken. Then again, that could be her fault too. Women are usually—'

Rory's arm snapped out and he smacked his cue against Patrick's with a sharp thud of wood on wood. Patrick lost his balance as his cue clattered to the floor and he flailed, grabbing onto the edge of the table to stop himself from falling on his face.

'What the hell!' he barked.

Rory loomed over him. 'Don't you ever, *ever*, say that in Emily's presence. D'you hear me?'

Patrick stared up, his expression a mix of ire and confusion. 'What—'

'The one thing she wants more than anything else on this earth is a baby.' Rory took a deep, controlled breath. 'And, whether by her fault or mine, 'tis looking more and more like the one thing she'll never have.'

Patrick was silent. He straightened and took a step backwards. 'I didn't realise,' he said quietly.

Rory felt his wrath leaking out of him as swiftly as it had risen. He stepped back too, his shoulders sagging. 'I'm just warning you there are lines you can't cross.'

Patrick nodded. 'Noted.' Brushing off his sleeves, he bent to retrieve his cue and inspected it for a moment. 'No damage done—at least, not to anything other than my dignity.' He shot Rory a wry glance.

Rory emitted an unsympathetic grunt, tempering it with a light tap of his cue against the table. 'So are you going to show me how a self-respecting gentleman plays this game or not?'

Patrick responded with a faint grin. 'Very well. But I must forewarn you: true mastery takes years of idleness.'

# Chapter 24

Jack's wide blue eyes stared into Cormac's. 'School?' he said in a soft voice.

Next to Cormac, Bridget put out a gentle hand to touch their son's arm. 'Only if you are open to the idea, my lamb. We wouldn't send you away against your will.'

They had decided beforehand upon Cormac's study as the appropriate venue for this serious conversation, but Cormac now wondered whether it placed too much weight on Jack's answer. Although they were gathered in a loose circle in the centre of the room as opposed to addressing the matter across the desk, perhaps the boy would have felt more at ease in a less formal setting. His gaze flicked nervously between them.

'Where?' he asked.

Cormac cleared his throat. 'Mr Humphrey recommended a school in Scotland,' he said, watching Jack carefully for his reaction.

Jack swallowed, the subtle protrusion of his undeveloped Adam's apple barely making a ripple beneath his skin. 'When would I start there?'

'This September may be a possibility if they have the capacity to offer you a place,' Bridget said, 'but we have not yet made any enquiry. Nothing is settled, and nor does it need to be if it's not the right course to follow.'

He chewed on his lower lip as he contemplated this. Slowly, he swivelled away from them and walked towards the window, skirting the large desk with an air of deference. As he peered out the window, Cormac and Bridget shared an apprehensive look. What was going through their boy's mind?

At length, he pivoted back to them. 'I think I want to go,' he said, his tone low but resolute.

Bridget blinked. 'You do?'

Cormac detected the hint of dismay in her words and realised that she had hoped Jack would reject this proposal.

Jack nodded. His head turned once again towards the window. 'I think I need to go,' he said, so softly that Cormac wasn't sure if he had meant them to hear it.

Something inside Cormac twisted with both grief and pride at his son's maturity. 'Well then,' he said, concealing his emotion beneath a veneer of pragmatism, 'in that case, we'll proceed with our enquiries.'

What followed after that was a series of letters: Mr Humphrey wrote to the headmaster of Balfour School to recommend Jack as a pupil, and Mr Cameron's response came with confirmation that a place could be made available for the next academic year, whereupon Cormac himself wrote to Mr Cameron requesting a visit to the school before they came to any decision.

While this was being arranged, he and Bridget debated the merits and drawbacks of persisting with the divorce and arrived at the conclusion that, as Patrick had intimated, the risk to Jack would likely be minimal if the school he attended was situated in far-flung Scotland. As for their other children, Gus would remain sheltered under their protection at Bewley Hall, but Emily would be particularly vulnerable to the negative effects of the scandal, given her art academy's location within England and its upper-class environment.

She happened to make her second trip back from Yorkshire while they were in the midst of their deliberations, so they took her aside to speak with her about it, divulging the prospect of the public statement that Bridget would be obliged to make.

'The repercussions might be even worse than we expected, gooseberry,' Bridget said morosely. 'We anticipate much contempt towards ourselves, of course, but it would also leave you quite exposed to gossip and derision, and we could not bear to be the cause of such pain for you. Thus, we believe you ought to have a say in this decision as well.'

'You must go ahead with it,' Emily replied at once. 'Of course you must.'

'But the impact it could have—'

She shook her head vigorously. 'You have lived twenty long years under Garrett's thumb. Seize this chance to set yourself free. There is not a single doubt in my mind that this is what you should do.'

She reached out to clasp their hands and Cormac grasped hers tightly in return, more grateful for her selflessness than he could articulate.

The next day, Patrick departed for London to convey their consent to Garrett that he could continue with his application for the divorce.

Although Patrick and Emily had been civil in each other's presence, her mood noticeably lifted after his departure. She only stayed for another two days, but when she left she was positively glowing. Cormac had absolutely no wish to think about the activities she and Rory had pursued behind the door of their suite to endow her with that glow, and yet he nevertheless hoped that the result would bring her the maternal happiness she craved.

In the meantime, he finalised the arrangements for his trip to Scotland. He would travel alone – there was no need for Bridget to undertake the lengthy journey too, not when she had just initiated plans for a new charity event involving a lecture by an eminent Anglo-Irish reverend. While it might be beneficial for Jack to get a sense of the school firsthand, on the whole it would be best to leave him behind on this occasion so that Cormac could engage in a frank discussion with Mr Cameron. He saw no point in building up Jack's hopes if the school turned out to be unsuitable.

On a mild day in the middle of March, he started out from Bewley Hall before the sun rose and endured a gruelling day's travel, taking the train from Bedford to London, where he switched to a railway line that carried him northwards, changing again just before the Scottish border to ride the Caledonian Railway as far as the station at Carstairs. Exhaustion set in hours before he reached his destination, his muscles aching from sitting for so long and his head throbbing from the constant clatter of the wheels on the tracks. This punishing ordeal would not encourage monthly trips like the ones Emily made from Yorkshire – even her journeys, though a little shorter, were hardly simple. Jack would probably only be able to come home between terms. At least gossip would also struggle to travel such a distance.

When Cormac disembarked from the final train at the Carstairs railway station late that night, a chilly wind buffeted him on the platform and he realised with a shiver that spring had yet to arrive this far north. Walking stiff-limbed along the village's main street, he located The Glenside Inn, which Mr Humphrey had recommended for his overnight stay, and took a room. Although he was worn out, his mind wouldn't rest and he tossed for the night, brooding over his impending interview with Mr Cameron the following day. The bed felt too big without Bridget beside him, and he found himself missing his nightly custom of tugging the bedcovers back from her side.

The next morning, the innkeeper offered the services of a local driver to take him up to the school in a gig, but Cormac opted instead to hire a horse. Though the day was cold, the wisps of clouds that scudded across the sky were too insubstantial to carry the threat of rain, and he yearned for the freedom of riding after the previous day's confinement.

On the winding road up to the school, he beheld the rugged landscape around him, patches of gorse dotting craggy fields which gave way to undulating hills in the distance. The trees on either side of the road were scarcely beginning to bud, winter clinging on here as long as it could. As he neared the school grounds, he observed signs of more careful stewardship: neatly trimmed hedges, stone walls, and a fenced pitch that appeared to be designated for sports, though its surface was somewhat uneven.

He passed through a set of open iron gates and followed a short avenue up to the school, which seemed to rise naturally out of the land in front of him, its architecture dignified but understated. As he approached the building, he noticed several boys crossing the grounds, their dark jackets and caps lending them a uniform appearance, although a closer look revealed varying levels of wear and repair. They wore sturdy boots, and on their chests they sported badges emblazoned with what he presumed was Balfour School's crest.

He dismounted next to a modest stables set apart from the main building and led his horse inside, securing it in an empty stall with a bucket of water. There was no one about, so he brushed down its coat himself before making his way back outside. Suppressing his nervousness, he strode up to the school's entrance, where he informed a porter that he had an appointment with the headmaster. Not long after that, he found himself seated in Mr Cameron's office, ready to discuss Jack's future.

The headmaster sat behind his desk, his greying hair neatly combed, his cheeks clean-shaven, and his eyes boring into Cormac's with a scrutinising intelligence. He consulted a page in front of him.

'Your son's name is Jack McGovern?' he said, his Scottish accent much thicker than Mr Humphrey's.

'Yes,' Cormac said. 'And his mother's name is Lady Courcey. You may not have heard of our family yet, but chances are you will before long.'

He saw no reason to prevaricate on the matter. If this was going to be an insurmountable issue for the school, then it would be better to find out now and have done with it.

'Aye, the forthcoming divorce,' said Mr Cameron, indicating the page on his desk. 'Humphrey divulged it in his recommendation letter. Do you deem it to be a barrier to your son's enrolment at Balfour?'

'I think it's a fair assumption. We're concerned that he'd face prejudice, in spite of the school's distance from the scandal. Word has a way of spreading, whether through the other pupils or via the tutors. We don't want to expose him to such discrimination. We know what these institutions can be like.'

There was a pause as the headmaster regarded him with quiet appraisal. 'Did you attend one yourself?'

'No,' Cormac said, his tone brittle. 'I rose to my position later in life. And that, by the by, is another strike against Jack's name. His father is lower class by birth.'

Mr Cameron rubbed his clean-shaven jaw. 'Not to mention, his parents are as yet unmarried, therefore we must also add illegitimacy to the laddie's list of shortcomings.'

Cormac willed himself not to redden with shame. 'Indeed. So if you feel it would be best to end our interview now, I'll spare us both the time and take my leave.'

He had known this would be a mistake. It was only a pity he'd had to travel so far to confirm it; he was already dreading the arduous journey back.

Mr Cameron tapped his finger meditatively on Mr Humphrey's letter. '"These institutions",' he murmured. 'Tell me, what comes to mind when you think of such places?'

Cormac wanted to be blunt, but he tried to choose his words carefully. 'One hears troubling things. Harsh discipline that crosses the line into excessive cruelty. A culture where younger boys are made to suffer at the hands of the older ones. Punishments meted out if they write home and disclose the extent of their abuse.' He grimaced. 'Perhaps the rumours are an exaggeration of the reality, but they are still disturbing, even if only a fraction of them are true.'

Mr Cameron leaned back in his chair. 'And you fear Balfour School perpetrates these practices,' he stated evenly. He cocked his head to the side. 'Do you not trust Humphrey's recommendation?'

'He spoke very highly of the school,' Cormac admitted. 'But I wondered if he was somewhat overstating it due to his natural optimism. He has a tendency to see the best in people and places, occasionally more than they deserve.'

Mr Cameron chuckled. 'Aye, that's true. The man is optimistic to an immoderate degree. Nevertheless, it pleases me to say that in this case he has not embellished the truth. Balfour School is not typical of its kind. I know because I attended it as a laddie myself, and taught Latin here for fifteen years before attaining the title of headmaster.'

'In what ways does it differ?' Cormac asked, holding the man's gaze and daring him to provide his rationale.

'The ones that matter,' Mr Cameron replied, unruffled. 'Our ethos is that every boy with the intellect to excel deserves the opportunity to do so, regardless of his background. No one will bat an eye at Jack's illegitimacy, because nearly every pupil in this school carries some supposed defect of his own. We teach bastards, orphans, wards, impoverished boys who can only attend on scholarship, youngsters who have disgraced their families and been packed off in shame. Some of our pupils come from Scottish nobility, or even from upper-class families south of the border, but very few have any right to lord it over their peers. And neither is that a culture we will tolerate, unlike certain other schools which shall remain nameless in this conversation.'

His tone remained mild, but Cormac caught the disapproving curl at the corner of his lip.

'Balfour is no paradise,' the headmaster continued, 'but it is a place where the pupils are judged by their abilities, not by their families' titles or wealth.' He spread his hands. 'I, myself, am the third of my noble father's four by-blows. I wouldn't have prospered with such a blemished pedigree, had I not been allowed to thrive on my own merit.'

Cormac blinked as his error of judgement became plain to him.

Mr Cameron arched an eyebrow. 'Has anyone ever presumed to know your character before they've even met you?'

The answer came to Cormac without hesitation. 'Yes.'

'And have you ever been guilty of the same?'

'I think, perhaps, today,' he said with a rueful smile.

'We shall overlook it,' Mr Cameron said wryly. 'Now that you have conducted your assessment of Balfour's suitability as a school, shall I conduct my assessment of Jack's suitability as a pupil?'

For the first time, Cormac felt a flicker of anxiety at the prospect that Jack might not secure a place at what he now recognised as a most commendable institution.

'Let's see,' Mr Cameron said. 'Mixed lineage, yes. Scandal in the family, indeed. How about studious? Well-mannered? Cooperative?'

'All of the above,' Cormac said, unable to hide his pride.

'How does he fare in social situations?'

'He can be a little shy,' Cormac conceded. 'Especially when he's in the company of stronger personalities. It's Mr Humphrey's hope that Balfour School might encourage him to overcome that trait and flourish beyond it.'

'Aye, I think we could be of assistance in that area. But Jack would have to play his part and make an effort to engage with the other pupils. We can't help someone who doesn't want to be helped.'

Cormac recalled Jack standing at the window of his study, and the soft words he had spoken. 'I believe he's ready for that challenge.'

'Then we would be very glad to welcome him here.'

'You would?' Cormac said, relieved.

'Most assuredly. Humphrey already had me convinced, for he recommended the laddie very highly. Still, I understand that this appointment was necessary for you to take our measure too.'

Although Mr Cameron had every right to be reproachful, there was an amused twinkle in his eye. Without any further ado, their discussion shifted to the practicalities of accommodation, meals, uniform and fees, as though Cormac's earlier preconceptions had never entered the room. At the conclusion of it all, he gave the headmaster a solid handshake and departed from the office with the distinct awareness that he had just relearned a lesson he had somehow forgotten.

Buoyed by this encouraging meeting, he no longer felt so daunted by the lengthy return journey to Bedfordshire that lay ahead of him. As he rode back to Carstairs to spend one more night at The Glenside Inn, he decided that, since he was already this far north, he would make a detour to Yorkshire to visit Emily.

He and Rory had both accompanied her to Harrogate before the start of her first term at Blake-Fletchley, so he knew exactly where to go when he reached the town the next evening, having taken two trains and a short carriage ride to get there. He made his way to the art academy, where he found its halls rapidly emptying as the students finished their classes for the day. He wasn't sure how he would locate Emily, but then he spotted a young woman in a brown bonnet dodging out of the way of a group of laughing young men who didn't even acknowledge her as they strode by.

Cormac approached her, tipping his hat politely. 'Pardon me, miss,' he said, 'but would I be correct in assuming that you are Miss Jane Lyndon?'

The young woman stared, taken aback. 'I am. Do I know you, sir?'

'We haven't been introduced,' he said, offering her a reassuring smile. 'But I believe we have a mutual acquaintance—Emily Carey. I'm her father, Cormac McGovern.'

Recognition flickered in Jane's eyes, and her posture relaxed slightly. 'Ah, yes. Emily's spoken of you.'

'She's spoken of you too,' he said amiably. 'I was wondering if you might know where I could find her?'

'Well, that's a very good question,' Jane said. 'She never showed up for our classes today, leaving me to argue alone with Mr Parrish over his exclusion of females from a lecture about techniques in military paintings.'

'She never showed up?' he repeated. 'Did she send a note to explain her absence?'

'Not that I'm aware of,' Jane replied with a shrug, her peevish expression suggesting that she had not won the argument with her drawing master.

With a prickle of alarm, Cormac took his leave and hurried from the academy in the direction of Bilton. Though there was no doubt a reasonable explanation, his paternal instincts still stirred with concern.

The previous month's snow had melted away, enabling him to march quickly from the busy streets of Harrogate into the more peaceful environs of Bilton. Dusk had fallen by the time he reached the Fieldings' home and light shone from its front window as he pushed open the garden gate.

When Louise Shelby answered the door in response to his knock, she stood there gaping at him for five whole seconds before she said faintly, 'Are you a clairvoyant, Mr McGovern?'

'Why do you say that?' he asked, his unease mounting to panic. 'Where is Emily? Has something happened to her?'

'She's here,' Louise said, stepping back to let him enter the hallway. 'And she hasn't come to harm. But she is in exceedingly poor spirits, and she said not one hour ago that all she wanted was to go home to her family.'

Louise led him swiftly down the hall. As they passed the open door to the parlour, he caught sight of the curly-headed Philippa peeping out at him. Louise stopped at a door at the end of the hall and knocked on it before opening it gently.

'Emily, pet?' she said. 'Your father's here.'

A muffled gasp came from within as Louise ushered Cormac into the tiny room. He found his precious treasure hastening to sit up on her narrow bed, wiping her palms over her wet, puffy cheeks.

'Oh, Papa!' she exclaimed, her voice thick with tears. 'What on earth are you doing here?'

There would be time enough to explain that later. He crossed the room in two strides and sank onto the bed beside her, grasping her hands and studying her stricken face. The glow she had exuded when she last left Bewley Hall was utterly gone.

'What has upset you, *a stór*?' he murmured. 'Tell me, and I will do everything in my power to put it to rights.'

His first guess was that some devil at the art academy had treated her in an abominable way, and he was prepared to stalk back there right away and thrash the living daylights out of whoever had hurt his little girl. But she shook her head sadly.

'There's nothing you can do.' Her lower lip trembled. 'There's nothing anyone can do. I think it's just not meant to be, no matter how much I might wish it otherwise.'

Her voice broke. Comprehending the source of her grief, he gathered her into his arms and rocked her – no longer a child, but forever his child, and yet she might never rock a child of her own.

'Do you want me to bring you home?' he said tenderly. 'To your mother? To Rory?'

She responded with a grateful sob.

# Chapter 25

'This, that, these, those,' Mr Humphrey said, standing ramrod straight and enunciating the words with elaborate movements of his mouth and tongue.

Rory's knees bounced anxiously beneath the table in the tutor's room as he wrestled with his distracted thoughts. When Mr Humphrey gesticulated meaningfully at him, he drew in a resigned breath and, on the exhalation, repeated, 'This, that, these, those.' He didn't imitate Mr Humphrey's exaggerated diction, but he did make an effort to pronounce the words with the proper 'th' sound, and not to fall back on the more comfortable 'd' sound he had used for most of his life.

'Very good, Mr Carey,' the tutor said, beaming. 'Please repeat several times over while I check on the young masters' progress.'

Jack and Gus were seated on the opposite side of the table, toiling over open books containing arithmetic equations. Jack's head was bent in concentration as his pencil scratched at the paper, while Gus chewed on the end of his pencil and stared dolefully down at several empty spaces on his page.

Mr Humphrey cast an eye over Jack's calculations and gave an approving nod. 'Excellent, Master Jack. Keep working like this and you'll do splendidly where your future studies take you.'

Jack coloured with quiet pleasure, but his expression faltered as his gaze flickered to his oblivious younger brother. Then Mr

Humphrey peered over Gus's shoulder and clicked his tongue, not in annoyance but in sympathy.

'Let us decipher these equations together, Master Angus,' he said cheerily, seating himself on the chair next to Gus. 'We shall soon unravel their mysteries.'

He cocked an encouraging eyebrow at Rory as he took possession of Gus's pencil. With some reluctance, Rory began to recite 'this, that, these, those' multiple times, taking care not to let his pronunciation slip and reminding himself that his elocution needed to be flawless whenever the Duke of Desmond was obliged to make an appearance.

After five or six repetitions, he let his voice trail away. Mr Humphrey didn't notice, preoccupied as he was with explaining to Gus how to identify the lowest common denominator in a set of fractions. Rory pressed his palms to his bouncing knees in an attempt to still them, but his mind would not settle.

Emily had returned to Bewley Hall with her father the previous evening, her air of melancholy palpable. In the presence of her brothers and the servants, she had explained that her father's spontaneous visit to Yorkshire had been fortuitous as she'd been feeling a little unwell and, not wanting to be a burden to her kind hosts, she had thought it best to spend a week or so at home until she'd recovered. But later, in the privacy of their suite, she had confessed the distressing truth to Rory: they had suffered another bitter disappointment in their efforts to conceive.

She had wept in his embrace until a troubled sleep had claimed her. This morning, she'd permitted Jennie to dress her but had chosen not to join the family at breakfast, although she had urged Rory to follow his normal routine, which he had done without enthusiasm. Now, sitting here in the tutor's room, he wished he had ignored her gentle insistence. Every instinct clamoured at him to go seek her out and offer her whatever scrap of comfort he could.

He stood abruptly. Mr Humphrey looked over at him in surprise.

'I've got something I need to do right now,' Rory said. ''Tis important.'

'*It's* important,' Mr Humphrey corrected.

Rory repeated the words properly, shifting his weight from one foot to the other. Mr Humphrey squinted at him in concern and then nodded. As Rory hurried towards the door, he heard Gus say, 'I've just remembered I've got something important to go do as well, Mr Humphrey.'

'That may be,' replied the tutor with a chuckle, 'but I'm afraid masters don't have the same liberties as misters.'

Gus grumbled as Rory let the door swing shut behind him.

He strode along the corridor, heading first to Emily's parlour, certain that this was where she would have retreated in her despondency. However, when he pushed open the door, he found an empty room and a blank sheet of paper clipped to the drawing board on her easel.

He hesitated. Perhaps she was with her mother, confiding her sorrow. If so, Lady Bridget would be far better equipped than Rory to offer counsel on such intimate female matters. The thought eased his mind and he was almost about to retrace his steps when, glancing out the parlour window, he spotted Lady Bridget herself skirting the lawn in her riding habit, a crop in her gloved hand. His momentary relief vanished. If the lady was heading out for a ride, then Emily would certainly not be in her company.

Guessing that her preferred companion was probably solitude after all, he made his way upstairs to their private suite and, indeed, that was where he found her, huddled on the window seat in their bedchamber with her knees drawn up beneath her skirts. She was slow to turn her head towards him in the doorway, giving him enough time to see that she had been staring listlessly out the window. How long had she been in that forlorn position? Since he had left her before breakfast?

He closed the door behind him and crossed the room to the window seat. Instead of sitting beside her, he leaned against the wooden panelling on the wall next to the alcove. Neither of them spoke for several minutes. She usually filled any silence between them with animated chatter, but today she was mute. He was no good with words and he cursed that failing now more than ever. Still, he had to try.

'You're sad,' he said, deciding to start with the obvious.

The corner of her mouth quivered upwards as though she were attempting a brave smile. In the end, she only managed a rueful wince. 'I am.'

He swallowed. 'I know 'tis hard, but d'you want to talk about it?'

He wasn't disposed to correct his pronunciation outside of Mr Humphrey's presence, not when there were more important matters to focus on. It felt like a bit of a cheat to put the burden of speaking back onto her, but she took a shaky breath.

'I haven't told you about a disconcerting conversation I had with Louise last month,' she admitted. 'With the kindest of intentions, she helped me to see that I was harbouring two incompatible ambitions. Though both could co-exist for the time being, I realised that I would ultimately be forced to choose between pursuing my art and raising a family. And so, after much contemplation, I chose.' Her voice grew softer. 'I decided I wanted to be a mother more than anything else, and I was prepared to set aside my other dream for the sake of this one. And when I returned home to Bewley Hall and you and I lay together, I felt certain that this was our time at last. It had to be, for I had finally committed myself wholly to the goal of motherhood, in mind as well as body. I believed my divided heart had been all that held us back.'

He remembered the happiness she had radiated upon her departure from Bewley Hall – she had seemed almost brighter than the sun.

Now, a swell of anguish moistened her blue eyes. 'I was thus devastated when my courses came a few days ago—even heavier than usual, to add insult to injury.' She bowed her head. 'It seemed to me the definitive sign that my dearest wish simply cannot come true. I am grieving for a future that will never transpire.'

Even as his heart cracked for her loss and his own, he floundered for some words of solace. 'Just 'cause it didn't happen this time doesn't mean 'tis never going to happen.'

She sighed. 'Only it wasn't just this time, was it? It was last month too, and the month before that, and the month before that.'

She could have kept going but she didn't need to; over a year and a half into their marriage, it had been more months than either of them wanted to count.

'Sometimes these things take a while,' he tried limply.

'Most of the time they do not,' she countered, looking up at him with a little more fire in her expression. 'My mother conceived her very first time. She confessed as much when she came to me here after breakfast, though I had to pry it out of her.'

He shifted uncomfortably, the panelling digging into his back. He had no inclination to picture his parents-in-law engaging in that private act. While he knew, of course, that it had been essential in order to bring his beloved Emily into the world, it only reminded him that all parents were implicated in that deed, which made him think of his own mother, and that was most certainly not a thought in which he wanted to indulge any further.

He moved on swiftly. 'You're still really young. We both are.'

Her gaze dropped to her knees. 'Mama was already with child at my age.'

'But you're not your ma,' he said forcefully. 'Comparing yourself to her doesn't help.'

She swivelled away to the window, clearly wounded.

'I'm sorry,' he said at once, scrabbling to recover. 'I just meant that your body is different to hers, in lots of ways. You can't ride a horse as well as her, and she can't paint as skilfully as you. It stands to reason that there must be other differences too.'

He was glad when she turned back to him and he discerned the tiniest flicker of hope in her countenance.

'That's true,' she said. 'I ought not to expect our situations to be exactly the same.'

He tried not to wonder just how many intimate details she had shared with her mother in her attempt to find comparisons. 'I hope it helps, even a little bit.'

'It does,' she whispered. 'Thank you.'

She put out her hand to him and he stepped away from the panelling to take it. As their fingers touched, she grimaced. He pulled his hand back as though he had burned her.

'What did I do?' he asked.

'Nothing,' she said wearily. 'It's just a particularly bad cramp.'

She withdrew her own hand to massage her belly. He stood immobilised in place. Yes, he was her husband, and yes, they had participated in extremely familiar activities with each other's bodies. Still, her secret aching and bleeding seemed like a female area into which he was not entitled to intrude.

And yet, he yearned to do anything he could to ease the contours of pain on her face. Cautiously, he stepped close and let his hand hover above hers in the space between her torso and her bent knees. She peeped up at him and her eyes filled with tenderness. Sliding her hand away, she allowed him to press his own to the flat plane of her stomach. He felt the stiffness of her stays beneath her dress and negotiated his way below the rigid material, seeking a softer region of her flesh but taking care not to venture too far downwards. He didn't want to signal the wrong intention – he knew she was in neither the mood nor the condition to engage in passionate pursuits today.

Gently, he rubbed the lower part of her belly and watched her eyelids flutter shut. The lines on her forehead softened and she looked more like her youthful nineteen-year-old self. They stayed like that for a long time, his palm massaging her without pause and her breathing becoming slow and relaxed.

At last, she murmured, 'I feel so much better. I think I am tranquil enough now to try to sleep.'

He didn't say anything. He just slipped his arms under her knees and her back, gathered her up in her mass of skirts, and carried her over to their bed. Laying her down on top of it with the utmost care, he tugged the covers over from his side and draped them across her fully clothed figure. She mumbled something unintelligible. He kissed her forehead and backed away from the bed. By the time he shut the door, she was asleep.

Over the next two days, Rory spent much of his time in the company of Mr Comerford, who had scheduled a meeting with Lord Sinclair's land agent, Mr Longridge, to discuss an area of tree felling that would benefit both the Bewley and Sinclair estates. They rode out both days to conduct lengthy surveys of the site in question and drafted preliminary plans to determine the most efficient way to carry out the work, including the construction of a sawmill to process the timber. However, the morning after that, he rejoined Jack and Gus for another bout of Mr Humphrey's tutoring, although he sorely wished he hadn't when he entered the room and saw that the table and chairs had been pushed to the side. He knew which component of their lessons required moving the furniture, and he always dreaded it.

'Now, now, no long faces,' Mr Humphrey trilled. 'Every young gentleman must know how to dance.'

Rory recognised his own reluctance in Jack's slumped posture. Gus, on the other hand, sprang to attention, straightening his shoulders and his tricorne.

'I want to be a good escort when the time comes for me to accompany a lady to a ball,' he declared.

Rory and Jack were more than happy to let Gus be the primary beneficiary of Mr Humphrey's instruction, encouraging him to serve as the volunteer upon whom the tutor demonstrated all the dance moves. Still, they could not avoid participation entirely and in due course Mr Humphrey beckoned to them to perform the steps themselves. Adopting the proper stance for bowing at the introduction of a dance was bearable, but Rory wanted to sink into the floor when the tutor made him take his hand and turn in a circle one way and then the other.

'You must be lighter of foot, Mr Carey,' said Mr Humphrey. 'Remember that you are a noble gentleman, not an elephant.'

Although Rory was in no doubt that his humble origins had far more in common with elephants than noble gentlemen, he suffered on, stumbling through the movements to the tune of Mr Humphrey's indefatigable enthusiasm. Next to him, Gus received praise for his exuberance, though the tutor tempered it with a gentle caution that excessive energy could result in the inadvertent crushing of a lady's delicate toes. A stoic Jack persevered quietly alongside them without drawing too much attention.

Mr Humphrey's patience was greatly tested throughout the dancing lesson and yet he somehow managed to reach the end with a bright smile still affixed upon his face. As soon as he brought the proceedings to a conclusion, Jack and Gus tore out the door – the former looking relieved at his escape, the latter chirping that he couldn't wait to tell his ma what he had just learned – leaving Rory and Mr Humphrey to push the table and chairs back into place in the centre of the room.

'Don't glower like that, Mr Carey,' the tutor said in an amused tone. 'Dancing is not as torturous as you imagine. You will get better. And you never know—someday you might even enjoy it.'

Rory endeavoured to shake off his frown as he shoved a chair under the table. 'I'm no good at it,' he muttered. 'If I ever try to do this in public, I'm going to make a fool of myself. Worse, I'll make a fool of Emily.'

'Aye, you certainly will,' Mr Humphrey agreed, 'at your current level of ability. But I have a reputation to preserve, so I won't permit you to dance in public until you're ready. And I promise that you will improve with practice. First, though, you need to remove this pressure you've put upon yourself. You cannot hope for positive results when you are wound so tight with the strain of striving to meet the expectations of others. Allow your body to loosen up and eventually it will find its natural rhythm.'

Rory thrust the last chair into place and didn't respond. How could he explain to the tutor that the expectations had not been put on him by others but by himself? He knew Emily and her parents wouldn't think any less of him if he proved to be utterly incapable of keeping time in a waltz, but he would not forgive himself if he couldn't achieve those standards. Emily deserved only the best. If that wasn't him, then he'd had no business marrying her at all.

After leaving Mr Humphrey's room, he went in search of her; he suspected his dancing woes would amuse her and he longed to bring a smile back to her face. Once again, she was not in her parlour, so he made his way to their suite of rooms. He dreaded finding her curled up on the window seat in another state of melancholy, but this time the seat was empty and instead the sound of voices drifted from the adjoining bathing room. As he dithered in the centre of the bedchamber, Jennie emerged through the bathing room door with an armful of wet towels. There was a briskness to her step, which always grew more pronounced whenever her mistress was back in residence. She came to a surprised halt at the sight of Rory.

'Oh, Mr Carey,' she blurted. 'Um, Mrs Carey isn't disposed to—'

'It's quite all right, Jennie,' Emily called through the doorway. 'I am decent enough for my husband's eyes.'

She appeared from the bathing room enveloped in a long, thin, cream-coloured wrapper, knotting its sash around her waist. Her feet were bare and her hair was damp, its golden hue darkened to a deeper shade of caramel.

'There's no need to come back for now,' she said to Jennie, her tone light. 'I should like to take a nap before I get dressed. I'll ring the bell when I'm ready.'

Whether Jennie believed the excuse or not, she didn't betray any reaction. Curtseying, she left the bedchamber with the wet towels. As soon as she was gone, Emily skipped across the room to Rory and wrapped her arms around him.

'I had a bath and now I feel clean and wonderfully refreshed,' she said, beaming. 'It was quite ridiculous of me to be so dismal these last few days. My spirits are much better again.' She squeezed him happily and peeked up at him through her eyelashes. 'In case you didn't guess, the nap was only a pretence. I'm not sleepy at all.'

He tried to chuckle, but even to his ears it sounded false. When he endeavoured to loosen her grip on him, she tightened her hold.

'I'm ready to try again,' she said eagerly. 'Let's make a baby. I know it will happen this time. I'm sure of it.'

He detected the subtle vein of desperation beneath her eagerness and his heart dropped. Even before they had begun, she had already placed so much expectation upon the act. And to what depth of despondency might she sink next time if they were once more unsuccessful? They couldn't keep going through this same cycle of highs and lows month after month.

With a more determined effort, he detached himself from the circle of her arms and backed away. Her brows knitted together.

'Rory?' she said. 'What's the matter?'

He didn't know how to say it – he never had the right words. But then the solution came to him with sudden, striking clarity.

Mr Humphrey had given him the words.

'You need to remove this pressure,' he said quietly.

She blinked. 'What pressure?'

'The pressure you've put on yourself. On us.' He drew in a breath and let it out slowly as he sorted through the things Mr Humphrey had said, trying to choose the best way to communicate them to Emily. 'Every time we join, we're wound up so tight with expectation, hoping against hope that it'll finally happen. But 'tisn't fair on either of us. How can we expect a positive result when our bodies are under such stress? Surely the more we strain towards it, the less likely it becomes.'

She stared at him, utterly silent. To his alarm, her chin began to tremble. But then she said in a small, choked voice, 'You're right, of course. We cannot force it through will alone.' Her eyes glistened. 'In truth, it is only wishful thinking at this stage. I am convinced it will never come to pass.'

His alarm increased even further. 'I didn't mean for you to lose all hope,' he said hurriedly. 'Just to take the weight off our shoulders. We have to give it more time.'

She pressed her palms over her abdomen. 'But I yearn for a child so very much,' she whispered. 'How long will our bodies make us wait?'

He stepped close to her again and folded her into him, her cheek resting against his chest, the damp curls on her crown grazing his jaw. 'Maybe if we stop asking the question, it will be answered sooner rather than later.'

She sniffed and nodded. 'We shall continue to be patient. It may yet transpire when the time is right.'

In the silence that followed, he found a small, selfish comfort: Emily was safe. Childbirth was fraught with danger – it had almost claimed her mother's life when Gus was born. If Emily never conceived, at least they would be spared that terror.

The thought didn't mend the hurt, but it softened its edges, just a little.

She made to step out of his embrace but he held onto her, clasping her slender frame against him.

'There's something I'd like to do,' he said softly.

She peered up at him. 'What is it?'

'I want to show you that your body isn't just for making babies. 'Tis important for you to remember that you can just enjoy it as it is, without pressuring it to live up to any expectations.'

A faint pink colour bloomed in her cheeks. 'Oh,' she said, the corners of her mouth curving upwards. 'Yes, perhaps that is a lesson worth learning.'

Her fingers skimmed down his chest, reaching for the buttons on his coat, but he caught her by the wrists and shook his head.

'You don't need to do that,' he said. 'Today is just for you.'

Her eyes widened. 'Oh,' she said again, her tone pitched higher this time. 'B-but that's not an equal way of going about it.'

''Tis the way I want to do it,' he said firmly. 'Will you let me?'

She bit her lower lip. Then she gave him a bashful nod.

He released her wrists and reached for the sash of her wrapper. He wasn't inclined to speak any more words for now; it would be far easier to show what he meant by revering her body with his own. He was determined to demonstrate to her that, regardless of what additional joy might or might not come to them in the future, what they already shared was truly enough.

# Chapter 26

When the imposing façade of the Palace of Westminster came into view, Bridget shivered, despite the oppressive August heat that brought a gleam of sweat to the foreheads of the Londoners brushing past them on the street. Somewhere inside that towering edifice was a chamber where men were waiting to humiliate her. Her grip tightened on Cormac's arm and he drew her closer to his side, the only physical comfort he could offer in public.

'There's still time to reconsider,' he said.

'There isn't,' she replied.

'The lady is correct,' Mr Carruthers said on Bridget's other side. 'We are committed to this venture now.'

The lawyer did not have a critical role to play today, but the House of Lords had consented to his attendance at the hearing in recognition of his legal capacity. Cormac, on the other hand, would not be permitted inside the building.

As they approached the seat of the English parliament, Bridget found herself both awed and intimidated by its striking Gothic architecture, the sharp lines and unyielding symmetry speaking of conformity and inflexibility. She, with her deplorable lack of morals, was categorically not welcome.

They passed through the shadow of an enormous clock tower still in the midst of construction and found Garrett waiting beyond it in the company of his own lawyer, a moustachioed fellow Bridget recognised from his occasional visits to Wyndham House during the years she had lived there. Garrett grimaced as they drew near, and she glanced up to discern a wary frown on Cormac's countenance. This was the first time the two men had come face to face since Garrett had proposed the divorce. She hoped Garrett would manage to retain some measure of the civility he had shown her in the unkempt gardens of Oakleigh the previous November. He pursed his lips as they reached him.

'I'm afraid a fresh complication has arisen,' he said without preamble.

Cormac's expression darkened further. 'What's happened?'

'I have just learned who will comprise the panel of peers at today's hearing.' Garrett wrinkled his nose in obvious distaste. 'Lord Woodbury has been selected to chair the panel. I've had no personal dealings with him, but his reputation precedes him and he is not known for his compassion. He will be quite merciless, I expect.'

Bridget's stomach roiled.

'That, unfortunately, is not the worst of it,' Garrett continued. 'Lord Woodbury will be accompanied by two others. One of them, Lord Swaneset, is an acquaintance of mine and not a cause for concern, I believe. Apart from being personally associated with me, he has three sisters and two daughters, and his customary solicitude in their regard leads me to presume that we can count on a certain level of sympathy from him towards the gentler sex in general. The other, however' – Garrett swallowed – 'is the Duke of Northrop.'

'Oh, God damn it,' said Cormac.

'Indeed,' said Garrett. 'I had originally deemed this to be merely an exercise in degradation, and that the outcome would be a foregone conclusion. I am a member of the House of Lords, after all—they would not deny a fellow peer willing to go to these lengths to achieve his ambition. But the duke is a different matter. He may well wish to exact revenge for the actions of my wayward son in relation to his wife. There's a strong likelihood that he will put his weight behind a motion to reject the granting of the divorce.'

Which would mean that Bridget's abhorrent task today might yet come to naught, and she would have disgraced herself for no worthwhile purpose. Her sweat felt cold on her skin.

Garrett's expression verged on apologetic as he said to her, 'I fear you are walking into the lions' den to be devoured.'

She recalled the biblical story of Daniel, who was saved from the lions only by the hand of God. How she dreaded the snapping, salivating jaws of the men awaiting her.

Cormac gave Garrett a razor-sharp look. 'Are you prepared to protect her in there?'

'I'm not divine,' Garrett said wryly, 'but I shall do what I can.'

He took out a pocket watch and consulted it. With a jolt, Bridget remembered her father's pocket watch which she had gifted to Garrett in the early days of their relationship, only to retrieve it from his possessions when she ran away from London with Cormac. They had never spoken of this reclamation – this theft, as he no doubt viewed it – in all the years since. How angry had he been when he had discovered it missing from his bedchamber? Did he guess that it was now in Cormac's keeping?

He made no mention of it as he stowed away the watch and said, 'It's almost time. I'll meet you in the hearing chamber. Pryor will guide you there.'

With a brisk bow, he strode away, leaving even his lawyer behind. Bridget understood that there was a special entrance into the palace designated exclusively for peers, while all visitors, including commoners, clerks and journalists, were obliged to use a separate access point and to present documentation attesting to their right to enter.

Garrett's lawyer, Mr Pryor, led the way to this other entrance, bringing them to a stone archway that was less grand than the rest of the building. Liveried guards stood sentry in front of it.

'This is as far as I may go,' Cormac said, his reluctance palpable.

Bridget dropped her hand from his arm but he captured it in both of his own and bent his head to hers, their foreheads almost touching.

'I desperately wish you didn't have to do this,' he murmured, low enough that neither the lawyers nor the guards could overhear. 'Just remember that you are worth a thousand times more than the person they will try to reduce you to.'

She gulped down the lump in her throat. 'I have the strength to do this,' she whispered, 'because I know that your faith and love go with me.'

'I'll be right here waiting for you afterwards.' He let go of her hand and brushed his left knuckles against her right hip before turning to Mr Carruthers. 'I'm relying on you to intervene if it proves necessary. Should they push too far, get her out of there.'

Mr Carruthers nodded. 'I'll monitor the situation closely.'

Cormac stepped back and Bridget, Mr Carruthers and Mr Pryor approached one of the guards, who held out his hand, unsmiling. Mr Pryor produced the documents Garrett had signed on their behalf and the guard retreated beneath the archway, disappearing from sight. A long, tense minute went by before he returned and handed the papers back to Mr Pryor with a curt gesture for them to proceed. His manner seemed even more dour after his brief absence and Bridget caught his fleeting look of disapproval as she passed him. Was it simply because she was a woman whose presence would taint these hallowed halls of masculine power? Or had he learned the scandalous purpose of her visit? She cast one final glance over her shoulder and drew courage from Cormac's unwavering blue gaze. Then she faced forwards again, straightened her spine and walked resolutely towards her fate.

Inside the palace, an attendant greeted them grimly and motioned for them to follow him. Mr Pryor affirmed that he already knew the way, but the attendant ignored him and set off at a brisk pace, leaving Bridget and the two lawyers to hurry along in his wake. The dim interior was pleasantly cool after the heat outside, though that was the only welcoming aspect of the building; its hallways seemed deliberately designed to intimidate with their vaulted ceilings, shadowed recesses and walls adorned with sombre portraits of long-dead statesmen whose gazes seemed to judge all who passed beneath them. Feeling both dwarfed and censured, Bridget nevertheless carried on, one echoing footstep at a time.

She lost track of the route they took through the cavernous passages and up long flights of steps, but eventually the attendant stopped at a solid wooden door and gave them a sharp nod before marching away. Mr Pryor went first, opening the door and stepping through. Mr Carruthers prompted Bridget to go next and followed close behind her as she crossed the threshold, her heart beating in her throat.

Although opulent in its features, the size of the hearing chamber was smaller than she had expected it to be. There was a dais at the top of the room, occupied by a wide desk and three empty chairs. In front of it stood two separate tables clearly meant for the litigants and their legal counsel – Garrett was not yet present. To the side, a clerk sat with an unimpeded view of both the dais and the litigants' tables; his own small table bore an open record book, an inkpot and three pens, and he already clutched a fourth pen, looking eager for the proceedings to begin. Against the back wall, a seating area included two rows of benches for journalists and other privileged spectators; Bridget winced upon seeing that it was completely full.

A low muttering rose up as she entered the chamber and the appraising stares of everyone present swung in her direction. The small room might seem like a private setting but this was very much a public hearing – she eyed the journalists poised to write in their notebooks and knew that her reputation would be in tatters by the morrow. Thank goodness the lecture she had arranged with Reverend Hartley had taken place earlier in the summer and the collected donations had already been distributed. Without the benefit of Frances's altruistic services beyond London, and buoyed by her and Cormac's comparatively mild reception from the theatre-goers in Dublin (at least, until the riot broke out), she had ventured to put her own name on her correspondence with the reverend. Their interactions had gone smoothly at the time, but she doubted whether he, or the wealthy patrons who had attended the lecture, would deign to have any further dealings with her after this. She felt a pang of selfishness that going ahead with the divorce would impinge upon her ability to help the people who were still suffering from the blight. However, it would not stop her altogether – she and Cormac would simply need to carry out their charitable efforts in total anonymity from this point forth.

Mr Carruthers pulled out a chair for her at one of the tables and she sat, careful not to make eye contact with anyone. It would have taken considerable influence or prominent connections to secure a place on the limited spectators' benches, so she could assume that those who had managed to claim a spot were especially keen to witness her downfall. She didn't want to know who harboured such a loathsome thirst. At least her back would be facing them for the duration of the hearing.

Garrett strode into the chamber a moment later and joined his lawyer at the other table without even a glance towards Bridget. She gritted her teeth and berated herself for having anticipated some kind of encouraging signal from him. In this room they could only be adversaries.

With both litigants now present, the air in the chamber seemed to thicken with expectation. She heard rustling and creaking behind her as the spectators shifted on their benches. The clerk's knuckles were almost white as he gripped his pen, his attention fixed on a discreet door in the wall behind the dais. Then the door opened and three figures came through it.

The first gentleman carried himself with an imperiousness that bordered on regal, his straight-backed posture and sweeping gaze redolent of a monarch surveying his court. When his haughty glare landed on the other litigant's table, Garrett visibly flinched and Bridget realised with a sinking feeling that this had to be the Duke of Northrop. The man adjusted his cuffs with measured precision and she caught sight of the signet ring on his little finger, a thick band of gleaming gold.

The second gentleman didn't exude any such superiority. Although not elderly by any means, his shoulders were markedly stooped, as if he were trying to take up less space. Expression inscrutable, he cast Garrett a single, brief nod before stepping aside to reveal the final figure.

Bridget blinked. The third gentleman was smiling graciously, the first smile she had seen all day. He had a handsome face, and laughter lines clustered at the corners of his mouth and eyes. Inclining his head courteously towards his fellow peers, he moved forwards to claim the middle chair on the dais. The duke settled himself on the man's right-hand side, leaving the stooped gentleman to take the third seat on his left.

The man in the centre paused for a moment before addressing the room in a honeyed tenor voice. 'This hearing is now in session, on the 14<sup>th</sup> of August, 1849. Presiding today are His Grace, the Duke of Northrop, the esteemed Viscount Swaneset, and myself, the Earl of Woodbury. We have convened to deliberate upon the petition for divorce put forward by Viscount Wyndham. The evidence presented and the testimonies given in this chamber will determine whether the matter will be brought before the House of Lords for further debate and ultimate resolution.'

Bridget swallowed at the obvious message in his words: their desired outcome was in no way guaranteed. She kept her focus trained steadily on the wall just above his head, unwilling to betray any sign that she felt daunted by the occasion. In her peripheral vision, she glimpsed the clerk scribbling swiftly in his record book.

Lord Woodbury carried on. 'We now acknowledge the key parties in attendance: the petitioner, Lord Wyndham, accompanied by his counsel, Mr Pryor, and the respondent, Lady Wyndham, accompanied by her counsel, Mr Carruthers.'

She cringed at the title, but of course she could not object to it – she was here, after all, in her role as viscountess. Under these circumstances, Lady Courcey was a secondary and irrelevant rank.

'The petition submitted by Lord Wyndham seeks to dissolve the marital union between himself and Lady Wyndham. According to documents lodged in advance of this hearing, grounds for divorce have already been established in the ecclesiastical courts, where a decree of legal separation has been obtained, and the litigants now wish to wholly end the marriage by a private Act of Parliament.'

A chorus of disapproving whispers rose up behind Bridget.

Lord Woodbury raised a hand for silence; unlike a judge in a courtroom, he had no gavel to command order. 'I must remind all present that this is a solemn proceeding, and that disruptions of any nature will not be tolerated.' He levelled a kindly gaze at Bridget and she wondered whether his harsh reputation was somewhat undeserved, especially when he continued, 'We understand that matters such as these are deeply personal and often painful, and we urge all parties to maintain composure and dignity throughout. Together, my fellow panel members and I will consider the merits of the petition in accordance with the statutes of our institution and the principles of fairness.'

Bridget chanced a glance at the Duke of Northrop; his features were steely.

'If there are no objections,' said Lord Woodbury, 'we will now hear from Mr Pryor on behalf of the petitioner.'

Garrett's lawyer pushed back his chair and stood. Bridget caught the flicker of discomfort in his countenance before he carefully schooled it into an expression of cool detachment.

'My lords, I am honoured to speak for Lord Wyndham on this grave matter. It is our submission that the evidence presented here today will fully satisfy the legal and moral grounds required for the granting of this divorce. I should like to affirm that Lord Wyndham is a gentleman of integrity and that he has no wish to promote any unnecessary conflict. Having endured considerable personal anguish throughout this process, it is his earnest desire to bring this lamentable chapter to a close with all due propriety.'

Bridget bit the tip of her tongue. Of course, Garrett had to be presented as the innocent, injured party in order to accomplish their goal, but the injustice of this fanciful depiction of his character nonetheless nettled her.

Mr Pryor delicately cleared his throat. 'My lords, it is with regret that I must draw your attention to the undeniable fact that Lady Wyndham has engaged in conduct contrary to the solemn obligations of her marriage. The particulars already provided to the ecclesiastical court have established beyond dispute that she formed an improper connection outside the bounds of matrimony, thereby violating the sacred trust inherent in the union. It is my understanding that Lady Wyndham herself intends to offer a candid acknowledgment of her actions in your noble presence today, thereby substantiating the grounds upon which this petition has been brought.'

He turned expectantly, and the heads of the three panel members swivelled towards Bridget. She gulped. Now? She had anticipated a lengthy spell of tedious legal discourse before she would be called upon to speak. Startled, she looked at Mr Carruthers, who withdrew the prepared statement from inside his coat.

'Good luck,' he murmured, handing it to her.

She accepted the piece of paper numbly and stared down at it. Although she had rehearsed her testimony before coming to the palace, the sentences now seemed to jumble together without making any sense. She blinked rapidly to try to clear her vision.

'My lady?' Mr Carruthers said, leaning closer in concern.

'I'm fine,' she croaked.

She rose from her seat, her pulse thundering in her ears. She could do this. She was facing the hardest part now, but it would all be worth it once she was finally able to become Cormac's wife.

'My lords,' she started in a wavering tone, and then stopped. No, that would not do. It was prudent to be compliant, but she would not cower before them. Clutching the page tightly, she read on in a stronger voice, 'I, Lady Wyndham, do hereby confess that during the course of my marriage to Lord Wyndham, I did knowingly and willingly engage in a relationship of an adulterous nature with Mr Cormac McGovern, with whom I have cohabited since my departure from my husband's household. I committed this transgression—'

At this juncture, she was obliged to stop once more because the gasps behind her drowned out her words. She expected Lord Woodbury to admonish the spectators into silence again, but he merely waited, allowing the scandalised reactions to continue without interruption. She felt the agony of every passing second – now that she had begun, she only wanted to finish her statement as quickly as possible and be done with it. Eventually, the noise petered out and she took a steadying breath.

'I committed this transgression in the year 1836 and have persisted with it to the present day, thus breaking the vows of my marriage and neglecting the duty owed to my husband. I make this admission freely and without coercion, on the understanding that it serves as evidence in these proceedings and that it corroborates the petition set forth by Lord Wyndham in seeking the dissolution of our union. I submit myself to the judgement of this panel and the consequences that may arise from my actions.'

When she ceased speaking this time, there wasn't a sound in the chamber; it seemed she had rendered her audience speechless. She resisted the urge to look over her shoulder and view their appalled faces. Instead, she concentrated on Lord Woodbury, who had steepled his hands under his chin and was regarding her with a furrowed brow.

'Thank you, Lady Wyndham,' he said at last. 'I have no doubt it took tremendous resolve to articulate those words aloud. May we ask some clarifying questions about your statement to ensure we have a full comprehension of the facts?'

'You may,' she said, as Mr Carruthers had forewarned her of this.

He smiled at her. 'How obliging of you. Frankly, my lady, I am impressed. Your lack of humility is quite stunning, though I daresay it is a fitting reflection of the vice in your character.'

She recoiled as if he had slapped her. The clerk paused in the midst of his frantic writing to gape up at the dais. Lord Woodbury's pleasant expression remained unchanged.

'You cannot be surprised that we would perceive you in this light,' he said. 'Your conduct has been a reprehensible insult to your entire sex. Did you not consider the damage you would do to your fellow females when you strutted down this path of immorality?'

As speechless as the spectators, she found herself unable to respond. She had not anticipated that the interrogation would be so direct and offensive.

'Come now, Lady Wyndham, you agreed to answer our questions. Kindly tell us: did it occur to you in the midst of your selfish passions to contemplate the broader ramifications? That your shameful behaviour would lead to a widespread reduction in general respect for so-called "ladies"? That we gentlemen would be impelled to suspect such wantonness lurks within every woman, though she bats her eyelashes innocently in public? You belonged to a distinguished circle of females granted rank and society status. These privileges came with responsibilities, which you so carelessly cast aside. Did you not pause to think of all the women who would be tarnished by their association with you?'

It felt like her throat was swollen with influenza, so difficult was it to get the words out. 'I did not.'

He shook his head in disappointment. 'How terribly self-centred. Do you believe it was worth it? Has your own carnal satisfaction outweighed the loss of honour suffered by the ladies of your class?'

She sent a desperate look of entreaty to both Lord Swaneset and the Duke of Northrop, but, though the former shifted uneasily in his seat, neither intervened. It appeared that they were there to make up the numbers and that Lord Woodbury was the driver of this inquisition. He raised his eyebrows at her in expectation.

'I-I cannot answer that,' she stammered.

He sighed. 'Let us ask you some easier questions, then. I trust these will be less taxing for you.' He tapped a finger against his cheek in exaggerated deliberation. 'When precisely did your improper relationship with Mr McGovern begin?'

She realised she was clutching her statement hard enough to scrunch the paper and loosened her grip slightly. 'February 1836.'

'And where did that act of criminal conversation take place?'

'At Wyndham House on Berkeley Square,' she said faintly.

'Dear me, you took him into the bed you shared with your husband? Your audacity truly knows no limits.'

She risked a glance in Garrett's direction. His gaze was fixed straight ahead on the dais, but she discerned the taut line of his jaw.

'Help us to detect some level of virtue in you,' Lord Woodbury said, pressing his palms together as though in plea. 'Did you discourage Mr McGovern in his pursuit of you? Did you remind him of your marriage vows and protest against his advances? Perhaps this affair only commenced because he forced himself upon you?'

'No,' she said in a clear voice that could not be misinterpreted. 'I accepted him willingly.'

Lord Swaneset winced and she knew she was saying nothing to ameliorate her situation. Nevertheless, she would not have false slurs against Cormac printed in the papers.

'So you surrendered to a reckless indulgence in your base impulses,' said Lord Woodbury, his tone grave while his eyes glinted with glee.

She bristled. 'Our connection was not the product of a fleeting moment of lust. I have known Cormac since we were childhood friends. We cherished a lifelong bond that became rooted in deep love.'

Did she hear a murmur of sympathy behind her? Lord Woodbury ignored it.

'If your acquaintance is so longstanding, should we thus infer that you had been on familiar terms with Mr McGovern during your engagement to Lord Wyndham? Were you unfaithful even before your marriage took place?'

She blanched. Her early friendship with Cormac at Oakleigh, as well as their later roles as employer and servant, had already been documented in the evidence submitted to the ecclesiastical court, but only on paper. If she allowed Lord Woodbury to pursue this line of questioning now, would he dare to go a step further and suggest that Emily had been conceived before Bridget wed Garrett?

Mr Carruthers stood quickly. 'My lords, the scope of this inquiry pertains strictly to events within the bounds of the marriage between Lord and Lady Wyndham. Scrutinising what may or may not have preceded it is irrelevant and beyond the remit of this esteemed panel.'

He sat back down and she tried to conceal her relief when Lord Woodbury nodded in acquiescence. He appeared unperturbed by the lawyer's intervention; she supposed his insinuation would be more than enough to feed the hungry journalists, who would spread their speculations without any further steering on his part.

'Let us turn to the matter of your motivation, my lady,' he said instead. 'Why would you ever consider straying from your husband? You made a fine match in marrying above your station.'

'Rank isn't everything,' she said in a low voice. 'Ours was an unhappy union.'

Lord Woodbury's expression filled with concern and he leaned forwards. 'I am very sorry to hear that, my lady. Was your husband abusive? Did he beat you?'

'No,' she admitted. For all his failings, Garrett had never been physically violent with her, although he had come close to it that day he burned the wooden bird.

'Perhaps he confined you to the house, then? Limited your social engagements? Deprived you of your household allowances?'

She compressed her lips. 'No.'

'I beg you to enlighten us. In what manner did he make you so miserable that you felt compelled to flee from him?'

'He was...cold.'

Lord Woodbury affected a look of horror. 'A severe crime, indeed. So he was not demonstrative enough in his emotions and you deemed that sufficient justification to abandon the sacred institution of marriage?'

She cringed. 'It was more than that. He—he never took my feelings into account. He insisted we move to London, though it was against my will, and—'

'Permit me to extend my sympathies for your grievous burden,' Lord Woodbury interrupted. 'He brought you to a luxurious home in a vibrant city, where you had substantial wealth and influence as a viscountess. What dismal circumstances to contend with.'

She ground her teeth. 'He made it plain that my preferences were inconsequential and that he would dictate the course of our lives.'

'Did you not promise to honour and obey him on your wedding day? It strikes me as a weakness in *your* nature, and not his, that you chose to dispense with the holy vows you made before God.'

It took all her willpower to hold back the tears threatening to surface. She wouldn't expect a man of privilege to understand what it was like for a woman to have no agency of her own.

'He had numerous mistresses,' she choked out.

Lord Woodbury cocked his head to the side, assuming an air of boredom. 'My lady, many husbands seek diversion outside the home. That is hardly a cause for objection.'

Her insides burned with outrage, though she was entirely unsurprised. By the standards of these lords, a wife's duty was to turn a blind eye and never dream of straying herself. The duke exemplified this hypocrisy – he indulged in his own affairs and yet demanded fidelity from his wife when she gave her attentions to Patrick. Bridget yearned to point out this duplicity, but it would not serve to antagonise a member of the panel while in her current precarious situation.

'And are these all of Lord Wyndham's faults?' Lord Woodbury pressed. 'He didn't do anything else to offend you?'

She wanted to growl with frustration. Of course Garrett had many other faults, but she was not at liberty to divulge them. If she told the panel how he had aided her mother in orchestrating Cormac's banishment from Oakleigh and then sabotaged his prospects of gaining employment on any other estate, she would once again run the risk of revealing their liaison before her marriage. If she complained about the fact that he'd had his agent follow her in Boston, the panel would only argue that a gentleman had every right to try to find his missing wife.

And his worst transgressions of all could never be uttered in public, for if she disclosed the abominable way he had treated Mary, or his deceitfulness in luring Emily to London, then she would also expose Patrick's illegitimate origins, which she simply could not bring herself to do, no matter how much it might bolster her own position.

Lord Woodbury smirked. 'I take it by your silence that you have nothing further to add.'

She didn't know what to say without implicating others in her accusations. She peeked sidelong at Mr Carruthers, but he gave her a rueful shrug, unable to offer any helpful intercession this time.

'In that case,' Lord Woodbury said jauntily, 'I feel obliged to propose a new motion for the consideration of this hearing. Evidently, Lady Wyndham does not have reasonable grounds for abandoning her husband, whose sins are minor at best. Before we proceed any further on the matter of their divorce, might we not recommend that Lord Wyndham put forward a petition for the restitution of his conjugal rights instead? Such a step would be far preferable in preserving the sanctity of marriage.'

Bridget gaped up at the dais as Lord Woodbury looked to his right and left, seeking the approbation of his companions. Surely she had not heard him correctly?

'It is a prudent proposal that calls for closer scrutiny,' the Duke of Northrop said with a terse nod.

Lord Swaneset shot a furtive glance towards the petitioner's table as though trying to divine which response Garrett would prefer. 'Perhaps it should be considered,' he said hesitantly.

A frisson of cold dread rippled down Bridget's spine. 'No,' she croaked, but her protestation went unheard as Lord Woodbury carried on with a warm smile.

'Wouldn't it be a more uplifting occasion today if, instead of sundering this marriage, we succeeded in reconciling the couple? We would most certainly welcome Lord Wyndham's altering of his petition if he would rather appeal to his spouse to rejoin him in their marital home and resume her wifely duties.'

Bridget's statement slipped from her frozen fingers and landed soundlessly on the table in front of her. A wave of nausea surged in her stomach. Next to her, Mr Carruthers jumped to his feet.

'My lords,' he said sharply, 'that is not the issue before you today.'

'But oughtn't it to be?' Lord Woodbury responded in a silky voice. 'From the scant evidence provided by the lady herself, it is clear that she has unjustly deserted her husband. Should he declare himself willing to maintain their union after all, then he would be within his rights to file a petition compelling her to fulfil her role as his wife again. I feel confident that we would find in his favour, as it would be a much happier outcome of this day's proceedings.'

There was a loud roaring in Bridget's ears. 'Reconciliation is not a viable option,' she managed to utter, fearing she would vomit.

Lord Woodbury contemplated her with polite scepticism. 'Is it not a woman's obligation, by both law and morality, to return to her husband if he demands it?'

'I endured a joyless life in Berkeley Square for as long as I could,' she said hoarsely. 'Returning to it would not preserve the sanctity of marriage—it would only mock it.'

In a gentle tone, he said, 'It behoves me to remind the lady that, were she to refuse to comply, she would face penalties as severe as financial sanctions or even incarceration.'

This could not be happening. Throat clogged with panic, she swung her gaze across to the petitioner's table. Garrett was still facing forwards, and Mr Pryor wouldn't make eye contact with her. Her stomach heaved again and she put her hand over her mouth.

Had this been Garrett's plan all along? Had his proposition of divorce merely been a ruse to lure her to this chamber and entrap her? She imagined the horror of being forced to go back to Berkeley Square after the hearing, crossing its threshold like a condemned prisoner, confined once more to that shadow of an existence.

No, she could *never* go back there.

And yet, the law had the power to compel her.

Her heart plummeted as she caught sight of Lord Woodbury's diabolical grin and realised that he must have acquired his copious laughter lines from cruel amusement, since there was no kindness in him. What a scoundrel. Still, it was possible that he was only a co-conspirator and not the chief architect of this vile scheme.

She dropped her hand. 'Look at me,' she hissed in Garrett's direction.

She didn't care who heard the terror and desperation in her voice. She would demand that he face her if he was going to betray her.

Slowly, so slowly, he turned his head towards her. And she saw it there in his eyes: his desire for victory. That same compulsion had driven him before – he had once confessed that he had married her, despite her infidelity, because he simply had to win. Every relationship in his life was a contest to be dominated and conquered. If the panel granted him the authority to drag her back to Wyndham House, he could claim her as a trophy of his triumph.

In that moment, she felt a spear of disgust go through her – not for him, but for herself. She had believed this man was actually capable of change. More fool her.

His gaze narrowed as though he could tell what she was thinking. He rose from his seat without any sense of urgency and swivelled to face the dais once more, straightening his coat sleeves.

'My lords,' he said, his demeanour wholly unruffled. 'I am gratified by your solicitude. It is truly flattering that you would demonstrate such eagerness for a reconciliation between Lady

Wyndham and myself. I can only thank you most sincerely for your generosity in proposing this alternative resolution.'

Bridget's heart thumped painfully against her ribs and she cast a fleeting look over her shoulder at the door. Should she make a run for it? It was a reckless idea, and she would likely get lost in the palace's maze of passages, but if she could find a place to hide until they stopped searching for her—

'However,' Garrett continued, 'I must decline the proposition you have suggested.'

Her head whipped back to the petitioner's table as shocked whispers emanated from the back of the room. Garrett was staring coolly at Lord Woodbury, who raised an inquisitive eyebrow in return.

'Indeed?' the gentleman said. 'May we enquire as to your reasoning behind that decision?'

Garrett's jaw tightened. 'Before I entered this chamber, I had already come to the definite conclusion that the lady and I are not suited to each other. I'm afraid this "happy marriage" you envision is a fanciful notion. Were she and I to live once more under the same roof, there would be nothing but unhappiness between us. I am entirely convinced that divorce is the best option for all concerned.'

Bridget's breath leaked out of her as she pressed both of her palms onto the table for support.

'What a pity,' Lord Woodbury said with a sorrowful shake of his head. 'You are quite sure you wish to proceed with your original petition?'

'I am,' said Garrett.

Bewildered by the rapid turn of events, Bridget's whole body started to tremble with shock and relief. Mr Carruthers put his hand on her arm to keep her steady.

'And what about the other guilty party?' Lord Woodbury asked. 'Are you of a mind to sue him for the debauching of your wife?'

Garrett pursed his lips. He seemed to struggle with his answer, but at last he said, 'No, I choose not to pursue that course of action either.'

Untroubled that his meddling had not yielded results, Lord Woodbury spread his hands. 'Then I believe we have heard all the testimony relevant to this hearing. It is now the responsibility of this panel to determine whether the evidence that has been presented warrants advancing the matter to the House of Lords.'

Bridget wondered whether the three gentlemen would withdraw to deliberate over their judgement, but the Duke of Northrop sat up rigidly and said, 'I recommend that the petition be denied.'

'It is my view that the petition should be granted,' Lord Swaneset piped up, seeming relieved to have identified which side of the dispute he was meant to be on.

Lord Woodbury looked down at Bridget with a smug expression; no doubt he was elated to hold the deciding vote. Her gut twisted as she anticipated his verdict and she dearly wished she had never come here today to be subjected to such brutal treatment for no reason at all.

But then he declared, 'I side with Lord Swaneset. At a majority of two to one, this panel has decided to progress the motion to the next stage of debate in the main house. Following that, a decision will be reached as to whether an act may be passed sanctioning the divorce.'

The duke's lip curled sourly but he didn't gainsay his fellow peers. Bridget stared at Lord Woodbury in disbelief. After pushing for the alternative, why would he now be so quick to approve this outcome? The corners of his eyes and mouth crinkled in delight, causing her stomach to heave yet again with revulsion. Had he just been toying with her all along? How could he call himself a gentleman when he behaved like such a beast?

At least there was one man who had proved himself to be better than she had given him credit for. Garrett gave the panel a curt nod in acknowledgement of their ruling as they rose to leave, before turning to murmur something to Mr Pryor. Should she approach him and offer her thanks for his rare display of integrity?

Mr Carruthers tightened his grip on her arm. 'My lady, I would advise you to make a swift exit.'

She followed his apprehensive gaze; the journalists had leapt up from their benches and were advancing towards her with open notebooks and avid expressions.

'Yes, let's hurry,' she mumbled.

However, they had barely stepped away from the table when the first man blocked their path.

'Lady Wyndham, what do you have to say about the state of your reputation?' he asked eagerly.

'Do you regret leaving your husband?' another called from behind him.

'Do you believe you've set a scandalous precedent for other women?' demanded a third as he snatched up her abandoned statement from the table.

'How can you justify your sinful choice?'

That one made her pause. She sought out the speaker, a youth hurriedly reaching for the chewed pencil tucked behind his ear. He looked scarcely old enough to shave, let alone grasp the breadth of the struggle that had brought her to this point.

'I chose love,' she said calmly. 'And I would choose it again without repentance.'

His mouth fell open in astonishment as she strode away to the door.

# Chapter 27

Smoke billowed past the window and the wheels clacked in their relentless, noisy rhythm as the train rattled along its tracks. Cormac and Jack sat opposite one another, their knees almost touching in the narrow compartment. Cormac surreptitiously eyed his son, whose attention remained fixed on the blurred landscape beyond the sooty glass; the boy hadn't uttered a single word since they boarded the Caledonian Railway just before the Scottish border.

Tapping his fingertips nervously against each other, Cormac continued to steal glances at Jack, desperate to know what he was thinking. At last, he blurted, 'Are you anxious, *a mhac*? It would be perfectly understandable if you are.'

Jack dragged his gaze away from the window. 'I am,' he admitted.

'Tell me what's troubling you,' Cormac urged, 'and I'll do my best to allay your concerns.'

Jack clasped his hands together and bit his lip. 'I'm worried about Gus.'

Cormac blinked. 'I see,' he said.

He, too, had been dwelling on how Gus would fare in Jack's absence – ever since they'd broken the news that his older brother would be going away to school, Gus had been far quieter than usual, and he had visibly struggled to hold back tears when Cormac and Jack had departed from Bewley Hall early that morning. However, Cormac was surprised that Gus was foremost in Jack's thoughts at this moment, considering the upheaval that was imminent in his own life.

'Are you worrying about how he will cope without you?' he asked.

'Yes,' Jack confessed. 'The longest we've ever been apart is a day, and now we won't see each other until I come home for Christmas. Those four months will crawl by if he's feeling very lonely.' Jack hesitated. 'There's also the concern that I won't be able to keep him in check when one of his more harebrained ideas occurs to him.'

It suddenly struck Cormac that Jack must have actively prevented some of Gus's wildest schemes from coming to fruition in the past, and he experienced a rush of thankfulness that Jack had always been there up to now to rein in his younger brother.

'Don't fret too much,' he said. 'We'll keep him busy while you're away, and Mr Humphrey will see to it that he works hard on his lessons. If he applies himself with enough diligence, he might even join you at Balfour School next September.'

Jack's eyes flickered with cautious hope. 'You think so?'

'I certainly hope so.' Cormac paused. 'Do you...have any other worries? About school, perhaps?'

Jack shrugged. 'Not really. I mean, I'm nervous, but I'm sort of looking forward to it too.' He met Cormac's gaze directly. 'And I know what's expected of me. I won't let you down.'

How did this conversation turn into the son reassuring his father, when it was supposed to be the other way around?

'You have nothing to prove,' Cormac said, forcing the words past an unexpected blockage in his throat. 'And also, I trust, nothing to fear. The headmaster seems to be a good man, and he has promised me that Balfour fosters an encouraging environment.'

Jack gave a buoyant nod, his manner so credulous that it made Cormac seize up with misgiving.

'Having said that,' he went on carefully, 'you won't be in a position to ascertain the truth until you're there. If anything feels amiss, you must write at once to let us know.'

Jack's expression faltered and Cormac felt guilty for planting the seed of doubt; he didn't want the lad to lose his optimism. Still, it was best to be prepared for less favourable eventualities.

'I'm only saying that it's worth being on your guard a little,' he said, grimacing as he dug a deeper hole. 'If you're unhappy in any way, make sure you tell us.' Conscious that these institutions had a propensity for monitoring their pupils' letters home, he added, 'You don't even need to put it in so many words. Just mention that you're missing your dog Jasper, and I will come for you without delay.'

'But I don't have—' Jack started with a frown, then cut himself off. 'Oh, I understand.'

Cormac winked at him, hoping to diffuse the tension he had created. Jack's responding smile was genuine, if a touch tentative. In the next instant, it faded and his brows knitted together.

'There's someone else I'm worried about,' he said timidly.

'Who?'

'Ma.'

'What troubles you about her?' Cormac asked, trying to keep his tone light.

'She hasn't laughed once since you came back from your trip to London last month.'

Cormac regarded his son in startled silence. The lad truly absorbed every detail around him with unerring perception. How much should he share with him?

'She...had a difficult experience there,' he acknowledged quietly.

In truth, he still shuddered when he recalled her pallor as she emerged from the palace after the hearing. She had hurried past the guards at the entrance, fled by Cormac where he stood waiting, and been violently ill against the sand-coloured stone wall of the building. When he caught up to her, all he could do was stroke her back and murmur soothingly to her in ignorance until Mr Carruthers had appeared and provided the details of what had transpired in the hearing chamber. By the time the lawyer had finished, Cormac found himself utterly despising the vengeful Duke of Northrop and the spineless Lord Swaneset, but it was Lord Woodbury whom he wished he could tear limb from limb.

'That goddamned blackguard,' he had snarled, shaking with rage. That he had dared to propose Bridget return to Garrett was both infuriating and frightening. If Cormac had known what was afoot, he would have stormed inside the building to confront those so-called gentlemen in unbridled fury. He had been on the brink of doing just that anyway, but Mr Carruthers's level-headed counsel restrained him – they had achieved their goal, and a reckless outburst on Cormac's part would accomplish nothing except perhaps to provoke the panel into reversing their decision.

And what a hard-won decision it had been. When Bridget had finally found the strength to speak of it, the anguish in her eyes had revealed the torment she had suffered under Lord Woodbury's ruthless interrogation. It was no wonder that Jack had noticed a pall of despondency lingering over her once they returned to Bewley Hall.

'You don't need to be apprehensive about your mother,' Cormac assured him. 'The divorce proceedings have taken their toll, but I promise you I'll look after her.'

'She'll have Gus too,' said Jack.

'Precisely,' Cormac said with a grin. 'No better chap to raise her spirits.'

A shadow flashed across Jack's face. Before Cormac could identify its cause, the train began to slow down; steam hissed outside their window and the brakes screeched, setting his teeth on edge and cutting off any further conversation. Nudging Jack's knee with his own, he offered him an encouraging smile, and they prepared to disembark at the Carstairs railway station.

They stayed overnight at The Glenside Inn, which was bustling with other fathers and sons also availing of the accommodation ahead of the commencement of the September term at Balfour. The dining room resounded with hearty greetings and animated chatter, but Jack kept quiet and close to Cormac, his gaze flicking covertly across the room as he observed the older boys with their confident, easy camaraderie. Cormac didn't push him to interact with them just yet; navigating this new social terrain required small steps, and there would be plenty of time for him to find his footing.

The next morning, they had to wait their turn to hire a local driver to take them and Jack's trunk of belongings up to the school in a gig. The school grounds were full of activity when they arrived and adolescent boys of all ages hailed each other raucously, bellowing goodbye to their parents as they dashed towards the building's entrance. Cormac sensed Jack shrinking in the seat beside him. Plenty of time, he reminded himself, though his unease nonetheless grew. Had the lad been feigning bravery on the train yesterday?

The driver brought the gig to a halt and muttered something in such a thick local accent that Cormac couldn't make it out.

'Right—ahem, would you mind waiting here for me?' he asked. 'I don't think I'll be too long.'

'That's what I *said*,' the man barked back, his tone both curt and amused.

With a chuckle and an apologetic dip of his head, Cormac jumped down from the gig and helped Jack lift out his trunk. As it thumped to the ground, he heard a voice call out a greeting and straightened to see the headmaster, Mr Cameron, approaching with brisk steps.

'Good morning, Mr McGovern. I trust your journey up from the south wasn't too arduous?'

'Not at all,' Cormac replied as they shook hands firmly. 'Mr Cameron, this is my son Jack.'

The headmaster regarded Jack with a smile. 'Welcome to Balfour, Jack. Are you ready to start this new chapter in your education?'

Jack glanced at his father before giving a small but earnest nod. 'Yes, sir. I hope I'll be able to prove myself worthy of my place here.' He blushed; it sounded like he had rehearsed the line beforehand.

'I'm sure you'll do just fine,' Mr Cameron said encouragingly. Turning, he beckoned to two broad-shouldered boys jogging past. 'Graham! Duncan! Help this laddie with his trunk and show him up to the dormitory, will you?'

They came to a swift stop and replied in unison, 'Yes, sir!'

As they trotted over to Jack's trunk, Cormac realised that this action brought him and Jack to the moment of parting. His chest tightened. It was going to be harder than he had anticipated, especially given the way Jack was staring up at him like the guileless lamb Bridget had dubbed him since he was an infant.

'Take care, *a mhac*,' Cormac said, striving for a bracing attitude to conceal the emotion that was squeezing his heart. 'I have every faith in you.'

He yearned to embrace his precious son but suppressed the impulse – the last thing he wanted was to embarrass Jack in front of his new headmaster and the other boys. Instead, he simply shook his hand, intending the gesture as an acknowledgement of the fact that today Jack was taking a significant step towards manhood. However, it felt hollow the instant their palms separated, and the disappointed look on Jack's face suggested that he might have actually welcomed a hug. Regret pierced Cormac, but it was too late – Graham and Duncan had hefted the trunk into their arms, each gripping one end as they waited expectantly.

Cormac cleared his throat and leaned in close to Jack as if to bridge the growing distance between them. 'Jasper will be pining for you,' he said meaningfully, 'but we'll be sure to take him on long walks while you're gone.'

The corner of Jack's mouth turned up – it was almost a smile, but not quite. He turned away to follow Graham and Duncan, looking small and insubstantial in the shadow of their bulkier frames.

After bidding a polite farewell to Mr Cameron, Cormac forced himself to turn away as well, resisting the urge to watch Jack until he disappeared from sight inside the school building. The weight of the moment settled heavily on his chest as he climbed back into the gig.

The driver muttered something incomprehensible again.

'Very true,' Cormac agreed vaguely, his voice dull. He knew that public school offered Jack opportunities he himself had never had, but the sacrifice of letting his eldest boy grow up so far from their tight-knit family was a hard price to pay.

# CHAPTER 28

Emily marched along the corridor at Blake-Fletchley, her steps purposeful and her head held high. She was thoroughly ready to impress her drawing master with the artwork she had created during the academy's summer break. Currently stowed in the flat leather case under her arm, its subject was a little daring for a female artist, but she was determined to prove that she could produce compositions just as bold and skilful as her male peers. Eager to show it to Jane as well, she looked forward to seeing what her friend had worked on since the end of the previous term.

There was no sign of Jane in the corridor, so Emily pressed on towards the drawing master's domain in Room Eight, skirting the clusters of smoke-shrouded young men milling about and ignoring their customary glares. She anticipated even more blatant disapproval from them this term, now that the news of her mother's divorce hearing had spread far and wide in the papers. No matter – she could handle their contempt, for it signified nothing to her; she was here to hone her craft, not to ingratiate herself with others. She hoped Jack's new academic environment would be more forgiving, however, so that he could make friends without prejudice.

Her father and Jack had departed from Bewley Hall the same day that she and Rory had headed for Yorkshire. Rory had stayed one night at Louise's home in Bilton, before accompanying Emily to the academy this morning. She could still feel the whisper of his sweet kiss against her cheek as he left her at the door to commence his journey back to Bedfordshire.

His kindness, too, lingered with her. He was such a remarkable man the way he had comforted her in the depths of her despair over their continued lack of a child. From that day to this, he'd made her feel like they had enough love to wholly fill their lives, even if there would only ever be the pair of them to share it. She'd taken his advice to heart and no longer allowed herself to dwell on the potential outcome whenever they lay together. A baby would come if their bodies were ready.

In the meantime, she had kept herself very busy, both with her studies in Harrogate and once she returned to Bewley Hall for the summer. She'd helped her mother make the arrangements for the charity lecture delivered by Reverend Hartley. She'd begun paying regular visits to Maud Jones, who still twitched at every unexpected movement but who had gained full hours at the lacemaking factory and finally seemed to be settling into her new situation – in the midst of this, she tried not to feel guilty for befriending Maud, and hoped Derval Carey would understand. And, of course, she'd spent countless hours labouring over the piece of art that she was bursting to present to Mr Parrish. When he saw it, he would not be able to deny that her demonstrable abilities entitled her to an equal education.

Arriving at Room Eight, she entered and spotted Jane sitting at an easel in the back row. There were two empty spots on either side of her, as though the male students feared she carried some contagion and didn't dare get too near. Snorting under her breath at the absurdity of it, Emily wove her way towards the back of the room to claim the easel on Jane's right.

'Good day to you, Jane!' she exclaimed as she reached her. 'Did you have a pleasant summer? I cannot wait to show y-you—'

She stuttered to a halt at the expression of horror on the other woman's face; Jane had reared back as if Emily were the one with the contagious disease.

'Don't speak to me!' she hissed through clenched teeth.

Emily goggled at her. 'I beg your pardon?'

Jane cast a fretful glance at the students in their vicinity whose collective attention was converging avidly upon the two females.

'I have no desire to associate with you any longer,' she snapped at Emily and shot to her feet with the clear intention of relocating to another easel.

'But whyever not?' Emily said, bewildered. 'Surely not because of my mother—'

'Of *course* because of your mother!' Jane gave her an incredulous look. 'How could you imagine it to be otherwise? It's hard enough being a woman in these surroundings, without also having to contend with the affliction of your family's scandal. Pray, do not have any further contact with me.'

Emily stared as Jane gathered up her drawing materials and flounced away, selecting a vacant easel at the end of the row – as she settled herself, the young man next to her unsubtly picked up his own things and abandoned his spot. Emily stood rooted in shock. She had expected scorn from the men in this institution, yes, but not from her only female companion. Did Jane not have any appreciation of her mother's difficult circumstances? How baffling that she could not show compassion for a member of her own sex.

Pressing her lips together, Emily decided to occupy Jane's vacated seat, in no doubt that the two places on either side of her would remain empty. As she sat and rested her leather case in her lap, Mr Parrish swept into the room. His gaze found Emily's at once.

He crooked his finger at her and inclined his head towards the door. 'Mrs Carey, if you please.'

She withered. Was she to be banished yet again from the lesson? Picturing Room Twelve as her site of exile once more, she began to suspect that she would be confined there for the whole term and not just when the subject matter was unsuitable for ladies. No, that simply would not do. She would need to make a strong argument in her defence, but she didn't wish to do so with an audience, so she rose meekly with her leather case and followed the drawing master out of the room.

As she trailed after him along the corridor, she envisioned their imminent confrontation – he would gesture to the dusty environs of Room Twelve and declare it to be an excellent spot for an uninterrupted devotion to her craft, and she would counter with an assertion that her skills merited greater respect than that, at which point she would display her artwork to him with a flourish. She wasn't naïve enough to presume that he would immediately shower her with praise, but she was certain that the quality of it would give him pause and that he would be obliged to rethink his attitude towards her, or else run the risk of neglecting a most promising talent. That last thought was quite vain, but she had to believe in herself and fight for the esteem she deserved, because no one else here would.

To her surprise, however, he strode past the doorway to Room Twelve and proceeded to the stairs at the end of the corridor, which he ascended with rapid, clipped steps. She hastened to keep up, wondering where they were going. On the next floor, he halted outside a stately panelled door bearing a brass plate engraved with the words 'Mr Blake, Director'.

'He wishes to speak to you,' Mr Parrish said grimly.

Her stomach dropped.

He rapped on the door, waited for a response from within, and then opened it, practically pushing her through ahead of him. They entered an antechamber where a sour-faced clerk glared down his nose at Emily before pointing to a door on the opposite side of the room. Once again shunted forwards and across the threshold by Mr Parrish, she found herself in an enormous office filled with luxurious couches and boasting massive, gilt-framed paintings on every wall. There was no desk, but an older man sat primly on one of the couches, as if posing for a portrait. He had a thick head of hair with one curl falling over his forehead in a manner that seemed far too deliberate to be accidental. His cravat was tied in a fussy knot and there were paint stains on the fingers of his right hand, although the room showed no evidence of a canvas in progress nor painting supplies of any kind.

'Be civil,' Mr Parrish warned Emily and withdrew from the room, shutting the door after him.

'Mrs Carey,' the man on the couch said, elongating each syllable. 'How full of regret I am that the moment of our first meeting is also the moment of our final parting.'

Her skin crawled in distaste at both his pompous voice and the implication behind his words. While her heart sank as she guessed what was coming next, she managed to say brightly, 'Good day, Mr Blake. I am pleased to make your acquaintance. To what do I owe the honour?'

He waved his hand as though to suggest he was only too delighted to bestow such an honour. 'Oh, I merely wanted to express my sincere thanks for your brief but, ah, memorable attendance at the academy, and to wish you all the best in your future studies wherever they take you next.'

She adopted an air of exaggerated puzzlement. 'That is very kind of you, but I have not yet completed my course of study here at Blake-Fletchley. When Miss Lyndon and I initially enrolled, it was agreed that we would continue as students until the conclusion of next year's Easter term.'

'That is true,' he said, nodding vigorously and making the curl on his forehead quiver in what he no doubt hoped was a debonair way. 'Which is why it grieves me to see you leave before you have achieved your full potential. But I do understand why you are unable to commence this term with us and very much appreciate you coming in person to inform us of that regrettable, yet unavoidable, fact.'

'On the contrary, I have no intention nor desire to leave,' she said innocently. She would not make this easy for him.

'Indeed, that's what makes this so distressing to bear,' he said, his tone dripping with sorrow. 'Nevertheless, bear it we must.'

He arched a well-groomed eyebrow at her, daring her to contradict him again.

She sighed. 'So you are expelling me then?'

'Good gracious, no!' he exclaimed, pressing his palm over his chest in horror. 'However, we comprehend your complicated situation and agree that it is best for all concerned that you choose to withdraw from the academy.'

She gripped her leather case tightly. 'What if I refuse to do so?'

He gave an oily chuckle. 'Well, that is not an option, my dear girl. You must see that this is for your own good. It will protect you from further humiliation, while also preserving the standards of our respected institution.'

'And do you believe that your respected institution, which is so earnestly dedicated to the noble arts, ought to stoop to the level of contemptible society gossip?' she demanded tartly.

His eyes widened. 'That is a bold insinuation, Mrs Carey, and not one becoming of a lady pursuing those same noble arts. We seek grace in our students, not brash defiance. I'm afraid it is by your own crude words that you demonstrate how unfit you are to remain under our tutelage.' He shook his head sadly.

She regarded him in silence, her shoulders sagging under the crushing weight of inevitability. Rubbing the pad of her thumb over the leather case, she knew that nobody in this building would ever lay eyes upon the artwork it contained. What a shame, for she had been so very proud of it.

Having been denied access to Mr Parrish's series of lessons on the human figure in motion, she had become fixated upon acquiring that knowledge some other way. Consequently, she had stolen out to the fields on the Bewley Estate over the summer and spent hours sketching the tenants at work, observing the tightening of their muscles, the arch of their backs, the sweat gleaming on their skin under the relentless sun. Her final composition, over which she had toiled for so long in her parlour, had become the greatest triumph of her portfolio to date: she had depicted two labourers during the height of the harvest, their shirts discarded in the summer heat as one of them wielded a scythe in a sweeping arc and the other tossed hay into a wagon with a pitchfork. She had captured them mid-movement, their masculine strength evident in every line of their bodies. Her choice to focus on the men rather than the idyllic landscape in the background would have dismayed the more conservative minds at the academy, but she had been certain that it would also have earned her admiration. She knew it was proof that she wholly deserved her place at Blake-Fletchley.

Except it was now being snatched away from her by this pretentious ignoramus, whose only concern was the fact that her mother's disgrace would undermine his academy's reputation. Emily had known there would be a price that she herself would have to pay when the divorce proceedings became public knowledge, but she had not expected it to be quite this steep. Her personal prospects had once again been eclipsed by her parents' love affair.

Her thoughts drifted back to her impetuous flight from Boston at fifteen, driven by the belief that her parents' choices had robbed her of the life of luxury that Garrett had so tantalisingly dangled before her instead. Well, she wouldn't be so foolish again. This time, she had the wisdom to accept the limitations of her situation, no matter how unjust it felt.

Furthermore, she resolved then and there not to divulge to her mother and father how she had been cast out of the academy. That was a burden of guilt which they did not need to bear. Instead, she would invent a plausible lie to justify her sudden return home.

It was too late to catch Rory, who was probably already preparing to board his first train, so she would stay a little longer with Louise and then make her way back to Bedfordshire in her own time, armed with a story good enough to convince her parents. After that, she would need to yet again re-imagine her future. It seemed like she had been knocked back so many times in her artistic endeavours that she had lost count at this stage.

Well, fine. It only made her all the more determined to succeed.

Mr Blake said something and she blinked to refocus on him. 'Pardon?' she asked, not much caring how he replied.

'I said,' he answered with an ugly smile, 'that your crudeness leads me to believe a less ladylike version of you exists beneath your dainty exterior.' He patted the couch next to his thigh. 'If you are receptive to a compromise of sorts, perhaps we could negotiate an arrangement for private lessons?'

She shuddered with revulsion. 'Nothing on this earth would induce me to make such an arrangement with you,' she said bluntly. His eyes bulged, but she carried on, 'Before I gladly take my leave, I want to assure you that Miss Lyndon is untarnished by her association with me. She made it quite clear that she wishes to sever all ties between us. Hence, her continued attendance at the academy will not threaten its prestige.'

Mr Blake's lip curled. 'Oh, we'll find some other reason to get rid of her. She won't last long either.'

Emily glowered at him, mentally adding him to the list of men she utterly despised. Her schoolmaster, Mr Miller, featured high on the list, of course, as did Mr Grover, the cad who had tried to trap her in a compromising position in the gardens of the Hutchville Estate before Rory showed up to rescue her. Mr Blake had now gained his own place of prominence.

And one day, she would prove her worth to them all.

# Chapter 29

Madam,

It is with a sense of deep repugnance that I pen this missive, for I simply cannot fathom the extent of your sinful conduct. Not only have you besmirched the sanctity of marriage by wilfully seeking a divorce, you have done so in the full knowledge that it would be reported to the public and that any persons connected with you would be inescapably stained by association. That you invited me to deliver a lecture in aid of your charitable cause mere months ago is now a source of horror for me. I cannot in good conscience continue to support your philanthropic endeavours, lest I appear complicit in condoning your brazen disregard for the Christian institution of marriage. The virtues of self-sacrifice and duty to one's vows, no matter how burdensome, are the cornerstones of a principled life and cannot be set aside upon a whim. What example does it set to the females

females in our flock when a woman of your station voluntarily descends to such a disgraceful low? This breach of the solemn oath you made before the altar undermines not only your own moral standing but also the sacred trust that binds the Christian household. Not to mention...

On and on the letter went, but Bridget stopped reading after the second page. She dropped it onto the breakfast table with a sigh, doing her best to suppress the wave of shame that swelled within her. Although Reverend Hartley's cutting accusations were not unexpected, that didn't make them any less excruciating.

'Can I see Jack's letter, Da?' Gus asked eagerly on the other side of the table.

Cormac passed him the single page they had received that morning, their first communication from Jack since he had started at Balfour. As soon as David had presented the post, Cormac had seized the letter from the silver tray, opened it in a hurry and hastily scanned it.

'No mention of Jasper,' he had said to Bridget, his relief palpable.

'Who's Jasper?' Gus had piped up.

'Nobody for you to worry about,' Bridget had told him with a smile as she reached for the letter on the tray that had turned out to contain Reverend Hartley's vitriol.

Now, Gus read Jack's letter with a hungry expression. 'He says he's learning to play football! I hope he'll teach me when he comes home.' Gus frowned down at the page. 'He forgot to mention anything about the food. I'd better ask him when I write back. He might need to be rescued if it's just too awful to eat.'

A hopeful note leaked into Gus's voice as he said this and he cast a wistful look down the table at the empty seats along it – not only were Jack and Emily absent, but even Rory had excused himself early from breakfast as he and Mr Comerford had arranged to meet Lord Sinclair's land agent again about the proposed tree felling, which they would finally be able to commence once winter arrived. Bridget's heart squeezed at the sight of Gus looking so small and forlorn by himself.

'Instead of, ah, "rescuing" Jack, perhaps we could send a package of tasty treats to him,' she suggested gently. 'I'm sure he would appreciate that, and I know you would put special consideration into what to include.'

'Mince pies,' Gus replied without hesitation. 'And a jar of blackberry jam, which I'll definitely ask Mrs Hawkins for permission before taking this time. And a box of those boiled sweets we had last Christmas that Jack liked so much. And—'

'All right, all right,' Cormac interrupted with a grin. 'Remember to limit it somewhat, so that it's not too heavy for the postman to carry.'

Gus returned the grin sheepishly. 'Good point. Can I go down to the kitchens right now? If Jack's starving, we'll need to send the package as soon as possible.'

'Aren't you forgetting something, my little miracle?' Bridget asked, raising her brows.

He opened his mouth as if to respond with his usual phrase, but then paused guiltily. 'Oh. My lessons with Mr Humphrey.'

'Mmm-hmm. You need to keep working hard if you want to be ready to join Jack at school next year.'

She was unsure whether that would actually be a convincing enough incentive for him to attend Balfour, given his doubts about the quality of the food there, but he straightened and said, 'I'll work hard, I promise.' It appeared that his brother trumped even his stomach.

Thus, after two more slices of toast, he departed from the breakfast table with an air of determination. Cormac also headed off to ride out and join Rory and the two land agents, who had requested the presence of both landlords for a brief time during that day's discussions to inspect the nearly completed sawmill. This left Bridget with unencumbered time to throw Reverend Hartley's vicious letter into the fire in the drawing room before settling at her writing desk to continue her charitable efforts in defiance of the reverend's disapproval, though of course she would now have to do so in anonymity. She had just concluded letters to three different churches in the county, imploring them to overlook the absence of her signature in favour of doing essential good in support of their Irish neighbours, when Sheppard entered the drawing room with a soft clearing of his throat.

'My lady,' he said, and she wondered with powerful curiosity who he was about to announce, for they had not received a single visitor since the hearing. 'Your daughter has returned from Yorkshire.'

She hardly had time to register her alarm when Emily appeared at Sheppard's side, a wry smile on her face.

'Oh, Mama, I've given you quite a shock, haven't I? Allow me to explain it all.'

Sheppard bowed and retreated from the room while Emily came over to Bridget's writing desk to embrace her. Bridget stood and hugged her daughter, but there was a subtle sense of rigidity between them. What had brought Emily back to Bewley Hall out of the blue like this? Had she suffered another pregnancy-related blow? But no, she certainly wouldn't be smiling in that case.

'Are you quite well, gooseberry?' Bridget asked tentatively.

Emily nodded with vigour. 'Yes, indeed. There is nothing to be concerned about. Come, let us sit down.'

She drew Bridget over to the sofa and they sat side by side. Her bright expression remained fixed in place, although her gloved hands were clasped rather tightly.

'I understand that this will come as a surprise to you and Papa, and perhaps also a disappointment,' she said, 'but I have decided not to continue my studies at Blake-Fletchley.'

Bridget regarded her with astonishment and confusion. 'My goodness, why have you decided that?'

Emily's fingers twitched in her lap. 'When I went back after the summer break, I realised that the academy's approach to instruction simply does not suit me. After the freedom I'd enjoyed over the summer, painting what I wanted, how I wanted, the structured lessons seemed stifling to me. In addition, I've told you before about some of the restrictions they have placed upon female students, and these have only become more frustrating, to the point that I no longer wish to tolerate them.' She pressed her lips together, her shoulders drooping a little before she perked up once more. 'I truly believe that I'll learn better in a different setting—perhaps with a private tutor, or even by travelling to study real works of art. I'm enormously excited to explore new paths of progress.'

Bridget blinked as she absorbed Emily's words. She appeared sincere, and yet a shadow veiled her eyes, as though she were keeping something shuttered behind them. Bridget didn't really know how she ought to respond – should she sympathise, or celebrate?

'This is...rather unexpected,' she began, but then she stopped.

Was it?

Or was this, in fact, precisely what she should have predicted?

Her mind whirled with sudden misgiving. The divorce hearing had taken place the previous month and the journalists had gorged themselves on it, analysing every salacious aspect in their newspaper reports. She and Cormac had worried about the impact it would have on all their children – but while Gus remained protected within their home, and Jack had moved largely beyond the reach of gossip, Emily's situation had been the most vulnerable. Was her newfound dislike of Blake-Fletchley genuinely due to its teaching methods, or had she been subjected to such abuse in the wake of the scandal that she could not endure it anymore? Or, worse still, had they outright expelled her from the institution because of it?

Bridget's breath caught in her throat. Of course. That had to be it. Why else would Emily abandon her place there, after working so assiduously to secure it? Shame flooded through Bridget, a hundred times more crushing than her reaction to Reverend Hartley's letter. This was her fault. She was the reason Emily could not pursue her dreams.

Again.

'Oh, my dear gooseberry,' she said in a broken voice. 'I think I comprehend—'

'Do not be distressed on my account, Mama,' Emily cut in swiftly, her tone bracing. 'I'm confident that I have made the right choice. However, it does mean that I have wasted your and Papa's money on the academy's fees, and I am so very sorry for that.'

She met Bridget's gaze directly, her earnestness so palpable that it only made the truth she sought to conceal more evident. Bridget swallowed. Why was Emily not distraught, or angry? She had every right to rail against her parents for what this divorce had cost her. Bridget searched her daughter's face, seeking any trace of resentment, but she found none. Emily's features stayed composed, giving the impression that she had already made peace with what had transpired. Bridget's chest tightened as understanding struck; Emily was trying to make this easier for her, suppressing the sadness of her loss so that Bridget would not have to bear it too.

'Oh, Emily,' Bridget choked out, overcome with emotion.

Emily lowered her gaze. Silence billowed between them, fragile with an unspoken acknowledgement of the reality they now both perceived. Bridget reached out a trembling hand to cup her daughter's cheek. When Emily looked back up, her blue eyes expressed only forgiveness.

There was no need to say anything else. Their conversation was like a painting that had been left unfinished, yet the brushstrokes indicated exactly what was meant to be.

# CHAPTER 30

Emily groaned as she set her basket down on Maud's doorstep, her arms throbbing. It had been quite silly of her to walk all the way from Bewley Hall to Gildham, when the more sensible option would have been to ride there. But the October afternoon had been crisp and dry, and she had convinced herself that her basket wasn't all that heavy as she had set out. Now, she had to acknowledge that her aversion to horses had not only resulted in utterly unnecessary aches and pains but also delayed her to the extent that she would end up walking back to the Hall in the dusk and would probably be late for dinner.

Knowing that she had no one to blame but herself, she stretched her sore wrists and knocked on the door – two quick taps, followed by a single tap, and finally two more quick ones. She heard footsteps from the hallway within, and then the door opened and Maud's face appeared in the gap. Although Maud would have expected it to be Emily by the knocking pattern they had established between them, she still looked momentarily cautious before smiling and pulling the door wide.

Inside the kitchen, Maud knelt in front of the hearth to resume her task that Emily had interrupted: sweeping up ashes strewn on the brick floor around the low-burning fire, using the brush and shovel from the fire irons to gather them in a bucket by her knees. While she did that, Emily put her basket on the nearby table and started unpacking its contents.

'A few tasty morsels from the kitchens up at the Hall,' she announced as she laid out three cloth-covered packages.

'Thank you, but there was really no need,' Maud said, brushing the last of the ashes onto the shovel and tipping them into the bucket.

'Oh, believe me, there was,' Emily replied with a laugh. 'These had to be liberated from Gus's latest parcel to Jack in Scotland. He had conveniently forgotten to tell the cook that the mince pies in the first parcel hadn't travelled well, arriving at the school in a stale, crumbling mess. I'm sure he planned to salvage this new batch for himself before they were posted off, but I spotted the "error" and claimed them for your children instead.'

Maud chuckled. 'My brood will certainly appreciate them when they get back. They're out at the moment collecting firewood for the Cobbs next door. Well, Alfie and Frankie are—May's just tagging along with her brothers, but she might pick up an odd stick here or there too.'

'Every little bit helps,' Emily quipped as she opened one of the cupboards and tucked the packages of mince pies away on a shelf.

This was how it had become between her and Maud: an easy companionship. If she were being honest, her visits had begun out of a sense of duty as Rory's wife, and she had sometimes wondered if Maud had resented her for it, suspecting that she was merely the recipient of Emily's pity. However, over time their bond had grown in quite a natural way and they had come to enjoy each other's company more and more. Emily still experienced a small stab of guilt whenever she thought of Derval Carey, but she reassured herself that the two relationships were very different – for the most part, she had known Rory's mother only as a girl, whereas she and Maud were both grown women, able to meet as equals. And though their personal circumstances were not the same, Emily felt an undeniable kinship with Maud, connected by a quiet understanding of loss in relation to motherhood.

Maud rose from her knees, swiping her frizzy hair off her forehead. 'I'd a letter from Elsie a couple of days ago,' she said, indicating a loose page resting on the plain mantelpiece.

'How is she faring?' Emily asked, shutting the cupboard.

'Fine overall, except the admiral sneezed twice in a row on Tuesday, which means a big change is on the horizon.' Maud shook her head wryly. 'She either said it was "a threat" or "a treat"—I'm not exactly sure, although that could be down to her bad writing or my poor reading.'

A figure passed by the window, its outline vague in the dusk already gathering outside. Maud flinched but quickly covered up her reaction by bending to hang the brush and shovel back on the fire irons.

'Did Elsie mention anything about Tommy?' Emily asked hesitantly.

Maud shrugged. 'Just that she's seen people traipsing in and out of the house from time to time. Usually his drinking mates or' – she coughed – 'women of a certain sort.'

Emily grimaced. 'Has he asked her about you?'

'No, and I trust her that she won't tell him. Besides, the only address she has for me is the post office in Bedford. They forward my post to Gildham, so it's just the locals who know where I actually live.'

Still, that didn't stop her from casting another anxious glance at the now-empty window.

'I should give you fair warning,' Emily said lightly, toying with the handle of her basket, 'that Gus might call by one of these days. Mr Comerford told him about a mysterious flickering light that's been seen at night moving through the fields between Gildham and Bewley Hall, so I think my brother is planning to question all the villagers to ascertain if they've spotted any strange activity.'

'A light?' Maud repeated, alarmed.

'There's no cause for worry,' Emily hastened to reassure her. 'Mr Comerford let us in on his secret—he's invented a mystery for Gus to solve, in an effort to distract him now that Jack's gone away to school. He's laying clues for Gus to follow, and the light is part of the scheme. It's not the first time he's concocted such a thoughtful diversion.'

'Oh, that's fine,' Maud said, albeit with a nervous twitch of her shoulders.

'I'll teach Gus my knocking pattern,' Emily promised her. 'There'll be nothing to fear.'

Maud gave her a weak smile. 'Thank you. I—' She broke off and her head whipped back towards the window. 'Was that the same person walking past again?'

'I'm afraid I didn't notice,' Emily said apologetically, feeling sorry for the poor woman who seemed to always exist on the edge of her nerves.

Flushing, Maud waved a hand to dismiss her insecurities. 'How are things for you up at the house? Have you settled back into a routine?'

Emily tilted her mouth in a wry expression. 'More or less.'

She hadn't yet established a clear path forwards for herself, although she had committed to painting daily in her parlour since her return. Rory had been astounded to find her at the Hall that day when he came back from fulfilling his duties out on the estate. She had immediately taken him aside to divulge what had really happened at Blake-Fletchley, for she couldn't keep it from him of all people. While he had fumed for days over the way Mr Blake had treated her, she had also sensed his sheer gladness to have her home again.

She could tell that her mother had seen through the tale she had invented, and assumed she'd shared the truth with her father in private, but none of them had directly addressed the blatant fact that she had been forced out of the academy as a consequence of the divorce proceedings. Instead, they had framed it as a new direction, a new season, anything but what it was: another door slammed shut.

Refusing to feel bitter or daunted, she said, 'It's starting to get dark in here. Why don't we stir up the fire?'

'Good idea,' Maud said, reaching for the tongs hanging on the fire irons. 'I've got a few pieces of coal in the bucket here, and the children will probably bring back some firewood when they—'

A loud knocking came from the front door – three heavy bangs that could not have been produced by Alfie, Frankie or May. Maud gulped back the rest of her words.

'I'll go answer it,' Emily said, keeping her manner as serene as possible in an attempt to put Maud at her ease. 'Are you expecting anyone?'

Maud shook her head.

'Not to worry,' Emily said cheerfully. 'Perhaps it's Ettie from next door, or a passing pedlar. I'll be back in a moment.'

As she trotted out into the hallway, she reflected that it was quite late in the day for a pedlar to be coming by, so the caller was most likely Ettie, who was robust enough to deliver those sturdy knocks. Still, she adopted Maud's customary caution as she reached for the latch and only pulled the door back far enough to peek out.

A man stood on the doorstep, his stature short and stocky.

Her stomach lurched. He had no pack strapped to his back, nor donkey and cart waiting nearby, so he was surely not a pedlar. She had never met Tommy Jones, but her hackles rose instinctively at the sight of this stranger. Then his mouth widened into a grin, revealing a large gap in his teeth on the right-hand side. She tensed with dawning horror.

'Is Maud here?' he asked in a distinctive Liverpool accent, confirming the awful truth.

'No, sorry, you've got the wrong house,' she said, hurrying to shut the door as fast as she could.

She wasn't fast enough. He shot out his arm and kept the door open with his broad palm braced on the wood. The edges of his nails were black with soot.

'Are you telling me lies, little missy?' he growled.

'No!' she squeaked and pushed hard on the door.

He managed to thrust his booted foot into the gap before it closed and then he shoved it wide. The force of it flung her back against the wall in the hallway – her hip took the brunt of the blow and she knew she would have a livid bruise by tomorrow. Disregarding the pain, she flailed her arms out as he strode past her, trying to haul him backwards. He shook her off and marched down the hallway.

'Maud!' she shrieked. 'Run!'

Although probably futile, she clung to a brief, desperate hope that Tommy might check the cottage's other room first, perhaps giving Maud time to escape through the window. But no, he made unerringly for the kitchen door which Emily had left ajar behind her. She rushed after him as he stalked into the room.

Maud stood frozen before the hearth like a frightened deer cornered by a hunter.

'There she is,' Tommy sneered. 'I've found you at last.'

Emily hurried to Maud, planting herself in front of her and facing Tommy with her hands on her hips. She knew her slight figure was an insubstantial barrier to his hefty weight, but she was determined to defend her friend if she could.

'Don't come any closer,' she snapped.

As she glared at him, she discerned a long, thin scratch down his left temple. He scowled back at her.

'I don't know or care who you are,' he retorted. 'Get out of my way.'

'E-Emily, love,' Maud stammered. 'Do as he says. Don't let yourself get hurt.'

Emily stayed put and squared her shoulders. 'I'm the wife of your landlord,' she spat, 'and I'm aware of the rental arrangement he made with you. You were a fool to come here—you've just thrown away the easiest situation of your life. He'll evict you as soon as he hears about this.'

Tommy barked out a laugh. 'I don't think so. I'm bringing Maud back with me to Liverpool, so evicting me would mean kicking her out onto the street too.' He smirked. 'Something tells me he'd be too noble to do that.'

Bile rose in Emily's throat at his smug attitude. Of course, he was right – Rory wouldn't do anything to put Maud at risk. If Tommy managed to snatch her away, he would have the upper hand. But the trouble was that he already did. Emily and Maud were here alone, while Rory was up at Bewley Hall, doubtless getting ready for dinner and oblivious to what was unfolding in the little cottage in Gildham. What were they to do?

Tommy cast an appraising glance around the room. 'Got a nice place here, haven't you, Maud? Too bad you'll have to leave it all behind. And just to forewarn you, there's a fair bit of work for you to do when we get back to Penny Close.'

He took a step nearer, but Emily held her ground, trying to block Maud from his view.

'She's not going anywhere with you,' she said stoutly.

'Now, now, missy, you keep your pretty nose out of our business. My wife and I need to get reacquainted. We've been apart for too long—nine months, if you can believe it. Just think, we could've had a baby in that length of time.'

Emily sucked in her breath at the horribly callous comment. Behind her, Maud whimpered. Tommy smirked again and held out a commanding hand.

'Come on now, Maud. Let's go home.'

Emily worried that Maud might capitulate out of fear, but she didn't move.

'No,' she said, her voice low but clear. 'Number 5 stopped being "home" when you set foot in it. This is my home now.'

Tommy's lip curled but he maintained a complacent air. 'Gone all high and mighty, have we? Don't worry, I'll soon beat that out of you.'

It sickened Emily that he could speak with such nastiness. There wasn't a shred of decency in him.

He further reinforced this when he continued coolly, 'If you refuse to obey me, I'll just wait around for your children to show up and get them to convince you. Does Frankie still have that limp? I can easily make it worse.'

Maud gasped. 'Y-you wouldn't.'

'I definitely would.' He winked as though he was promising a special treat. Then he looked around the room again. 'Got anything to eat while we wait? I'm starving.'

He wandered across the room like it was his own domain. After checking Emily's basket on the table and finding it empty, he bent to open the cupboards. Emily felt a tug on the back of her dress and glanced over her shoulder. Maud's eyes were wide. At first, Emily thought it was with panic, but then she realised Maud was trying to communicate something to her, widening her eyes even further and throwing her gaze frantically towards the door to the hallway. Emily understood. She gave an almost imperceptible nod.

'Wait,' she mouthed. They would need to time it just right.

Tommy had found the packages of mince pies and was unwrapping the cloths. 'Bloody perfect,' he exclaimed and broke one in half, stuffing a generous chunk into his mouth.

As he chewed, he brought the rest of them over to the table and made himself comfortable on the wooden settle, leaning against its high back and propping his feet up on the table's surface. Yes, make yourself right at home, you louse, Emily thought. The more relaxed, the better.

'How did you discover Maud's whereabouts?' she asked aloud.

'Did Elsie tell you?' Maud added in a trembling voice.

'Dear old Elsie,' Tommy said, crumbs spraying from his lips. 'She's a tough nut to crack, that one.'

'Oh no, please don't say you hurt her,' Maud moaned.

Tommy reached for another mince pie. 'Nah, it was her cat who took the brunt,' he said with an amused snort.

'What did you do?' Emily asked, scarcely wanting to know.

'Elsie wouldn't tell me where she was posting her letters, so I threatened to chop off her cat's tail. That made her give in, but I still did it afterwards for good measure. It got me back, though, the little ginger monster.' He pointed to the scratch on the side of his face with a huff of annoyance.

Emily stared at him, horrified. Did his cruelty have no limits? Feeling queasy, she hoped poor Elsie would be able to overcome the trauma of that dreadful ordeal. Her recent letter to Maud had contained no warning, so she must have sent it before Tommy barged into her house to terrorise her and her unfortunate cat. With that thought, Emily frowned.

'But how did you find Maud here? The postmasters in both Bedford and Gildham have been informed that she's in a difficult situation and that they're not permitted to disclose her address to anyone.'

He jutted out his jaw, causing a scattering of crumbs to fall from his chin to his chest. 'I bribed a lad at the Bedford post office to tell me where letters for Maud Jones were headed. I wondered if she might have switched to Pratt or even Carey, but no, she'd stuck with her married name, so that was easy enough. The village proved trickier, however—it seems even the young brats around the place have been warned not to talk to strangers about her. But as it turns out, the blacksmith isn't too keen on outsiders and he eventually told me where the woman with the odd accent lives.'

Tommy flicked a bit of soot from under his nail and grinned at his own cleverness.

'Why on earth did you come after her, though?' Emily demanded, trying not to let her gaze stray to the kitchen door. 'You had a bachelor lifestyle and practically all of your wages at your disposal. Those were ideal circumstances.'

'Were they?' he challenged. 'Seems to me like I was given a raw deal.'

She scoffed. 'After the way you abused this family, what more did you think you deserved?'

His eyes flashed. 'I'm still paying rent, even if it's only a shilling a quarter. If your fella wants me to stay away, then *he* can pay *me*.'

So he didn't really care about getting Maud back. He was here for money.

'What took you so long to come up with that ingenious plan?' she said witheringly. Any thug with an ounce of cunning would have seized that opportunity from the outset, not nine months later.

He threw her a baleful look. As he took an enormous bite out of yet another mince pie, he muttered something about being sick and tired of his mates jeering at him because his wife had scarpered.

Did that mean he wasn't even the impetus behind his own scheme? She almost laughed but managed to hold it in; were she to provoke him any further, he might forget about his belly and decide to drag Maud from the cottage without waiting to use the children as leverage.

She reached back surreptitiously and Maud clasped her hand. If they could just make it out onto the road and call for help, someone in the village would surely come to their aid – unless, by sheer misfortune, the first to respond happened to be the blacksmith, who apparently couldn't be counted on.

Tommy crossed his ankles and said, 'There'll be no more mockery when I get back to Liverpool with my pockets loaded. I'm positive I can get your fella and his posh friend to pay me to stay quiet, else I'm going to the peelers about how they kidnapped my wife.'

He tilted back his head to thrust another lump of mince pie into his mouth.

Emily squeezed Maud's hand hard.

Together, they ran for the door.

Emily reached it first and dashed across the threshold as Tommy's bellow of rage followed them. The hallway was dim but she could see that the front door was still partly open after Tommy had pushed his way through. They only needed to get outside—

Behind her, Maud screeched in pain. Emily's footsteps faltered briefly, but she was certain she would better serve her friend by running for help, so she dashed onwards to the door and was just stretching out her arm to pull it wide when something yanked on her hair and a searing agony tore across her scalp. Gasping, she fell backwards and landed on her back with enough impact to snatch the air from her lungs. For a frightening moment, she struggled to inhale at all, but finally she managed to suck in a shallow breath. Wheezing as badly as Gus on a cold winter's day, she looked up through blurry eyes as a stocky figure stepped over her and slammed the door shut, cutting off the last vestiges of daylight and leaving them in almost complete darkness.

'Get up,' he snarled and jerked her roughly to her feet, shoving her ahead of him.

She stumbled back into the kitchen to discover Maud crouched on the floor, weeping and clutching her shoulder. The remainder of the mince pies lay in a trampled mess next to the table leg. Emily rubbed the base of her head and several golden strands came away tangled in her fingers. How she wished she had thought to scream while the front door was open. They had missed their chance.

'Stupid bitches,' Tommy flung at them. 'Get away from the bloody door, you!'

He pushed Emily further into the room, causing her to pitch forwards. As she tried to catch her balance, her foot knocked against the bucket in front of the hearth and it toppled over with a dull clatter. Ashes spilled out of it in a cloud of thick, grey dust, billowing up into her face and making her cough violently. Maud scuttled over to her and thumped her back.

'I'm fine,' Emily spluttered, scooting away a few paces to gulp clearer air.

Maud turned her pleading gaze to Tommy; the glow from the fire's embers highlighted the tracks of tears on her cheeks.

'Please let Emily go. And don't involve the children either. I'll leave with you if you let them stay here.'

His eyes lit up with sinister triumph. 'I want my money too,' he said warningly.

Fury rose in Emily. No, he could not win; it would be an unspeakable injustice. They needed another distraction so they could try to escape again.

She scrabbled towards the fire irons on the hearth and seized the tongs, then shot to her feet and swung it at Tommy. Before it could make contact, he clutched it with both hands and wrenched it from her grip, hurling it away. It rattled across the floor and disappeared beneath the table.

'You interfering hussy!' he barked. 'This has nothing to do with you!'

He aimed his fist in her direction and she ducked out of reach. When she swivelled towards Maud to urge her to run, she saw that Maud had grabbed the poker from the fire irons. It was a heartening sight, despite the obvious tremble in her arms – she needed to stand up for herself and not surrender to this despicable brute. But Tommy was glowering at Maud with his teeth bared, and he was already advancing on her to pull the poker from her grasp. What could Emily do to give Maud the best chance to flee?

She hunkered down, scooped up a mound of the ashes into her cupped hands and flung them into Tommy's face. He coughed and spluttered just as she had done, and reeled to the side. But he didn't see the bucket by his feet and stumbled on it, losing his footing and lurching forwards again, right towards Maud.

Who was still holding up the poker to defend herself.

Emily gasped and Maud stiffened in shock as Tommy's momentum carried him onwards. He and Maud fell against the hearth, their bodies pressing together with the poker between them. Tommy let out a roar of pain as they tumbled, narrowly missing the grate and sprawling across the bricks that Maud had been sweeping earlier. For one macabre moment, it looked like they were locked in the throes of passion until Tommy groaned, and it wasn't a sound of pleasure but of agony. When he reared back on his knees, Emily clapped her hands over her mouth.

The point of the poker was lodged in his abdomen, below his right ribs. He stared down at it in disbelief, while Maud gaped up in horror. Tommy attempted to speak but the words came out in an incomprehensible gurgle. With weakening arms, he grasped the poker and tugged it out of his body, letting it roll away on the floor. Blood gushed up from the wound, running down his clothing and onto Maud's skirt. His features turned grey as he collapsed sideways, his limbs spreading limply in the scattered ashes.

Maud scrambled to her knees and Emily darted to her side, putting a hand on her shoulder to steady her as she wavered. When Emily looked back at Tommy, his mouth was slack and his breath was whistling in jagged spurts through the gap in his teeth. Then the whistling noise ceased and his body became utterly still.

Maud shuddered beneath Emily's grip. 'Is he dead?' she whispered.

'I-I think so.' Emily didn't want to go any closer to check.

An expression of sheer panic swelled on Maud's countenance. 'I killed him,' she said, her voice strangled.

'It was an accident,' Emily tried to reassure her.

'I'll be hanged for this!' Maud exclaimed. 'Oh God, what'll happen to my children?'

'They'll be fine, and so will you,' Emily said, although her own alarm was mounting rapidly. She didn't have a clue what the authorities' standpoint might be in this scenario. Would they believe her and Maud that the outcome of the confrontation had been entirely inadvertent, or would they even bother taking the word of two women into account? Perhaps, upon seeing the corpse, their only objective would be to ensure that the culprit faced justice, no matter the actual truth.

Full of misgiving, Emily said, 'We can't deal with this by ourselves. I must go fetch Rory, and my father too. They will know what we ought to do.'

Maud gave a jerky nod of agreement, her attention fixed upon the wound in Tommy's abdomen; the flow of blood had slowed but it was still seeping out and soaking his clothes.

'Will you be all right?' Emily asked tentatively. 'If I leave you alone with…?'

Maud grimaced. 'I'll cover him in a sheet.' She blanched. 'What about the children? They'll be back soon—I can't let them see this!'

'I'll run next door to the Cobbs on my way and ask Ettie to keep the three of them with her and Ethel for the evening.' Emily squeezed Maud's shoulder. 'Build up the fire and keep warm. I'll make haste and return as quickly as I can. Don't answer the door unless you hear my knocking pattern.'

Keeping her gaze averted from the body, she hurried out of the room, down the hallway and out into the night, desperately wishing that she had decided to ride instead of walk to Gildham that afternoon.

# CHAPTER 31

Rory stared down at the glassy-eyed corpse of Tommy Jones and felt no remorse. The world was better off without him.

However, he hated what Emily and Maud had been forced to endure. They were currently huddled together on the wooden settle with a blanket wrapped around their shoulders. Maud's features were pasty and her breathing was shallow; Emily looked a little healthier, although she kept rubbing her hip and wincing.

Mr McGovern was hunkered on one knee next to the body, pulling back more of the sheet to reveal the gruesome injury. The blood had thickened to a dark, sticky mass and a small pool of yellow liquid had accumulated on the floor beneath Tommy's thighs. The stenches of gore and urine mingled in the air.

As Mr McGovern appraised the body, his forehead creased. Reaching out, he slid his hand warily into the pocket of Tommy's trousers and withdrew...a cut-throat razor.

'Jesus,' Rory muttered.

A muscle ticked in Mr McGovern's jaw as he glanced from the razor over to the two women. Then he fished out a handkerchief from inside his coat, wrapped it around the razor and slipped it into his own pocket without a word.

After he tossed the sheet back over the corpse, he stood and led Rory across the room to Emily and Maud. Maud kept her head lowered, but Emily looked up at them both. Although she had washed her face up at the Hall, she had evidently hurried the task because a smudge of ash still remained near her left ear.

'What do you think should be done?' she asked tremulously.

Mr McGovern gave his daughter a sympathetic look, but his mouth was tight and Rory could tell that he was just as livid as he was about what she had gone through that evening.

'We have a couple of options,' he said. 'However, time is not on our side. The body isn't rigid yet but there is some stiffness. We will need to decide upon our path forward before it fully sets in.'

Maud gagged and pressed her fist to her lips.

'I'm sorry, Maud,' he said with utter gentleness. 'I understand how difficult this is for you. Nevertheless, though the manner of it was horrific, I honestly believe that what happened tonight was for the best.'

She goggled up at him, aghast. His expression remained composed.

'Had events not transpired the way they did, and had it been possible to put him to flight on this occasion, he would only have come back for you again in the future.' Mr McGovern's voice was calm. 'You would have spent the rest of your life looking over your shoulder in fear. And the next time he showed up, you might not have survived.'

She dropped her gaze again, but not before Rory caught the flicker of comprehension in her eyes.

Mr McGovern turned back to Emily. 'You were right to be cautious about notifying the authorities. The circumstances here are too ambiguous for the law to protect Maud. England's justice system is not designed to favour a woman from the working class whose husband has been found dead in an apparent case of murder. Not to mention, you would also likely be implicated as an accomplice.'

Emily gulped.

'My gut tells me that we cannot involve the authorities without risking a sentence of hanging or transportation, and I absolutely refuse to stand by and let that happen to two innocent women, especially when one of them is my daughter. Which means we need to handle this ourselves.' He grimaced. 'Rory and I will have to dispose of the body covertly and cover up our tracks.'

Maud's frame quivered with palpable horror, while Emily's countenance turned green. Rory, however, was unsurprised and prepared to do whatever it took to shield his wife from harm. Hanging was for criminals and transportation was for miscreants like the Sandlers, not his beloved, sweet, precious Emily.

'I know it's distasteful,' Mr McGovern said. 'But it's necessary to avoid the prospect of the courts meting out a most unjust punishment. We have no other choice.'

Emily bit her lip. 'But what if you get caught in the process of...the disposal? That would lead to equally unjust consequences.'

Rory shook his head. 'No, we carry more of the blame here. We started this back in Penny Close when we took Maud and the children away. Now we're the ones who have to finish it.'

'I don't want either of you to be in danger!' Emily's pitch rose in panic as she gazed from her father to her husband.

'We won't be,' Mr McGovern replied with such assurance that even Rory was inclined to believe him. 'We'll make his death look as natural as possible to evade suspicion.'

Rory gave him a quizzical glance. 'I figured we'd just bury him in a deep grave where no one would find him.'

Mr McGovern chewed the inside of his cheek. 'I've considered that option, but I don't think it's feasible. We haven't got the time to find a remote enough location and dig that size of a hole. Furthermore, if anyone stumbled across the freshly turned soil, or wild animals dug it up, we'd have to contend with the fact that the body has suffered a very obvious injury. There would be an immediate assumption that a murder had taken place.'

'And the blacksmith would be able to identify Tommy and connect him to Maud,' Rory said with a sinking feeling. 'What d'you suggest instead, then?'

Mr McGovern hesitated. At last, he said reluctantly, 'The river.'

'To make it look like a drowning?' Emily asked in a small voice.

He nodded. 'To the unaware, it will appear to be nothing more than an unfortunate accident. Whoever comes upon him will probably think that the fellow was drunk and lost his footing at the edge of the water.'

'But won't they question the wound?' she said, frowning.

He cleared his throat uncomfortably. 'My plan is a little more elaborate than merely letting him fall in.' He broke eye contact with her, as if he were too ashamed to meet her gaze. 'It entails keeping him underwater for long enough to start decomposing, so that when he is finally discovered he will not be recognisable to anyone, not even the blacksmith.'

A startled silence fell. Emily and Maud sat totally still on the settle. Rory shifted his feet and found himself toeing a messy mound of mince pie remnants on the floor. He took a step back from it.

'So, uh, how will we manage to do that?' he asked, puncturing the silence.

Though Mr McGovern's compunction was plain in his remorseful blue eyes, he nonetheless spoke with resolve. 'We need to keep him trapped below the surface for a period of time. And as our dubious luck would have it, the very solution lies just over the border on the Sinclair Estate.'

Rory's brows knitted in puzzlement for several moments before it dawned on him. 'The sawmill?'

'Indeed.' Mr McGovern eyed Emily and Maud, who were both still mute. He winced at Rory. 'You and I can discuss the finer details once we're on our way.'

Emily blinked. For a second, Rory wondered whether she would ask to be made privy to those details. But she only said cautiously, 'It sounds like the river is the best choice.'

'I'm afraid there are no good choices, *a stór*,' Mr McGovern replied. 'Only bad or worse. But we will see it done.'

All of a sudden, Maud said, 'What about the folk back in Liverpool?' Her words were hoarse like she hadn't spoken in days. 'What will Tommy's drinking mates think when he doesn't return?'

'I'll take care of that,' said Mr McGovern. 'I can find a way to ensure that a rumour spreads through the pubs there that Tommy has decided to seek his fortune overseas. His friend Ned might guess there's more to his disappearance than that, but he'll be too scared to pry because he knows what I'm capable of.'

The tension in the room conveyed that they were all quite aware that he was not someone to be crossed.

Emily turned to Maud. 'Will you wish to return to Penny Close, now that Tommy's...gone?'

Maud stared at her knees for so long that Rory began to doubt if she had heard the question at all. But at last she said, 'I can't go back there—it'd raise suspicion if I showed up right after he left. Besides, I don't think I want to. That house holds too many bad memories.' She shot a grim glance at Tommy's covered corpse and wrinkled her nose. 'And that's saying something.'

'There's a home for you on the Bewley Estate for as long as you wish to live here,' Mr McGovern promised.

'Thank you,' she mumbled. Then she hiccupped and squinted at Rory. 'But this means there'll be no tenant at Number 5.'

'Don't worry about that,' he replied. 'I'm sure Mr Martins can find me a new tenant. That's a problem for another day.'

'Yes,' Mr McGovern agreed. 'We have a more pressing matter to deal with first.'

They had to wait another couple of hours before they could tackle it, however. It wasn't until close to midnight, when they could be quite sure that the village's inhabitants were asleep, that they deemed it safe enough to remove Tommy's body, swathed head to toe in a pair of blankets, from the cottage. This proved to be a challenging task because it had already grown stiffer, making it difficult to manoeuvre onto the back of Mr McGovern's horse, Orion, who had been tethered patiently alongside Rory's mount, Bran, at the rear of Maud's cottage all evening.

Once they finally had it roped in place, they went back inside. Maud was still hunched on the settle, but Emily had risen and was contemplating the stains on the floor where the corpse had lain.

'We'll clean up while you're gone,' she said, her lips pinched with revulsion.

Mr McGovern nodded. 'We should be back by dawn, I hope, unless there are unforeseen complications. Don't answer the door to anyone but us.'

'Two taps, one tap, two taps,' she reminded him.

He gave her a faint smile before cocking his head at Rory. Rory touched his hand to Emily's and then followed Mr McGovern out the door. As he pulled it closed behind them, he heard Maud's quiet, resolute declaration.

'I am never, *ever*, getting married again.'

Rory's heart was in his mouth as they set off. A half moon hung above them, casting just enough light to guide them, yet not so much as to easily give them away. They could only go at a walking pace due to the load on Orion's back, and they would have to avoid the roads, travelling across fields and through woods to reach the border between the Sinclair and Bewley estates. Mr McGovern had estimated that it would be at least an hour's ride each way.

A dog barked in the distance as they left the village behind and approached the gate to the nearest field. Rory dismounted to open it and led Bran through after Orion. As he was about to close the gate, he glanced over his shoulder and jolted in fright when he caught a flutter of movement back down the road. Bran jerked at his reaction but he held tight to the reins and the horse didn't bolt.

'Sir,' he croaked softly. 'I think we're being followed.'

Mr McGovern's figure went rigid but he didn't make any sudden motion. Casually, he turned his head to scrutinise their surroundings. After a minute, he straightened in his saddle.

'I see him,' he said, his tone surprisingly serene. 'Let's wait for him to catch up.'

To Rory's amazement, Mr McGovern waved an arm in invitation. Rory swivelled and watched a shape emerge timidly from the gloom.

'Christ, Alfie!' he gasped. 'You scared me half to death.'

He couldn't distinguish his half-brother's expression until the lad came up right beside him – it was a mixture of sheepish and fervent.

'Sorry,' he said. 'I spotted you from the back window of the Cobbs' cottage. I think I can guess what that is.' He pointed to the bundle secured behind Orion's saddle. 'Tommy came after Ma, didn't he?'

Rory grimaced. 'Yes.'

'She's not badly hurt?'

'No, thank God.' Emily had said that Maud's shoulder and back would have some bruising, but she'd had a lucky escape otherwise.

'And now you need to get rid of him,' Alfie said matter-of-factly. 'Can I come?'

Rory glanced at Mr McGovern.

'It might be useful to have a lookout,' his father-in-law said. 'You can ride with Rory, Alfie. We must warn you, though: this won't be pleasant.'

'That's fine,' Alfie said, his features grim in the dim moonlight. 'I'm just glad the bastard's dead.'

Thus, with the momentary alarm of discovery dispelled, they set off again, Alfie settled somewhat awkwardly on Bran's back in front of Rory. All three of them stayed on the alert, but everything seemed quiet in the surrounding landscape. Thankfully, Lady Bridget had expressly forbidden Gus to investigate the mysterious flickering light in the fields at night without the assistance of his father, so they didn't need to worry about bumping into the young detective. As they rode, Rory told Alfie in low murmurs what had happened at his mother's cottage that evening. Alfie simmered with anger, but his simultaneous relief was unmistakable.

'He didn't deserve to live,' he said simply, and Rory had to agree.

They made it the rest of the way without incident. When they reached the new sawmill, they found the site deserted, but cart tracks and hoof prints were visible in the soil throughout the area.

'That's good,' Mr McGovern muttered. 'We won't need to be too concerned about what marks we leave behind.'

He led them towards the sound of flowing water and presently the mill's main building loomed out of the dimness, perched on the bank of the river. Next to it was the round, hulking shape of the millwheel, half submerged in the water. Rory had viewed it several times in daylight when he and Mr Comerford had come to inspect the site, but it seemed a lot more ominous now, shrouded in moonlight and shadow.

Alfie shivered in front of Rory. 'Why isn't it moving?'

'It's braced in place, see?' he answered, pointing out the wooden beams wedged between the wheel's paddles and bound with iron chains to the mill's wall. 'It doesn't need to turn until the workers are ready to begin the tree felling, which can't start until the trees become dormant for the winter.'

'And that suits us perfectly,' said Mr McGovern. 'From what Mr Comerford and Mr Longridge said at our last meeting, they expect to have it operational by December. Two months ought to be sufficient for our purpose.'

'What exactly are you planning to do?' Alfie asked.

'We're going to ensure that our companion here gets caught in the spokes of the wheel below the water. By the time the bracing beams are removed in a couple of months, the river will have done its job and his face shouldn't be recognisable. When the wheel starts to turn, it will carry his body above the surface but it will likely bruise and batter him in the process, obscuring his original injury among numerous others.'

Rory swallowed, taken aback by the deep level of thought Mr McGovern had put into this grisly enterprise.

His father-in-law sighed. 'While the sawmill is a joint venture between both of our estates, the most suitable location for it happened to be on Lord Sinclair's land. It's hardly the neighbourly thing to do, orchestrating this here. But since it will appear to be an accident, the Sinclairs should face no troublesome repercussions—except, of course, the distress of having a man's unexpected death occur on their property.'

With that glum observation, he swung down from his horse. Rory and Alfie followed suit, the latter cringing and discreetly rubbing his buttocks. Mr McGovern started untying the rope.

'Alfie, please stand near the horses and keep watch,' he said. 'Alert us at once if you notice anything out of the ordinary.'

'Yes, sir,' Alfie said, squaring his slight frame.

As the rope fell away, Mr McGovern said to Rory, 'I'll take the shoulders if you take the feet?'

Rory nodded and moved into position, trying very hard to pretend that they were just preparing to carry a large sack of grain or potatoes. The illusion shattered as soon as his hands registered the unyielding mass beneath the coarse weave of the blankets. They struggled to lower it from Orion's back; it was heavy and uncooperative, and he almost dropped his end before firming up his grip just in time. Without speaking, they trudged towards the river bank with their load. At the water's edge, they set it down.

'I'm going to take away the blankets now,' said Mr McGovern, a subtle warning to Rory if he wished to avert his eyes. He did just that, keeping his gaze focused on Tommy's sooty bootlaces as they came into view.

'Do you know how deep the water is?' he asked, like he was making light conversation.

'It's difficult to tell in the dark, but it shouldn't be more than four or five feet.'

Rory heard a soft thump and peered up to see that Mr McGovern had removed his right boot and let it drop to the ground. As he took off the left one, he said, 'There's no need for you to get in the water too. Just help me guide it from the bank and I'll do the rest.'

Rory didn't argue. There was something quite intimidating about the darker side of this man. It was also extraordinary how much he was willing to take upon himself so that others wouldn't have to.

After removing his hat and coat as well, Mr McGovern crouched by the water and then slowly lowered himself into the steady current. 'Oh, hell, that's cold,' he blurted.

By the time he was standing with it up to his ribs, he had let loose a string of curses in both English and Irish with such rapidity that Rory couldn't grasp most of them, although he thought he caught the phrase 'twelve devils' in there.

Gritting his teeth, Mr McGovern faced the river bank. 'All right, let's slide it in.'

Rory pushed the body to the water's edge and Mr McGovern gripped it and pulled it towards him. It plunged into the river with a heavy splash. Despite its weight, it didn't sink at once, so Mr McGovern waded through the current with his hand guiding it in the direction of the millwheel. When he reached the wheel's curved rim, he looked back at Rory kneeling on the bank.

'Won't be long,' he said with a resigned tilt of his mouth. He pressed down on the body with firm pressure to force it below the water's surface, and then, taking a deep breath, he ducked under himself.

As Rory waited anxiously for him to re-emerge, he pictured him manoeuvring the body between the wheel's paddles and tangling its limbs sufficiently on the spokes so that it wouldn't come loose. However, when the seconds lengthened into a minute and more but still Mr McGovern didn't reappear, panic began to climb Rory's throat. Could he have become stuck himself somehow? Should Rory go in after him?

'Sir?' he rasped, doubtful whether Mr McGovern would be able to hear him. 'Sir, do you need help? Cormac!'

Just as he had decided to jump in, the surface of the water broke and his father-in-law materialised, gasping for air.

'Thank Christ,' Rory uttered with unspeakable relief.

He reached down and heaved him, dripping, onto the bank before fetching the abandoned blankets to wrap around him. Cormac accepted them gratefully, neither he nor Rory mentioning the fact that they had served as a shroud mere minutes ago. He sat hunched with the blankets around his shoulders, catching his breath.

'It's done,' he said at last, pushing his hand through his sopping hair. There was a haunted look about him, which Rory thought was fairly self-explanatory until he murmured, 'That wasn't the first time I've put a body in the water.'

Rory flinched. 'I'm sorry,' he said. 'I don't think any of us really know just how much you've sacrificed over the years. I respect everything you've done for this family.'

Cormac swatted the words away with a shower of droplets from his sleeve. 'Enough of that. We still need to get rid of the razor—I believe it would be wisest to toss it into the river at least a half mile downstream.'

Rory didn't budge. 'I mean it, Cormac. Thank you.'

They shared a wry smile of acknowledgement. There were some things that inevitably left a man on first-name terms with another, and disposing of a body together in the dead of night was one of them.

# Chapter 32

*The torment of drawing breath, already breathing death.*

Cormac stared down at the words of despair written in Oliver's elegant hand. He had discovered the young man's notebook of poems tucked away in a desk drawer in the study several months after the family had moved into Bewley Hall. Lord and Lady Bewley had kept it all those years, and they must have pored over it hundreds of times, judging from the worn edges of its navy cloth cover. Now, he toyed with a corner of the page and let his mind stray back to his encounter with Oliver that had begun when they met on the deck of a ship and ended when he consigned Oliver's body to the sea.

Lost in his bleak thoughts, he jumped at the sudden sound of Bridget's voice.

'Cormac? Did you not hear me knocking?'

Looking up swiftly, he found her standing in the open doorway of his study, a letter in her grasp.

'No, I didn't,' he said guiltily, closing the slim notebook and slipping it back into the drawer.

She let it pass without prying; he had shown her the book of poems before, and she was aware that Oliver had frequently preyed on his mind since October. However, it was now the new year, so he resolved to put last year's melancholy behind him.

'Do you have a moment?' she asked, coming further into the room.

He registered her troubled expression and frowned from her to the letter. 'What's that?'

She sighed. 'A remarkable coincidence, and a grave disappointment.'

His skin prickled with dread. Had there been further complications with the divorce? But she held out the page to him across his desk and, taking it, he saw that it was signed by a clergyman from St George's Church in west Bedfordshire.

She crossed her arms. 'That's one of the three churches I wrote to seeking support for victims of the blight, and the only one that responded. Reverend Procter and I had been discussing how best to collect the donations from his congregation...until now.'

'What changed?' Cormac started to scan the letter and discerned the words 'inconceivable deception'.

'A connection I couldn't have foreseen,' she said despondently. 'Reverend Procter happens to be an acquaintance of Reverend Hartley. They met recently at a theological assembly and he mentioned the relief efforts of St George's in the course of their conversation. Hartley's mistrust was raised by the fact that the anonymous letters were coming from "a concerned lady" and he asked to see them. Unfortunately, he recognised my handwriting.'

Cormac swore under his breath. 'And he warned Procter off.'

She nodded. 'His letter makes it plain—he and his church will have no further dealings with me, thanks to Hartley's intervention. It seems that the stain of scandal is always ready to resurface, no matter how hard I try to scrub it away.'

Cormac set the letter down with disgust. 'Is there any way to convince him? Appeal to his supposed Christian goodness?'

She shook her head. 'It would be no use. Even if he were inclined to forgive the folly of my heart, he now sees me as possessing a deceitful character for having concealed my identity on account of an immoral reason rather than a humble one.'

They exchanged a look of quiet resignation.

'We'll shift the focus of our endeavours elsewhere, then,' he said. 'The churches in Dublin?'

'I do believe we might find a more sympathetic response from those with influence in Ireland,' she agreed. 'They are much closer to the suffering than anyone here in England.' Her countenance lifted with hope. 'Ought we to consider travelling back there soon? I would very much like to go back for our own sakes as well. We've remained at Bewley Hall longer than we intended yet again.'

Jack was the main reason for that; Cormac had been reluctant to leave the country in case they received a plea from their son begging for his swift rescue from school. And yet, no such plea had ever come. In all his letters, Jack had made no mention of Jasper, nor had he expressed any misery or regret. When he returned home for a brief visit at Christmas, he had spoken of his experiences at Balfour with enthusiasm. Cormac was astonished and relieved by how well he had settled, and it had been much easier to see him off in January than it had been in September. It appeared that there was nothing to fear after all, and whether they were at Oakleigh or Bewley Hall hardly mattered while Jack was far away in Scotland, thriving rather than in need of saving.

'Maybe we should consider it,' he said at last.

'Ahem.'

Cormac glanced past Bridget and spotted Sheppard in the open doorway.

'Apologies for disturbing you, sir, my lady,' said the butler. 'Mr Carruthers has arrived and requests an audience with you both at your earliest convenience.'

Bridget stiffened. 'We'll see him right away. Won't we?' she added quickly to Cormac.

'Yes,' he said, his prickle of dread returning. 'Please send him in, Sheppard.'

By the time Mr Carruthers entered the study, Cormac had paced the length of the room ten times, while Bridget had chewed at least two of her fingernails. They both whirled towards the lawyer as he came in carrying a leather case similar to the one Emily liked to store her important artwork in.

'Do you have news for us?' Cormac asked without preamble.

'I do,' Mr Carruthers replied, betraying no hint of whether that news was good or bad. He pointed to the desk. 'May I?'

Cormac motioned his assent and Mr Carruthers strode across the room to place his leather case on the desk's surface. Opening it, he withdrew a document of stiff parchment and turned to Bridget, presenting it to her with a courteous bow.

'Official confirmation of your divorce, my lady.'

She didn't say a word. Neither did she reach out to take the document. She just stared at it, her chest rising and falling with rapid, soundless breaths. Cormac approached warily, half expecting the parchment to disintegrate into a pile of dust.

'It's real?' he asked.

'Yes. The original Act must be kept in Parliament's records but this is a certified copy. It verifies that the dissolution of the marriage between Lord and Lady Wyndham was passed by the House of Lords and the House of Commons, and subsequently received royal assent. It also explicitly states that both parties are at liberty to remarry.'

Cormac's heart pounded against his ribs.

'There's more,' Mr Carruthers said, turning to retrieve another document from his case, this one made of ordinary paper. 'Here is a signed declaration by Lord Wyndham, conferring the ownership of the Oakleigh Estate irrevocably upon Lady Courcey as part of the divorce settlement. He no longer retains any claim to the property or its assets.'

A tiny gasp escaped Bridget's lips and her dark brown eyes began to glisten.

'I will leave you to absorb the news,' Mr Carruthers said, the corners of his mouth curving upwards. He set the two documents carefully on the desk and departed from the study.

Cormac felt so overwhelmed that he could hardly look at Bridget. He didn't know what to say – no words seemed big enough. He just took one stumbling step towards her and then she was in his arms, her cheek pressing against his torso, his fingers sinking deeply into her hair. They clung to each other as the path towards their future became crystal clear.

Eventually, she mumbled something into his chest and he coaxed her back a few inches to tilt her head up.

'Come again?' he said with an affectionate grin.

Her eyes crinkled. 'I said, I could hear your heartbeat. It was going at an extraordinary gallop.'

'Can you blame it after the news we just received?' He winked.

'No,' she said breathily. She blinked in wonderment. 'It's as though shackles have fallen away from my ankles. I feel like I am light enough to float. Has this truly happened?'

'It has, unless Carruthers is playing a cruel and elaborate prank on us that would guarantee his immediate unemployment.' He said that loud enough for the lawyer's benefit, in case he was still within the vicinity to hear it.

'He wouldn't do such a thing,' she said with a bubble of laughter. 'This really is happening.' She peeked up at him eagerly. 'The wedding should take place at Oakleigh, don't you think?'

'What wedding?' he said innocently.

She gave him a mock glare.

'I haven't proposed yet,' he reminded her.

'Well, you'd better hurry up and do it.'

'You hardly expect an old man in his forties to get down on one knee, do you?'

'At this rate, I'll be an old woman in my eighties by the time you get around to it.'

'Are you sure you'd prefer not to be fettered with another set of shackles?'

Her humour transformed into solemnity in an instant. 'Not shackles. An anchor.'

His heart skipped a beat. What an honour it was that this woman had such faith in him. He would do anything and everything in the world to make her happy.

Grasping both of her hands and keeping his eyes locked on hers, he lowered himself to one knee and gazed up at her.

'*A rún mo chroí,*' he said. '*An bpósfaidh tú mé?*'

'*Cinnte,*' she replied, the Irish word reflecting the certainty in her voice.

He surged back to his feet and pressed his mouth to hers, kissing her thoroughly. She returned the kiss with fervour, her tongue meeting his in an act of passion that was so familiar and yet suddenly seemed brand new again. They had shared their first kiss as lovers at the age of nineteen; now, after all these years, they could finally marry. Elation streamed through him and he felt like he might burst apart with the joyful force of it.

When they eventually separated, she beamed up at him, her lips rosy from his attentions.

'So now that we've established that a wedding will indeed occur,' she said, 'do you agree that Oakleigh is the right place for it?'

'Absolutely.' He hesitated. 'We won't be able to get married in St Mary's, though.'

Her expression dimmed a fraction. 'No, that door is closed to us.'

The Roman Catholic church would not recognise her divorce – according to its doctrine, she was still bound by marriage and would not be free to marry again until Garrett's death made her a widow.

'What about St Canice's?' she asked. 'Would they permit you to wed there?'

'I've already made some enquiries regarding that,' he admitted. 'A Catholic may marry in a Church of Ireland establishment if the bishop of the diocese grants a dispensation.'

'Then that's what we'll do,' she said firmly. 'How long might it take?'

'Weeks or months, depending on the bishop's cooperation.'

She deflated a little. 'I hoped it might happen sooner than that.'

'Let's look at it from a positive angle,' he urged. 'If we plan for a summer wedding, that means Jack can complete his year at Balfour before we travel as a family to Ireland.'

'Yes, true,' she said, brightening again. 'And it will give us more time to make the arrangements.' Then she paused, biting the tip of her tongue. 'However, it will mean lingering in England in the immediate wake of the divorce. Once the newspapers report that it has been finalised, that will no doubt prompt a fresh wave of scorn.'

'It will,' he said, for there was no point in denying it. Society's contempt would grow even more vociferous once they learned that the wanton woman at the centre of the scandal had managed to accomplish her disgraceful objective, conveniently ignoring the fact that Garrett had been the one to instigate the proceedings. 'I suppose there are two different paths we could take in response.'

She cocked her head to the side. 'Which are?'

'We could seclude ourselves here, retreating indefinitely from all public life. Or we could confront the situation in a direct manner.'

'Would I be correct in guessing that your preference would be the latter?' she asked wryly.

He nodded. 'But only if you are also in agreement.'

'Hmm,' she said. 'What do you suggest?'

'The Grand National is taking place next month at Aintree, just outside Liverpool,' he said, the idea forming quickly in his mind. 'Lord Sinclair has recommended to me on a number of occasions that I should make the trip. If we attend as a couple, it would be an ideal setting to test the waters of public opinion.'

'That is quite a daring move,' she said. 'There's a risk that they will run us out of there for showing our faces.'

'And in that case we will know where we stand,' he said with a shrug. 'But the onus will be on them to abandon civility. We'll merely be indulging in a legitimate interest in horse racing.'

The more he thought about it, the more certain he felt that this was the better path to choose, even if it wasn't the most prudent. Rather than creeping timidly around the fringes of society, it would be simpler to make a decisive appearance, showing that they were unshaken by the gossip and using the opportunity to gauge who their allies were. The result would set the tone for their future place within, or outside of, respectable circles.

'Let's go for it,' Bridget said, lifting her chin.

He couldn't wait to call this courageous woman his wife.

# CHAPTER 33

Rory trailed Mr Comerford across the sawmill site, the January frost crunching beneath his boots and his pulse hammering in his throat. A ghostly mist hovered over the river, dampening the voices of the millworkers who called to each other as they went about their morning's labours. Try as he might, Rory couldn't prevent his gaze from straying towards the skeletal shape of the millwheel looming out of the mist. It still remained stationary, the bracing beams holding it in place as they had all winter.

But for how much longer?

Forcing himself to look away, he caught up to Mr Comerford, who was surveying their surroundings with the keen eye of a man already composing a report in his head. As Rory drew his coat tighter against the chill, Lord Sinclair's land agent, Mr Longridge, emerged from the large doorway of the mill's main building and approached them, rubbing his gloved hands together.

'Quite a nip in the air, isn't there?' he remarked.

Never one for idle chat, Mr Comerford only grunted in response. Feeling obliged to fill the silence, Rory said, 'For sure. It's the sort of morning that wakes you up whether you like it or not.'

He thought it came out rather awkwardly, but Mr Longridge gave an amused chuckle.

'At least the water isn't frozen,' he said, gesturing towards the river. 'That would have wholly impeded today's inspection.'

Rory went stock-still. 'I thought we were meeting to discuss the budget for supplies?' he managed to utter, barely keeping his voice from sounding strangled.

'We'll get to that too,' Mr Longridge said, nodding. 'But the foreman came to me as soon as I arrived on the site and proposed testing the wheel today. I agree—it's time. There's no sense in putting it off any longer, and we want to make certain it's fully operational before being brought into service.'

Mr Comerford had been the one to suggest delaying the launch from December until January, citing the need for a few extra weeks to better acquaint the men with the general workings of the mill, and thus minimising the risk of accident during the wheel's initial rotation. However, Rory knew it had been Cormac who had quietly sown the seed of that idea. It had been a clever ploy...but it had only postponed the inevitable.

'Fine with me,' Mr Comerford said. 'Today's the day.'

Rory tried to school his countenance into a neutral expression, even as his mouth went dry. Christ, he wasn't ready for this.

His feet felt like lead as Mr Longridge led them towards the riverbank, where they met the foreman, a thickset fellow with a tattered scarf knotted at his neck.

'Morning, sirs,' the man said, grinning. 'Ready to get started? We're all keen to see her come to life at last.'

He gestured to the other workers who were beginning to gather around, their faces alight with anticipation. Rory's breakfast churned in his stomach.

Mr Longridge motioned to the foreman. 'Let's proceed.'

Rory swallowed hard as the foreman gave a sharp whistle, prompting a flurry of activity. The workers swarmed around the millwheel and proceeded to loosen the iron chains that had kept the wooden beams wedged between the paddles for so long. The foreman shouted orders, coordinating the men's movements, and the chains fell away with a clang of metal. Then the workers extricated the beams, tossing them onto the bank before jumping out of the way themselves. The wheel gave a groan like a waking beast. Rory's heart lurched.

Water flowed through the paddles and the wheel began to turn without impediment, slowly at first, and then more surely, its great arms creaking. Cheers went up from the nearby men and Mr Longridge clapped his gloved hands, while Mr Comerford grunted with approval. Rory tried to paste a pleased smile onto his face.

That was when the wheel faltered, not with a harsh jolt but with a dull, dragging sound. It struggled to rotate, as though invisible hands were holding it back. The cheering died away and a few voices uttered exclamations of confusion and disappointment.

In the next instant, the wheel jerked and moved again, wrenching free from the unseen obstruction below the surface. One of the workers resumed whooping but cut himself off as a dark mass emerged from the water and became visible even through the mist.

Rory's breath caught.

In the crook of the paddles, a limp shape was tangled around the mossy frame. Limbs bent at unnatural angles. Clothing in tatters. Boots. Flesh.

'Is that what I think it is?' someone choked.

A horrified silence fell.

Mr Longridge was the first to pull himself together. 'Stop the wheel,' he barked. 'Brace it now.'

White-faced, the foreman yelled a frantic command and several of the men leapt forwards to ram the wooden beams back into place. Others swung the iron chains back over and secured them. The wheel came to a stuttering halt, leaving the body in full view.

'God above,' Mr Comerford muttered, looking as pale as a sheet.

Mr Longridge turned and seized the shoulder of a young millworker standing immobile nearby, his mouth agape at the grisly sight.

'Ride to Bedford,' the agent ordered. 'We need to fetch a constable.' He shook the man's shoulder. 'Immediately!'

The young man blinked and straightened before sprinting away. Mr Longridge swivelled back to the foreman.

'We have to remove it,' he said, his voice calm and firm. 'Carefully. Use planks and ropes. Get the timber shed's door off its hinges—it can serve as a stretcher.'

The foreman relayed his instructions and the workers obeyed without question, moving silently, the cheerful atmosphere from earlier completely eradicated. Rory watched numbly as a number of the men hurried away from the riverbank, while those who remained set about extracting the body from the wheel with palpable reluctance. When one of them balanced himself on a broad paddle and reached forwards to take hold of an arm, the sodden sleeve slipped off with a sickening squelch, dragging a layer of skin with it. He jerked his hand back in dismay, but the damage was done – beneath the torn cloth, pale flesh sloughed away like wet parchment. The unfortunate fellow turned his head away and retched into the water below. After that, the men carried out their abhorrent task with exceedingly slow and deliberate movements. Guilt flooded Rory; when he and Cormac had disposed of the body, they had not given enough thought to the horror they would inflict on these unsuspecting souls.

With the help of a length of rope, the men manoeuvred the body off the spokes of the wheel and onto a floating plank to bring it across the water. As they hoisted it up onto the grass beside the riverbank, the stench hit Rory like a punch to his gut. It was all he could do not to gag. The foreman pulled his tattered scarf over his nose and mouth before stepping closer to peer down at the waterlogged corpse.

'Who were you, you poor devil?' he muttered.

Rory clenched his fists as hard as he could in an effort to remain blank-faced. He was the only person on the site who shouldered the burden of that knowledge.

The other men returned a few minutes later, carrying a shed door between them, its edges ragged where they had hastily detached it from its hinges. They set it down and managed to heave the body onto it without any further gruesome slippage of skin.

'Take it to the timber shed,' Mr Longridge said grimly.

Led by the foreman, they bore their ghastly load away, but the smell lingered behind, a rotten tang that clung to Rory's tongue and clogged the back of his throat.

'You all right?' Mr Comerford asked him gruffly.

Rory just nodded, not trusting himself to speak in case vomit or a confession came pouring out.

Mr Longridge approached and leaned in to speak to them in a low voice. 'We'll need to report this at once to Lord Sinclair and Mr McGovern. I wonder how long he's been underwater.'

'God knows,' Mr Comerford said with a grimace. 'Weeks, or even months, by the state of him.'

Mr Longridge looked a little green. 'This is extremely serious. It could well be an accident, but...'

His words trailed away and Rory's pulse skittered.

'Hmm,' said Mr Comerford. 'Do you suspect foul play?'

Mr Longridge frowned. 'It's too hard to tell at this stage. There'll need to be an inquest to try to determine what happened to the fellow. The constable will know who should take charge of the matter. We'd better keep everyone else away until he comes.'

He strode off after the workers, and Rory and Mr Comerford followed. When they reached the timber shed, they found that the men had already deposited the body within and were now hovering uncertainly around the open doorway. Mr Longridge beckoned to them and they clustered in front of him.

'Thank you for carrying out such an immensely difficult task,' he said gravely. 'As you no doubt understand, no further work will take place on the site today. You may all return to your homes.'

As the men pivoted towards their foreman with worried demands about that day's pay, Rory sidled past the group and up to the shed. Two hinges dangled off the door jamb. Against his better judgement, he edged over the threshold.

Inside the dim building, the fetid stink intensified, and he pressed the back of his wrist to his mouth as he stared down at the body laid out on the shed door. There he was. Tommy Jones.

Or what was left of him.

The remains of his coat clung to the grey, swollen mass of him. His features were bloated and distorted, and his hair had slid away in patches. His shirt had torn at the belly but there was no obvious wound beneath the rot and filth, just a mess of putrid flesh.

Rory closed his eyes. The gash from the poker was gone – that was a mercy. Still, the presence of the body raised many questions. Soon, people would begin to ask them. They weren't safe yet.

Mr Longridge's voice drifted into the shed from outside as he assured the men that they wouldn't be penalised for the regrettable event that had occurred that morning. Before his absence became too prolonged, Rory stepped back out into the daylight, the cold air a relief after the stench within.

Across the sawmill site, the mist was lifting from the river, revealing the millwheel more clearly. It stood still once more, its secret now dragged into the open.

# Chapter 34

The grounds at Aintree Racecourse teemed with spectators poring over their programmes as they waited eagerly for the forthcoming races. Bookmakers wove among them, shouting out odds and taking bets. Concealing his nerves beneath a calm façade, Cormac led Bridget through the crowds, Emily beside them on Rory's arm. The grandstand was visible in the distance; he glanced around and wondered what were the odds of them reaching it without someone making a show of their disdain towards them.

'If this proves to be a categorical disaster,' he said, 'then we may just have to accept our social exile.'

The three of them nodded soberly. At least one point in their favour was the fact that the throng consisted of all classes, from aristocrats to commoners; this wasn't an exclusive occasion where they would stand out for being the only ones beneath the ton's esteem. The working-class folk were as numerous as the nobility, and, on a further positive note, they probably wouldn't have even heard of the adulterous Lady Courcey and her paramour, given that the majority lacked the means or ability to read the papers that carried the scandalous story.

'Good *gracious*!' an appalled voice burst out. 'The indecency of it!'

Swivelling his head quickly to locate the owner of the voice, he spotted her about a dozen feet away wearing a wide-brimmed bonnet and a sour expression. He felt his own expression curdle at the sight of her: it was Lady Talbot, the woman who had walked out of a gathering at Sinclair Manor because Cormac and Bridget had been in attendance. Next to her stood her husband, Lord Talbot, and their son, Mr Grover. Cormac clenched his fists; Mr Grover had been an utter cad to Emily on multiple occasions and deserved nothing but vilification for his poor opinion of women.

In an act that no one could misinterpret, Cormac turned purposefully away from the trio, steering Bridget in the opposite direction and trusting that Emily and Rory would follow suit. Even above the noise of the crowd, he heard Lady Talbot's affronted gasp; he hoped it had galled her not to be the one to deliver the snub.

As he strode on, he noticed several people in ordinary clothing eyeing them, though their gazes seemed to be curious rather than accusing. No doubt rumours would spread during the course of the day and these folk would ultimately find out why the fancy lady had been so dismayed. Remembering that the whole point of today was to show their fearlessness, he slowed his pace so that it wouldn't appear like they were trying to run away from the situation.

'Mr McGovern!'

He halted, as did Bridget, Emily and Rory. When he turned, he perceived the straight-backed figure of Lord Sinclair marching towards them and gritted his teeth. This would be a true test of who they could rely upon to stand by them. Apart from a rocky beginning, Lord Sinclair had been perfectly gracious in all his private interactions with Cormac. How would he now behave in full view of his peers?

The viscount came to a stop and regarded Cormac shrewdly from beneath his heavy brow. 'Audacious of you to show your face here, is it not?' he said. 'You certainly know how to set tongues wagging. The ink has hardly dried on the newspaper reports.'

'Audacity was not our intention,' Cormac said warily. 'We merely decided to grasp the nettle instead of waiting to be stung.'

Lord Sinclair barked out a laugh. 'Indeed. I don't know whether to commend you or question your sanity. Still, let me assure you that you do not need to fear a sting from me or my family.' He gestured behind him, where three figures hovered at a distance. 'I have warned them to be civil.'

It looked like Lady Sinclair had swallowed the warning with some difficulty, judging by her pained expression. The Sinclairs' son, Mr Bertram, only radiated boredom, while their daughter, Harriet, offered a hopeful wave in Emily's direction. Emily returned the gesture cautiously.

'Thank you, my lord,' Cormac said with genuine gratitude. 'It's encouraging to learn that we are not entirely without allies.'

'I see no reason to sever our acquaintance. You have amply demonstrated that a man's worth ought to be measured by his character, not his breeding. The lady, too, has proven that true worth is calculated in how one rises above adversity.' He inclined his head towards Bridget with respect and she bobbed a startled curtsey in response. 'Others, meanwhile, have made it plain that noble birth does not always yield noble conduct.'

This time, he shot a scathing glance over at Lady Talbot, who was watching them with blatant revulsion. Shaking his head, he returned his attention to Cormac, leaning in to lower his voice.

'While I don't wish to delay you, I do want to briefly apprise you of the latest developments with regard to that unfortunate discovery at the sawmill.'

Cormac sensed Emily tensing nearby, but he kept his own demeanour as composed as he could manage. 'Has the man been identified?'

'Regrettably, no,' Lord Sinclair replied. 'Apart from a missing tooth, his features were unrecognisable, and his presence doesn't align with any reported disappearances in the area. The authorities checked as far as Bedford.'

'How puzzling,' Cormac said, loathing himself for lying to the gentleman after he had just asserted his steadfast support for him.

'They've concluded that he was probably a traveller passing through, and that he must have been intoxicated and strayed too close to the river. There's no telling when he fell in or how far he drifted before reaching the mill. The chances of him getting caught in the wheel had to have been one in a hundred thousand—quite a ghastly discovery for the millworkers when they removed the bracing beams and let the wheel turn for the first time.' Lord Sinclair shrugged and sighed. 'Aside from that, they are making satisfactory progress, and we should see profits before the year is out.'

'That's good to hear,' Cormac said, forcing a nod. 'I hope the work will continue without any more...interruptions.'

'As do I. Now, I'll leave you to enjoy the day with my fervent wish that you won't be subjected to any further recriminations. By the by, there are a couple of horses running that might take your fancy as they have an Irish connection.'

With that, Lord Sinclair shook Cormac's hand and bowed to Bridget before returning to his family. Emily released a jagged breath.

'Does that mean it's over?' she asked shakily.

'It does,' Cormac answered, relieved. 'Maud is safe, and so are you.'

Not to mention, they had won the explicit backing of Lord Sinclair, a fine confidence boost at this juncture. Encouraged, Cormac snagged the attention of a passing vendor and purchased two programmes, one of which he handed to Rory. Flicking open the programme, his gaze landed on a list of the competing racehorses.

'Ah, look at that—there's a runner called Tipperary Boy. Might be worth a punt, don't you think?'

***

As they approached the grandstand, the crowds grew even thicker and Emily lost sight of her parents. Clinging more tightly to Rory, she heard him murmuring under his breath, 'This, that, these, those. This, that, these, those.'

She brushed her fingers along the inside of his elbow in reassurance, though she was certain he didn't need it—she had every confidence that he would rise to the occasion. He had continued to persevere in his lessons with Mr Humphrey and she knew how much he had refined both his education and his etiquette. In fact, given the consistency of his dancing instruction, he was likely a far more accomplished dancer than she was now. The timing, however, was unfortunate – after her mother's divorce, would there be any opportunity for him to put those hard-earned skills to use? Ahead of their excursion to Aintree, Emily had presumed that the family would never be invited to another social gathering. Still, Lord Sinclair's lack of prejudice gave her hope that they would not be ostracised forever. Perhaps she ought to join Rory in his dancing lessons, if only to ensure that she could keep pace with him when the time came.

Another student intent on improving himself was Gus, who had recently voiced a desire to become more involved in the family's exploits, since, with Jack away at school, he was now the only one being left behind. He had been sorely disappointed to be excluded from the expedition to the races, but he'd had no grounds upon which to object – a severe cold had settled in his lungs, confining him to bed for days with a rattling cough. Emily suspected that her parents had been quietly relieved to have a valid reason to keep him at home; it was another way to delay his exposure to society a little longer, though that day was drawing ever nearer, considering how attentively he'd been applying himself to his lessons of late. To console him for missing the trip, Mr Comerford had promised Gus that as soon as he'd recovered they would undertake a bout of night-time surveillance to investigate the source of the flickering light in the fields. Thus, when the rest of the family embarked on their journey to Liverpool, they'd left Gus sitting up in bed, a mustard plaster warming his chest as he enthusiastically sketched maps and compiled lists of necessary provisions.

As Emily glimpsed the racecourse beyond the grandstand and contemplated the sketches it might inspire her to create, she heard a tentative voice behind her.

'Emily?'

She and Rory both twisted around to find Harriet Bertram hovering there.

'Um,' she said. 'Good day, Harriet.'

She didn't really know how to feel towards this woman. Although they had come to reasonably amicable terms when they last met, Harriet had still been a chief collaborator in a scheme to ruin Emily's reputation on the Hutchville Estate, along with the detestable Mr Grover.

Harriet cringed as though she could tell what was running through Emily's mind. 'I won't intrude on your day,' she said softly. 'I just wanted to say hello and enquire after your wellbeing.' She glanced from Emily to Rory. 'I hope married life is everything you wished for, and more.'

Perceiving no guile in her demeanour, Emily replied, 'That is kind of you. Yes, we are very happy.' An image of a rocking cradle crept into her thoughts, but she resolutely pushed it away.

Harriet looked genuinely relieved. 'I'm pleased to hear that. May you have an enjoyable time today at Aintree.'

She made to turn away, but Emily said quickly, 'And you? Are you well?'

Harriet paused. 'Oh. I'm fine, thank you.' She hesitated. 'I...you might be interested to know that I...received a marriage proposal. From Lord Dartry.'

Emily tried to mask her surprise but she was sure her wide eyes betrayed her. 'I-indeed? Allow me to offer my congrat—'

'No need,' Harriet cut in. 'I refused him.'

This time, Emily couldn't hide her astonishment. She knew her own reasons for rejecting Lord Dartry and had no regrets, but what could have led Harriet to turn him down? Granted, he had probably asked for her hand in order to gain her dowry, and yet the marriage would have elevated her to the rank of countess.

'I was at least his fifth choice for a bride,' Harriet said. 'A kind-hearted acquaintance taught me to have more self-respect than that.'

Emily blinked and then smiled. Harriet smiled back. A bubble of sincere warmth swelled between them...only to be punctured by a sneering tone.

'What a charming reunion—so very touching.'

Emily's skin crawled as Mr Grover materialised out of the milling crowd, clutching a race programme. Rory went rigid, his hand flexing at his side. Emily reached for his wrist and squeezed it. While Mr Grover himself was a most unpleasant sight, at least there was one gratifying feature to note: a distinct crookedness to his nose.

Harriet stepped back in distaste. 'Excuse me, I must return my mother,' she said and hurried off.

Mr Grover's gaze followed her retreat with amusement. 'Poor, dear Miss Bertram. A spinster in the making, without a doubt.'

'Go away,' Emily said, disinclined to afford him even a shred of civility.

He ignored her. Flipping through his programme with exaggerated interest, he said, 'Have you decided yet where to place your wagers?'

'No,' Rory said shortly.

'Neither have I, although I've ascertained where I won't be wasting my money.' He pointed to a name on the list of racehorses. 'This one is going by the nickname Little Ab because he's so diminutive. However, his size isn't his greatest shortcoming. He has an Irish trainer, and I can't think of a worse gamble than backing a horse trained by an Irishman. There's no way he's finishing the race today.'

Emily frowned, trying to grasp the thread of his insult.

'The Irish have quite a lot of trouble finishing what they started, don't they?' Mr Grover grinned. 'I seem to recall reading about some disturbance in Ireland that they fancifully called a "rebellion". That was, what, a year and a half ago? And yet, not a whisper about it since.'

Emily despised him all the more because his assertion was unfortunately true – the Young Irelander rebellion had not turned into a more lasting resistance. It had sputtered out, leaving Ireland still shackled to British rule.

Rory exhaled a slow, controlled breath. 'You mistake endurance for surrender. The Irish are a patient people—we know how to wait for the right moment. And when our time comes, well...' He let the words hang in the air, his gaze steady. 'You may find we finish things in a way that leaves a permanent impression.'

Mr Grover gave a derisive laugh. 'Is that so? And here I thought you Irish preferred raising glasses to raising rebellions.'

'It's easy to mock from the safety of English soil, isn't it? I suggest you exercise some discretion.' Rory's voice remained smooth, but there was an unmistakable steel beneath it. 'Unless you fancy having that nose of yours broken again, of course. This Irishman can certainly finish what he starts.'

Mr Grover's hand twitched towards his face for just a second before he scoffed. 'I hardly think you'd be foolish enough to instigate a brawl in public.'

Rory shrugged. 'Maybe. Maybe not. I suppose you should pray that I'm feeling civil today.'

Mr Grover hesitated. His bravado didn't completely crack, but his feet shifted as though he was considering whether to stand his ground or make a dignified retreat.

'I see no point in arguing with a fellow who thinks only with his fists,' he muttered, before turning and stalking off into the throng.

Emily stared up at Rory in awe. 'I am so impressed,' she said admiringly.

He blushed. 'The Duke of Desmond put on a good display.'

She shook her head. 'You know what? I believe that was all Rory Carey.'

He rubbed the back of his neck, looking disconcerted but quietly pleased.

And then, to top it all off, Little Ab won the Grand National later that day.

# CHAPTER 35

'There he is!'

Gus waved frantically as Jack came into view further down the docks, and Cormac raised his own arm in enthusiastic greeting, elated to see his eldest boy again. Jack picked up his pace, trotting forwards until he was almost running to reach them. They embraced in a three-way hug, beaming. Gus, of course, launched into his patter right away.

'Ma, Emily and Rory have already boarded the ship with Polly, Jennie and Mr Varley. Just wait until I tell you what happened!' He drew in a breath – it had taken four months to shake the worst of his February cold, but his voice had mostly settled back to its usual wheezy state. 'We finally solved the mystery of the flickering light in the fields! Ettie Cobb thought it might be smugglers, but her nan said it could be the spirit of a local farmhand who lost a flock of sheep in a bad storm and kept searching for them until the day he died. I reckoned that was the strongest theory, so Mr Comerford and I lay in wait to see if we could spot the light, and when it appeared I swear to God I felt the air get colder like we were in the presence of a ghost, only guess who it turned out to be?' He paused dramatically, giving Jack time to adopt a look of avid anticipation. 'It was one of the tenants, Harry Barnes! He's been sleepwalking, going back and forth across the fields at night with a lantern!'

'You don't say!' Jack replied.

'Mr Comerford helped Harry's wife put a lock on their door so he won't wander off anymore.' Gus bounced on his toes. 'I think it's still worth investigating the background of the farmhand, though. For all we know, he could be roaming restlessly too, trying to figure out what happened to his poor sheep. I'll look into it as soon as we get back from Oakleigh.'

'Good idea,' Jack said, nodding seriously. 'It's definitely worth investigating further.'

Cormac stared at him in astonishment. A small smile was playing at the corner of the lad's mouth; he was clearly only humouring Gus. When had he stopped believing in ghosts? Had he guessed that Mr Comerford had roped Harry Barnes into performing the role of the sleepwalker? Perhaps Jack's year away at school had accelerated his maturity beyond what they had anticipated, with the unsought consequence of widening the gap between him and his brother. He seemed to be crossing the threshold into adulthood right before Cormac's eyes.

But there were other signs of that as well. Jack had been capable enough to travel alone from Scotland at the end of the school term, meeting the family in Liverpool before they sailed to Ireland. He wasn't shaving yet, and yet a slight thickening of the hairs on his upper lip and jaw line indicated that he couldn't be far off it. A strange mixture of pride and loss settled in Cormac's chest.

'All went well over the final term?' he asked.

'Yes. The school will post out the results from my summer examinations, but Mr Cameron said he already had a quick glance and I've nothing to be worried about.'

'Well done, lad,' Cormac said warmly. 'And, uh, any cause to mention Jasper?'

'No,' Jack said, a touch wearily. 'You don't need to keep asking me that.'

'I just want to be sure—'

'Everything's fine, Da,' Jack interrupted with a somewhat brittle smile. 'I promise.'

Cormac let it go, but he couldn't shake the feeling that his son had just lied to him for the first time in his life.

When they boarded the ship, they discovered that Emily and Rory had already gone below deck so that Emily could endure the misery of the sea crossing in the privacy of their cabin; she would have a long night ahead of her. After Jack shared an affectionate reunion with his mother, he and Gus headed off to explore the vessel before twilight set in. There was a sheen in Bridget's eyes as she watched them go.

'Whole again,' she said softly, and Cormac understood exactly what she meant.

They began to stroll along the deck as the ship moved away from the docks. Cormac felt giddy like a child; when they next stood on land, it would be Irish soil and they would be another step closer to Oakleigh and to their wedding day. It was all falling into place: the bishop had granted the dispensation, St Canice's had been confirmed as the venue, and the staff at Oakleigh were preparing for the upcoming celebration with the joy of those who had been too long deprived of a reason to be happy. This would be a summer to remember.

'Are you sure the crew loaded Jack's school trunk?' Bridget asked.

Cormac nodded. 'The hackney he hired at the railway station brought it directly to the wharf. I watched them take it aboard myself.'

'We will have a great deal of luggage to collect when we disembark,' she remarked.

His lips twitched, but he elected not to comment on the excess baggage she had decided to bring. 'I'll brief Varley—he'll see to it that none of our belongings get lost in the chaos of unloading.'

Her brow furrowed. 'Why won't you see to it yourself?'

He hesitated. 'I'm hoping to make a slight detour before we travel on from Dublin.'

She contemplated him for a moment. 'You mean to visit Henrietta.'

'I do,' he said, matching the evenness of her tone with his own.

She turned her head away to gaze out over the ship's gunwale. He waited uneasily for her to decide upon her response, conscious that this conversation had been in the offing for a while.

At length, she looked back at him, her expression pained. 'The last thing I desire is to create friction between us. Nevertheless, I feel compelled to express my discomfort regarding this situation.'

He didn't like that she referred to Henrietta as a 'situation', but he couldn't blame her. The circumstances were so very complicated.

'You can be honest with me,' he said. 'And I'll be the same.'

She sighed and stopped to grasp the gunwale with both of her gloved hands. He halted on her left and faced her so that her countenance was in profile.

'I realise that I must come across as a jealous lover,' she said, 'and I suppose that is what I am. It's just that it upsets me how much you care for a girl who isn't our daughter but the daughter of a woman who shared an experience with you that I wish had been mine alone. I know it's irrational, of course—when that happened, neither of us expected to ever find our way back to each other. And after all, I also shared a bed with another.'

He was glad she pointed that out because otherwise her line of reasoning would have felt rather unjust.

She pursed her lips. 'But you've had many opportunities to leave Henrietta, and her mother, in the past, and yet at sporadic intervals you bring her back into our lives, sometimes against her will. Granted, I went to seek her on one occasion, but only because I knew you would want me to. Why must we revive this connection every time we go to Dublin? It seems like she is an afterthought that only crosses our minds when we are reminded of her by happenstance.'

He swallowed. 'I appreciate how you might perceive it that way, but she's not an afterthought to me. I've maintained regular correspondence with Mr Dunhill since we discovered Henrietta's whereabouts at the Theatre Royal, and I've been sending intermittent packages to her, even though she can't—or chooses not to—write back.'

Bridget looked shocked. 'What have you been sending her? Why didn't you tell me this?'

'Sheet music, for the most part,' he replied, trying and failing to repress his guilt. 'I didn't purposely conceal this—in fact, I told Emily about it once. But I suppose I didn't declare it too loudly either, probably in an effort to avoid this very confrontation.'

'And why did you want to avoid it?' she challenged. 'What did you not wish to admit?'

He winced, knowing that she would have no desire to hear this. Still, he had promised honesty. 'That, God help me, I do regard her as another daughter. I've endeavoured not to, and I understand how it must pain you, but I can't seem to stifle these feelings.'

Bridget was silent. The scar on her cheek tightened, suggesting that she was clenching her jaw quite hard. He wanted to touch her, but he held himself back.

'Mr Dunhill has sent me handbills from the theatre's performances since it reopened after the riot. I've experienced an absurd amount of paternal pride in learning that Henrietta has publicly performed some of the songs I gifted her.' He exhaled dispiritedly. 'I'm sorry.'

Bridget turned to him. He was prepared for her resentment, perhaps even her anger, but not for the rueful smile that curved her mouth.

'Don't be,' she said. 'You can't help how big your heart is. It would be like apologising for the colour of your hair or your eyes. You have a capacity for compassion and love that is sometimes hard to fathom. Maybe I'm envious that I must share it with so many others, but I can also recognise that you have enough for us all.' She paused. 'I'm convinced that, had he lived, you would have adored James like he was your own son, regardless of who his father was.'

'Of course I would have,' he said with absolute sincerity.

'And the truth is I love you all the more for being such a generous, kind-hearted man—even towards Henrietta, despite the fact that she has not offered you the same affection in return. I think that is often the fate of a parent, to cherish their child more than their child cherishes them. At least, until the child becomes a parent themselves and truly comprehends what it means to love unconditionally.'

He pressed his lips together as her words resonated deeply. 'I've been careful not to place any conditions or expectations on Henrietta. She's had a difficult life and has every reason to be wary of others, including myself. I'll give her all I can and continue to be content with whatever she's willing to give in return.'

'That's as much as you can ask of her,' said Bridget. 'And you have not asked too much of me. You have my blessing to go see her when we dock, and in the future too.'

She lifted her hand and grazed the back of her gloved fingers against his cheek.

They didn't speak of Henrietta again, but the candid exchange – and the relief it brought – made Cormac's step even lighter when the ship docked in Dublin early the next morning and the family disembarked, setting foot on Irish soil once more. After relaying instructions about the luggage to Mr Varley, and reiterating them to Rory in case the aging valet missed anything, he gave Bridget a swift kiss and hurried away from the docks.

Upon reaching Hawkins Street, he found the Theatre Royal utterly still and silent. That made sense; it wouldn't stir into life until the next performance that evening. What alarmed him was the great bill plastered to the front door proclaiming an alteration to the listing of performers that month: 'The Theatre Royal regrets to announce that Angelica, the girl with the voice of an angel, will not appear on stage during June. In her place will be the stunningly talented...'

He didn't bother to read the rest of it. His insides coiled with apprehension. What had happened to Henrietta?

He tried the door of the theatre, expecting it to be locked, but it opened easily. When he stepped inside, he discovered a stooped woman with a long-handled brush in the lobby, sweeping up discarded handbills, ticket stubs and other bits of detritus left behind by the previous night's audience. She jumped at his appearance.

'My apologies for intruding,' he said at once with a quick bow. 'I'm looking for Mr Dunhill.'

Even as he said it, he realised that the theatre manager was likely at his home on Frederick Street, given the time of day, but then the woman nodded.

'He's up in his office,' she said in a thick Dublin accent. 'Although he's sure to be asleep at this hour.'

'We have a scheduled appointment,' Cormac lied smoothly. 'He'll be expecting me, so I'll just head on up.'

She shrugged and went back to her sweeping. He strode across the lobby to the inconspicuous door that led backstage and let himself through it. As he climbed the stairs, he wondered whether Henrietta might be sleeping in her dressing room, but when he reached the door with the nameplate 'Angelica', he found it ajar and the dim room within empty. There were no blankets on the cot, while a few roses lay abandoned on the dressing table, their petals faded and withered. The air held no trace of fresh perfume and only a single pair of wings hung from the otherwise bare costume rail.

Misgivings rapidly mounting, he charged along the corridor to Mr Dunhill's office and didn't pause before banging on the closed door. He heard a yelp in response and decided he would wait no more than five seconds until he barged right in. If he discovered Henrietta in there with the theatre manager, he would wring the bastard's neck.

On the fourth second, he perceived muffled footsteps, and on the fifth, the door opened and Mr Dunhill peered out blearily wearing just a shirt and trousers. He squinted and then his eyes sprang wide.

'M-Mr McGovern?' he stammered, his round face full of shock. 'What brings you here, and at this ungodly hour of the morning?'

'We need to speak. May I come in?' Cormac demanded in a way that sounded like an order rather than a request. If the man refused him entry, that would all but confirm that something untoward had been going on behind the door.

Mr Dunhill faltered before stepping back. Cormac marched into the office...and found it as empty as Henrietta's dressing room. By the light of a high, small window, he could make out a rickety desk covered in ledgers, handbills and receipts, with a creased waistcoat and cravat tossed carelessly over them. Next to the desk stood a large cabinet, its open doors revealing haphazard stacks of props, while a low cot lay opposite with rumpled blankets and a flattened pillow. The air had a stuffy, sleep-laden quality to it and, after a discreet glance behind the door, Cormac could tell that there wasn't a single place where Henrietta could be hiding. Mr Dunhill had definitely been sleeping alone.

Though somewhat abashed, Cormac didn't show it as he turned to the befuddled theatre manager.

'I saw the bill on the door of the theatre,' he said tersely. 'Why isn't Hen—Angelica performing this month? What's happened to her?'

Mr Dunhill's expression cleared with understanding and became morose. 'Ah, yes. Most regrettable. The poor girl. She's not well.'

'In what way?' Cormac nearly barked, wishing the man would get to the point.

'Such unfortunate luck,' Mr Dunhill said, shaking his head. 'She's taken ill with typhus.'

Cormac gaped, his alarm rising further. 'Is her life in danger?'

'I don't believe so, although it's made her very sick and weak. The rash and fever have been quite severe, and of course the coughing has extinguished her singing voice, although I do hope that will only be temporary.'

Cormac gritted his teeth. 'How did she catch it?'

Mr Dunhill rubbed sleep from his eyes. 'It's rampant in the city at present with the flood of refugees from the countryside. I suspect the costumier may have passed it on when she came to measure Angelica for new wings, as I heard afterwards that she'd also been struck down with it. I'm lucky it didn't spread to the rest of the performers or my theatre would have been ruined. Again.' His gaze darkened.

'Where is she?' Cormac demanded. 'I want to see her.'

Mr Dunhill looked horrified. 'Mr McGovern, no, I cannot allow that! Only imagine if you caught it off her—that would be disastrous.'

That made Cormac pause. The last thing he wanted was to transmit the disease to any of his family; he could easily envision the havoc it would wreak on Gus's lungs in particular.

'Tell me where she is, at least,' he said, his tone clipped.

'She's at Frederick Street. My wife is taking good care of her. We sent our daughters to stay with her sister, and she has barred the door to prevent anyone from going in or out. Hence why I am currently sleeping in my office.' Mr Dunhill raised his arms in a helpless gesture. 'The show must go on.'

Cormac chewed the inside of his cheek. 'And you're certain she's not at great risk?'

'I truly hope not—the long-term loss in ticket sales would be shattering.' At Cormac's glare, Mr Dunhill hastened on, 'But naturally my angel's health is the most important priority. We are all praying for her swift recovery.'

Cormac kept his expression stony. 'Don't push her back onto the stage too soon. Give her enough time to recuperate fully.'

'Yes, yes, of course,' Mr Dunhill said quickly.

Cormac ran a hand over his jaw, which was bristly after the overnight crossing. 'Is there any help I can provide to aid her convalescence? Do you require money for medicine?'

Mr Dunhill hesitated. 'That's very generous of you. However, the doctor said all we can do is let the fever run its course. She just needs to rest.'

He sent a hopeful glance towards the door, but Cormac crossed his arms.

'Why didn't you notify me about this? You're aware of my concern for her welfare—you ought to have written as soon as she fell ill.'

'I'm almost certain I wrote you a letter,' Mr Dunhill said with a frown, starting to rummage around the debris on his desk. He unearthed a crumpled page from beneath a mound of receipts. 'Ah, here it is,' he said with a wince.

Looking over the man's shoulder, Cormac could see that the page contained only the words 'Dear Mr McGovern'.

'I'm very sorry,' Mr Dunhill bleated. 'It must have slipped my mind. It's been a stressful time, you understand.'

Cormac suspected he was referring to the toll that Henrietta's absence had incurred on his theatre, rather than his distress over the girl's wellbeing. He took the page from Mr Dunhill's unresisting fingers, fished a pencil out from among a pile of handbills and wrote on it.

'This is the address where I'll be staying in Carlow for the time being. Please ensure you write to me if her condition worsens by any degree. I'll travel back up to Dublin next month in the hope that she'll be well enough to receive visitors by then.'

He would wait until after the wedding, just to be cautious. Bridget had been remarkably understanding about Henrietta, but there were limits to even her patience – postponing their wedding because he had contracted typhus from Henrietta would surely test them to breaking point.

After receiving fervent assurances from Mr Dunhill that he would write to Carlow with any significant news, Cormac left the office and made his way back down to the lobby where the stooped woman and the rubbish on the floor had disappeared. He emerged from the silent theatre onto the footpath and immediately advanced in the direction of Frederick Street. When he located Mr Dunhill's house, the address of which he knew from their correspondence, he halted on the opposite side of the street and observed the tall, narrow building. Like the theatre, there was no sign of movement, and its lower windows were tightly shuttered. He pictured Henrietta curled up on a bed within, twisting in the throes of her fever, and his fingers itched to stroke her hair back from her face and tuck the blankets more closely around her, no matter if his only reward would be another rebuff.

'Feel better soon, *a éan ceoil*,' he murmured.

His songbird.

# Chapter 36

As Ashbrook Lodge came into view, Rory's chief thought was that if this was what passed for a 'small' estate then he didn't understand the meaning of the word. To be fair, it didn't match the size of Bewley Hall, or even Oakleigh, and yet it still boasted three large storeys with bow windows on both the ground and middle levels, while a pair of stout columns flanked the front door, giving the place a stately air.

He and Cormac reined in their horses before the house as the two carriages rolled to a stop behind them. They had arranged to make this visit on their way down to Carlow upon the request of Patrick, which was such a rare invitation that the family had all agreed it could not be declined. It also proved to be a welcome break in their journey, since the June heat had only intensified from the morning to the afternoon, turning the railway carriage into a stifling box of dead air – opening the windows had admitted more dust than breeze, leaving them all thankful to disembark at Kildare railway station.

Dismounting from his horse, Rory approached the nearest carriage as its door swung out.

'Thank you, Rory,' Bridget said as he helped her and Emily to descend.

'You're welcome, Bridget,' he answered and she gave him an affectionate smile. Once he started calling Cormac by his first name, addressing his mother-in-law as Bridget had become easier too.

Jack and Gus jumped down after them, looking around eagerly. Alighting from his own mount, Cormac assisted Polly and Jennie from the other carriage, while Mr Varley followed with an audible creak of his spine as he straightened.

The front door of Ashbrook Lodge opened and Patrick emerged. If Rory didn't know better, he would have said the fellow seemed nervous in the way he tugged at the cuffs of his coat. His gaze slid restlessly from his guests to the corner of the house and eased when a pair of stable hands came trotting into sight.

'Thanks, chaps,' he called and they gave him deferential nods before reaching for the reins of Rory's and Cormac's horses. As they led the animals away, he came forwards to greet the family. 'It's my pleasure to receive you here,' he said. Although his words were somewhat stilted, he bowed with exemplary courtesy.

Cormac shook his nephew's hand, while Bridget smiled and said, 'Thank you for inviting us.'

'Do you have a billiard table here, Pat?' Gus asked, almost bursting with enthusiasm beneath his tricorne. 'I've been practising with Da!'

'Is that so?' Patrick said, the corner of his mouth lifting. 'It sounds like I might have a formidable opponent on my hands. We'd better make time for a game later.'

Gus's face flooded with a blend of excitement and determination.

Patrick turned back to the rest of them. 'Would you care for some refreshment? Given the fine weather, I took the liberty of arranging it in an outdoor setting.'

'That sounds delightful,' Bridget answered on everyone's behalf, her brows drawing together with curiosity. She flicked her glance to the side where Polly, Jennie and Mr Varley stood waiting unobtrusively.

'All are welcome,' Patrick said, acknowledging the servants with a polite dip of his head. 'We don't stand on ceremony at Ashbrook. My agent, Blanchard, will likely join us too. There are no precedents to abide by, seeing as you're the first guests I've entertained here.'

As the stable hands returned to take care of the carriage horses, Patrick led the way around the other corner of the house and the rest of them followed, family and servants alike, Gus jogging to the front of the group so he could apprise Patrick of every detail relating to the solved mystery of the flickering light. Walking along, Rory noted the tidy lawn at the side of the house that sloped down to a well-maintained stone wall and, beyond that, an expanse of barley fields. This didn't appear to be the province of a man squandering his inheritance.

When they reached the grounds at the rear of the house, Patrick guided them towards a wooden arbour, where two maids were laying out jugs and glasses on a linen-covered table. The frame of the arbour was covered in flowering honeysuckle; stepping beneath its fragrant shade was a pleasant relief. The maids bobbed curtseys to Patrick and, at his appreciative nod, they slipped away towards the house.

'I can personally vouch for this claret cup,' he said, gesturing to the table. The jugs contained a deep red wine, chilled with ice and speckled with slices of citrus and some sort of greenery that Rory didn't recognise. 'It's a splendid thirst-quencher. By the by, that jug to the side has been diluted with extra soda water for our younger company.'

Cormac chuckled and reached for the jug in question to pour glasses for Jack and Gus, who looked crestfallen but resigned. Rory speculated that there was a time when their cousin would have actively encouraged them to drink the stronger beverage, and he wondered when that time had passed.

Bridget set about pouring everyone else's drinks; the iced liquid fizzed and clinked as it flowed into each glass. Polly and Jennie flushed at being served by their mistress, while Mr Varley located a bench on the far side of the table and sank onto it with a weary sigh. Rory sipped from his glass and relished the sensation of the cool claret running down his parched throat. Next to him, Emily took a deeper gulp – she had been delicate ever since the ship, but now the drink brought some colour back into her wan cheeks.

Cormac raised his glass to his nephew. 'Thank you for your hospitality. May we look forward to returning the same next month?'

Patrick nodded. 'Yes. I'm hoping to travel down two days before the wedding.'

Bridget beamed. 'That's marvellous.' After a slight hesitation, she said, 'Have you been in touch with your father lately?'

Patrick stared meditatively into his drink. 'We've maintained regular correspondence since the beginning of the year. I'm keeping him informed of estate developments here at Ashbrook...and I recently communicated that he will not be refused at the door the next time he chooses to visit.'

Patrick looked up, and Rory thought he discerned a trace of reluctant pride in his eyes.

'I've regained a measure of faith in my father,' he admitted. 'It seems he does possess the capacity to be selfless, after all. He even said in his last letter that he wishes you well, my lady.' Patrick gave an amused grunt. 'Although I don't expect his magnanimity will extend as far as him attending your nuptials.'

Rory highly doubted whether Bridget and Cormac had even issued an invitation to Garrett, but then their sense of honour had always been a peculiar thing, obliging them to act with fairness even towards those who had wronged them. If they had sent word to London, surely it would only have been out of duty rather than any real expectation that Garrett would appear.

'I'm glad you are on good terms with him again,' Bridget said sincerely. 'And also that you're evidently making a success of your time here.'

Patrick shrugged self-consciously. 'Without a pedigree to rely on, I figured I'd better make myself useful in other ways.'

Rory felt Emily tense at his side. However, before the moment became awkward, Patrick pivoted smoothly and waved to an approaching figure.

'There's Blanchard now.'

The arrival of the land agent, a stout man with a shrewd expression, prompted a round of introductions, followed by a discussion regarding the condition of the estate. When Cormac enquired about their use of crop rotation, Blanchard grew quite animated.

'Turnips and barley proved to be sound choices,' he declared. 'The tenants weren't convinced at first, although after last season's yield they're not so quick to grumble anymore. Another healthy harvest might make believers of them yet.'

'We even took a gamble on planting a small potato crop this year,' Patrick added. 'It's too early to say whether the blight will return later in the summer, but for now we are cautiously optimistic.'

By the time the jugs were emptied, a genuinely convivial atmosphere had settled over the arbour. Cormac, Rory and Patrick had all unbuttoned their coats and loosened their cravats, while Bridget idly fanned herself with a folded napkin. Emily and Jennie were smiling and blinking languidly, the claret apparently having had a strong effect on them both. Mr Varley's chin had dropped onto his chest and he was snoozing; Polly delicately eased his glass from his slackened grip and placed it back on the table. At the edge of the arbour, Jack and Gus were sprawled on the grass, tossing pebbles at a mark on the ground.

'Can we play billiards soon?' Gus asked hopefully.

Patrick checked his pocket watch. 'It's nearly time to get ready for dinner. But if you can exercise just a little more patience, we'll have a game afterwards. What do you say?'

'I'll eat quickly so we can start sooner!' Gus declared, earning a few quiet chuckles around the group at the unlikely notion of him abandoning the dinner table early.

This exchange was enough to stir everyone from their drowsy contentment. Polly gave Mr Varley's shoulder a gentle tug and he startled awake with a sheepish expression. In a leisurely trickle, they all began to leave the arbour, dispersing towards the house where the two maids emerged promptly to show them to their rooms.

Patrick cleared his throat. 'Rory, could I have a quick word?'

Surprised, Rory cast a glance after Emily, who had gone on ahead, leaning sleepily on her mother's arm. With a hesitant nod, he held back. Cormac and Jack were the last to step out into the sunshine; Cormac acknowledged Rory and Patrick with a brief tilt of his head before steering Jack after the others.

Patrick fidgeted with the items on the table, lining up the empty glasses and dropping an errant lemon slice back into one of the jugs. Rory watched him with a frown.

'What d'you want to talk about?' he asked, his tone on the edge of impatience.

Patrick stepped away from the table. 'Ah. Yes.' He stuck his finger inside his cravat and loosened it even further. 'There's something I wanted to mention.' He cleared his throat again, his discomfort palpable.

'Which is?' Rory prompted.

Patrick pressed his lips together. 'Look, I won't blame you if you decide to give me a box, and I won't stop you if you try.'

Dipping his hand into his pocket, he withdrew a folded piece of paper and held it out. Rory took it, his brows furrowed. Before he could unfold it, Patrick spoke again.

'It's the name and address of a doctor. He wasn't easy to find—it's not a branch of medicine that's commonly studied. But this fellow has gained a reputation for his particular interest in the area.' Patrick paused, noting Rory's blank face. Wincing, he said, 'His practice centres on the ailments and other impediments that may hinder a family's natural increase.'

Rory's mouth fell open.

'I'm aware that it's a very sensitive matter,' Patrick hurried on, 'and I have no desire to intrude on this private affair between you and my cousin. However, when we last spoke of it, I got the impression that you had resigned yourself to the situation. And I thought it worth encouraging you not to give up hope yet.'

Rory stared at him in dumbfounded silence.

'Right, go ahead,' Patrick muttered, letting his arms fall to his sides and offering his chin. 'I deserve it.'

Rory swallowed. 'I'm not going to hit you.' He clutched the paper tightly as if it might blow away, even though there wasn't a breath of wind on this hot June day. 'I think a handshake might be more in order.'

Patrick eyed him warily.

'This is—' Rory stopped. He didn't know what to say. ''Tis really unexpected.'

Patrick rubbed the back of his neck. 'I just wanted to make up for...past transgressions. You don't have to tell Emily where you got the information, if you decide to use it.'

Rory nodded. 'Thanks, Pat. Thanks a lot.'

Patrick tossed his head. 'Consider it my last good deed of the day. I fully intend to trounce you on the billiard table later.'

# CHAPTER 37

Bridget stood at her bedchamber window in her shift, stays and petticoats and stared out glumly at the lashing rain. Rain on one's wedding day was supposedly good luck, but did that include a deluge of such torrential proportions? She could scarcely see past the sheet of water streaming down the glass.

With a sigh, she turned away from the window and glanced about the room. Oakleigh's household staff, led by Ellen, had continued to work hard in Bridget's absence, and the manor had at last been furnished to a very pleasing level of comfort. A freestanding mirror with a mahogany frame stood in the corner, its brass fittings allowing it to tilt with ease, while a pair of sheepskin rugs covered the floor on either side of the bed, which now boasted an abundance of pillows and an ivory-coloured counterpane with a quilted floral design.

On top of the counterpane lay the crowning piece of her wedding ensemble: a beautiful taffeta gown in a warm shade of copper. Although white had apparently become quite a fashionable colour since Queen Victoria wore it a decade ago, Bridget simply could not resist the copper fabric – and besides, the purity of white did not seem fitting for a second marriage. Cormac had poorly hidden his amusement at the volume of luggage she had brought from England, but she hoped he would reconsider his stance once he set eyes upon what the extra trunk had contained.

Approaching the bed, she brushed her left hand over the lustrous material. Her fingers were bare – Cormac had taken the gold ring from her the previous night and wouldn't return it until they stood together before the altar in St Canice's Church. Her heart fluttered with nerves and excitement.

She took another look around the bedchamber and her gaze landed upon the wooden carving resting on the mahogany mantelpiece: the figurine of their family that Cormac had carved so many years ago in Boston. It had travelled with them from America to England, and now to Ireland, for she couldn't have left it behind on this important journey – it was a testament to the life they had built on their own terms, a life they could finally make lasting and secure. She hugged herself as a thrill of anticipation ran through her.

A knock came at the door and Polly entered, carrying an ornate wooden box in her arms.

'Here it is, my lady,' she declared.

She had been somewhat downcast since leaving Bewley Hall, and Bridget had felt guilty for obliging her to part from her mother and uncle yet again, but now she came forwards with a beaming smile as she placed the box on Bridget's dressing table and lifted its heavy lid. The circular mirror on the lid's underside reflected the array of necklaces and brooches within, all of which had once belonged to Lady Bewley. As Bridget took in the dazzling display, Polly opened several of the box's drawers to further reveal numerous bracelets, rings and pairs of earrings, as well as a separate compartment containing the precious pearl necklace Emily had used for her still life painting (which now took pride of place in the drawing room downstairs).

'What do you favour on this special day?' Polly asked.

Bridget felt a lump form in her throat. Her emotions were already simmering quite close to the surface, and this gesture only added to the momentous occasion, demonstrating that Polly truly deemed her to be worthy of Lady Bewley's treasured jewellery.

'What would you suggest?' she managed to choke out.

Polly cast her gaze over the various pieces. 'This,' she said, reaching into the box and extracting a gold locket. 'It will complement the colour of your gown.'

She held out the locket and Bridget accepted it gingerly. The weight of it felt solid in her palm as she admired its oval casing engraved with undulating rococo patterns, the swirls and flourishes redolent of the previous century. Its hinge gave a faint creak as she undid the clasp, revealing an empty space within.

'Her ladyship used to keep a miniature of his lordship in it,' Polly said softly. 'Before she passed, she asked that it be taken out and placed into her hand so that she would not be alone under the soil.' Polly's voice shook and she blinked hard.

Bridget couldn't recall if she had ever noticed the locket on Lady Bewley, but perhaps the lady had kept it hidden beneath high-necked dresses, a quiet token of devotion unseen by the world.

'It would be my honour to wear it,' Bridget murmured. As she refastened the clasp, she resolved to ask Emily to paint a miniature of Cormac so that he would always be close to her heart.

Polly smiled and began to push in the drawers of the jewellery box, while Bridget moved to lower the lid. Their hands fumbled across each other and the lid slipped between their grips, slamming shut with a heavy thud. A muted crack followed. They exchanged wide-eyed glances before Polly cautiously raised the lid again. A fracture had appeared in the round mirror, running right through the centre of it. Bridget gulped.

'Are you superstitious at all, Polly?' she asked weakly.

Polly paused for just a little too long before saying robustly, 'Of course not.' Flinching, she closed the lid with extreme care, even though the damage was already done.

The bedchamber door opened, and this time Emily and Ellen entered. Emily, dressed in a charming gown of cream muslin, carried two posies of white myrtle, while Ellen had brightened her plain housekeeper's garb with a sprig of lavender pinned to her bodice. She still wore a black ribbon around her upper arm and, given that it was now more than three years since Liam had died, Bridget wondered whether she meant to wear it for the rest of her life.

'John is ready with the carriage,' Ellen announced. 'He said he will bring it as close to the door as possible,' she added with a wary look at the rain still pelting the window.

'Time for you to finish dressing, Mama,' Emily said, her eyes already sparkling with tears. How strange it was for a daughter to be present at her own mother's wedding.

Bridget sat on the edge of the bed to don her stockings and shoes – low-heeled, satin slippers in a soft shade of bronze – and then stood to allow Polly to slip the taffeta gown over her head. Once Polly had fastened the tiny hooks at the back and arranged the bell-shaped skirt neatly over all her petticoats, she guided Bridget over to the mirror and tilted it to give her the best angle.

'Oh, Mama,' Emily breathed.

Bridget was surprised to perceive a woman in her reflection who looked younger than forty-one. The gown's off-the-shoulder neckline exposed the elegant slope of her collarbones, and the pleating at its waist somehow concealed the fact that she had birthed four children in the past. Her chestnut curls were drawn back into a chignon at the nape of her neck, and the clever styling had all but banished her grey hairs. Polly must have cast some sort of spell, or perhaps it was only joy that made Bridget's cheeks glow like a fresh-faced debutante.

'Now for the final touches,' Polly declared.

She tied the gold locket around Bridget's neck and it settled in the hollow at the base of her throat with a satisfying weight. Next, Polly helped her slide on a pair of ivory, elbow-length gloves, the silken fabric cool and smooth against her skin. Lastly, she draped a lace mantilla over Bridget's hair.

'Beautiful,' Ellen whispered. 'If Maggie McGovern could only see you now.'

How telling it was that she had thought of Maggie and not Bridget's mother in that moment.

After a collective, pensive silence, Polly said brightly, 'Let's get you to the carriage, my lady!'

They were just about to head out the door when Bridget exclaimed, 'My perfume!'

She hurried back across the room to her dressing table and reached for the thick glass bottle, but in her haste she managed to knock it over instead. It rolled off the edge of the table and fell to the floor, dislodging the stopper and spilling its contents onto the floorboards. The scent of lilac saturated the air at once, overpowering in such a concentrated volume.

'Oh no,' she moaned.

Her gaze connected with Polly's. Was this a consequence of the broken mirror? No, she refused to believe that; it had just been an accident.

'What a shame,' she said unhappily, picking up the empty bottle and setting it back on the table's surface. 'I'll have to do without.'

Polly scurried over to her and fished out a few handkerchiefs from one of the dressing table's drawers. 'I'd better clean it up right away, or it'll discolour the boards. You're lucky it didn't splash your skirt, my lady. Please step back now.'

After Polly had mopped up the wasteful puddle of perfume, they rejoined the others at the door, Bridget steadfastly ignoring the small seed of anxiety that had taken root in her stomach. Accepting one of the posies from Emily, she inhaled the sweet fragrance of myrtle and willed herself to be calm.

Down in the manor's entrance hall, they found John Corbett hovering with a black umbrella he'd procured from Mr Enright, who, according to John, had gallantly recognised that the bride's need was greater and resolved to face the elements in only his hat and coat. Opening the umbrella on the threshold, John held it above Bridget's head as she scuttled from the front door to the carriage waiting with two harnessed horses, and then he provided the same service to Emily, Ellen and Polly. Once all four women were safe and dry within the carriage, he stowed the umbrella under one of the cushioned benches, shut the carriage door and tugged his cap low over his forehead as he hurried around to the driver's seat. Moments later, they set off down the gravelled avenue with the rain still pouring outside.

Bridget thought she would feel better once they were on the move, but her nerves only clamoured louder as they rattled along, following the winding lanes towards Ballydarry. All sorts of troubling scenarios raced through her mind. What if the church had been flooded by the rainfall? What if Cormac had had an accident on his way to the village? He'd been planning to ride there with Rory, Patrick and the two boys, but what were the chances that his horse had thrown a shoe or lost its footing on the muddy road? Or what if someone stood up during the ceremony and declared that they had an objection to the continuation of the wedding?

This last one worried her most of all. As the water ran in rivulets down the carriage window, she stared out at the sodden hedgerows passing by in a shaky blur and imagined those words

'I object!' echoing through the church. Who might be the speaker?

Garrett, of course. With a quiver of dread, she saw it play out in her mind's eye: he would stride up the aisle to the altar and announce that the divorce had been a hoax and the official parchment a forgery and that she was still his lawful wife, forbidden to marry anyone else. Her crystal-clear future with Cormac would shatter into pieces. Tormented by these qualms, she yearned even more desperately to get to the church and bind herself to Cormac as soon as possible, sealing their union before anyone could stop them.

She felt so convinced that something bad was going to happen that it didn't even surprise her when the carriage suddenly lurched, jolting the four of them as it came to an abrupt stop. Polly gasped and Ellen grabbed the edge of her seat with white knuckles.

'What was that?' Emily exclaimed.

Bridget peered out the window, her heart thumping. 'John will explain—I can see him coming back to us now.'

The former stable master opened the door and stuck his head inside, giving them a rueful grimace from beneath his drenched cap. 'We're mired in mud and still a mile out from the village. I'll just need a few minutes to get the horses to pull us free.'

Bridget bit the tip of her tongue, certain that this delay would yield another ruinous consequence of some kind. John ducked back out and she shifted restlessly on the bench, wringing her gloved hands. Then she reached down and seized the umbrella.

'You should all stay with John,' she urged the others. 'But I simply cannot wait.'

With their protests resounding in her ears, she darted out of the carriage, her feet landing in a patch of squelching mud. She sighed with regret as she opened the umbrella – there would be no saving her lovely bronze-coloured slippers. However, she gathered up as much of her gown as she could in one hand, while in the other she balanced both the umbrella and her posy. She hurried to the front of the carriage, where she found John urging the horses forwards, their muscles straining as they heaved against the weight of the carriage. He goggled at her as she hastened past him.

'My lady!' he blurted. 'Where are you—'

'I'll see you at the church!' she called and strove onwards, her shoes struggling to find good purchase on the muddy ground. The rain hammered on the canopy of the umbrella and the delicate blooms of her posy were being crushed against its shaft, but she wouldn't go back to the carriage. She needed to keep moving. She needed to get to Cormac.

The lane began to slope downwards and, lifting the umbrella higher, she glimpsed Ballydarry in the distance, the spire of St Canice's standing out even through the downpour. She gripped her skirts tighter and tried to walk faster, despite being hampered by the mud and her entirely inappropriate footwear. If she had been cursed with seven years' bad luck because of that mirror, then she supposed there was every likelihood that she might turn her ankle. But she didn't slow down.

By the time she reached the vestibule of St Canice's Church and dashed into its shelter, her slippers were soaked and filthy. Dropping her skirts, she discovered that her efforts to save her gown had not been successful; the hem was smeared with mud, and she cringed at the sorry sight. Perhaps her bad luck had been her own reckless decision to leave the carriage behind.

The doors leading from the vestibule into the nave were closed, but she thought she could hear faint murmurings beyond them. Was Cormac in there? Her whole body itched with her urgent need to know. Hastily closing the umbrella, she propped it in the corner of the vestibule and approached the doors, her posy dangling limply from her hand. She would just take a peek without anyone seeing her – once she had assuaged this irrational sense of foreboding, she could wait for the others to arrive.

Unfortunately, she hadn't counted on the ear-splitting creak that the door made as she pulled it back – she could hardly have announced her presence more loudly. Numerous heads turned in her direction from the pews, but she peered past them, seeking the one face that mattered most.

And there he was, standing to the side at the top of the aisle. He was angled towards the altar but he turned at the deafening noise of the door. Her heart settled back into place as she took in his tall, handsome figure, present and unscathed. How striking he looked in his black frock coat, fitted at the waist and flaring down to his thigh – although a damp sheen to its shoulders indicated that his day had not been without its tribulations either.

His smile slipped into an expression of concern, and she wondered just how shambolic she appeared. She shook her head, trying to convey that there was nothing to worry about, but she instantly realised her mistake when his eyes widened in shock. Oh, dear God, how had he misconstrued the gesture? Had it seemed like she was saying no, like she was refusing to go up the aisle?

She was prepared to sprint straight up there to disabuse him of that notion when she heard a frantic whisper behind her.

'Mama!'

Glancing over her shoulder, she found Emily, Ellen, Polly and John standing in the vestibule. All three women had mud splatters on the hems of their dresses, while John was filthy up to his knees. She let the door creak shut and gaped at them.

'The horses eventually pulled the carriage free,' Emily said, her features full of distress, 'but not until after we'd got out and ended up in the mud ourselves. And then poor John tripped when he was climbing back into the driver's seat. Oh, Mama, we are all in such an awful state!'

Bridget couldn't help herself – she laughed. 'We are! And there's nothing we can do about it, so let's go in there, shall we?'

'Wait, wait!' Polly said quickly. She stepped forwards and adjusted Bridget's lace mantilla, then smoothed the gown over her petticoats as best she could. 'Take small steps so your shoes don't peek out,' she advised.

'And here, use this,' Emily said, holding out her posy. 'It's in fresher shape.'

Bridget sheepishly swapped one posy for the other. 'We'd better hurry,' she said. 'Otherwise, Cormac's going to think I've called off the wedding.'

Alarmed, Polly and Ellen both hastened through the door into the nave. They must have given some sort of indication that all was well, for in the next moment an organ began to play.

'Off you go, gooseberry,' Bridget said with a smile, moving back to let Emily through.

That left just her and John in the vestibule. She had seriously considered walking up the aisle alone – after all, it was her second marriage and she did not need to be 'given away' this time. But if fate had been kinder and she had married Cormac from the start, John would have undoubtedly stood in for her late father. It felt only right, then, to have him by her side for this new beginning.

He held open the creaky door and guided her through on his arm, prompting everyone in the church to rise. This time, she let her gaze focus on the pews and she experienced a dart of astonishment to see them so full – a great many of Oakleigh's tenants were in attendance, despite the fact that this wasn't a Catholic ceremony. Among them, she recognised Ben Bracken and his sister, Annie, standing next to Maisie McKinty and her husband, while even Dr Lynch had come. Polly and Ellen had slipped into a pew occupied by Ellen's three children, along with the maid Cathy, whose attention appeared to be drifting towards the bridegroom instead of the bride. Further up, Bridget spotted Mr Enright, his hat and coat saturated, as well as Mrs Kavanagh and Denis, who seemed to be competing over which one of them could beam the brightest.

For a brief moment, a pang of sadness swept over her for those who were absent on this special day. If only Orlaith and the rest of the family in Chicago didn't live so far away. She dearly wished they could all be here – yes, even Tess.

Then her spirits brightened as she and John approached the top of the aisle and the occupants of the front pew came into view. Gus's tricorne wobbled on his head as he waved energetically at her, while Jack just smiled in his own quiet way. Beside them were Rory and Patrick, who had become noticeably more cordial with each other since the family visited Ashbrook Lodge.

Bridget felt a particular rush of fondness towards Patrick, for he was the reason they were all here today. If he hadn't provoked Garrett into bettering himself for the sake of his son's respect, the divorce would never have happened. They truly owed Patrick so much.

And then her eyes found Cormac's. He stood waiting ahead of her, his hands clasped calmly before him, but the shining emotion in his face belied his composed stance. She felt her feet quicken until she was leading John instead of the other way around. When they reached Cormac, he extended his hand to John and grasped his arm with unspoken gratitude. John clapped him on the shoulder and kissed Bridget on her cheek before stepping back into a pew. Cormac turned to Bridget and his fingers closed around hers, warm and sure. Her anchor.

'I'm glad you made it,' he murmured. 'I was halfway down the aisle to find out what was going on when Ellen and Polly came in and shooed me back up to the altar.'

'I'm so sorry for causing unnecessary alarm,' she mumbled. 'And also for my dishevelled appearance.'

His mouth curved upwards. 'Dishevelled is always how I've liked you best.'

He winked and she blushed.

They faced the celebrant, who was the only stranger in the church. She would have much preferred to be married by Father Macken, but of course he couldn't officiate within these walls. The celebrant began to speak, welcoming them all, especially the bride and groom – if he harboured any disapproval of her divorced status, he kept his opinion to himself, for which she was thankful.

His words washed over her in a happy blur until he enunciated in a very serious tone, 'If any man can shew any just cause why they may not lawfully be joined together, let him now speak, or else hereafter for ever hold his peace.'

She tensed.

Silence fell.

And it remained unbroken.

She let out a breath as the celebrant carried on, guiding them through their vows. Cormac spoke them first and she thrilled at every word of commitment he uttered, feeling the promise of them settle in her very bones. When it was her turn, she poured every ounce of devotion into her oath, declaring before their family and friends that she belonged to this man and no other. The rain continued to beat against the church windows, a reminder of all the storms they had weathered to reach this point.

Then Cormac produced the gold ring that he had taken from her the day before. Its metalwork depicted two hands cradling a crowned heart, and it embodied the truth of all that they had pledged to one another – their friendship, their loyalty, and their love, woven together in an unbreakable bond.

At this juncture, Emily moved forwards to take Bridget's posy, beaming even as tears streamed silently down her cheeks. Bridget passed her the posy and cupped her chin tenderly before turning back to Cormac, who lifted her left hand.

'With this ring, I thee wed,' he said in a clear, steady voice.

He discreetly touched the ring to the knuckles of her thumb, index finger and middle finger, before slipping it onto her fourth finger – a subtle nod to the Catholic custom. It settled back where it belonged and she felt a sense of deep fulfilment.

There was no ring for him, but she caressed his left wrist where the leather band lay hidden beneath his cuff and whispered, 'With this, I thee wed.'

He gave her a look full of affection, and they both comprehended the band's new significance.

The celebrant's voice rose once more. 'Those whom God hath joined together, let no man put asunder.'

The hypocrisy of the pronouncement pricked at her conscience. By its decree, her first marriage should not have ended. But she had made those vows to Garrett against her will – how could that be considered sacred? This second union, however, she had chosen freely and entered into it wholeheartedly. It would endure until she and Cormac took their final breaths.

After the celebrant finished his blessing, they signed the marriage register, and then it was done. She gazed up into Cormac's warm blue irises, her heart brimming with joy. Finally, after all these years, they were husband and wife. He bent his head and kissed her, the touch of his lips gentle and reverential.

When they turned to the pews, she sought out the faces of their children first. All three of them were glowing with pride.

Beyond them, the church was a sea of smiles. As Cormac led Bridget down the aisle, murmurs of congratulations pressed in on them from all sides. Mrs Kavanagh waved her handkerchief before blowing her nose loudly.

They reached the vestibule, at which point Bridget expected they would need to make use of the umbrella again. But then she peered out the doorway.

'I think the rain has stopped!'

She and Cormac emerged into the churchyard to find that the deluge had indeed passed over at last. What was more, it had left a stunning rainbow in its wake, arcing across the sky through breaking clouds.

'How breathtaking!' she marvelled.

'My breath is taken away for an entirely different reason,' he said and he swept her into a passionate embrace for one swift second before they were inundated with well-wishers coming out of the church behind them.

They didn't have another moment to themselves until much later that evening, when he tugged her gently away from their family and friends who were still celebrating inside the manor – every single person seemed determined to make the most of this rare occasion to be joyful after so many blight-ravaged years. Leaving them to their merriment, he led her down to the kitchens and out the back door into the cobbled courtyard. The sky above was streaked with the orange of sunset. She assumed he wanted to bring her to the orchard, but instead he guided her past the stables and to the furthest hay barn. Inside, he glanced around the dim space and then steered her to an empty point near the centre.

'I think this is it,' he said with a nod.

'This is what?' she asked, nonplussed.

'The exact spot where we first said "I love you" to each other.'

Her pulse pounded.

'The haystacks are obviously not in the same places,' he said, gesturing to their surroundings. 'But there was one right here that night, and this is where we sat.'

She swallowed as the memories heated her skin. 'I remember.'

He tucked a wayward curl behind her ear. 'Wife,' he said softly, as though seeing how it tasted on his tongue.

She smiled and murmured, 'Husband.' It tasted wonderful. 'I love you.'

'I love you.' He cupped the back of her neck and leaned his forehead down to touch hers. 'God, how I love you, Mrs McGovern.'

# What's Next

The story of the McGovern family is far from over! If you'd like to be part of the growing community of readers eager to continue following this family's journey, be sure to join my Readers' Club at **bit.ly/susie-murphy-readers-club**. You'll be the first to hear all the latest news, and you'll also receive free short stories, exclusive updates and special discounts for my online bookstore.

Please help more readers discover this series by leaving an honest review about A Class Liberated on Amazon and/or Goodreads. A short review will make a huge difference in spreading the word about A Matter of Class. Thank you so much!

The next book in the series will be A Class Divided.

## Acknowledgements

The very first person I must thank is YOU. There has been quite a long gap between the last book and this one, and all I can say is thank you so much for not giving up on me. The past year and a half has been really challenging for me on a personal level and there were many days when I couldn't see light at the end of the tunnel. But I persevered and you held on, and I can't express how grateful I am for your patience. I hope the story was worth the wait!

An author might be able to write a book on their own but they need a team to successfully get it out into the world. My amazing team includes my editor, Averill Buchanan, my cover designer and web designer, Andrew Brown, my narrator, Gary Furlong, my accountant, Oliver Clare, and my ads manager, Bryan Canter. High fives all round!

Thank you to my beta readers and to my advance reader team for the joy you always bring to your reading. My deep gratitude goes to the very generous author community, in particular Lisa Boyle, Kelsey Gietl and Pam Lecky, and to these lovely book reviewers as well: Claire Bridle, Valerie Whitford, Lisa Redmond and Mandie Griffiths.

I wouldn't be where I am today without the unfailing support of my friends. You all kept believing in me when I struggled to believe in myself, and I know how incredibly lucky I am to have so many special people in my life. These include my school girlies (you know who you are!); my library gals, Sarah and Lindsay; my DCU gang, near and far; my oldest friend, Mary Claire; my pen pal, Elizabeth; the CG book club (too many to name!); and Elle and Julia of the Tortured Writers Department: you all deserve tight hugs for keeping me uplifted.

I'm so thankful for my wonderful extended family on both the Bourke and Murphy sides. Thanks especially to my mam and dad, who are constantly supportive and always there to listen.

My husband, Bob, deserves the final mention. You've discussed plot points with me to the nth degree (east wing!), and you've kept my brain from leaking out of my ears on countless occasions. You are my favourite person.